KINGDOM
OF
SOULS

KINGDOM OF SOULS

RENA BARRON

HARPER TEEN
An Imprint of HarperCollins Publishers

Library of Congress Control Number: 2019939328
ISBN 978-0-06-287095-7

Typography by Jenna Stempel-Lobell
19 20 21 22 23   PC/LSCH   10 9 8 7 6 5 4 3 2 1
❖   ˙
First Edition

To everyone who dares to dream,
dares to live their truths,
dares to stand against atrocities,
dares to say *I am enough*,
this book is for you . . .

. . . and for my family.

PART I

For she will rise from the ashes alit in flames.
For no water will ever quell her pain.
For no redemption will befall her.
For we will never speak her name.
—Song of the Unnamed

PROLOGUE

Be still, Little Priestess.

My father kneels before me with a string of teeth threaded between his fingers. They shine like polished pearls, and I square my shoulders and stand a little taller to make him proud. The distant echo of the djembe drums drowns out his words, but it doesn't tame the twinkle in his eyes as he drapes the teeth around my neck. Tonight I become a true daughter of Tribe Aatiri.

Magic of all colors flutters in the air as gentle as wingbeats. I can't be still when it dances on my father's dark skin like lightning bugs. It flits along his jaw and leaps onto his nose. My hand shoots out to catch an ember of gold, but it slips through my fingers. I giggle, and he laughs too.

Girls gossip as their mothers fix their kaftans and bone charms. For every one the magic touches, it skips two, like the rest of us are invisible. My chest tightens, watching it go to others when it's never come to me—not even once.

The few girls who speak Tamaran ask me what it's like living so far away in the Almighty Kingdom. They say that I am not a true Aatiri because my mother is not of the tribe. Something twinges in my belly, for there is truth in their words.

I hold my head high as my father straightens my collar. He's the only man in the tent, and the other girls whisper about that too. I don't care what they say; I'm glad he's here. "Why doesn't magic come to me, Father?"

The question comes out too loud, and silence falls upon the tent. The other girls and their mothers stare at me as if I've said something bad. "Don't worry, daughter," he says, folding the sleeves of my orange-and-blue kaftan, which matches his own. "It will come in due time."

"But when?" I stomp.

It isn't fair that many of the Aatiri children younger than me have magic already. In Tamar, I'm the only one among my friends who can see magic at all, but here, it flocks to the other children and they can make it *do* things. I can't.

"Maybe never, little *ewaya*," says the oldest girl in accented Tamaran. She glares at me and I wrinkle my nose at her. I'm not a *baby*, and she's wrong. It will come.

The girl's mother clucks her tongue and fusses at her in Aatiri. Her words slide over my ears without meaning, like all the strange and beautiful languages in the markets back home.

"Even if the magic never comes," my father says, "you'll still be my Little Priestess."

I poke my tongue out at the girl. That'll teach her not to be so mean.

Another girl asks why my mother isn't here. "She has more

important things to do," I answer, remembering how my father had begged her to come.

"Why the sad face?" my father asks, squeezing my cheeks. "Imebyé is a time of celebration. Tonight, you begin the long journey into adulthood."

The djembe drums stop. I bite my lip, and the other girls startle. It's time to go stand in front of the whole tribe so the chieftain can bless us. But for once, my legs still as the other girls hurry from the tent with their mothers.

"I want to go home, Father," I whisper as the last girl leaves.

Some of the light fades from his eyes. "We'll go home soon, okay?"

"I want to go home *now*," I say, a little stronger.

He frowns. "Don't you want to take part in Imebyé?"

I shake my head hard enough to make my bone charms rattle.

My father comes to his feet. "How about we just watch the ceremony together?"

The chieftain walks into the tent and I tuck myself against my father's side. Her silver kaftan sweeps about her ankles and stands out against her midnight skin. Salt-and-pepper locs coil on top of her head. "Do my son and granddaughter plan to take part in a ceremony they traveled fourteen days to attend?" she asks, her deep voice ringing in the tent.

My father wraps his arm around my shoulders. "Not this year."

The chieftain nods as if satisfied. "May I speak to my granddaughter alone, Oshhe?"

My father exchanges a look with her that I don't understand. "If it's okay with Arrah."

I swallow. "Okay."

He squeezes my shoulder before leaving the tent. "I'll save you a spot up front."

The chieftain flashes me a gap-toothed grin as she squats on the floor. "Sit with me."

The tent flap rustles in my father's wake. My legs ache to follow, but the sight of the great Aatiri chieftain sitting on the floor roots me in place. I sit across from her as she raises one palm to the ceiling. Sparks of yellow and purple and pink magic drift to her hand.

"How do you make the magic come to you, great chieftain?"

Her eyes go wide. "I'm your grandmother before all. Address me as such."

I bite my lip. "How, Grandmother?"

"Some people can pull magic from the fabric of the world." Grandmother watches the colors dancing on her fingertips. "Some can coax magic to come with rituals and spells. Many can't call magic at all. It's a gift from Heka to the people of the five tribes—a gift of himself—but it's different for everyone."

She offers me the magic, and I lean in closer. I hope this time it will come to me, but it disappears upon touching my hand. "I can see it," I say, my shoulders dropping, "but it doesn't answer me."

"That is rare indeed," she says. "Not unheard of, but rare."

The feather strokes of Grandmother's magic press against my forehead. It itches, and I shove my hands between my knees to keep from scratching. "It seems you have an even rarer gift." Her eyebrows knit together as if she's stumbled upon a puzzle. "I've never seen a mind I couldn't touch."

She's only trying to make me feel better, but it doesn't mean anything if I can't call magic like real witchdoctors—like my parents, like her.

Grandmother reaches into her pocket and removes a handful of bones. "These belonged to my ancestors. I use them to draw more magic to me—more than I could ever catch on my fingertips. When I focus on what I want to see, they show me. Can you try?"

She drops the bones into my hand. They're small and shiny in the light of the burning jars of oils set on stools beneath the canopy. "Close your eyes," Grandmother says. "Let the bones speak to you."

Cold crawls up my arm and my heart pounds. Outside, the djembe drums start again, beating a slow, steady rhythm that snatches my breath away. The truth is written on Grandmother's face, a truth I already know. The bones don't speak.

Charlatan.

The word echoes in my mind. It's the name my mother calls the street peddlers in the market, the ones who sell worthless good luck charms because their magic is weak. What if she thinks I'm a charlatan too?

My fingers ache from squeezing the bones so hard, and Grandmother whispers, "Let go."

The bones fly from my hand and scatter on the floor between us. They land every which way, some close to others and some far apart. My eyes burn as I stare at them, straining to hear the ancestors' message over the djembe drums.

"Do you see or hear anything?" Grandmother asks.

I blink and tears prick my eyes. "No."

Grandmother smiles, collecting the bones. "Not everyone's magic shows so early. For some, the magic doesn't abide until they're nearly grown. But when it comes so late, it's very strong. Perhaps you will be a powerful witchdoctor one day."

My hands tremble as the Aatiri girl's words come back to me: *Maybe never.*

"Come, child, the celebration awaits," Grandmother says, climbing to her feet.

Tears slip down my cheeks as I run out of the tent without waiting for Grandmother. I don't want to be a powerful witchdoctor one day—I want magic to come now. The heat of the desert night hits me, and my bare feet slap against the hard clay. Sparks of magic drift from the sky into the other children's outstretched arms, but some of it flits away. I dart through the crowd and follow the wayward magic, determined to catch some of my own.

It weaves through the mud-brick huts like a winged serpent, always staying two beats ahead of me. Beyond the tents, the drums become a distant murmur. I stop when the magic disappears. It's darker here, colder, and the scent of blood medicine burns my nose. Someone's performed a ritual in the shadows. I should turn back, run away. The wind howls a warning, but I move a little closer. Fingers like crooked tree roots latch on to my ankle.

I yank my leg back, and the hand falls away. My heart beats louder than the djembe drums as I remember all the scary stories about demons. During a lesson, a scribe once warned: *Don't get caught in the shadows, for a demon waits to steal your soul. The younger the soul, the sweeter the feast.* A shiver cuts down my arms at the thought, but I remind myself that those are only tales to scare children. I'm too old to believe them.

It isn't until the outline of a woman comes into focus that

I breathe again. Magic lights on her skin, and she writhes and thrashes against the sand. Her mouth twists into an ugly scream. I don't know what to make of her; she looks both young and old, both alive and dead, and in pain.

"Give me a hand," says the woman, voice slurred.

"I can get my father," I offer as I help her sit up.

Her brown skin is ashen and sweaty. "Don't bother." She wipes dirt from her lips. "I only need to rest a spell."

"What are you doing out here?" I ask, kneeling beside her.

"I could ask the same, but I know the answer." A flicker of life returns to her vacant eyes. "There is only one reason a child does not take part in Imebyé."

I glance away—she knows.

"I don't have magic either," she says, her words seething with bitterness. "Even so, it answers my call."

I swallow hard to push back the chill creeping down my spine. "How?"

She smiles, revealing a mouth of rotten teeth. "Magic has a price if you're willing to pay."

ONE

Every year, the five tribes of Heka gather for the Blood Moon Festival, and I tell myself that this will be *my year*. The year that wipes the slate clean. The year that makes up for the waiting, the longing, the frustration. The year that magic lights on my skin, bestowing upon me the gift. When it happens, my failures will wash away and I'll have magic of my own.

I'm sixteen, near grown by both Kingdom and tribal standards. My time is running out. No daughter or son of any tribe has come into their gifts beyond my age. If it doesn't happen *this year*, it won't happen at all.

I swallow hard and rub my sweaty palms against the grass as the djembe drums begin their slow and steady rhythm. With the tribes camped in the valley, there are some thirty thousand people here. We form rings around the sacred circle near the Temple of Heka, and the fire in the center ebbs and flows to the beat. The drummers march around the edge of the circle, their steps in sync. The five tribes look as if they have nothing in common, but they move as one, to honor Heka, the god of their lands.

Magic clings to the air, so thick that it stings my skin. It dances in the night sky above endless rows of tents quilted in vibrant colors. My tunic sticks to my back from the heat of so many bodies in tight quarters. The sharp smell in the valley reminds me of the East Market on its busiest days. My feet tap a nervous beat while everyone else claps along with the music.

As Grandmother's guests, Essnai, Sukar, and I sit on cushions in a place of honor close to the sacred circle. It isn't because we're special. We're quite the opposite: ordinary and outsiders at that. Some people glare at us to make sure we don't forget. I wish the looks didn't bother me, but they only raise more doubts. They make me question if I belong here. If I deserve another chance after years of failing.

"I suppose your gawking means the magic is coming," says Sukar, wrinkling his nose. The tattoos on his forearms and across his shaved head are glowing, so he knows as well as I that the magic is already here. "Either that, or you're missing *someone* back home . . ."

A flush of warmth creeps up my neck. We both know who he means. I try to imagine Rudjek here, perched on a cushion in his fancy elara. He'd stand out worse than me and love every moment of it. The thought brings a smile to my face and eases my nerves a little.

Sukar, Essnai, and I made the journey from Tamar with the caravan, crossing the Barat Mountains at the western edge of the Almighty Kingdom to reach the tribal lands. Some two hundred people had come, but many more Tamarans of tribal blood hadn't bothered. "We should've left you in the Kingdom too," I tell Sukar, casting him a scathing look. "Some of us are respectful enough to pay attention to the ceremony, so please stop distracting me."

"Well, if it's a distraction you need . . ." He winks at me.

"Back me up, Essnai," I beg. "Tell him to pay attention."

She sits cross-legged on the opposite side of Sukar, her face stony as always. My father brewed a blood medicine to color her hair last night, and the shock of red looks good against her ebony skin. As usual, she's caught eyes, although she never seems to notice. Instead Essnai looks like a lovesick puppy without her *ama* Kira at her side.

She shrugs, watching the drummers. "He won't listen anyway."

I sigh and turn back to the sacred circle. The moon has settled into a crimson hue, deeper red than only an hour before. In Tamar, we're taught that the moon orisha, Koré, cries blood for her fallen brethren on this night. Five thousand years ago, she and her twin brother, Re'Mec, the sun orisha, led an army to end the Demon King's insatiable thirst for souls. But the tribes believe the blood moon represents their connection to Heka. For it is only during this time that he returns to give his gift to future generations.

Even from this distance, the fire draws beads of sweat from my forehead. Or at least, I pretend it's the fire that has me on edge. I wish I could be like Essnai and Sukar. They don't care about not having magic, but it's different for them. Neither of their parents have the gift. They don't have to live up to the legacy of two prominent bloodlines.

When I think of the *other* reason I'm here—the tests—my belly twists in knots. The drums stop, the sound as sudden as the calm before a storm, and my muscles wind even tighter. The musicians stand almost as still as the statues in the scholars' district in Tamar. Silence falls upon the crowd. The moment we've been waiting for has finally come, but it stretches a beat too long to spite me. In that space of time, the what-ifs run through my mind. What if it doesn't happen? What if it *does*, but my magic isn't strong like my parents'? What if I'm destined to become a charlatan peddling good luck charms?

Would that be *so* bad?

I draw my knees to my chest, remembering the woman at Imebyé writhing in the sand. *Magic has a price if you're willing to pay.* Her words ring in my ears, the words of a charlatan, the words of someone desperate for magic. I push her out of my head. There's still a chance for me—still time for Heka to give me his gift.

A hum rises from behind me and I crane my neck to see the witchdoctors weaving through the masses. They will perform the dance to start the month-long celebration. The blood moon casts them in eerie crimson shadows. Save for their voices, the entire valley quiets. No whispers, no children fooling around, only the whistle of wind and the rustle of feet in the grass. I want so badly to be in their ranks, to belong, to measure up to my family's legacy. Instead, I'm stuck on the side watching—*always* watching.

For the ceremony, seven witchdoctors stand for each of the five tribes. Under their chieftains, the other six make up the *edam*, the tribal council. Although many of the tribal people have Heka's grace—his magic—witchdoctors stand apart. The chieftains gifted them the title because they show a mastery of magic above others. Of all the tribal people, only a hundred or so have earned this prestigious appointment. They are the ones that the others revere and the ones I envy the most.

As the witchdoctors grow closer, their chants rattle in my bones. What would it be like to command magic with the ease of taking a breath? To reach into the air to collect it on one's fingertips, or walk in the spirit world? To not only see magic, to tame it, to bend it, to *be* magical?

First come the Tribe Litho witchdoctors: four women and three men. Their tribe lies southwest of the Temple of Heka in the woodlands. White dust covers their bodies and vests of rawhide. Their intricate crowns, made of metal and bone and colorful beads, jangle in the breeze. The ground shifts beneath their feet, moving as gentle as ocean waves, gliding them to the sacred circle, which only the *edam* are allowed to enter.

As the procession draws closer, the djembe drummers start again, moving away from the circle to settle in an open spot on the grass. Their slow beat surges faster when the Litho chieftain enters the sacred circle.

Tribe Kes comes next—the smallest of the five tribes, whose lands border the valley to the northwest. Their diaphanous skin and near-colorless eyes remind me of the Northern people. Two are as white as alabaster and their bright clothes stand out in stark contrast. With each step they take, lightning cuts across the sky and sparks dance on their skin. They fan pouches of smoke that burns my nose. It smells of bloodroot, ginger, and eeru pepper: a cleansing remedy I've helped my father make in his shop at home.

The tribe from the mountains south of the Temple arrives next. The Zu witchdoctors leap above our heads, their feet supported by air. Tattoos cover their bodies and they wear crowns of antlers, some curved, some hooked, some large, some small. Some fashioned out of slick metal with edges sharp enough to sever a finger. With one misstep, an antler could fall upon the crowd, and it wouldn't be pretty. I tuck my fingers between my knees just in case.

Sukar nudges me, a lopsided grin on his face. His family is Zu, and although he's got at least two dozen tattoos, he doesn't have nearly as many as the *edam* from his tribe. "As always, the most impressive of the five," he whispers.

I swat Sukar's arm to shush him at the same time Essnai slaps the back of his head. He winces but knows better than to protest. It's the Aatiri's turn, which Essnai and I are anticipating the most. Even with her short-cropped hair, there's no denying that her high cheekbones and wide-set eyes mark her as an Aatiri. We'd become friends after she'd found me in the desert at Imebyé with the charlatan.

Relief washes over me as Grandmother steps from the shadows, leading Tribe Aatiri. I hadn't expected anyone else, but she's the first familiar face among the *edam*. I sit up taller, trying to look like even a shadow of the great Aatiri chieftain.

The Aatiri do not walk or leap, for clouds of magic carry them. Grandmother's silver locs coil on top of her head like a crown, and she wears a half dozen necklaces of teeth. The Aatiri are tall and lean with prominent cheekbones and wiry hair braided like mine. Their skin is as beautiful as the hour of *ösana*.

My father is the last of them to enter the circle, and my heart soars. He's tall and proud and magical, more so than any of the *edam* aside from Grandmother. He stands upon his cloud with his traditional staff in hand and a knife carved of bone in the other.

He is an honorary Aatiri *edam* as he doesn't live with his people, but they don't deny that he's one of the most powerful among them.

I'm not foolish enough to think that if . . . *when* . . . my magic comes I'll be as talented as he is. But seeing him fills me with pride.

The Mulani come last. They live the closest to the Temple of Heka.

It was a Mulani woman Heka revealed his presence to when he first descended from the stars a thousand years ago. Now the Mulani chieftain serves as his voice. The position would belong to my mother had she not left and never looked back. When she was only fourteen, the tribe named her their next chieftain and emissary to Heka because she'd shown such remarkable powers.

I could never live up to that legend either, but it doesn't stop me from wanting to.

Unlike the witchdoctors of the other tribes, who vary in gender, Mulani witchdoctors are all women. I cover my eyes before the flashes of light that always come when they enter the sacred circle. Sukar curses under his breath because he's too busy *not* paying attention to remember. From the groaning around me, he isn't the only one. When their auras cool, the Mulani stand facing the crowd. They have broad shoulders, curvy bodies, and skin ranging from deep brown to alabaster. My amber eyes and some of my color come from them, while my lean build favors the Aatiri.

"I speak for Heka." The Mulani chieftain's words echo in the valley, silencing all. "I speak for the mother and father of magic. I speak for the one who gave of himself when the orishas withheld magic from mortal kind. I speak for he who has no beginning and no end."

The Mulani chieftain is my mother's first cousin, and her voice rings with authority. *Almost* as much authority as my mother's: Arti is soft-spoken, but she commands as much respect in the Almighty Kingdom as her cousin does in the tribal lands. I tell myself I don't mind that she's not here. It isn't so different from how things are at home. There, she spends most of her time at the Almighty Temple, where she and the seers serve the orishas. When my mother left the tribal lands, she adopted the gods of the Kingdom too.

When I was younger, I begged my mother to spend more time with me, but she was so busy even then. Always busy or unavailable or unhappy—especially about my lack of magic. A pang of resentment settles in my chest. If I'm honest, a part of me still wishes things could be different between us.

"For a thousand years Heka has come to us at the start of every blood moon," the Mulani chieftain says. "So it will be again. On this night we gather in worship so that he may show favor to our people. We shall share our *kas* with him so that he can look into our souls and judge us worthy."

Anticipation quickens my heartbeat. Every year children from the very young to sixteen come into their powers after Heka's visit. This year has to be my turn—before I'm too old and it's too late. Magic will stop my cousins from looking at me like I don't belong.

Magic will finally make my mother proud of me.

After the Mulani chieftain has delivered her speech, the dance begins. The witchdoctors move around the fire, all thirty-five of them, chanting in their native tongues. Their songs fit into an intricate pattern that's at once odd and beautiful. The ceremony will go on for hours, and the drummers adjust their tempo to match the *edam*'s rhythm.

Farther back from the sacred circle, campfires crop up between the tents. The smells of brew and roasted meat fill the air. People pass wooden bowls through the crowd, and when one reaches me, I take a sniff that burns my nose. I recoil before I can stop myself.

"You of all people should be used to a little blood medicine," says Sukar, his voice smug.

"I'll take the next pass," I say, shoving the bowl into his hands.

He laughs, then takes a dramatic gulp.

Someone thrusts another bowl into my hands, and I almost drop it when my gaze lands on Grandmother. She's broken ranks and stepped out of the sacred circle. Now she towers above me, and my breath hitches in my throat. No *edam* has ever left the circle during the dance.

"Drink, Little Priestess."

Her voice carries on a secret wind, loud and clear despite the noise from the crowd, the curses, the dirty looks. It's only a pet name when Oshhe calls me that, but there's weight in Grandmother's words. She looks down at me, hopeful and hesitant, as she studies my face.

I'm not a priestess. I'm only going to disappoint her.

Unable to refuse, I take a sip. Heat trails across my tongue and down my throat. It tastes herbal and metallic and rotten. I clench my stomach to keep from gagging. Grandmother nods, takes the bowl, and passes it to Sukar, who swallows hard. "Thank you, Honored Chieftain," he says, bobbing his head to her. He looks surprised that she's here too. None of the other *edam* have left the sacred circle.

"Have you been practicing?" Grandmother asks me with a toothy grin.

This is the real reason that I've been on edge all night. Each year at the Blood Moon Festival, Grandmother tests whether I have magic, and each year I fail.

"Yes," I stutter as the medicine starts to take hold.

I don't tell her that for all my practicing, with Oshhe and alone, nothing has come of it.

"Tomorrow we will talk more," Grandmother says.

Next to me Sukar falls on his face in the grass as the blood medicine takes him first. Essnai rolls him on his side with her foot. A rush of warmth spreads through my body and my tongue loosens. "I still don't have magic," I blurt out without meaning to, but I'm too drowsy to feel embarrassed.

Grandmother starts to say something else but stops herself. A pang flutters in my stomach. I can't read her expression and wonder what the ancestors have shown her in my future. In all these years, she's never told me. "Our greatest power lies not in our magic, but in our hearts, Little Priestess."

She talks in riddles like all the tribal people. Sometimes I don't mind the way she and Oshhe try to soothe over my worries about not having magic. Sometimes it's infuriating. They don't know what it's like to feel you don't belong, to feel you're not worthy. To not measure up to a mother who all the Kingdom admires.

Before I can think of something to say, the blood medicine lulls me into a state of peace. The burning in my throat cools into a smothering heat, and my heartbeat throbs in my ears. Behind Grandmother, the other *edam* move at an incredible speed. Their faces blur and their bodies leave trails of mist that connect them to one another. Their chants intensify. Before long, most people lie in trances—Essnai, the elders, almost the entirety of the five tribes.

The djembe drums fall silent, and the witchdoctors' song echoes in the valley.

Grandmother grabs my hand and pulls me into the sacred circle. "Let Heka see you."

This is wrong. I don't belong in the sacred circle. Only the *edam*, and honored witchdoctors like my father. Never someone like me—without magic, an outsider.

I shouldn't be here, but I can't remember whether I mean in the circle, or in the tribal lands. My mind is too foggy to think straight, but I'm warm inside as I join the dance.

Magic swirls in the air. It's purple and pink and yellow and black and blue. It's all colors, tangling and curling around itself. It brushes against my skin, and then I am two places at once, as if the bonds that tether my *ka* to my body have loosened. No. I'm all places. Is this what it's like to have magic, to *feel* it, to wield it? Please, Heka, bless me with this gift.

One by one, the witchdoctors fall into a trance and drop to the ground too. There is no sound save for the crackling of the fires set around camp. The Mulani chieftain—my cousin—sweeps past me, her steps as silent as starlight. She's the only other person still awake.

"Wait," I call after her. "What's happening?"

She doesn't answer me. Instead she climbs up the Temple steps and disappears inside. Something heavy pulls against my legs when I try to follow her.

I glance down and my breath catches at the sight of my body lying beneath me. I'm standing with my feet sunk to the ankles in my own belly. I gasp and my physical body mimics me, chest rising sharply, eyes wide. Is everyone else's *ka* awake too? I can't see them.

Can they see me? I try to move again, but the same strong pull keeps me rooted in place.

My *ka* holds on to my body with an iron grip—a chain around my ankles. I wonder how I can let go—and if I want to. According to my father, untethering one's *ka* is tricky business. Only the most talented witchdoctors can leave their bodies. Even they rarely do it, for fear of wandering too far and not finding their way back. The blood medicine alone couldn't make this happen. Grandmother must have performed some magic when she pulled me into the sacred circle, so I'd have a better chance at being seen by Heka. That has to be it.

My body calls me back. The call is a gentle beckoning at first, then grows in intensity. My eyelids flutter and I fight to stay aware as bright ribbons of light set the night sky on fire. I fall to my knees, the pull growing stronger, the source of the light drawing closer. It's both warm and cold, both beautiful and frightening, both serene and violent. It knows me and something inside me knows it. It's the mother and father of magic. It's Heka.

He's going to bestow his grace upon me.

I can't believe it's happening after all these years. My body lets out a sigh of relief.

My mother would be proud if I showed a sliver of magic. Just a sliver. I shut my eyes against the intense light and let his power wash over my skin, his touch as gentle as brushstrokes. It tastes sweet on my tongue, and I laugh as it pulses through my *ka*.

Then the light disappears, and I'm left empty as the magic flees my body.

TWO

The morning after the opening ceremony, I'm in a foul mood as Oshhe and I deliver gifts to his countless cousins. He watches me like a hawk, but I don't know why. I'm still the same magicless girl I was the night before. Nothing has changed. I want to believe that some magic rubbed off on me—that this year will be different.

My hands tremble and I keep them busy so he doesn't notice. I have my tests with Grandmother at the hour of *ösana*. I can't face her right now, not after entering the sacred circle. Not after feeling magic at my fingertips, feeling it in my blood, and then feeling it abandon me. That's when the trembling started—as if the magic snatched away a piece of my *ka* when it left.

I catch the scent of cinnamon and clove and mint on the air and it reminds me of home. Every year my father brings me here so we can spend time with his family and I can get to know my mother's tribe better. When older Mulani look at me, they see Arti: it's only the rich brown of my skin that sets us apart. For my mother was not much older than I am now when she left her tribe for the Kingdom and never looked back. I can't hide from my own reason for coming, the one fueling my anticipation.

We only stay for half of the month-long celebration. Oshhe has his shop to run back in Tamar, and I have my studies with the scribes. A part of me is anxious to return home, where I'm not so much of an utter failure, especially after last night.

Our Aatiri cousins bombard Oshhe with questions about the Kingdom most of the morning. They ask if Tamarans are as ridiculous as they've heard. If the Almighty One is a bastard like his father before him. If Tamar smells of dead fish. If leaving his tribe for the lure of city life was worth the trouble.

While my father talks to old friends, I eavesdrop. I don't understand everything they say in Aatiri, but I follow enough to stay abreast. They complain about the council that represents their interests with the Kingdom. They want more in return for the precious metals mined from the caves beneath their desert lands. Many times, friends have asked my father to help with trade negotiations, but he always refuses. He says that Arti is the politician in the family. To call my mother a politician is an understatement.

A witchdoctor asks after the health of the seer from Tribe Aatiri who serves in the Almighty Temple. He is very old and wants to return home. The tribe will meet in three days and Grandmother will ask for a volunteer to replace him. They say that only the very old will go because no one else wants to live in the Kingdom. Oshhe laughs with them, but his eyes are sad.

I thread my fingers together to keep them steady while my father hands out the last of the gifts. They're still shaking from the ritual, but also because my great-aunt Zee has just asked me about Arti.

When a simple shrug doesn't deter her, I say, "She enjoys being *Ka*-Priestess of the Kingdom very much."

With a nod and a laugh, Zee tells me that Arti *could* have married the Almighty One had she been clever enough. Joke or not, this is news to me, but it doesn't come as a shock. My mother has done well for herself in Tamar. Having risen from nothing, she holds the third-most powerful position in the Kingdom, behind the Vizier and the Almighty One himself. Not a day goes by that she lets anyone forget it.

"If you were a princess," Zee says, "you wouldn't need magic then."

At her slight, I forget her comment about my mother.

You wouldn't need magic then.

Everyone knows about my little problem. My younger cousins at least pretend they don't, but some of the elders are blunt about it, their tongues sharp. Zee's the sharpest of them all.

"If I were a princess, Auntie," I say in a slippery sweet voice, "I wouldn't have the pleasure of seeing you every year. That would be such a shame."

"Speaking of shame," Zee says, fanning a worrisome fly away. "I can't for the life of me understand why my sister would risk angering the other *edam* by bringing you into the sacred circle." She draws her lips into a hard line. "What did she say to you last night?"

Grandmother had said surprisingly little, but I won't tell Zee so she can spread rumors.

"I see you still like to gossip," Oshhe cuts in, fixing his stony eyes on his aunt. "A wonder your tongue hasn't fallen out from talking too much."

Several people cluck at Zee and she rolls her eyes.

Late afternoon, my father is asked to step in to mediate a dispute between two friends from his youth. He fusses about leaving me until I tell him that I'm going back to my tent to rest before my tests with Grandmother tonight. I'm supposed to meet up with Essnai and Sukar, but I decide to take a walk to clear my mind first. I'm still seething at my great-aunt and seething at Heka too.

In Tamar, hardly anyone has magic, and no one cares that I don't either. But here magic plays on the wind like dust bunnies, teasing and tantalizing, forever out of reach. Most tribal people have some magic, even if it's not as strong as Grandmother's and the other witchdoctors'.

As I move through the patchwork of bright Aatiri tents, a cousin or an old friend of my father greets me at every turn. They ask about last night, but I want to be alone, so I leave camp, hoping for some peace. I weave through the white Mulani tents nearest the Temple of Heka. The Temple stands on the north edge of the valley, the golden dome shimmering against the white walls. A group of Mulani decorate it with flowers and bright fabrics and infuse the stone with magic. I walk by as a procession of women, each with a basket of water balanced on her head, march across the stone. The art is so detailed that you can see the water sloshing around in the baskets.

I slip between the Zu tents covered in animal hide and pause to watch elders carving masks out of wood. It's getting late by the time I roam into the maze of Litho tents, separated by sheets draped across wire. There isn't much privacy in the valley, but the camp is quiet aside from the rustle of the cloth in the wind. Most of the tribe has gathered around the firepits to prepare for the second night of the blood moon.

My wandering doesn't bring me much peace, not like it does when I lose myself in the East Market back home. There's always a merchant selling something interesting to keep my mind busy there. Or I can listen to the stories of people who come from neighboring countries. Meet people like the Estherian, who tosses salt over her shoulder to ward off spirits. Or the Yöome woman who makes shiny boots that patrons line up in the early morn to buy. But most of all, I wish I were lying on the grass along the Serpent River with Rudjek, away from everyone and everything.

If the Aatiri camp was orderly, the Litho tents are a mess of confusion. I become so turned around that I end up in a clearing. By the smell of blood and sweat, I can tell that it's a makeshift arena. Had Rudjek come to the tribal lands, he'd spend every waking moment here.

I'm halfway across the clearing when two Litho boys around my age step into my path. When I try to move around them, they block me again, stopping me in my tracks. They're up to no good. It's written in their white ash-covered faces. Both stand a head taller than me and wear vests of animal hide dyed stark red. We stare at each other, but I don't speak. I'm not the one sneaking around like a hungry hyena. Let them explain themselves.

"We want to know why a *ben'ik* like you got to enter the sacred circle," demands the boy with a black dorek tied around his head. He looks down his nose at me. "You're nothing special."

The way he spits out *ben'ik* makes my skin crawl. I wander so much in Tamar without fear because of my mother's reputation. No one would dare cross the *Ka*-Priestess. In the tribal lands, I should know better. I'm an outsider and people like me, *ben'iks*, are even less liked for our lack of magic. It can't help that they're angry Grandmother broke the rules for me.

My blood boils. I should've been more careful. I turn to go as two more boys appear out of the shadows. "Don't make a mistake you'll regret," I say, lacing my words with equal venom. "My grandmother is chieftain and won't take kindly to any trouble." I immediately realize my mistake. People shrink upon hearing my mother's name at home, but here my empty threat only makes things worse. The Litho boys cut me with glares that set my heart racing.

One of them waves his hand and the air shifts to encase the whole clearing in a shimmering bubble. Everything outside it seems to disappear. I suspect that the bubble will keep anyone from seeing or hearing what's happening inside, too. "We know your grandmother and your *owahyat* mother too," the boy says, his face twisted in disgust.

"We know you as well, Arrah," the dorek boy snickers. "It's rare to meet a *ben'ik* with a lineage so rich in magic. But then, the sins of the mother often fall on the daughter."

My eyes land on a staff propped against a rack as sweat glides down my back. It may be useless against them, but at least it's something. My chances would be better if I had a hint of magic, even a smidgeon. Enough to keep me safe. I clench my hands into fists, thinking of when Heka's magic touched me last night. It drew my *ka* from my body, then left me like a fleeting wind. I can *almost* understand why some charlatans risk so much to lure magic to them.

I keep all four boys in my line of sight. "If you call me *ben'ik* one more time . . ."

"We're going to teach you a lesson," the dorek boy says. "*Ben'ik*."

I run because they have magic and I'm outnumbered. Before I get far, I crash into the edge of the bubble and fall down. They've made sure I can't leave.

My pulse drums in my ears as I climb to my feet and lunge for the staff. It feels balanced in my hands, offering me the faintest feeling of security. If I had a weapon of choice, this would be it. *Any Aatiri worth a grain of sand knows their way around a staff*, Oshhe would say.

The Litho boys laugh.

Let them.

I shift my stance. "Touch me and I will break every bone in your miserable bodies."

"The *ben'ik* can fight?" The third boy cracks his knuckles. "I don't believe it."

"Believe it when you eat dirt, you swine," I say.

My words sound braver than I feel, but I mean them. Even if they have magic, I won't go down without a fight.

"She's bluffing," says the bubble boy.

Magic crackles in the air like a summer thunderstorm and I brace myself, the staff ready. They close in around me. The third boy pounds his fist in his other hand, and the ground trembles. I take several steps back, keeping the barrier at my rear.

"Well, what do we have here?" someone asks from behind me.

Sukar appears out of thin air. The three tattoos across his forehead sparkle like stars in the night. He runs his hand over his shaven head, looking as amused as ever. The Litho boys take one look at his slight physique and roll their eyes. Their mistake.

Essnai steps into the clearing behind him—statuesque and poised, a head taller than both of us. Purple powder covers her forehead down to her long lashes. The red beneath her midnight eyes and the gold dusted on her nose stand out against her umber skin. Her lips are two different shades of pink. She's changed her hair back to black. Even the Litho boys are too caught up in her beauty to notice her deceptively relaxed grip on her staff.

I sigh in relief. My friends never fail to make an entrance.

Essnai clucks her tongue at me. "Always wandering off and getting into trouble."

Heat creeps up my neck, but I answer her accusation with a shrug.

"Someone forgot to invite us to this little party," Sukar says.

"Your protection tattoos won't save you, Zu." The dorek boy spits on the ground.

Sukar pulls a pair of sickles from scabbards across his chest. "They broke through your ward easily enough, but I have these just in case."

Even his curved blades have magic symbols engraved in them—made by his uncle, the Zu seer in the Almighty Temple.

"What're two more *ben'iks* to beat up?" the third Litho boy asks with a laugh.

Essnai says nothing as she lifts her staff into the same position as mine.

"You should leave before you get hurt," I warn the Litho swine.

"You're bold for the daughter of an *owahyat*," says the bubble boy.

Before the words clear his lips, I hurl a rock, aimed for his face. It's clear from the malice in his voice exactly what he thinks when he calls my mother a prostitute. He doesn't know her and if anyone can talk crap about Arti, it's me, not him. But the boy knocks the rock from its path with a gust of wind.

"Nice try, *ben'ik*," he says.

I spit in the dirt.

So they're talented in the elements. Dirty, arrogant swine. They think because we don't have magic, we're defenseless. Another mistake.

"Are we going to talk all night or fight?" Sukar yawns. "I vote fight."

Even magic isn't foolproof. I know that better than most from watching my father in his shop. The only way out is through the boy holding the bubble intact. He hasn't moved a muscle since he conjured it, as if he needs to stand still to keep it steady. That's my opening. I don't second-guess as I charge at him. My fingers tighten against the staff, but the ground shifts and I land hard on my face. The fourth Litho boy's outstretched arm trembles as the dirt under me groans and settles again.

Sukar and Essnai spring into action. My friends bat away the rocks two of the Litho boys hurtle at us with their magic, neither lifting a finger. I catch a rock and send it flying. It hits the boy who knocked me down square in the chest. He lets out a little squeak and I can't hide my satisfaction. Serves him right.

I'm on my feet again, my eyes narrowed on the bubble boy. He calls for help, but Sukar and Essnai already have his friends battered and bruised on their knees. The bubble falters before I even reach the boy, and he runs away. I don't bother going after him. He got the point. Once the bubble's gone, the sounds of the night's celebrations rush back into the clearing. The rest of the Litho boys run away too.

My hands shake as I clutch the staff. They weren't even that powerful. Yet, if not for Sukar and Essnai's help, things could've ended much worse. How could Heka bless scum like that with magic and skip me? At the first beats of the djembe drums, dread slips between my ribs like a sharp blade. It's time to face the thing I've been dreading all day.

My tests with Grandmother—the great Aatiri chieftain.

THREE

Grandmother's dome pavilion looms over the smaller, squat tents in the Aatiri camp. Its patchwork of bright cloth billows in the gentle breeze in the valley. My legs ache as I weave through the throng of people preparing for the second night of the blood moon. I wish I could lose myself in them and find a place to hide from my tests. I don't want to fail again.

I suck in a deep breath as I finally reach the tent. My cousin Nenii pins back the flap and ducks inside. She and Semma clear away teacups and wash down the long, low table. Magic strung in glass beads, draped along the walls, lights the room. I'm always amazed by Grandmother's endless ways to bend magic to her will.

I press two fingers to my forehead and dip my head in a slight bow. "Blessed night, cousins," I say in Aatiri. The greeting twists on my tongue, but the girls don't make fun of my accent. These cousins have always been kind and accepting, even if I'm an outsider. Still, it's hard not to wonder if it's only because of Grandmother. Plenty of people are polite to me in Tamar out of respect for my mother.

They chime back, "You honor us, granddaughter of our great chieftain."

"Join me, Little Priestess," Grandmother calls from another room.

Her voice brims with authority, but it's not unkind.

Nenii and Semma give me encouraging smiles as they fluff pillows.

Before I slip into Grandmother's private quarters, Nenii whispers, "Come by our tent later so we can help you braid your hair." My cheeks warm, but I'm glad for the offer. It's long overdue and would take me forever. I shake off my doubts about my cousins. Not everyone cares that I don't have magic.

I pull back the curtain that separates the salon from Grandmother's private quarters. She sits cross-legged on a mat in the middle of the floor. She isn't wearing her bone charms, only a yellow kaftan with colored beads across her shoulders. Light flickers from the jars of burning oil in the corners and leaves the rest of the room in shadows. Her quarters smell of cloves, cinnamon, and cardamom—the spices of her favorite tea. "Grandmother," I say, bowing to her. "Honored Chieftain of Tribe Aatiri, blessed night."

"Welcome, granddaughter." She smiles. "Sit."

Grandmother clutches her hands on her lap, and when I squat on the reed floor facing her, she flips her wrists and lets the bones fly. They land between us in the same position they did all those years ago when she first tried to teach me magic. As they do every year. Her whispers fill the room as she channels the ancestors' spirits through the bones. Several voices come across at once. My belly twinges at the clipped, guttural words that are neither Aatiri nor

Tamaran. The language doesn't sound like that of any nation near the Kingdom or the tribal lands. In the corner, one of the candles flickers and goes out.

Grandmother has never told me what the message means. Whenever I ask, she answers, "The time is not yet right for me to say."

Still the question burns on my lips. *What does it mean?* I almost beg for an answer but bite my tongue. It isn't fair that she's keeping it from me. Why would she? Unless it's something bad, or if it means that I'll never come into my magic. The blank expression on her face gives nothing away.

"People are upset about me entering the sacred circle," I start, then my words catch in my throat. She had to know they would be. Grandmother stares at me with one eyebrow arched in anticipation. She bears the angular face, prominent cheeks, and proud nose common among the Aatiri. Her look, as always, is one of slight amusement—as if she's privy to a secret that no one else knows.

The phantom of Heka's magic still lingers on my skin. It was the first time that magic has ever come to *me*. It didn't just brush by on its way to answer someone else's call. It sparked in my soul like a vital organ I hadn't known was missing. I want to tell Grandmother this, but I'm afraid of what it means that the magic didn't stay.

She risked angering the other *edam* and the entirety of the tribal people—for *what reason?* I bite my lip and drop my gaze to my hands. "Why did you do it?"

"People should mind their own business," Grandmother says, her voice sharp. When I meet her eyes again, she smiles. "As for your question, let me try to explain." She waves her hand over the bones and they arrange themselves into a neat pile. "Our magic presents in different ways. It's no small thing that you can see magic and your mind resists it. I've long wondered if, perhaps, your magic is simply asleep. I brought you into the sacred circle in an attempt to awaken it."

A flush of heat creeps up my neck. "I guess there's only one way to see if it worked."

"Take the bones," Grandmother says. "Tell me what you see."

So begin my tests.

The bones feel smooth and polished, and slippery against my hands. They don't hum with magic or speak to me. It's no different from Imebyé all those years ago, or any blood moon since then. I clutch the bones with my eyes closed, my pulse pounding in my ears. I will them to tell me their secrets. *Please let this work.*

When I can't stand waiting any longer, I throw them.

The bones scatter in a random pattern that means nothing to me. Grandmother studies them, her eyes lingering on each bone, then lets out a soft sigh. They don't mean anything to her either.

Why do I keep failing at this? What am I doing wrong?

She allows me no time to lament, only snaps her fingers. Nenii enters the room carrying a mortar and pestle, a knife, and piles of herbs. Once she's gone, Grandmother says, "Make a blood medicine of your choice."

That I can do. I've learned how to make dozens while helping my father in his shop. But without magic, all blood medicine does is give a person a stomachache. Or a hangover.

I crush herbs, adding a bit at a time to get the right consistency. The medicine calls for white nightshade smoothed into a paste and a dozen other herbs. It isn't long before I'm lost in the work, my mind at peace for the first time at the festival. I've always found making blood medicine calming, even if challenging. Juices stain my fingers green and a pungent odor stings my nose by the time it's done.

To seal the spell, I need to add my blood, but I hesitate. I don't want to disappoint Grandmother or myself again. After this, we'll know if last night had been worth it, if my true magic was only asleep. I nick the tip of my finger, add blood, and whisper the incantation in one breath.

It's done.

If my measurements were off by the smallest amount, the work would be for nothing. Without magic it *is* for nothing. I always go through the motions because of Grandmother, but after Heka, I hope a spark of magic will finally show. This year has to be different. It's now or never.

Grandmother's silver locs are loose and reach her waist. Even without her adornments, she still looks every bit the chieftain that she is. She raises an eyebrow. "You intend to turn your hair blue?"

"It's very popular in Tamar." I smile down at the bowl. If it works, I'll make Essnai all the hair color she could dream of. I'll find a thousand frivolous, fun things to do with magic. I'll be useful in my father's shop, and one day open a magic shop of my own.

"Indeed." Grandmother gestures at the bowl, a grin dancing on her lips. "After you."

We both drink and nothing happens. Aside from the atrocious taste. Another failure.

On to the next.

We spend hours going through the tests.

I fail to read minds.

I fail to manipulate water.

I fail to see into the future.

I fail to call upon the ancestors.

I fail to heal the cuts on my fingers.

I fail to detect what ails a sick woman.

We work late into the night, people coming and going for various tests. My head throbs and my stomach twists in knots as the hour of *ösana* approaches. Magic is at its most potent in that space of time between night and sunrise. Grandmother never loses patience and encourages me to keep trying. I wish my mother would be that way instead of voicing her constant disapproval.

"Are there any *easier* tests?" I ask the moment we are alone again.

Grandmother throws the bones again. "Those *were* the easier tests, Little Priestess."

I wince. "Please don't call me that. It only makes things worse."

She frowns but doesn't look up. Something in the bones has her full attention. She points to two bones that lie crossed together. This is new. They've never landed like that before.

The sacred circle *did* change something.

My heart races as I lean forward in anticipation. Could this finally be it?

Grandmother's finger shakes as she speaks in two voices. One is a low hiss that comes from her throat, and the other sounds like glass shattering. Both are so terrible that they send chills down my spine. Her head snaps up. "Who are you?"

I shrink when her eyes land on me—only the whites visible. "What?" I ask, not knowing what else to say. I've seen her in trances before but never anything like this. Something shifts in the air. "Grandmother, what's wrong?"

"Leave!" she shouts, staring over my shoulder. I jump to my feet and whirl around. The tent flutters and the unlit jar of oil sparks to life. I back away. No one's there, but a new, unfamiliar magic rushes into the room. Magic not coming from Grandmother and definitely not from me. Magic that I *can't* see, only *feel* slithering on my skin. "You do not belong here, green-eyed serpent!"

Spittle shoots out of Grandmother's mouth as she barks the last words. Sparks of magic—*tribal magic*—fill the room. It lights on her skin. Her whole body begins to glow. The bones rise from the ground and spin, caught in an impossible windstorm.

I clench my fists as her magic sweeps through the tent. It flits against my arms like moth wings. I want to flee, but I don't move. It won't hurt me.

Grandmother's head snaps backward so hard that her spine cracks. I gasp. Soon we're both shaking. She leans to one side, sweat pouring down her face. For the first time, she looks old and fragile. I kneel next to her.

"It will pass," she says, straightening herself up again, though she's still panting.

"What . . . what was that?" I stutter.

"Have you seen the green-eyed serpent in your dreams, child?" she asks, her voice sharp.

"What?" My teeth chatter, and I hug my shoulders. The tent is cold in the aftermath of the strange magic. The space feels too small, the air too thin. Something bad was here—something powerful enough to challenge Grandmother. "I don't understand."

She clucks her tongue, then glances at the curtains separating us from the rest of the tent. They stand as stiff as sheets of metal until she draws a loop in the air with her finger and they become cloth again. "Enter, Oshhe."

My father bursts through the curtains with so much force that he halfway rips them from the ceiling. His expression is panicked as he looks between us. Upon seeing that we're all right, he lets out a deep sigh. "Honored Chieftain," he says, bowing. Then his voice softens. "Mother, what happened?"

"It's hard to put into words," Grandmother says. "Please join us, son."

Oshhe squats beside me, his eyebrows pinched together. "Are you okay?"

I nod and lean against his side. He wraps his arm around my shoulders. He's warm and smells of grass and sunshine, and his embrace calms my nerves. "To answer your question, Grand-mother," I say. "No, I haven't seen a serpent, green-eyed or not, in my dreams."

"I think you better explain, Mother," Oshhe says, his voice calm—too calm. He only uses that voice when he's *not* happy.

"There was someone here . . . *something*." Grandmother shakes her head as if clearing away cobwebs. "Someone who does not belong. Perhaps a relic from the past, I do not know, or an omen of the future . . ."

Again Grandmother speaks in riddles, but her voice shakes a lit-tle. Whomever, or whatever, this thing is, it's rattled the great Aatiri chieftain, and that scares me too.

"She—the green-eyed serpent—possesses magic I do not know," Grandmother finishes. "Magic that feels very old and very power-ful."

"Magic you don't know?" Oshhe questions, one brow raising. "Was it . . . an *orisha*?"

"An orisha here?" I blurt out. "In the tribal lands?"

I can't imagine the orishas in the tribal lands any more than Heka in the Kingdom. Though the tribes acknowledge that the orishas exist, they hold Heka above all. In the Kingdom, the orishas take precedence, but the citizens come from all walks of life and so do their deities.

"No, not an orisha," Grandmother says, her tone reluctant. "Something else."

"A rebirth, perhaps?" Oshhe says. "A powerful witchdoctor who has cheated death."

Grandmother massages her temples. "I can't be certain. I need to talk to an old friend who will know more. It will take time to reach her, for she does not walk these lands."

A chill runs down my spine. Grandmother is the Aatiri chieftain. I've never known her to not have an answer. She's one of the most powerful witchdoctors in the tribal lands, in all the world.

"You haven't said what this green-eyed serpent—what *she* has to do with me," I say, unable to hold my question back any longer.

Grandmother regards me again, her eyes bloodshot. "In truth, I do not know, Arrah."

Her words knock the taste from my mouth. The Litho boys would've beaten me if not for Essnai and Sukar's help. The boys' magic had been feeble and nothing special, yet still too much to handle on my own. Now this? My mind slips back to the sacred circle again. Why couldn't Heka gift me with magic? "Am I in trouble?"

"I will not lie to you," Grandmother says. "I do not think she means you well."

"But you have an idea of what *she* is," Oshhe says, his face blanching.

Grandmother's voice drops low—the way one utters an unspeakable secret. "I don't want to speculate." She scoops the bones into her lap, her hand shaking. "It's best if I consult with the other *edam* first . . ."

"Grandmother!" I beg. "*Please* . . . you know, don't you?"

She worries her fingers across the bones, still refusing to meet my eye.

"Mother," Oshhe says, his jaw clenched, "speak your mind."

"The green-eyed serpent," Grandmother says after a weary breath, "is said to be a symbol of demon magic."

Silence falls upon the room and Grandmother's words hang like a noose between the three of us. Demons are myths, legends. Stories that parents tell to scare their children into behaving. The scribes teach us that the orishas saved mortal kind from them. Back home we call someone who sucks the joy out of life a *soul eater*. It's meant as a harmless insult—one inspired by the tales that demons feasted upon *kas*. Everything I know about them comes from those half-forgotten stories. People fill in the gaps in the folklore with their imagination. The scribes say that the orishas erased the full memories of demons from our minds to protect us. Now Grandmother's telling me that demons are real, and one is very much alive.

"It's *impossible*," my father whispers, the news stealing the strength from his voice. "There has to be another explanation. Demon magic has been gone for thousands of years."

"Yes, I know," Grandmother says, closing her fist around the bones.

I rub the back of my head, feeling the onslaught of a headache. The vision has Grandmother scared too. She's trying to protect me, but I want the truth. I need to know if the green-eyed serpent is a demon . . . *how* could it be possible and what does it mean? Could this be the reason my magic is asleep, or why Heka's grace had only touched me in passing in the sacred circle? I'm reaching for straws, but I ask anyway, "Does this *demon* have anything to do with my magic not showing?"

"It's possible," Grandmother says, her voice so very tired. "There's much in this world that even I cannot perceive. As I said, I must consult with the other *edam*. Together, we may be able to find an answer."

My father's practiced calm gives away to frustration. "How do I keep Arrah safe?"

Grandmother thinks long before answering, "I do not know, but we'll find a way."

I don't miss the uncertainty between her words. I'm irritated that they need to protect me. If I had magic of my own, I could protect myself. My mind reels with the grim news. Not only has Heka forsaken me his gift, but things are much worse. I once laughed at stories about demons, and now I know that one may walk in my shadow.

She does not mean me well.

RE'MEC, ORISHA OF SUN, TWIN KING

Tell me again, sister, why do we tolerate such disrespect from these tribal people? I have a mind to stomp out their lives like the ants they are. They think magic is a gift. A gift! How can they be so foolish? Magic is a curse for mortal kind, and in time they will use it to destroy themselves. Who knows that better than us? We saved their world once, and I'm not of the temperament to save it again. I should take another nap. Twenty years wasn't enough. I grow tired.

Heka is to blame for our new troubles. Had we not lost so many of our brethren in the War, we could have stopped him from giving them magic. Now we find ourselves in this new predicament.

It's not that I'm sentimental. This world can burn today and I will have forgotten it by tomorrow. It means nothing to me. It's the principle of the matter. We gave everything to protect them from that bastard Demon King, everything. Now this is how we're repaid for our sacrifice, our kindness?

I'm sorry, dear sister. I know that the blood moon is your time. It is your way of remembering our fallen brethren, as the Rite of

Passage is mine. As he's done for a thousand years, Heka has come back to ruin your bereavement. His very presence is an act of pissing on our siblings' graves, if we had bodies to bury. Or do they burn bodies now? I forget what's popular these days.

You don't have to remind me of our failures, Koré. They haunt my every thought. I should've known that we'd only postponed the inevitable. After five thousand years, I hoped that it wouldn't come to this, but the beast stirs even now. We must act before it's too late.

Alas, sister, as always you're right. I could not stand by and let this world come to an end. I couldn't do it then, and I won't do it now. I love it too much, and that is my greatest failing above all else.

FOUR

It's never easy returning to Tamar after spending time in the tribal lands. I'm bone-tired and more than a little cranky from sleeping in a tent the entire time. The whole trip took a month. Eight days of travel each way with the caravan, and two weeks at the festival. We arrive in the middle of the night, and I'm so relieved to be back home that I go straight to bed. Mere hours later, I wake buried in pillows and sheets that smell of lavender and coconut. They were fresh and cool last night, but now they're ruffled and sweat-stained. The curtains around my bed keep out most of the sunlight, but some slips between the gaps and I can't fall back asleep.

This was supposed to be my year—the year that I can finally say that I have magic too. The year that I hold a light in my mother's shadow. Even an ember would've been enough for me. I tell myself for the one hundredth time that there's still a chance, that I can't give up. But hope is a fleeting thing when met with repeated failure.

Since the first night of the blood moon, I've dreamed about magic. The good dreams always end with some version of me possessing

Heka's gift. I step out of the sacred circle so powerful that the *edam* name me a witchdoctor on the spot. I glide on a cloud like the Aatiri in the opening ceremony. I leave my body to wander the spirit world and find Heka waiting for me underneath a palm tree. I come back to Tamar and tell Rudjek, and for once he's speechless. When I wake up, still on the edge of sleep, a sense of peace settles over me. But the moment never lasts.

In the bad dreams, I step into the sacred circle and the *edam* stop their dance. The valley falls silent and one by one they turn their backs to me. Or the Litho boys drag me out of the circle, kicking and screaming because I don't belong. Or as punishment a witchdoctor turns me into a *ndzumbi* to live out the rest of my life doing their bidding.

I shake my head. Dreams aside, Heka's magic rejected me. That was real. And that's the hardest thing to wrap my mind around. Yes, I have *gifts*, but what good are they if I can't use magic? What will these *gifts* do to protect me from the green-eyed serpent if she decides to show herself again? What if next time she can't be sent away? Seeing how powerful she'd been against Grandmother—it's possible that she's the reason my magic hasn't shown.

I pull the sheet up to my neck and screw my eyes shut. Terra is shuffling around my bedroom, so I pretend I'm still asleep. She usually hums to herself while she prepares my bath, but this morning she's quiet. Ty, our matron, along with Nezi, our porter, have been with our household all my life. Nezi bought Terra's indenture contract two years ago, after her father's debtors caught up with him. Terra told me that they would've cut off his hands had she not agreed to work off his debt.

Before I can bury my face in a pillow, she pulls the curtains back and the full brunt of the sun blinds me. In Tamar, the sun is also called the eye of Re'Mec, but right now more colorful names cross my mind.

"Twenty-gods," I curse, shielding my eyes. "Is it eighth morning bells already?"

Someone clears her throat and I bolt upright—it's not Terra. A short, stout woman with gray cornrows stands at the foot of my bed with her fists on her hips. She purses her lips in that way that leaves no doubt that she means business.

"Ty!" I slip out of bed in an instant. "Pardon my language. I thought you were Terra."

She stares at me and blinks twice, and I brush the wrinkles out of my nightgown and stand a little straighter. Ty never comes herself. This isn't her domain. She does all the cooking, and Terra takes care of the rest of the chores.

She shakes her head and taps her foot, a sign that she wants me to hurry up.

My cheeks warm as I rush into the washroom where my bath is waiting. I don't linger long. Then I slip into a fresh cotton robe that smells like home. I inhale deeper, taking it in, trying to push the tribal lands out of my mind. When I return to my room, it's pristine. The white sheets are as smooth as stretched papyrus, the pillows stacked in a neat row. Cold stabs through my slippers as I pad across the stone floor to my vanity in search of my favorite balm.

Ty sorts through the shelves of clothes in the armoire next to the window. When she doesn't find what she's looking for, she crosses the room to the closet by the door. On the way, she fluffs one of the velvet pillows on the settee in the center of the room. She's not the most cheerful person, but today she's more somber than usual. It isn't one of her bad days, but definitely not one of her good days either.

While she's searching through my clothes, I go to the shrine next to the bed. Dust coats my collection: my very first bone charm, the one that my father gave me at Imebyé. The Kes necklace made of crystal beads to bring good luck. Two clay dolls, which Oshhe and I made to honor two of his favorite aunts, long since passed. In the right hands, these things amplify magic and our connection to the ancestors. But in my hands, they are only trinkets. No one touches my shrine, as is the Aatiri custom, so the whole lot of it needs cleaning after weeks away. I reach for a rag, but Ty clears her throat behind me again.

"Yes, you're right." I sigh. "I can do that after my lessons with the scribes."

I mean after I see Rudjek. I wrote him a letter before we reached the city and gave it to Terra to deliver. If all goes well, he'll meet me after my lessons in our secret place by the river.

When I turn to face Ty, she holds up a flowing teal sheath. It's breathtaking, the way the sun catches on the beads and gathers on the fine silk. Essnai and her mother gave it to me on my last birth day. Ty may not usually help with my clothes, but she should know the sheath is too formal for lessons with the scribes.

"I don't think that's *quite* appropriate," I say, heading to the armoire. I dig through piles of folded clothes and pull out my sea-blue tunic and matching pants. Ty shakes her head and lays the sheath on the bed alongside a beaded belt and jeweled slippers.

Before I can protest again, my mother sweeps into my room, her gold *Ka*-Priestess's kaftan rustling in her wake. The space between us feels too small and I cringe, as if caught doing something wrong. The morning light glows against her honey-golden skin, and her amber eyes shine like rare gemstones. When Oshhe and I got back last night, Arti was at the Almighty Temple. The seers sometimes hold vigils for days, so it's never a surprise if she's not home. I've always counted myself lucky then. It's easier to avoid her.

My mother is the definition of beauty. Her ebony hair flows down her back in loose curls, threaded through with pale crystals. She bears Tribe Mulani's softness and curves and small stature compared to the Aatiri. I am somewhere in the middle, taller than my mother, but much shorter than my very tall cousins. Although the resemblance between us is unmistakable, next to her, I might as well be a squat mule.

She never comes to visit me here. I can't guess the meaning of this—unless she's talked to my father already, and she knows.

Arti peers around the room, examining its condition, before her eyes land on Ty. The two women exchange a look—one of understanding that I've seen shared between them many times before.

Ty has never spoken to me, nor to anyone for that matter. I've heard her mumbling in the kitchen when she's alone, but she stops as soon as someone else comes near. I don't know why she doesn't talk. My childhood questions about it always went unanswered. No different from Grandmother hesitating to answer my questions about the green-eyed serpent.

"You may leave us, Ty," Arti says, tilting her head to show respect.

When Ty is gone, Arti's sharp amber eyes fall upon me. "I trust that you're well."

"I am, Mother," I say, resisting the urge to glance away. "Thank you for asking."

"Your father told me what happened at the Blood Moon Festival." Her attention shifts to the altar, and she wrinkles her nose. I can't tell if she disapproves of the mix of tribal trinkets or the dust. "It's time to let go of this foolish dream of having magic. Mulani show their gifts at a very young age. If it hasn't happened by now, it won't happen at all."

My mother speaks in a matter-of-fact tone that sets my teeth on edge. She might as well be talking to a stranger on the street. Her words sting in my chest and leave me speechless.

She brushes her hand across the sheath. The luminous pearl of her *Ka*-Priestess's ring shimmers in the sunlight. As her hand glides over the fabric, the color of the pearl changes from onyx to slate to cyan. "It's a shame to come from two powerful bloodlines and have no magic at all. No Mulani in my family has ever been without. But there is nothing to be done about it."

"There's still a chance." My words come out feeble and desperate.

"What makes you think so?" Arti says in a voice devoid of any emotion. "This year the Aatiri chieftain positioned you directly in Heka's path, and he didn't see fit to give you magic. It was a bold gesture, and commendable, but has anything changed?"

Warmth creeps up my neck at the slight. She very well knows the answer, but she wants me to say it. "Grandmother had a vision," I say, rallying my nerves. "A demon could be blocking my magic." That wasn't exactly what Grandmother saw, but it's the most plausible reason for my magic not showing.

"I do wish your grandmother would stop giving you false hope," Arti says after a deep sigh. "And this talk about demons?" She laughs. "That's the stuff of old wives' tales, Arrah. They've been gone for five thousand years, and if they were back, what would one want with you? A girl without magic."

Her words are a well-honed slap to the face—*yet* another reminder how much of a disappointment I am to her. What can I say? How can I fight back, when she'll have an answer for everything? I believe Grandmother, but it's not worth arguing. There's no winning with my mother—no convincing her of anything other than what she chooses to believe.

"I know that magic is important to you, daughter," Arti says, her words softer. "But don't be so obsessed that you'd do something foolish for a taste of it."

I bite my tongue as fire spreads through my belly. She's eyeing the bone charm on the altar now. Does my mother think I would stoop so low that I would consider trading my years for magic? Yes, I want it, but I'm not a fool. I'm not that desperate either. My mind falls on the night of Imebyé and the woman writhing in the sand. That was her choice. There are moments in your life that leave lasting impressions. The woman's sallow skin and rotten teeth, the way magic came to her, the way it was destroying her—every detail has stayed with me over the years.

I didn't know at the time what she'd done, but my father explained it to me after we returned home. In his shop one day, I asked if the charlatans in the market were like the woman in the desert. The ones who looked like they had one foot in life and the other in death. He said that some tribal people without magic had learned how to trade years of their lives to possess it. Upon finding this out, I bounced on the balls of my feet with excitement, because it meant I could have magic too. Oshhe squeezed my cheeks between his big hands. "No magic is worth your life, Little Priestess. That is not our way."

He stared into my eyes, his expression so serious and grave that the excitement fled as fast as it had come. "Promise me you'll never do anything like that no matter what." His deep voice echoed in his shop. "Promise me, daughter."

"But why, Father?" I said, jutting out my bottom lip.

My father sighed, his patience waning. "When you barter your years for magic, it takes of you what it will. It could be five years, or your whole life as payment. It does not matter the complexity of the ritual, spell, or charm. There's no way to tell until it's too late. Even I cannot reverse the damage that comes from such foolishness."

Magic has a price if you're willing to pay.

I, in fact, am not willing to pay. If I can't have magic gifted to me, I'll do without. I still have my pride, and that means something. I lift my chin and face Arti.

"Is there a reason you've come to see me this fine morning, Mother?" I say, my jaw set. "I need to get ready for my lessons."

Arti glances up at that, her face impassive. It's a wonder my parents ended up together. Oshhe is full of stories and laughter while my mother is sharp-tongued and *efficient*. I have to believe that once she was warmer, long before she became the third-most powerful person in the Kingdom.

"Suran plans to name his youngest son his heir at the assembly today." Arti folds her arms behind her back and begins to pace. "Not that he has much choice, since the other two are an embarrassment to the so-called Omari legacy."

I clutch the tunic against my chest as if it can protect me from the animosity in her voice. It's no secret that the Vizier and my mother hate each other. "Is that so?" I say, forcing my voice to sound bored and uninterested.

The Vizier is the right hand of the Almighty One. He governs the Kingdom. As head of the Almighty Temple, my mother is the voice of the orishas. It's said that Re'Mec himself visits the seers on occasion—when the mood strikes—but Arti never speaks of it. Because the seers come from the tribes, she also oversees trade with the tribal lands. Relations with all other countries, such as Estheria, Yöom, and the North, fall under the Vizier's domain.

"Two can play Suran's game," Arti says. "You will attend the assembly with me."

"But why?" I swallow the bitter taste on my tongue. It goes without saying that I have no place or reason to be there. I've never dreamed of being *Ka*-Priestess one day. Even so, it hurts knowing that without magic I'd never even be considered.

The Almighty One handpicks the Vizier and *Ka*-Priestess. The title of Vizier always falls to an Omari, close cousins of the royal family. As for the *Ka*-Priest or *Ka*-Priestess, the Almighty One chooses the most powerful of the seers. It's a small mercy that my mother's position isn't a birthright, or I'd be an embarrassing end to *our* family legacy. "We will make a statement of our own," Arti says on her way out. "Be ready at half bell to ten."

"But . . . ," I protest.

My mother pauses in the doorway with her back to me. "Did you say something, Arrah?"

What's one more slight to add to a treasure trove of them? "No, Mother."

Once a month, the leaders of the Kingdom meet to debate taxes and tariffs and new decrees. The Almighty One and his two sons, Crown Prince Darnek and his younger brother, Tyrek. The Vizier and his four guildmasters, and my mother with the four other seers from the Temple. When I go to the assembly with Essnai and Sukar, it's fun, but I dread attending with my mother.

With Arti gone, I slip into the sheath, admiring the splash of bright beads that run from the neckline to the hem. It's fitted through the hips, flaring just below my knees. I loop the belt low around my waist and toe on the sandals. Although it's quite pretty, I prefer my trousers. They have pockets.

While I'm adjusting the sheath in the mirror, Terra strolls into my room with a jeweled box tucked under her arm. She smiles, her freckles standing out against her bronze skin. She looks regal with her golden hair done up in braids. It's nice to have someone my age in the villa. There's never a dull moment with her. She collects gossip like some people collect figurines.

"I bet Ty gave you a scare," Terra says, her voice bright and musical.

"You could've warned me," I grumble. "She was in a mood this morning."

At that, Terra descends upon me with a little too much gleam in her eyes, like I'm a plaything to mold to her wishes. She massages oil into my scalp before twisting my braids in an elaborate crown with strings of pearls woven between the strands. While I can't deny it's beautiful, it's also very heavy. Terra spends what feels like forever powdering my face in shades of golds and silvers. When she's done, she grins at her handiwork and rushes me outside. Nezi has already opened the gate, and the litter waits in front of it. Eight men stand with their eyes downcast, the sun glistening off their brown skin.

The red curtain is half-drawn, and my mother waits inside. I swallow hard and join her. The compartment is cool and smells of wood polish laced with her sweet perfume. We sit facing each other, but Arti doesn't see me. Her eyes are vacant as she stares into a corner. She's so lost in thought that she doesn't stir when Nezi commands the laborers to proceed.

"Get going now," our porter yells, "and take care with them." There's a subtle "or else" in Nezi's voice, a warning. I wouldn't put it past her, if an accident were to befall us, to personally seek retribution.

The men lift on three, and we're on our way. Our villa sits on the north edge of the district, among other fine estates owned by families of import in Tamar. I steal glimpses of the city between the curtains, soaking in the bright colors. We travel down back roads to avoid the crowds of the West Market. Most people will go about their regular business today. It's only those with influence that attend the assembly. My father never comes, citing his allergy to politics.

After a long silence between us, Arti says, voice low and calculating, "When we arrive, follow my lead. Do not speak, do not smile, do not sit until after I've taken my place on the first tier. Do you understand?"

I startle at the sudden fire in her words.

"Yes," I say, knitting my fingers together.

Long before we reach the coliseum, we hear the roar of the crowd. Towering orisha statues stand in a row guarding the most prominent families of the city. Soon the crowd is as thick as bees, as scholars, scribes, and heads of families clamber into the coliseum. The building is a honeycomb-shaped mammoth with doors large enough to accommodate giants. When people see our litter, they slink to the side, the laborers never slowing.

Tenth morning bells strike when we are mere moments from entering the dome, which means we're late. There's no mistaking that my mother's up to something.

She's got a scheme brewing in her eyes.

FIVE

A gong echoes in the West Market, marking the start of the assembly. If my mother's even a bit mad about being late, she hides it well. The look of disinterest never slips from her face.

The crowd on the streets hushes and the Vizier's words fill the silence.

"You honor us with your presence, Almighty One, Crown Prince Darnek, and Second Son Tyrek." His voice blasts in the West Market. "May your wisdom guide our hearts and minds. May our orisha lords look upon the Kingdom favorably for as long as your great family reigns."

The Vizier pauses a heartbeat. "If the public will allow me a small indulgence, I would like my son, Rudjek Omari, to join me on the first tier."

My stomach sinks. I hope Rudjek isn't as caught off guard as I was this morning. In the new silence, I imagine him weaving through people and climbing the steps to reach his father.

I hold my breath as we draw closer to the coliseum. I expect the laborers to stop at the giant doors, but they rush us straight into the heart of the assembly. The crowd gasps, drowning out the Vizier's next words. When the laborers set the litter down, Arti gives me a meaningful glance. *Follow my lead, or else.*

As she descends from the litter, her head held high, triumph flashes in her amber eyes. The pieces fall into place. She *wanted* to be late so that she could interrupt the Vizier as he introduced Rudjek as his heir.

The voices fall silent upon seeing the *Ka*-Priestess. I follow my mother, resisting the urge to shrink beneath hundreds of stares. The Vizier stands on the first tier of the raised platform, shiny shotels sheathed on either side of his waist. His swords look like they belong in a museum, not like they've ever seen a day of battle.

My eyes find Rudjek, and when his dark gaze meets mine, my stomach flutters. I hold back a smile. He stands beside his father, clad in a purple elara to the Vizier's white and gold. The handles of his half-moon swords are dull and well-worn. His face is angular and lean, and recently met with a sharp razor. There's a shadow of a bruise under his right eye, no doubt from a fight in the arena. I should've known he couldn't stay out of trouble while I was gone.

He doesn't have his father's rich brown skin, but they share the same lush eyebrows and chiseled jawline. His coloring is between his father's shade and his Northern mother's paler, diaphanous skin. His hair is a mess of tangled black curls. I soak up everything about his face, as if we haven't seen each other in ages when it's been mere weeks.

He and his father both wear a craven-bone crest pinned to their collar, a mark of their family's importance. It signals their rank above all others in the Kingdom, except for the royal family. While the Omaris' crest is a lion's head, the royal family's—the Sukkaras'—ram is a symbol of their blood connection to the sun orisha, Re'Mec. There are others in the audience with crests that show their rank or position. And many more royal cousins proudly displaying their crests too.

"Don't let me interrupt," Arti says, her sweet voice echoing in the coliseum. Behind us the laborers take away the empty litter with practiced stealth. "By all means continue."

"*Ka*-Priestess," the Vizier spits out her title. "I'm glad you were gracious enough to join us. Although the assembly starts at tenth morning bells, in case you've forgotten."

Arti looks up to the second tier, which sits high above the first. The Almighty One and his sons lounge in velvety thrones with an attendant at each of their sides.

"My apologies, Almighty One, for my tardiness," Arti says, casting her glance to the floor. "I am late for reasons that will become apparent during the assembly."

The Almighty One leans forward on his throne, his eyes combing the length of her body, then says, "Begin."

While the Vizier's attention is on the Almighty One, Rudjek seizes his opportunity. He's halfway down the stairs before his father even notices. He returns to his empty seat, while I'm stuck counting down the moments until I can do the same.

The crowd perches on benches facing each other that stretch up the curved rotunda. Some sit so high that shadows shroud their faces. There's two thousand of the most influential people in Tamar here. People with an interest in the outcome of political decisions.

They're as polished as the quarry stone that makes up the round building. And they glow too, for the mosaic ceiling casts a prism of colors upon them. My sheath pales in comparison to the beaded kabas and jeweled headwraps worn by some of the women. Not to be outdone, the men dress in fancy agbadas, elaras, or the latest imported fashion.

The platform where the assembly meets is a two-tiered crescent moon. On the right of the first tier is a curved table and high-backed chairs for the Vizier and his four guildmasters. On the left, Arti and her seers sit in an identical arrangement. A spiral staircase leads up to the second tier. It's more for show than anything else. There's a pulley concealed behind a curtain that lifts each of the royals up to their private booth.

When Arti finally takes her place, I look for a seat. Sukar waves to get my attention. He and Essnai are sitting across from Rudjek, on the opposite side of the coliseum. Two blue-robed scribes look put out when I squeeze between my friends, forcing them to move over.

"Uncle said the *Ka*-Priestess was up to something," Sukar whispers, a gleam of excitement in his eyes. "I didn't think it was this. Interrupting the Vizier in his moment of glory . . . well played."

"Bring forth the first order of business." The Vizier barks the command to the courier standing at the edge of the first tier. The man steps forward and clears his throat as he unties a scroll that reaches to his knees. He begins reading a summary of today's agenda. Taxes, tithes, plans for a new public building, and another million mundane things that buzz in my ears. I'm starting to think that like my father, I'm allergic to politics.

"Does he have to stare like that?" Sukar whispers. "He looks like a lost puppy."

I don't ask who. I know who. Instead of listening to his father and my mother bickering, Rudjek is fanning himself with *my letter*. There's an expertly drawn donkey on the front—he knows the reason why. He grins at me and starts flourishing his hand in bolder strokes. I have a sudden urge to poke my tongue out at him but think better of it.

High above us, the Almighty One carries on a hushed conversation with Crown Prince Darnek. The only royal who seems interested in the proceedings is Second Son Tyrek. He's the same age as me, two years younger than his brother. He leans forward on his throne and follows the debate. But the Almighty One is never called upon to vote unless there is a tie, and today there are none.

I spend the entire assembly counting down the time to freedom. After two solid hours of debating and voting, the Vizier turns to the audience. "Does the public have any concerns to bring forth today?"

In the few times I've been in attendance, no one in the audience has brought an issue for debate. People seem content to sit and listen to the squabbles between the Guild and the Temple instead. I sit up straight, itching for him to adjourn the assembly. From the bored looks around me, I'm not the only one.

"With no further concerns," the Vizier says, "I hereby close—"

"I'd like to raise a concern that we have overlooked," Arti says from her perch among the seers. Her kaftan shines the richest gold while the other seers' kaftans are pale yellow. The striking contrast leaves no doubt that she, and she alone, is the voice of the Almighty Temple. Much the same as Rudjek's father in his pristine white elara.

In all the Kingdom, only the Vizier wears white silks. His guildmasters wear a variety of colors. The Master of Arms, Rudjek's aunt. The Master of Scribes, the Master of Scholars, the Master of Laborers. Half of whom look utterly disinterested in the proceedings.

"By all means, speak," the Vizier says. "We hope it's not to ask for yet another increase in tithes for the Temple. Please have mercy on our pocketbooks."

Nervous laughter rumbles through the coliseum, and people cast curious glances at each other. Even the guildmasters crack smiles.

The seers do not. Each of them wears a grim expression.

"There is a matter of grave importance." Arti rises from her chair. Her face is even grimmer than the other seers', and my pulse quickens. Nothing ever gets under my mother's skin. If she's worried, then it must be something bad. The room quiets as she glides to the center of the tier, and the Vizier huffs before yielding the floor to her. He whisks back to his seat, irritation etched on his face. "It pains me to say that a number of children have disappeared under the City Guard's watch." Arti pauses, her voice breaking. "Some from the orphanage, some not."

The audience turns to one another in collective whispers. I glance at Sukar, who shakes his head, and then at Essnai, who mouths, her voice low, "Did you know about this?"

"No," I say under my breath. I'm as shocked as everyone else, and don't understand why my mother waited this long to share such important news. It should've been first on the agenda.

"I've heard of no such report," the Vizier says, his brows creasing into a deep frown.

"While praying to the orishas on our recent vigil," Arti says, addressing the audience, "I saw something very disturbing. When I commune with the orishas, my *ka* wanders our great city, and our lords reveal things to me in strange ways."

I glance up at the Almighty One's booth again. Second Son Tyrek leans over to get his father's attention, but the Almighty One waves him off. He's busy laughing at something Crown Prince Darnek just whispered in his other ear.

"There's a vile person stalking the city and stealing children in the night," Arti says, her voice quiet. "A person I can only glimpse but not see clearly, because something protects them against my sight."

The Vizier's elara ruffles as he whirls around to face the Master of Arms, his twin sister, who sits to his right. "Is there any truth to this news?"

General Solar and the Vizier share the same sharp features and dark eyes. She leads the military forces of the Kingdom: the gendars, the guards, and the shotani.

"I received a report this morning." General Solar's voice is as cold as her brother's. "I am confident that the head of the City Guard will discover and arrest the culprit with speed."

"I wish I shared your confidence," Arti says, "but this is no ordinary child snatcher, to hide from our magic."

Barasa, the Zu seer, adds, "It must be the work of anti-magic."

The audience gasps, and my eyes land on the crest on the Vizier's elara. Anti-magic comes from craven bones. No one possesses it outside of the Omaris and the royal family. It isn't something you can buy. No one has seen a craven in centuries. Not since they slaughtered a legion of the Kingdom's army in one night.

It isn't hard to figure out what Arti and the seers are insinuating. Everyone knows the story of the Vizier's—and Rudjek's—ancestor who fought the cravens in the Aloo Valley. He'd slain a craven and later made trinkets of its bone to protect against the influence of magic. The bone could be the only thing to hide its wearer from the seers.

The Almighty One leans forward, his shaved head glistening with a dusting of gold. "Are you accusing the Omaris?"

I notice how he doesn't include *his* family—the Sukkaras.

"That is a bold accusation," Arti says, neither confirming nor denying it. "I'm only saying that the fiend must be wearing craven bone. That much I know from my vision." She casts a sidelong glance in the Vizier's general direction. "No one would question the Omaris' good name . . . but have we forgotten the incident in the market so soon?"

As Arti lets her words settle, everyone in the coliseum holds their breath. She means after the Rite of Passage. Re'Mec mandated the Rite to remind us of the orishas' sacrifice to save mortal kind. A hundred and twenty of them fell in their struggle to stop the Demon King and his insatiable thirst for souls. There's script on the Temple walls with instructions for the Rite, but there's no telling when Re'Mec will demand another one. Until the last Rite of Passage, there hadn't been one in twenty years.

For the Rite, the seers designed deadly obstacles for volunteers to undergo to test their mental and physical fortitude. Last time, they faced a hostile desert with nothing but the clothes on their backs. Looking to make their mark, the Vizier's older sons, Uran and Jemi, volunteered together. In the end, the Rite broke their minds just as it had done to so many before them.

The last Rite was five years ago—the only one in my lifetime. Fewer than a third of those who attempted it came back. Very few returned whole.

I wasn't in the market the day Jemi killed a merchant. Witnesses say he became enraged over a perceived slight. He was haggling with an Estherian over the price of a gossamer veil he wanted to buy for his mother. The argument went too far, and he cut the merchant's throat. After that, the Vizier sent him and his squadron on an assignment far from the Kingdom. He's been there ever since. The Vizier made his other son, Uran, an ambassador to the North. Rudjek says that he spends most of his time locked away in his rooms, refusing to see anyone, even his wife. He flies into sudden rages, and his attendants must restrain him.

A chill crawls down my back at how blank Rudjek's face has gone. I ache to go to him, but I know that would only make matters worse. We've come this far without our parents guessing how close we are.

"Where are your sons, Vizier?" Arti says, her voice bright. "I'm sure they'd want to clear their names."

My mother has wielded the news of the kidnappings at the assembly to strike at the Vizier, and doesn't care who else she'll hurt. She never does. Even so, the question of the missing children hits a nerve. From the whispers in the coliseum, I'm not alone in wondering who would do something so vile. My gaze finds Rudjek again, and my stomach sinks when he refuses to look at me.

SIX

According to my father, everyone has a little magic in them—only our family has more than most. He says that to the patrons who come to his shop to make them feel special. He knows it's not true, but people need something to believe. The crowd filing out of the coliseum certainly has no magic, and it would seem, no heart or conscience either.

They talk about the missing children like they're the latest scandal, and it annoys me to no end. To attend the assembly you must have property and standing. No one here will worry about their children, for none are without attendants day or night. I push through the throng of people, losing a few beads from my sheath along the way. There are so many of us that the gray-washed West Market feels alive for once. Alive and teeming with petty gossip.

"She'd better watch herself, lest she ends up like the former *Ka*-Priest," a man leans toward his friend to say. He's loud enough that some people mumble their soft agreements. Others rally to my mother's defense.

I only glare at him. It isn't the first time someone has flung that particular threat at my mother. It still stings. I don't like that Arti and the Vizier are always bickering. Sometimes it turns nasty. That said, she's done good for the Kingdom. When the Vizier joked about raising tithes again, he left out why the Temple asks for money. My mother and the seers run all public services in the Kingdom. Free education for those who can't afford private scribes, meals, shelter for orphans. Programs that my mother created when she became *Ka*-Priestess.

The former *Ka*-Priest, Ren Eké, was before my time, but people still sing his praises. He was beloved for his wise and quiet nature, and he and the Vizier got along well. People say there was better collaboration between the Guild and Temple back then. As an Eké of Tribe Litho, he bore the honored position of head of his extended family. Yet, one foggy morning, a fisherman found the *Ka*-Priest impaled on a hook in the bay. Naked, his body mutilated.

So even if my mother and I don't always see eye to eye, I worry about her. It's no small feat to kill any public figure, but to attack a witchdoctor would be even harder. Still, his death remains as mysterious as this child snatcher on the loose, one who can hide from magic.

Witchdoctors, real witchdoctors, can mend a broken bone with a word or ward off a storm with a ritual. Powerful ones like Grandmother can see across time. Arti can too, even if she doesn't bear the title *witchdoctor* since leaving the tribal lands. My father can reverse aging and extend a person's life beyond their natural years. I've always thought my family safe because of their magic, but now I'm not so sure.

A shiver creeps across my shoulders as I duck down alleyways chock-full of bins of rotting food to avoid the crowd. Grandmother had seen a green-eyed serpent while reading the bones and believed it to be a demon. Now Arti had only gotten a glimpse of the child snatcher. She and the seers think it's the work of anti-magic. What if it's something else?

A demon and missing children. It doesn't seem to make sense, but the timing is too close, the circumstances too strange. Why would a demon be in a vision about *me*? I'm nothing special. Yet, as impossible as it sounds, even I could feel the wrongness of the magic in Grandmother's tent. It was nothing like the feather touch of tribal magic. The magic had been invasive and curious, hostile. The situation with the children is far worse. The biggest question is why; what reason would anyone have to take children?

I slip out of the alley and into a different crowd in the East Market—my nerves on edge. I keep remembering the way Rudjek refused to look at me after my mother all but accused one of his brothers of being the child snatcher. If he doesn't want to see me, I can't blame him. Not after this morning. As I brace myself for the possibility that he won't come, dread sinks in my chest. I miss our routine—I miss *him*.

I pass people haggling over day-old bread, overripened fruits, cured meat, and charms. Donkeys laden with sacks of grain kick up a fury of red sand. The market writhes like the Serpent River after a rainstorm, and reeks of sweaty feet and dung.

As everyone goes about their business, hard faces stare at me. Soft faces. Kind faces. Faces of all colors. Faces leathered from too much sun. Faces so structured they look carved from stone. Jovial, round faces. The people in Tamar come from everywhere—across deserts, across seas, across mountains. The city is home to all who embrace it. Most noticeably so in the East Market, which is why I love coming here.

There's comfort in knowing that, like me, no one in this crowd quite fits. It always fascinates me how a person can at once blend in and stand out here. That would be the greatest advantage for the child snatcher, becoming invisible. My pulse throbs in my ears as I glance around again—seeing the market with new eyes.

Barefoot boys in tattered trousers and girls in dirty shifts duck through the crowds. Their small hands are quick as they slide them into pockets, lifting a money pouch here, a bracelet there. When a woman catches a little boy trying to steal her armlet, an unseen child on a rooftop strikes her with a pebble. Distracted and rubbing her head, the woman lets the little thief slip away with his prize. I don't condone what the orphans do in the market, but I don't judge them for it either. City life is hard for those who don't come from a family of status. Unlike in the tribal lands, where magic is all that matters, money and influence rule here.

The sun beats down on my back as I cross a street dense with food merchants. A plume of smoke from their firepits chokes the air and waters my eyes, but it smells wonderful. Roasting chestnuts, spicy stews, plantains fried in peanut oil. My stomach growls a reminder that I haven't eaten today. But I can't stop for food; I'm too focused on getting to the Serpent River to see Rudjek, too anxious that he won't be there.

He'd slipped out of the assembly before his father adjourned the proceedings. I'd watched as he'd tried to hide his anguish behind a blank, bored stare, but his is a mask that I can see straight through. I know him too well. My mother had dealt him a nasty wound. He'd already hated the way his father treated his brothers after the Rite and blamed himself for not being in the market that day to calm Jemi down.

I startle at a faint rustling at my side and catch one of the little thieves trying to lift my bracelet. I grab his arm—not too tight but firm enough to stop him from wiggling his way loose. The boy looks up at me with sad eyes, his lips trembling. Little con artist.

Before he drops a tear, someone slaps the back of his head. "Scat, or I'll call the Guard."

"Ouch," the boy protests, and whirls around, holding his head. "You're one to talk, Kofi!"

The would-be thief must be new to the market—I've never seen him before. From the hidden pocket under my belt, I dig out a silver coin and pass it to him. "You could've asked first, you know?"

He smiles sheepishly. "Next time I will."

When the boy runs off, Kofi steps into his place. At twelve, he isn't much older than the would-be thief. Fish scales cover the apron he's wearing, and he smells fresh from the docks, which is to say like rotting entrails. His eyes go wide as he takes in what I'm wearing. "Why are you dressed like *that*?" he asks me.

I purse my lips and glare at him, even though he's right, of course: my sheath is impractical and too conspicuous. Wearing something like this in the East Market proclaims me an easy mark to any thief. At least my family doesn't wear a crest like Rudjek's. "The better question is, why do you have a silver coin behind your ear?" I retort.

He grins as he reaches for one ear and finds nothing.

"The other ear." I tap my foot.

His hand moves quicker this time as if the money will disappear in the blink of an eye. When he retrieves the silver coin, he tucks it inside his apron, a blush of joy warming his brown skin. I've snuck him enough coins lately that he no longer protests that he must work to earn its value. Our family has more money than we need, and like Oshhe always says, a coin hoarded is a blessing missed.

Kofi's father is among the many fish merchants in the market. I came across their booth a year ago, drawn to where Kofi stood on top of a crate, selling outlandish tales to a crowd. "Desperate to flee a river of ice," he said, "the fish swam all the way from the North." When I shouted to him that this was unlikely, he changed his story, quick as a whip. "You're right! This batch swam from the Great Sea seeking refuge from a giant serpent. Only they didn't know that we eat fish too!"

Days after, I saw him with a woman who I later learned was his father's new wife. She grabbed Kofi by his shoulders, her teeth gritted. "You're so useless, boy," she spat. "Can't you do anything right?" Without provocation, she slapped him. The strike cut through me. I stepped in to stop her, but the next day Kofi came to the market covered in welts.

When I saw the woman again, I introduced myself as the *Ka-Priestess's* daughter. I told her if any more harm came to Kofi, there would be serious consequences. That was the first time I relied upon my mother's position to gain an advantage. It worked: Kofi's stepmother stopped hitting him after that. Instead of beatings, she now ignores him. I know what that feels like, so I decided to be his pretend-sister from that moment on.

"Did you hear about the giant sea turtle that rolled in with the tide this morning?" Kofi starts to say, but my attention lands on Rudjek. He's wading through the thicket of people, making a direct line toward me. The effect he has on the market is immediate. Girls flash him smiles and some try to catch his eye by stepping into his path. People stare at the craven-bone crest pinned to his collar.

Whenever anyone from a family of status comes to the East Market, there's always a ruckus. But he loves the market as much as I do: it's our second-favorite place to meet, aside from our secret spot by the river.

Merchants clamor for his attention, but Rudjek's gaze doesn't leave my face. He sidesteps a man selling the tiny bells favored by followers of Oma, the god of dreams. He's grinning from ear to ear, his pale brown skin flushed. I let out a breath and the tension in my belly eases.

"This morning was interesting," he says, interrupting Kofi. Up close the shadow of purple bruising on his right cheek matches his fancy silk elara. His obsidian eyes sparkle in the sun beneath long dark lashes.

I shift onto my heels. "Are you okay?"

Rudjek waves off the question, though his body tenses. "You missed my glorious match yesterday. I came in second." He glances to his right, where his attendant and best friend, Majka, stands clad in a red gendar uniform. I didn't notice him until now. "Only because *he* cheated."

"By 'cheated' I think you mean 'wiped the arena with your ugly face,'" Majka says. He presses two fingers to his forehead and flourishes a slight bow to me in the way of my father's tribe. The perfect

Tamaran diplomat's son. More so than Rudjek, Majka has the look of a typical high-bred Tamaran—rich brown skin, hair as thick and black as night, and deep-set dark eyes. I return the greeting with a smile.

Kira—to Rudjek's left—clears her throat. She's also clothed in a red uniform, a single black braid across her shoulder, her face as pale as a Northern winter. Unlike Majka and Rudjek with their double shotels, she has a dozen daggers strapped to her body. A merchant tries to shove a crossbow into her hands and another one waves tobachi knives to get her attention.

Families of import rarely set foot in either of the markets, not if they have attendants to send in their stead. Some families either can't afford attendants, or choose not to have them. We have Nezi, Ty, and Terra, but to my relief, none with the sole purpose of following me around everywhere. Rudjek isn't so lucky.

"I see you're enjoying your new post, Kira," I say as she shoos off the merchants.

Her face contorts into a frown. "I wouldn't call guarding *him* a real post."

Rudjek grabs his chest in mock offense, his eyes wide. "You wound me."

I shake my head, still not used to Majka and Kira in their new gendar roles. At seventeen, they're only a few months older than us, but old enough to begin careers. Majka's mother is a commander under the Master of Arms, Rudjek's aunt; his father is the Kindgom's ambassador to Estheria. Kira's father is the Master of Scribes. Both of them grew up competing in the arena with Rudjek for fun. After they joined the gendars, he petitioned to have them replace his old attendants. It's a high honor to serve the royal family and their closest cousins, the Omaris, and Kira and Majka hadn't earned the rank to be considered. But Rudjek's father agreed, if only to strengthen political alliances with their respective families.

"Hey, I was talking to her first," Kofi says, crossing his arms. "Wait your turn."

Rudjek laughs and pats Kofi's head. "Hello to you too."

I cast an apologetic glance at Kofi. "I'll stop by to see you tomorrow, I promise."

Kofi pokes his tongue out at Rudjek before darting off into the crowd.

"That little runt." Rudjek feigns indignation. "I have half a mind . . ."

"Shall we go?" I ask.

Without waiting for an answer, I head for our spot along the river, taking one route while they take another. It wouldn't be so secret if four people marched straight to it. Rudjek has had many attendants over the years, and he's bribed them to keep our secret. When coins haven't worked, he's turned to subtle and sometimes not-so-subtle persuasions. He really can be charming when he wants. Not that I'd tell him, lest it go to his head.

As I push through the crowds, an ice-cold chill runs down my back. Familiars slink across the market like a pack of rabid cats ready to pounce. No longer than my arm, their shadowy bodies are shapeless and ever changing, as fluid as a breeze. As they flood the streets, their presence sucks the warmth from me. I take a deep breath, watching as dozens of them swarm around a young girl. They crawl across her face and cling to her limbs, and she's none the wiser.

A few others in the market see them—the ones with tribal blood. Their faces have gone stark and they whisper to each other. But most people don't see the Familiars at all.

One or two Familiars are a nuisance, with the way they slither over everything, but a horde means only one thing: something bad is coming. Thinking of the missing children, I realize that the bad thing *is* already here.

In a daze, I cut through the mud-brick houses on the bank of the Serpent River and travel upstream from the docks. There are no Familiars here, but cold gnaws at my bones. The tribes believe that Familiars are the relics of a people destroyed by the demons long ago. In the demons' lust for *kas*, they ravaged a whole realm before Koré and Re'Mec, the Twin Kings, waged war to stop them. Familiars are the only things left of that time. Restless ghosts with no souls, seeking what they cannot have again—*life*.

When I reach our well-worn spot amidst the tall reeds, I see Majka and Kira standing guard on the riverbank—far enough away to give us privacy. Rudjek sits on a yellow blanket spread across the grass. "Father's putting on a big fight to celebrate the end of the blood moon," he says after a yawn. "You must come. I'm undefeated in the swords competition three years straight. I'm only the best swordsman in Tamar. Well, outside of the gendars, *I suppose*."

"I don't think that's a good idea after this morning," I say, my throat parched.

His eyes, darker than the hour of *ösana*, widen in question. With his full attention on me, the space feels smaller, the air warmer. "What's wrong, Arrah?"

His voice cracks when he says my name and his boasting fades away. As I sit beside him, his scent of lilac and wood smoke sends a tinge of heat up my neck. I should say something to distract him or pretend that I don't like the way my name rolls off his tongue, but I don't. Not immediately. I let this strange, wonderful thing linger between us. He's my best friend, and insufferable half the time. But lately I imagine something else—I imagine something more.

Guilt settles in like an old friend, and I glance away. Even if our parents didn't hate each other, a wrongness edges into the back of my mind. Yes, I want more, but I don't want to ruin what we have now if it goes wrong. One moment I'm on the verge of confessing to him and the next I bury my feelings under a rock.

"Nothing," I say quickly, before our conversation veers off-course. So many thoughts tangle in my head. The Familiars, the child snatcher, the green-eyed serpent. On the surface they're unrelated, but together they remind me of moves in a game of jackals and hounds. A game built upon strategy, evasion, and misdirection. I could be drawing connections where none exist, but I don't believe in coincidences. I shake my head and smile at him. "Why the fancy blanket today?"

I smooth my hand across the quilt, feeling the intricate patterns of the stitches. He knows me so well that he doesn't protest when I change the subject.

"I didn't want you to ruin your *fancy* dress on the grass." He rearranges his scabbards, which lie next to him on the ground. "It's very pretty."

"Thank you," I say, staring at the boats ambling down the river. It's so wide that the water seems to stretch on forever.

After a long and awkward pause, we both try to speak at the

same time. We laugh and some of the tension eases. "You go first,"
I say.

"About this morning," he says, his voice catching in his throat.
"My brothers would never do something so vile. Jemi and Uran
haven't been themselves since the Rite of Passage, but my father . . .
my father keeps them in check. He has a gendar who sends regular
reports on Jemi's squadron, and Uran is *never* without his attendants. When I say never, I mean *never*."

I reach out for the family crest affixed to his collar, but I stop
myself. "May I?"

Rudjek scratches his head, looking sheepish. "Of course."

I run my fingers across the smooth craven bone carved into the
shape of a lion's head. It's cold even in the heart of a much-too-warm
day. Had I any magic, it would repel me. But nothing happens. Its
yielding touch is a reminder that I should listen to my mother. Maybe
it's time to give up my dream.

"What does it feel like when someone with magic is near you?"
I've never asked before, avoiding anything that could lead back to
my lack of magic. *What would it be like if I had magic and we were
close . . . closer than we are now?* That's the true question burning
on my lips.

Rudjek shrugs. "I don't know. . . . It vibrates a little if the magic
is directed *at* me; otherwise, I don't feel anything."

I move from the crest on his elara to the pendant that hangs around
his neck. My fingers brush his throat and we both tense. He leans a
little closer to me, his voice dropping to a whisper. "I missed you."

Majka clears his throat and we jump apart. "Am I interrupting
anything?"

"No!" we both yell in unison.

"Nothing at all," I add, piqued.

"Of course not." Rudjek frowns at him. "What do you want?"

Majka glances over his shoulder at Kira, who is still on watch. "I am to remind you that your father expects you at the council meeting at fourth afternoon bells."

Rudjek grimaces at his pant legs, dusty from the market. "Give us a moment, will you."

Majka nods with a crooked grin and pads off to where Kira is waiting.

"I'm sorry, I do have to go." Rudjek sighs. "Father will be in a mood after this morning."

"It's true, then," I say, my throat dry again. "He's going to name you his heir?"

Rudjek winces and looks away. "It is. I . . . don't know how I feel about it yet. I'm the youngest. I never thought the responsibility would fall to me. My father's expectations—well, everyone's expectations—of me have changed."

I don't want to think about what this will mean for our friendship. If he—no, *when* he becomes Vizier one day, he won't be able to shun his duties to sneak off to meet me by the river.

"What about the gendars? All you've ever talked about is joining their ranks." I regret my question when he glances longingly at his shotels. "How will you survive if you can't fool around in the arena all day?" I add to cheer him up.

"I'll make do." Then under his breath, he says, "I can be quite crafty."

I pick at the beads on my sheath. "You can't turn it down, can you?"

"No." He scoops up a rock and flings it into the river. "My mother sent a message to her childhood matron in Delene asking her to come teach me proper etiquette." He forces a humorless laugh, somber like both our moods. "What do the Aatiri say? 'A man's character lies not in his fine clothes, but in the purity of his soul.'"

"The purity of his *ka*," I correct him.

"I'm sorry," Rudjek says with a shy smile. "Here I am rambling on and on, and I haven't asked you about the tribal lands. How did things go?"

I groan. "Not well."

Rudjek arches an eyebrow. "You want to talk about it?"

"Another time." I'm not ready to tell him about the Blood Moon Festival and Grandmother's vision. It's something I'm still trying to wrap my mind around, and he'll only worry. I've done enough of that on my own.

"One more thing before I go." Rudjek rubs the back of his neck. "Mother sent an invitation to my Coming of Age Ceremony to your father's shop. I thought if *your* mother got her hands on it, that would be the end of it. But . . . you're coming, right?"

I wrinkle my nose, reminding him what I think about his *Coming of Age Ceremony*—hence the donkey on my letter to him. Before I can answer, he adds, rushing his words, "True, it's a bit archaic, but . . ."

"You mean with the half-naked dancers?" I cross my arms. "It's a silly tradition."

"Pretty please." He bats his lashes at me and I can't help but laugh.

It isn't that our parents don't know we're friends. There's only so many of the scholar district's ceremonies one can go to and not know everyone your age. I've seen Rudjek compete in the arena countless times. This should be no different, yet I hesitate to say yes.

"I'll think about it," I say, but I know what Arti's answer will be if I ask her.

I utter a goodbye as Majka and Kira drag him off. Staring at the river again, I can't stop thinking about the Familiars swarming the East Market. Enough people can see them that the scribes have come up with an official explanation. They call them harmless, wayward shadows, but I've never believed that. Even without real magic, I can't deny the signs.

Wherever the Familiars go, death soon follows.

SEVEN

After another restless night I crawl out of bed before dawn. So many dreams spin in my head. One about a *real* green-eyed serpent slithering through the East Market. No bigger than a river snake, it moved through the throng of shuffling feet with ease. In another, the child snatcher stalked the tribal lands with a string of children bound by rope. Then I saw Rudjek standing on the edge of a forest as dark as night, with the eye of Re'Mcc at his back. Some connection between the three had been clear in the dreams, but now sleep fog clouds my mind.

If I hurry I won't miss my father before he leaves for his shop. I slip into the sea-blue tunic and trousers I wanted to wear yesterday and carry my sandals to not wake the others. Terra will be put out when she finds me gone at eighth morning bells.

The sun peeks over the horizon as I pad down the long hallway. Our villa curves around a courtyard where my father grows herbs for his blood medicines. My parents' twin rooms are at the opposite end of the villa. Ty and Nezi have their own rooms, and Terra's is next to mine.

Mosaic figurines dance along the wall, twisting, twirling, and leaping to keep pace with me. The magic is Mulani, one among many traditions of my mother's tribe. From the dancers to the white curtains to the silk pillows in the salon, Mulani staples decorate our home. Even if Arti never visits the tribal lands, she must miss something about her life there, to keep these small mementos. I pause to stare at one of the dancers, and he stops too. When I was little, I used to press my hand against the wall to feel the hum of magic. Arti tried to teach me how to make the dancers move, but I couldn't. She knew what it meant even then. Years later, the unreadable look on my mother's face in that moment still haunts me.

Oshhe squats over the roots of a kenkiliba bush in the courtyard, running his fingers through the soil. "You're up early, Little Priestess," he says, his back to me. "Can't sleep?"

After I inhale a deep breath, I say, "I have a lot on my mind."

"Help me collect herbs." He offers up a pair of shears. "It will put your mind at ease."

My father cuts leaves from the bush while I settle in front of a thicket of tangled matay vines. I snip at the small red buds, careful not to prick my fingers on their thorns. He doesn't press me to talk; instead he quietly fills a small sachet with leaves. The courtyard is his sanctuary. Nezi manages the gardens surrounding the villa, but my father cares for his medicinals.

"I received an invitation at my shop yesterday—one I know you were expecting." Oshhe moves on from the kenkiliba bush and begins collecting seeds from a neem tree. "You have my blessing to attend, but we'll need to convince your mother."

I do want to go to Rudjek's ceremony, but with all the things that kept me up last night, it's the least of my concerns. "What she did yesterday was awful."

My father's face pinches. He says he wants nothing to do with politics, so it's a subject rarely discussed in our household. I figured out long ago that it's not politics he doesn't want to hear about: it's my mother's schemes.

"It was cruel," I say, unable to hold back my words. "She made a spectacle of the missing children just to strike at the Vizier. What kind of person does that?"

"Still your tongue, daughter," Oshhe says, "before you say something you may regret."

I snatch another vine so fast that a thorn pricks my finger. I bring my thumb up to my lips but think better of it. Matay causes sleepiness in small doses and hallucinations if one ingests too much of it. My father nods his approval when he sees that I remember.

"I don't agree with your mother's ways," Oshhe says, "but her animosity toward the Vizier is not unwarranted. He is not a kind man, daughter. I need you to understand that. I know that you and his son are close. I was hesitant all those years ago when you asked if you could go play with him by the riverbank. I only allowed it because one cannot judge the son by the father. Children are innocent."

Rudjek has always wanted to keep our friendship from his father. I assumed his reason was the same as mine, since our parents hate each other, but I'm no fool either. The rumors about the Vizier are even worse than the ones about my mother. People say the Kingdom has no enemies because he orders the assassination of anyone seen as a threat. "Father, I didn't come to talk about the ceremony."

He gives me a sheepish grin. "Sometimes it's better to ease into difficult conversations."

It's hard to know where to start or what to say. Everything that's happened since the Blood Moon Festival tangles in my mind. Disappointment, fear, and disbelief eat at me, but I refuse to let them win. I have too much pride for that. I'm too stubborn.

"Do *you* think the green-eyed serpent is a demon?" I finally work up the nerve to ask. "Could one have survived the war with the orishas and hidden herself this long? What would a demon want with *me*?"

My last question strikes a nerve, and my father flinches. It pains me to admit that my mother has a point. There's no reason a demon would have anything to do with me. I dig my fingernails into my palms. I'm grasping for connections, a reason, but nothing makes sense. Before my father can answer, another, more desperate question rolls off my tongue. "Do you know when the first child went missing?"

Oshhe cocks an eyebrow, waiting to see if I'm done. When I don't speak again, he inhales deeply. "It's hard for a parent to not have the answers their child seeks . . . but I sense that there may be a link between the Aatiri chieftain and Arti's visions. Whether this is the work of craven anti-magic or demon magic, I cannot say. We must hope it's anti-magic. If demons are back, then there will be much trouble ahead."

My father pauses, studying the tangled matay vines on my lap. His eyes brim with the shine of fresh tears held back. He wants to be strong for me and I want to be strong for him too. "To answer your other question: the first child went missing at the start of the blood moon. You are right to make that connection," he says, his voice strung tight. "I need you to be very careful, Arrah. I know you like to visit the markets and go to the river, but these are not safe times."

I tuck my hands between my knees, trying to push back the sinking feeling in my chest. There's no mistaking the fear in my father's eyes. A look so foreign on him that it tears out a piece of my heart. He can't bring himself to say the rest, so I do it for him. "You think Grandmother's vision means the child snatcher or demon, whatever it is, will come after me."

My father's posture straightens—his jaw clenches. "I won't let that happen."

"You wouldn't need to protect me if I had magic of my own," I say, bitter. "When my magic comes, I . . ." My words trail off at his pained expression.

"Arrah." My father's voice is gentler, almost placating. "It doesn't matter if you ever have magic. You'll still be my favorite daughter, and I'll protect you until my very last breath."

I'm your only daughter, I almost say to be spiteful, but I can't bring myself to hurt my father even in anger.

That's it, then.

Even my father has given up on me ever having magic. The news is too much to bear.

Every day at eighth morning bells, the Almighty Temple opens to the public. Most people climb the precipice to the Temple on their own, but some take litters. The Almighty Palace gleams against the western sky, even higher than the Temple, overlooking the city proper and the ambling Serpent River to the east. The Vizier's estate sits on a cliff opposite the Temple at the southern edge of the city. It's a palace in its own right with tan walls that glow in the morning sunlight. But my mind is far from the magnificent views of Tamar right now.

Dread crawls through my belly as I remember my father's words. It may not matter to him that I never have magic, but I'm not going to sit around and do nothing. If I want to know more about demons, the Temple's the best place to start.

Robed scholars and scribes sweep up the path beside street merchants wearing their very best. No matter their social status or family name or religion, everyone comes to the Temple. For the morning lessons are also the time to pay tithes.

Attendants in earth-toned robes direct people through the gates. Along the edge of the cliff, five stone buildings curve around a half-moon ingress. Several scholars veer toward the gardens and ponds to confer in private. While most people funnel into the central buildings for lessons, I head for the Hall of Orishas.

A tang of blood lingers in the air as I cross the courtyard, where the shotani practice in the dead of night. The elite assassins train with the seers from a young age. Over the generations, their families moved from the tribal lands to the Kingdom. They have magic—not enough to gain status in the tribal lands, but much more than the street charlatans. Most of what we know about them is speculation since they always move in shadows.

Magic clings to the Temple walls. More even than at the sacred Gaer tree where the first *Ka*-Priest's body was buried. In the day, it only looks like specks of dust out of the corner of your eyes. It's at night, especially during the hour of *ösana*, that it comes to life.

Sukar and another attendant stand outside the Hall of Orishas on the northeast edge of the cliff. He waves me over. "So many people confessing their wrongdoings." He rolls his eyes when I reach them. "They tithe to rid themselves of their guilt. It never gets old."

Sweat glistens against Sukar's shaved head, and his tattoos glow. They only do that when he's near someone with the gift. I glance at the other attendant as she waves people along. The echo of her magic dances across my skin, taunting me. Sukar excuses himself from his duties, and we duck into the long ingress and enter the Hall of Orishas. Shifting torchlight along the walls casts nefarious shadows across the chamber. It's the perfect place to talk—and to brush up on my history.

The hall is home to the statues of the orishas who survived the war with the Demon King. They molded their own images out of stardust darker than the darkest night. It's hard to look straight at them, or stare too long, for their figures begin to blur around the edges.

When I was younger, Sukar, Essnai, and I used to make a game of it. Who could stare the longest? I won once, if you can call it winning. I stared so long that the darkness around Essi's—the sky god's—statue bled into my eyes and left me blind for half a bell. Sukar ran to get my mother, who sent his uncle in her stead. I wasn't the first child to tempt fate and pay the price. I don't repeat my mistake now.

On our way to a private spot, we pass a few patrons prostrated in meditation at the feet of their favorite orisha. As we go deeper into the hall, we see fewer people and it's only the echo of our footfalls that disturbs the silence. The glowing script on the walls stands out in stark contrast against the dark. I've never had a reason to question the holy texts, nor the history I was taught about the tribal lands. But the scripts say that the orishas destroyed *all* of the demons. If the first scribes got that wrong, then what else don't we know?

The sun orisha, Re'Mec, wears an elaborate headdress of ostrich feathers and pearls, his ram horns as thick as a man's arm. His eyes glow with fire above a sharp beak that ends in a point. He's naked, his shoulders broad, the chiseled lines of his muscles further asserting his dominance. A glass sphere sits upon his lap. The gray mist inside it represents the souls of the orishas who sacrificed themselves to stop the Demon King.

Re'Mec's twin sister, Koré, sits across from him on a dais beneath a glass dome that shrouds her in shadows. She has the sculptured face of an Aatiri woman, sharp angles and prominent cheeks. Her hands are talons, and long braids flow like rivers across her breasts. She holds a bronze box with a chain around it. Two women wearing the sheer white headwraps common among the Twin King's worshippers kneel at her feet. They each offer their patron god a small box of trinkets with moons carved inside the lids.

The wall next to Koré tells the story of the Demon King's fall. She poured her magic into a box to trap his soul, yet it wasn't enough. It took twenty of their most powerful generals to seal the box. They volunteered their own *kas* to bind it forever. Other orishas had fallen in the war, but it took their sacrifice to end it.

I wrap my arms around my shoulders, unable to imagine what that would've been like. To give the part of yourself the tribal people considered the most sacred, the most pure. I have more questions about the demons than I started with. How were they as powerful as the orishas if they weren't gods themselves? Why did they eat souls? How did they do it? We only know fragments of stories about them, made whole by imagination.

Sukar clears his throat, encouraging me to hurry up. But I look at each orisha as we amble down the hall. We leave behind Koré and Re'Mec, passing by Essi, then Nana, the orisha who shaped the earth.

"Have the seers had any more visions about the child snatcher?" I whisper to not disturb the patrons lying at the feet of Mouran, the master of the sea. Across from him, two more patrons kneel before Sisi, the guardian of fire. I skim every holy script we pass, but nothing immediately jumps out at me. Much of it describes the war in bloody details.

"If you mean have we heard of more visions from your mother: no," Sukar says. "Whoever the child snatcher is, they're able to block my uncle and the others from seeing them at all. The *Ka*-Priestess is the only one powerful enough to get a glimpse. And even that hasn't been much help."

I wince at the news, and silence stretches between us as we walk past Yookulu, the weaver of seasons. His followers have sprinkled rain daisies at the base of his dais to celebrate Su'omi—the season of renewal, when all the flowers bloom after the cooler months of Osesé. We come upon Kiva, the protector of children and innocence. Oma, the orisha of dreams. Kekiyé, the orisha of gratitude. Ugeniou, the harvester. Fayouma, the mother of beast and fowl. Fram, the balancer of life and death. All of the orishas appear giant in stature.

"And you, my friend," Sukar asks, his usual playfulness gone. "Any news since the Aatiri chieftain's strange vision?"

I shake my head, recalling the conversation between my father and me. Now is not the time to say, not until we know more. "Nothing yet."

"Be as patient as a lion stalking the night." He winks at me. "The *edam* will find an answer."

At the end of the hall, we come upon the fourteenth orisha, called the Unnamed. Her face has no memorable features, so there's little to recognize her by, save for the cobras around each of her arms. I pause to examine her, or rather the serpents with their heads poised to strike at her wrists. The other statues are majestic, intimidating, but this one feels *wrong*. Staring too long at her, darkness begins to seep into the corners of my eyes and my heartbeat quickens. The room seems to tilt, and panic unfolds in my mind. I force myself to look away.

I'm in the middle of reading another script when Tam, one of Rudjek's sparring partners, ambles toward us. He has kinky golden hair with the sky-blue eyes and bronze skin of a Yöome set against Tamaran features. A face that's lean and athletic, noble. His look is striking, one that draws eyes, and he knows it. He was recently named a first-year scribe and has been teaching at the Temple.

Tam clucks his tongue, a sly grin on his lips. "Is the *Ka*-Priestess's daughter skipping lessons again?" He casts a pointed look at me, then turns to Sukar. ". . . and the Zu seer's nephew shunning his duties. Need I remind you that the orishas demand our fealty, and such disregard is frowned upon?"

Sukar rolls his eyes. "Get lost, Tam. Can't you see we're busy?"

"Barasa is looking for you." Tam shrugs. "Something about misplaced scrolls."

"Twenty-gods," Sukar says after a deep sigh. "I swear my uncle is hopeless without me."

"A Temple attendant swearing in this sacred place." Tam cringes, his sly grin fading. "That doesn't bode well."

"Shut it, will you, Tam," Sukar snaps, then excuses himself before rushing to answer his uncle's summons.

When Sukar is gone, Tam leans against the throne upon which the orisha of life and death sits. Fram is duality and balance, depicted with two heads to represent their fluid nature.

"They didn't want any part in the war with the Demon King." Tam tilts his chin up at Fram. "For them, life and death are different sides of the same coin, so they refused when Re'Mec and Koré asked for their help. The whole duality thing is a double-edged sword . . . but they eventually came around."

I cross my arms. "I never thought you'd end up a scribe; you love the arena too much."

"I considered the gendars"—he grins again—"but my real talents lie in education."

He says it with such sarcasm that I laugh. I'm about to write him off when I think again. Maybe he can help me find out more about demons.

"So tell me something about the orishas that most people don't know."

"The universe began with a bang." He whistles, drawing death stares from the other patrons in the hall. "You call it the Supreme Cataclysm, but it has many names. Think of it as a void of profound darkness that destroys and creates without beginning or end. Over the course of eons, the first orishas crawled from its belly and cut their umbilical cords—so to speak. Each of them possesses some piece of the Supreme Cataclysm's nature. Like the Cataclysm, the orishas love their creations." Tam adjusts his position, his focus turning to the Unnamed. "Unfortunately for us, a god's love is both beautiful and terrifying."

"I've never heard the origin story told quite like that," I say, surprised.

"I embellished it a little," he admits. "I became a scribe so I can tell lies once in a while."

"Tell me about her . . . the Unnamed." I point up. "The truth."

"We don't speak of her." Tam shakes his head, his words clipped. "There's nothing to tell."

My eyes linger on the serpents again. *There was someone here . . . something*, Grandmother had said. *Someone who does not belong. Perhaps a relic from the past, I do not know, or an omen of the future.*

"A green-eyed serpent." I swallow. "Is that a symbol of demons?"

Tam startles and stares at me with one eyebrow quirked. "That's an interesting question."

"Why interesting?" I say, catching the somber note in his voice.

"That's the name the orishas gave to the demons, yes," Tam confirms. "For though they possessed many forms, they all had green eyes, a mark of their race."

My dread from earlier comes back in full force. If my father is right about the connection between both visions, then I have my answer. I know what a demon would want with children . . . with *me*.

This can't be possible. It can't be. The demon race perished in the war with the orishas, but had one survived? Could there be more? If demons have an insatiable hunger for souls, there are none more sacred and pure than the *kas* of children.

EIGHT

Long after leaving the Temple, I struggle to catch my breath. I take a shortcut near the sacred Gaer tree on my way to the East Market. The tree stands naked and alone in iridescent dark soil—its black branches crooked and bare. The magic here is so thick that it's palpable. I don't linger, but as I pass, the branches shudder. Outside the Almighty Temple, it's the most magical place in Tamar. How powerful had the first *Ka*-Priest of the Kingdom been to cheat death by taking up roots and becoming a tree?

When I set foot in the East Market, I see Familiars swarming like a nest of agitated wasps. Hundreds slither among the crowd and crawl across every place imaginable. Dogs howl at them, while most people are none the wiser. They draw the heat from the air, and even though it's midday, a cool draft settles over the market. The sun is behind the clouds—a rare thing in Tamar, which enjoys sunshine on more days than not. Does the sun orisha Re'Mec feel the disturbance too?

On the surface, everything looks normal. People haggle over prices, and merchants outbid each other to attract patrons. Some older children play an upbeat tempo on the bottoms of wooden crates, and people drop copper coins in a bowl in front of them. But bad energy hums through the crowd like the charge in the air before lightning strikes. Several fights break out and the City Guard steps in. It hits me at once. All the amulets with the orisha Kiva in the market today—now that the news is out about the children. When I was little, his bulbous face and lopsided eyes scared me. But Kiva protects the innocent. People wear his likeness when disease sweeps through the city, or when crops are poor. It's a sign of fear.

I spot Rudjek ahead, fending off a street charlatan trying to peddle him charms. The charlatan wears a dozen bone necklaces and another two dozen on each arm. He gapes at Rudjek, his cataract-laden eyes stretched wide. His cheeks are sunken, his skin ashen and weathered—his movements slow and lethargic. People might think he's drunk, but his face bears the signs of someone who's been trading years for magic. Not all the charlatans do it, but this man clearly has.

"You need protection," he proclaims, his voice like cracked egg-shells. "I have a necklace for you. All the way from the tribal lands. Blessed by a great witchdoctor."

The charlatan's words stop me cold in the thicket of the crowd before I reach Rudjek. Patrons divide around me, some yelling to get out of their way, but I can't move. I've always thought the charlatans weak. In truth, some have more magic than me even without trading their years. They flood this corner of the market, offering charms, sacks of herbs, and potions promising to deliver your heart's desire.

I know what it feels like to want magic so bad that it hurts. To watch your parents impose their will on magic with the snap of their fingers, but not be able to touch it yourself.

A bitter taste sours my mouth and I swallow hard. What I can't understand is why someone would trade their years to make petty charms. If you're going to do it, do it for a better reason. Do it because you have no other choice.

It isn't fair to judge the charlatans, but when I look at them, I see my own reflection. I see a yearning to belong. I see my desire to protect myself when the demon comes after me—for it will. I have no doubts about that now. Grandmother's vision had been a warning for *me*.

Rudjek frowns. "I don't need trinkets made from chicken bones."

The charlatan sweeps his arms wide, rattling the bones. "Trinkets? These are genuine charms."

"Which tribe are they from?" Rudjek arches one eyebrow at the tiny bones strung together.

"Tribe Kes," the man says with a lazy wave. "Only the best bone charms from them."

Rudjek rubs his chin. "Aren't the Aatiri the bone charmers?"

The man grimaces, his expression so exaggerated that he belongs on a stage. "Where did you hear such lies?"

"He heard such truths from me," I say, stepping forward.

Rudjek greets me in the way of the Aatiri, touching his forehead and flourishing a little bow. His cheeks flush and he's grinning like a fool again. I can't stop myself from blushing too. I try not to stare into his obsidian eyes or at his lips that look as soft as velvet, or his broad shoulders. Instead, I make the mistake of shifting my attention to the smooth brown skin visible between the slit in his elara. I catch a glimpse of the curve of his throat, his collarbone, and a pang of warmth spreads to my belly. So much for less conspicuous places.

"She's the expert on all things tribal." Rudjek nods at me, his deep voice ringing in my ears.

"Waiting for someone?"

"You, of course," he utters under his breath.

"And who are—" The charlatan cuts off mid-question when his eyes land on me. He looks decades older and his hair is whiter since I last encountered him, months before the blood moon.

"Many blessings, young priestess." He bows, glancing to the ground. He must see my mother in my features. Most people do. The amber eyes, the high set of my cheekbones, the proud nose. "I meant no disrespect. May I offer a silver coin to the Temple to show my penance?"

I shift from heel to heel, looking everywhere but the charlatan's face. He makes a show of digging in his pocket and his hand trembles so much that he almost drops the coin. Some of the other charlatans watch with curiosity. What do they expect me to do? I'm not my mother, nor will I ever be like her.

"Please don't curse another one," Rudjek begs me. "Not after what happened to the last one who crossed you."

My lips purse in protest, but as much as I cringe in embarrassment, the charlatan looks equally distressed. People always believe Rudjek when he lies about my purported magic, even if I've never shown a drop of talent.

Before they realize who I am, strangers don't give me a second glance. I'm only another person in the market to swindle out of a few copper coins, or a silver one if I'm foolish enough. When they find out who I am—who *she* is—people look at me with a mix of horror, admiration, and longing. A little envy too. Like the charlatan staring at me right now. It's the same way I gazed upon the witchdoctors at the Blood Moon Festival, and for a moment I pretend it's true. I pretend that magic will obey my every whim. And the first thing I'll make it do is shove a rag in Rudjek's big mouth.

I glare at him as he pulls me away. A shock of warmth flows between our hands and crawls up my arm. His hand's much larger than mine, his skin calloused from handling shotels in his father's arena. My heart flaps like a skyward bird. Rudjek looks down at our interlocked fingers and blushes again as he lets go. We're both doing an awful lot of that lately.

I huff a frustrated breath. "I wish people wouldn't act like I'm her."

"Your mother inspires a special kind of terror," Rudjek says. "She and my father both."

What Tam said about Fram, the orisha of life and death, comes back to mind. They saw life and death as different sides of the same coin. Our parents could be described that way. Both ruthless in their own right. No wonder they hate each other.

Rudjek touches my arm and warmth pulses between us again. We've touched many times before, and this should be no different. Yet I'm not mistaking the spark in his midnight eyes. "Everything okay?"

Several people take notice of how we are together and another blush creeps up my neck. It's hard not to notice him. The Vizier's son in his fine purple elara with gold-plated shotels at his sides. His mess of black curls. He starts to say something but bites his lip. An awkward moment stretches between us, until finally I nod.

As we wade through the market, I tell Rudjek everything in a rush that leaves me breathless. I talk for a long time, the distraction of weaving through the crowd and having him near making it easier. I wasn't ready to talk about Grandmother's vision before, but it's a relief to finally get it all out. With Rudjek, I can let myself be vulnerable, I can let my guard down. "How could any of this be possible?" I wonder once I'm done. "Demons . . . after all this time?"

He stares at me, stunned. Whatever he'd expected, it isn't this. Ask a friend what's wrong, and they'll say they had an argument with their partner or they have a toothache. Ask me what's wrong, and I deliver news that a demon's come to roost in Tamar. It sounds grim even to my ears.

"What you're suggesting . . ." Rudjek clutches the hilts of his shotels and cranes his neck to peer into alleys. Even Majka and Kira linger closer than usual today. They're on full alert, eyes sharp, hands on their weapons, too. "Demons can't be back . . . It would mean . . ." He can't bring himself to finish.

I cross my arms. "Why are you so jumpy, then?"

Before Rudjek can answer, a Familiar flits between his feet and slides into a shaded area behind him. Dozens of them crawl up closed doors and walls and merchants' stalls. They perch like birds on the rafters of an apothecary as two guards push through the crowd. Four fishermen travel in their wake, carrying another man on a stretcher. The man has a whale hook clear through his shoulder, and both Rudjek and I stare at him in shock. There's so much blood that it overpowers the air. I hold my throat to force the acid back down. The men file into the apothecary and the Familiars follow them. There are always accidents on the docks, but I haven't seen one this bad in a long time. I remember the story about the former *Ka*-Priest, how someone impaled him on a hook in the bay.

"I wish you could see all the Familiars in the market right now." I shake my head in disbelief. "It's an omen."

"Familiars?" Rudjek tugs at his tunic. "You mean the wayward shadows?"

I wince, not wanting to hear another lecture about what the science scribes say. The scribes want us to forget about the souls that walked the world long before humans. But some didn't ascend into the afterlife. They're still here, hiding in plain view. Their presence pricks against my skin like needle points. There's no time to argue with Rudjek about this again. The trail of blood left in the fisherman's wake is making me light-headed.

"I don't care what your science scribes say," I snap.

"People have been talking about the wayward shadows—the Familiars—since . . ." Rudjek's gaze darts around, and his voice drops to a husky whisper. ". . . since the first child disappeared. My father keeps dismissing the reports as tribal superstition. I . . . I wish I could see them too." His hands fly to the hilts of his shotels at a sudden commotion behind us. When he sees it's only an overturned cart, he turns to me again, his eyes full of dread. "Another child was taken last night. The count is at six now."

"Six missing?" My voice shatters as a young girl slips under a patron's arm and steals his money pouch. The man is unaware as he peruses a stall of tobachi knives. I seek out all the children in the market, as many of them as there are adults. My heart thunders in my chest. If I had magic I could *do* something, *do* anything. Am I supposed to sit around, let this demon take the most vulnerable among us, and then wait my turn? How easy it was, a year ago, to utter a single mention of Arti and stop Kofi's stepmother from hitting him.

Kofi.

Without warning, I take a sharp turn, shifting our path in the direction of the fish merchants. I have to make sure my friend is okay.

"The shotani have been combing the city," Rudjek says, keeping pace with me. "Now that a scholar boy's missing, the Guild has grown a heart."

Shotani magic wafts through the crowds even now. It's heavy and oppressive, like sinking into a tar pit. Compared to them, the City Guard is little more than a nuisance. "Have they found . . ." I swallow, unable to say *bodies*.

"No." Rudjek snags his fingers in his mess of curls. He doesn't seem to know what to do with his hands, not even finding comfort resting them on his swords as he usually does. "There've been no leads at all. It doesn't seem right. I mean, they're the *shotani*, for gods' sake. Blessed by the orishas themselves."

"If Arti can't see the child snatcher in her visions," I shoot back, "then the shotani don't stand a chance."

Rudjek puts his hands on his hips. "Is she really trying?"

As his words sink in, the color drains from his cheeks. His accusation punches me in the gut. He doesn't have to say more. It's written on his face. Our parents hate each other, and either would do almost anything to see the other fall. "I don't know." I duck my head. There should be no doubt in my mind that my mother would do the right thing, yet . . .

"I'm sorry," Rudjek says, glancing away. "I shouldn't have suggested . . ."

I bite the inside of my lip. "Would your father help her if the situation were reversed?"

Pain flashes in Rudjek's eyes. "I don't think he would."

We walk on quietly, passing crowds gathering in front of merchant stalls. A vein of pent-up frustration and fear underlie their low whispers. This will get a lot worse if someone doesn't stop the child snatcher. The city will riot.

I ease out a sigh when we reach the fish merchants, and Rudjek gives me a reassuring smile. Kofi stands on his crate covered in scales. He smells atrocious, but he's okay. He grins at me and then rolls his eyes at Rudjek. Same old Kofi.

"How goes business?" I force brightness in my voice. "Selling like hotcakes?"

"Terra bought seven threadfish this morning." Kofi glances at his father, who's haggling with a patron over the price of shrimp. "I gave her an eighth one for free since you're good customers."

Rudjek leans close to my ear. "Is that little runt flirting with you?"

Kofi crosses his arms and scowls at Rudjek, standing face-to-face from his vantage point on the crate. "You going to buy something or what?"

"Should I challenge him to a match in the arena?" Rudjek looks sideways at me. "I'll do it with my eyes covered to make it fair."

Time to go.

I flip Kofi a silver coin and he catches it midair. "Stay close to your father and be careful, okay?"

"I will." Kofi looks at his father again, and the two exchange a nod. "Promise."

"See you later," I say before dragging Rudjek away.

"I'll get him a guard." Rudjek pitches his voice low so only I can hear him. "I know I can't do much, but at least I can make sure he's safe. I wish I could do it for the other children too." He scratches the back of his neck. "As future Vizier, I should be able to do something useful for once."

I beam at Rudjek. He'll be a better Vizier than his father one day. Now that I know Kofi will be okay, my fear eases a little. But then a Familiar slinks across my shoulder, and I stop cold. A tremble shoots down my spine, leaving my skin prickling with ice in the midday heat. More Familiars rush behind me—a horde of them. My breath catches in my throat as I whirl around. A dozen swarm Kofi, slithering across his face, arms, legs, like a cloak of nightmares.

Their meaning is unmistakable. The child snatcher isn't finished.

My friend is next.

NINE

Arti sits across from me at the low table in our salon, staring at a wall as she stirs her fish soup. She hasn't said one word. Though she's never one for small talk, she's especially quiet tonight. Worry lines crease her face; she looks tired and worn, and it makes me worry too. For the first time I can recall, there are dark circles under her eyes, as if she's not slept in days. It's moments like these that I remind myself that although my mother can be cold, she isn't unfeeling.

Her face shows signs that she's been hard at work performing rituals. Trying to uncover the child snatcher. I shouldn't have doubted my mother. Of course she would help.

We sat down to our evening meal only moments ago, but I can't stop squeezing my hands between my knees. I tell myself that Kofi has a guard now. He'll be okay. I've never been more thankful for Rudjek's familial ties to the Vizier than today. He put the word out, and within half a bell, there was a guard at Kofi's side. A gendar, one of the elite soldiers from the Almighty Army. Still, I can't wait until morning so I can go check on him myself. I promised I would look out for him.

Oshhe clears his throat at the head of the table, interrupting my thoughts. "I take it things aren't going well at the Temple."

Arti blinks as if clearing the cobwebs from her mind, a weak smile crossing her lips. She reaches for his hand and he reaches for hers. A look of longing, of sadness, of something lost, passes between my parents. "I wish things could be different," she says, her voice quiet.

My father smiles, resignation in his words, a sense of defeat. "As do I."

Ty bustles into the salon with Terra on her heels and my parents move apart. Our matron snatches up Oshhe's bowl, and still-hot soup spills on her hands and apron. She doesn't notice as she roughly puts the bowl on the empty tray in Terra's arms and moves to take Arti's. My father and I exchange a glance, and dread crawls through my belly. Ty's eyes are blank. She might as well be leagues away when she's like this. She's retreated someplace deep in her mind, where the horror that haunts her has taken hold.

"Ty, will you eat with us tonight?" Oshhe offers, his deep voice gentle. "Terra can take care of the dishes."

Families of status frown upon an attendant joining the household for meals. I didn't know that for the longest time, since it's commonplace for Nezi and Ty to eat with us. It came up in a conversation with Rudjek after my twelfth birth day. He was so excited upon hearing this that he asked his mother if his attendants could eat with them. He got a firm talking-to from his mother, and later a tongue-lashing from his father.

Ty doesn't accept or decline my father's invitation. She brushes away breadcrumbs from the table, her hands trembling. Terra puts the tray down and slips out to get Nezi. That used to be my job before she came. Whenever Ty had an episode, I'd run for Nezi, the only one who can calm her. The episodes always pass in time, but it's hard to see her like this.

"The soup was exceptional tonight," I comment, trying to bring her back. "It's your best yet."

She grunts, but her lips don't move, and silence eats her words. I wonder if the news about the children disappearing has upset her. By the time she's done clearing the table, her skin is gray. She stops cold and Arti goes rigid across from me too. Ty backs into a corner, shaking her head, her eyes as wide as two battered copper coins.

"You've only to ask, Ty," Arti says, her voice wound tight. "And I can make it go away."

I bite my lip and clench my fists between my knees. Like Grandmother, one of Arti's gifts is to manipulate the mind, but there's a limit to her powers. She can't make memories go away forever, only bury them for a time. Ty doesn't answer Arti either.

When Nezi hobbles into the salon with Terra, I ease out a breath. Her gaze rakes over us, a grimace painting her face. Ty is the oldest of our household and Nezi is next. Her black locs are streaked through with silver and stick up every which way. I stare at her scarred hands, gnarled and crooked like tree roots. She used to tell me that she burned them while plucking magic from the sky.

"I'm here." Nezi's husky voice echoes in the room. She doesn't approach Ty; that'll only make it worse. I learned that the hard way at a very young age. Nezi scratches at her old scars. She always does when she's upset or agitated. "Do you want Arti to help you?"

Ty's head snaps around, her eyes landing on her friend. There's understanding between the two. Some secret language that the other women of my household speak, but I'm not privy to. Ty blinks her answer, her nails clawing into the stone wall, her breath coming out sharp and short. Soon the feather touch of my mother's magic tingles against my skin. It sweeps through the room, and Ty squeezes her eyes shut and lets out a long groan before growing calm again.

While Ty's recovering, my father tells Terra to take away the dishes. By the time she returns, Ty has already slipped from her corner, her strict matron mask back in place. She and Terra serve our next dish: pepper-crusted broiled fish and mint rice. Ty dips her head to Arti, who returns the gesture. There's a shadow of peace on our matron's face as she retreats back to the kitchen with Nezi and Terra. I can't help but feel relieved too.

Arti looks so very tired. Magic takes from all—even the powerful. She sighs, her skin sallow, her eyes even more red-rimmed. But she'll recover: unlike charlatans who borrow magic, it doesn't take my mother's years. It gladly answers her call. Oshhe looks tired too. He always does after a long day. We're only halfway through our meal, and I'm still shaking from the episode with Ty, when Oshhe announces, "I must leave in the morning to hunt for a white ox."

I don't need to ask why. I've helped in his shop enough to know what he wants with the white ox. "I don't need a protection charm." I poke at the threadfish on my plate. "I need my own magic."

Arti's jaw tightens, but she holds her tongue.

My father swallows hard, his throat bobbing as he does. "I don't know if this is a demon, for we only know them in stories. I've tried to perform the ritual to see across time and space, but the magic will not obey me. I'm not talented in that particular gift."

I graduate from poking at the threadfish to jabbing my knife between its ribs.

If only I'd inherited some of that gift from Arti and Grandmother, I could help. I could do something to stop the child snatcher and protect Kofi instead of doing nothing. "I will make you the strongest protection charm known in the five tribes." Oshhe dismisses my protest outright. "I shouldn't be gone more than a few days; I must go to the Aloo Valley to seek out the beast."

"The Aloo Valley?" I blurt out. "That's near the Dark Forest. That's craven territory."

No one's seen a craven since they attacked the Almighty Army in the Aloo Valley generations ago. It's not a place that many in the Kingdom travel, for no one wants to tempt fate. The Aloo Valley is where the Omari family legacy began.

As the childhood fable goes, Rudjek's distant ancestor, Oshin Omari, was the last to fight the cravens. Oshin led a crusade to push them back into the Dark Forest when they threatened the Kingdom's borders. He set up his army in the Aloo Valley between the southernmost point of the Kingdom and the Dark Forest. The cravens, clever and illusive, killed half his men in one night.

Tired of losing, Oshin stalked into the forest alone, ordering his men not to follow. He hiked into the marshes, not seeing a craven until he came upon a clearing. There, they all surrounded him. He pulled his shotels, ready to die with honor, but they did not attack. His bravery impressed their leader, and she offered to fight him to the death in an even match. Swords against claws and teeth and tree-bark skin. The craven was fast and cunning, but Re'Mec honors the brave. Oshin won and the cravens conceded to his prowess in battle. As his reward, they promised not to invade the Kingdom, for they had gained respect for its people. He took the fallen craven back with him, and later discovered the anti-magic in their bones.

"*Near* the Dark Forest," Oshhe repeats, "not *in* the Dark Forest, daughter. The Aloo Valley has been peaceful for generations. It's where I have the greatest chance to find the ox. It isn't only the child snatcher that we must worry about; it's also people who let fear control their actions."

My pleading eyes find my mother's. If there's one thing my parents have in common, it's that they're both stubborn. I don't want my father to go, but I know there's no point in begging him not to. With so much uncertainty, we should stick together. No one is safe. "You and the seers will be able to find the demon, won't you?" I ask my mother, my voice a whisper.

Arti's *Ka*-Priestess ring clinks against her plate. It's changed to the color of an emerald tonight. "Demon or not"—she sighs—"I've done everything in my power. Now let Suran clean up his own mess. The protection of the Kingdom is his domain."

"If he can't, then what?" I spit out. "More children will go missing."

My mother meets my gaze, her sad eyes bloodshot. "I fear it will be so."

TEN

Every morning, I say a blessing for the missing children over the ancestor altar. It's been three days since my father left and the routine calms me. I clutch my charm from Imebyé while reciting the words. If I followed the Mulani tradition, I would make a doll from well-worn clothes. The Kes require a doll too, but one made of clay. The Litho tradition asks for a sacrifice, usually a chicken. The Zu perform a dance under the moonlight. I add an amulet of Kiva, the orisha of children, for good measure. I can't trouble myself worrying about mixing two faiths. The tribal people honor one god, Heka. The Kingdom worships the orishas. Right now, whoever decides to answer my prayers will have my eternal devotion.

But without magic, I know the ritual is meaningless. Whatever inkling I might have of Heka's gift, it isn't worth much. What good is it to see magic in the night sky if you can't touch it? I guess I should be grateful that my mind resists the influence of it, but I'm not. It isn't enough to make a difference. I can't believe I'm meant to hide in our villa and do nothing. If my fate is somehow tied to the green-eyed serpent—the demon—our paths will cross sooner or later. I should be doing something to prepare, to *protect* myself.

I miss my father. I need him here with me. I need him to tell me everything will be okay. The entire time he waited to board the ship for the Aloo Valley, I pushed down tears.

"Don't worry, Little Priestess," he said with a big smile. "I will be back before long."

"I don't want you to leave," I begged, my voice raw. "What if something happens while you're gone?" *What if the demon comes after me.*

"Rely on your mother." Oshhe squeezed my shoulder. "I know that she is difficult, but she loves you no less."

I turned away, a bitter taste in my mouth. *Difficult* was putting it kindly.

My father gently tugged my chin until I faced him again. "She is not as invincible as she pretends to be; she hurts too. More than you know."

I startle from the memory as Terra sweeps into my room for morning ablutions. She chats about the latest gossip from the market but avoids the topic of the missing children.

I skip my morning lessons with the scribes again to check on Kofi—and meet up with Rudjek in the East Market. He's been skipping his private lessons too. Even with his griping that Kofi is a little con artist, Rudjek doesn't hesitate to help with the watch. And I know that underneath the teasing, Kofi likes him too. I once came upon him defending both Rudjek and me to a group of older children. He had tears in his eyes when they told him that we were only his friends because we pitied him.

After I shooed the children away, he asked me if it was true. It hurt that he didn't know the answer, but I understood. I told him the truth: I was his friend because, like him, I knew what it felt like to not quite fit in at home. And Rudjek was his friend because he thought that Kofi was brave and liked to hear his stories. That was true too.

Even with fear and so much uncertainty in Tamar, the market is thick with people. Smoke from the firepits chokes the air and waters my eyes. Citizens argue with the gray-clad City Guard about the missing children. People say the child snatcher is hiding in the underbelly of the city. No one is quite sure where, so they argue about that too. I push through the throng. When I come upon the place where Kofi and his father usually stake their booth, another merchant is there.

"Can I interest you in a reading?" A slight woman in a dirty shift steps into my path and thrusts a bowl in my face. The woman has strange pale eyes, and long, loose braids frame her dark skin. "For only three copper coins, I'll tell your future."

I give her an apologetic look and turn back to the merchant who shouldn't be here. "Excuse me." I push to the front of the merchant's line. Her patrons grumble and curse under their breath at me. "Where's the regular fish merchant who sets up here?"

"Wait your turn, missy." The woman clucks her tongue, her teeth rimmed in gold. "There's enough of my famous cured whale fat for everyone. It's still early yet."

I repeat myself, louder this time, and the woman shrugs. "I don't know about no fish merchant and his son. This is a first-come, first-served market. The spot was empty, so I took it."

My heart slams against my chest as I back away from her booth. Kofi and his father were on this corner yesterday selling fresh catfish and tilapia. It's their favorite spot.

I chew on my lip, searching for them. My gaze flits from face to face. Not him. Not him. Not him. Where is he? The market's endless parade of people passes before my eyes.

I ask the merchants nearby if they've seen Kofi's father, but they brush off my questions and suggest I buy their wares. I have half a mind to tell the greedy swine where to shove their trinkets, but I slip back into the throng to keep looking.

It would be so much easier if I had magic. I could use a charm that would map a path to Kofi on a scroll instead of relying on hearsay. I swallow, but it does nothing to quell the frustration seething inside me. My whole body shakes with it.

"Arrah!" I hear Rudjek call, and turn to see him cutting a path to me. "Wait up."

Majka and Kira shove through the crowd. With their red gendar uniforms, no one dares push back. I take a sharp breath of relief. The three of them can help me look.

"I can't find Kofi or his father's booth." I peer over Rudjek's shoulder, still searching. "Have you seen him?"

Rudjek grabs my arm, his face grim. I don't like that look; I don't like it at all.

"He's gone, Arrah." Rudjek shakes his head. "Last night . . ."

"No!" I pull away from him. "He's around here somewhere."

A Familiar slips between my feet and I startle. Familiars had swarmed around Kofi four days ago in the market. Too many to count. He promised me he'd be careful. He *promised*.

Rudjek closes the space between us. His scent of lilac and wood smoke is both soothing and suffocating right now. "I'm sorry, Arrah." His words cut through me. "The gendar on duty last night stepped away for just a moment and when he came back, Kofi was . . . gone."

"What do you mean *gone*?" My mind reels, not quite absorbing what he's saying.

The noise in the crowd rings in my ears. It's not too late. It can't be.

"I'm going to find Kofi," I tell him, my decision made.

Rudjek rests his hands on the hilts of his shotels and shifts from heel to heel. "Arrah, what do you mean . . ."

I can't stand to meet his eye. "There's a way."

"I don't like the sound of this." He frowns. "What way?"

When I don't answer, Rudjek bites back his next question. He follows me to the part of the market the charlatans frequent. We find two dozen of them selling protection charms—some silver, some gold, some bone. Amulets with Kiva, Re'Mec, Koré, and other orishas. People line up to buy them and push and shove to get the one they want. I cringe at the sight of the desperate skirmishes. Some of the charlatans are mere con artists who knowingly sell fake charms.

It's not long before I spot the charlatan who offered to sell Rudjek a protection charm. "Give me a moment."

"Only if you promise you'll tell me what's going on." Rudjek draws his mouth into a hard line to let me know he means it.

"I will," I assure him as Kira and Majka catch up.

At that, I leave him and push through the charlatan's line. "Can we talk?" I shout over the commotion. He's showing a woman two sachets of herbs; one, he says, will ward off bad luck and the other will bring good luck. The woman can't decide which is better.

The man raises an eyebrow when I speak out of turn. It isn't my imagination that his face is more gaunt and his hair not only whiter—but thinner. His cataracts have grown worse too. "The *Ka*-Priestess's daughter." He dips his head. "Can I offer another coin to the Temple since you refused the last?"

"I need to speak to you on another matter." Heat flushes up my back, and I swear that the other patrons have stopped their business to watch me beg for help. "A private matter."

The man smiles, the look on his face smug. He knows what I want. It's a mistake to come here, but what choice do I have? There's no reason to believe that it'll work. My grandmother and Arti are both talented seers, but most of all, the demon appeared in a vision about *me*. That has to be something I can use to find Kofi and the other children. I have to try.

"Of course," he mumbles, his voice slick. Then he speaks loud enough so that others might hear him. "I'm always in service of the Temple."

Once he excuses himself from his patrons, we step into an alley to talk in private. From the corner of my eye, I can see Rudjek pacing back and forth at the mouth of the alley, out of earshot. Kira and Majka stand guard with their hands on their weapons.

"What can I do for the daughter of the greatest seer the King-dom has ever seen?" he asks with so much spite that it curdles in my belly. "Surely *I* can't be of any help to *you*."

"I need . . . I need." I'm hardly able to get the words out. I look around again to make sure no one else can hear my request. My parents would be so ashamed of me right now. I'm ashamed of myself.

"I need to know the secret to trading years for magic."

The man's smile widens into a full grin, and I bite back my shame. This is for Kofi.

"I'll pay for it." I fumble for my coin purse. "How much?"

"For you . . ." His sly cataract-clouded eyes find my gaze again. "It's free."

He adjusts the sachet across his shoulder and lifts the flap. Inside, there's a mess of bottles, trinkets, herbs, charms, and papyrus scrolls. Squinting, he sifts through them, until he finally hands me a scroll sealed with red twine. "You only have to do the ritual once to create the bridge for magic to come to you," he explains. "After that, every ritual will take your years, so use it with care."

I swallow the bile at the back of my throat, my belly filling with anguish. I hadn't known or considered the full consequences of trading years. This was something my father didn't tell me when we talked about the price of magic. If I create the bridge, then am I giving up on ever coming into my own magic? Every ritual I perform will draw from this horror bargain.

I stare down at the scroll, my hands shaking. If this isn't something that I can take back, can I live with it? Can I live with knowing that I traded away my last chance at having gifts of my own?

I want to ask if there's a way to burn the bridge—to disconnect it after one ritual, but I bite my tongue. It doesn't matter if there's a way. I made a promise to Kofi and I intend to keep it. If the bridge is for life, then it's up to me to resist the temptation to use it again.

"Don't make this decision lightly, child," the man warns, snapping me out of my thoughts.

I thank him and cram the scroll into my pocket. When I turn to leave, he adds, his voice cheerful, "Next time you see one of us in the market, do try not to look down your nose."

If there was ever a time I wished I could disappear into thin air, it's now. I've never had much to do with any of the charlatans—not the ones who dare call themselves *witchdoctors*. It's a prestigious title they haven't earned, a title that I always thought was my birthright. But I haven't earned it either and never will. I still don't wholly agree with trading years, but who am I to judge these people now? "I'm sorry." I bite my lip. "I'll do better."

I don't so much as walk out of the alley as flee, sweat pouring down my back, struggling to catch my breath. Rudjek steps in my path and snaps me out of my panic. He frowns, his face riddled with concern. I can't imagine how wild-eyed I must look to him right now. Can he see the fear in my expression? Can he feel it radiating from my bones?

"Tell me," he demands, his voice a deep rumble in his chest.

I brush his concern off with a wave. "He's given me a special ritual."

"A ritual." Rudjek pales and the veins in his face stand out like his mother's. His hands go limp against the hilts of his shotels. "Twenty-gods, Arrah," he says, his voice low. "Tell me that it isn't what I think. I know the rumors about the charlatans . . . what they do for magic."

It's exactly what he thinks.

I will trade my years for magic to find Kofi and stop the child snatcher.

ELEVEN

On our way to my father's shop in the West Market, the eye of Re'Mec emerges from behind the clouds. It knocks some of the chill from the air. But even under Re'Mec's favor, Familiars still flock to the streets like flies.

As we cross the merchants' row houses that separate the two markets, the ground turns from packed dirt to polished cobblestones. Gray walls replace the vibrant colors. Scribes and scholars hurry about their business flanked by hired guards. The chaos of the East Market hasn't reached here, but it stirs beneath the surface, waiting to breach. Kira and Majka hang back to give us space to talk.

Rudjek steps in front of me to block my path. "You haven't answered my question. What kind of ritual is this, Arrah? How can you perform one without magic?"

I want to tell him, but he'll try to convince me not to do it. "Can you just trust me?"

"Funny you should ask," he shoots back, glaring at me. "I would say the same."

I raise my chin and meet his midnight eyes. "My father suspected a link between the green-eyed serpent and the child snatcher. Since the seers have given up, and the serpent was in a vision about me—I hope that I can use that connection to find Kofi. The ritual that the charlatan gave me should help." I cross my arms, waiting for him to argue. "So now you know."

"It shouldn't be your place to do something so dangerous," Rudjek counters, his face stark from the news. "If the seers can do nothing, they should call upon their masters. The whole city tithes to the Temple, so the least the seers can do . . . the least the orishas can do is help for once."

People eavesdrop on our conversation—not even trying to hide it. I hiss at them, and the gossips scurry across the cobblestones like the rats they are. "I don't have any love for the orishas." He pauses, shifting his hands to his hips. "You saw what their barbaric Rite of Passage did to my brothers." His voice cracks open, each word laced with his pain and sorrow for what became of Jemi and Uran. One sent away in disgrace—the other living out his life under watchful guard. "But if this child snatcher is stronger than the seers, then the orishas are our only hope."

He palms the craven pendant around his neck, stroking the bone like it's a soothing song. His pain isn't only for his brothers; it's for himself too. His father expects him to measure up to a legacy never meant for him. My heart aches, and I wish there was something I could say to make it better. I know the burden of not living up to a parent's expectations all too well, but I need him to understand that what I do next is my choice.

"I can't stand by while this monster steals children," I say, my voice quiet. "I couldn't live with knowing that I could've done some-thing to save Kofi, and I didn't *try*."

"You're right. We can't stand by and do nothing, but . . ." His eyes are shiny black lakes of endless depth, reflecting hope and despair and something deeper, something warmer. A fire kindling. "You . . . you and Majka and Kira are my best friends. I don't know what I would do if I lost you."

"I'll be careful." I try to reassure him.

His eyebrows lift. "Can I stay with you?"

"You're allergic to my father's shop, remember?" I hide my own despair now, not knowing what other nasty surprises I'll find when I read the scroll. And I want to do this alone, in case I fail again. "It wouldn't be a good idea for you to come."

"He could stand to dust more often"—Rudjek waves for his friends—"but I'll manage."

If only Majka and Kira would drag him off to another one of his father's council meetings, then I could go in peace.

"I don't know what you're up to now," Kira juts up her chin when they catch up with us, "but I'm not going to like it, am I?"

Majka crosses his arms, grim-faced. "Whatever favor you're about to ask, Rudjek, the answer is no. The Vizier's in a foul mood and I'd rather not incur his wrath."

Rudjek gestures with his hand. "It's only a small favor."

"No." Kira grimaces. "For once, Majka's right."

"Come now, we're all friends here." He flashes Kira a winning smile. "I wouldn't be asking for a favor if it wasn't important."

Majka points at me. "Arrah we trust." Then he narrows his eyes at Rudjek. "You, we absolutely don't."

The bell tower looms over the West Market, taunting, as the hour approaches midday. I have no idea how much time the ritual will take. It could be anywhere from mere moments to days. I don't have days. Neither does Kofi. But I have to believe he and the other children are safe for now—the alternative is unthinkable.

"You wound me." Rudjek grabs his chest. "I'm very trust-worthy."

"Trustworthy?" Kira shakes her head. "A few days ago you snuck out of your rooms at night."

"Got accosted by some thieves on the docks," Majka chimes in.

"Lost a game of jackals and hounds and couldn't pay up." Kira taps her foot.

"Got yourself a black eye," adds Majka.

That explains Rudjek's bruises at the assembly, which he implied were from the arena. I give him a look sharp enough to cut and he ducks his head.

"Didn't they threaten to cut off your jewels?" Kira finishes.

Rudjek stands with his hands on his hips, staring at his friends with his mouth open. "You're one to talk, Majka. It was your idea to sneak to the docks. And Kira, you threw the first punch."

Majka's brown eyes shine with feigned innocence. "We're *your* attendants. Not the other way around. If you decide to go to the docks for a little fun, well then, we don't have a choice but to follow you."

"You three are *all* insufferable," I cut in, or else they'll argue for a solid bell. A little banter between them usually lightens my mood, but right now I'm anxious to get going.

"So back to that favor . . ." Rudjek clears his throat. "We need some time alone."

Majka's eyebrows raise. I don't know who blushes harder, Rudjek or me.

"Don't be absurd," I say, rolling my eyes. "It's nothing like that."

Majka sighs. "And here I thought you two would finally—"

"Shut it, Majka," Rudjek grumbles under his breath.

"Need I remind you," Kira says as she casts a scathing look at Rudjek, "you have afternoon lessons." Then she turns to me. "As do you."

My scribes aren't going to report me to Arti for skipping. They're afraid of her. "Yes, I know, *Mother* Kira." She can't help herself, I guess, being the daughter of Guildmaster Ny, the head scribe. Though I can't imagine her donning a scribe's tunic over all her shiny knives.

"Slip them a silver coin for me." Rudjek winks at Majka. "It won't be the first."

As the midday bells toll, I rock back on my heels. I can't fathom what the ritual will entail or what else I'll be giving up to make the bargain. I wipe away a string of sweat from my brow, trying to push down my doubts. "We'll be at my father's shop." I speak before either Kira or Majka can argue some more. I don't want Rudjek to come, but it's the only way to end this conversation. "You can drag him from there if you must."

We don't wait for them to answer before setting off for the shop again.

"One of these days they're going to confess to your father," I say to distract him.

He laughs, but it's forced. He's worried about Kofi too and covers it with thinly veiled humor. He gives me an ember of hope that things can be normal again. "As long as it's after my Coming of Age Ceremony"—he shrugs—"I don't care."

The bell on the door announces us to the empty shop. It's dark inside, and when I step across the threshold the fire lamps along the walls flare to life. The shop is warm and filled with rows of neatly stocked shelves. The hint of cloves in the air reminds me of sipping tea with my father between lessons. On my free days, I usually help him prepare his blood medicines. The memories calm my nerves a little.

Before we left for the Blood Moon Festival, I hid behind a shelf of animal carcasses and watched him extend the life of an old scholar woman. Oshhe squatted in the center of the room, where the cauldron boiled beneath a bushel of herbs. Kohl covered his already dark face, his teeth painted crimson. His eyes stretched wide as the smoke wrapped around the woman. It encircled her feet first, then curled up her legs. Slow and methodical, rising like a winged serpent.

The scholar stood as still as the dead, her pristine elara a flush of silver. A deep hum rose from Oshhe's throat as he guided the smoke. It snaked around her waist, and she didn't make so much as a sound. The regulars never did. I moved closer to get a better look, peeking between the bloodroot and woodworm. Always in awe of my father's work, I quietly straightened the medicinals on their shelves the entire time. Opium, cannabis, myrrh, frankincense, fennel, cassia, senna, thyme. Too many to count.

Once the smoke reached the woman's head, the fire beneath the cauldron winked out. The scholar's wrinkled skin rippled like a pebble breaching the surface of a pond. It smoothed along her temples and forehead. Her gray hair deepened into a rich auburn. My father's magic had halved the woman's age.

Rudjek fans his hand in front of his nose. "How can either of you stand the smell in here?"

Hints of thyme and lavender and clove lace the air. It smells better than a perfumery. If this were a better day, I would soak up the smell and settle in for a peaceful afternoon with my father. It's my favorite place to come outside of the East Market, but I'll find no comfort here either. "There's nothing wrong with the smell," I shoot back, more than a little annoyed.

He grimaces as he cracks open a window. "This place needs some fresh air."

I cross my arms. "What exactly about herbs and flowers do you find so offensive?"

"Herbs?" His eyes water and he wipes away tears. "That's a quaint description."

"What do you mean?" I ask. "The air's charmed to smell pleasant."

Rudjek frowns again. "The magic doesn't seem to be working."

I head for the shelves of scrolls at the back of the shop. "What does it smell like to you?"

"Like something gone rancid." He tugs at the collar of his elara. "It burns my nose and chest."

Rudjek *actually* might be allergic to something in the shop.

"I warned you," I mumble under my breath.

The scroll feels heavy in my pocket, and I can't wait any longer even if Rudjek's still here. I take up the wrinkled paper between sweaty fingers and untie the twine. I read the ritual written in

Tamaran so fast that my pulse drums in my ears. If I do this, make the trade, the connection can only be broken if magic decides to come to me of its own free will. I suck in a breath through my teeth, both relieved and devastated. There's still hope. If my own gifts come and they're strong, that will break the connection. But Arti said no Mulani came into their gifts late. Even my father doesn't believe it will happen. The only other way to break the connection is *death*.

I force myself to keep reading, my hand shaking as I do. The ritual requires a place where magic gathers in abundance. Here in Tamar, that means the Almighty Temple or the sacred Gaer tree. Since the Temple is out of the question, it has to be the tree. I've become no better than the people my mother ridicules. If she knew my plans she'd look down her nose at me, the same way I looked down my nose at the charlatans. The one in the market had made sure to rub it in my face. A pang of shame heats my belly, but I won't let it sway my decision. I'm doing this for Kofi and the others. My pride is the least of my concerns.

When I glance up, Rudjek has slid to the floor with his back against the wall. Sweat soaks through his elara. He's waiting for me to tell him what the scroll says, but I can't bring myself to do it.

"Are you okay?" I ask instead. "You really don't look well."

"I'm fine." He palms his family crest. "It'll pass."

I frown, wondering if the craven bone is reacting to the magic in the shop, and if it is, would it react to the ritual? I can't risk it interfering with my plans.

"Would you like some tea?" I ask, and his face blanches. "What?" I frown. "Do you think the tea smells bad too?"

"No, it's not that." He shakes his head and glances at his hands.

"Now that I'm coming of age, I've been learning more about the customs of my mother's people. In the North, offering tea can be . . . *misinterpreted*."

"Misinterpreted?" I laugh. "How?"

Rudjek draws his legs against his chest and rests his chin on his knees. He looks like the skinny little boy I first met along the Serpent River all those years ago. He was dreadful then, with his tangled black curls falling into his eyes as he yelled at two grown men. His attendants stood back while he tinkered with his fishing pole. One snickered at his frustration, and the other looked like he wanted to slap the boy across the back of the head.

Oshhe and I had been gathering mint grass by the river. The boy struggled with his line for the longest time, until finally I grew impatient. I asked my father if I could help, and without waiting for an answer, I stormed off toward them, to find the boy near tears. "They're not showing you the right way."

He looked up at me with eyes darker than night. Then he flashed the two attendants a crooked grin. "I told you, but you never listen to me!"

"Do you want me to show you?" I shrugged. "My father taught me."

Pain flashed in his eyes and he replied in a small voice, "I'd like that."

"In my mother's country, Delene"—Rudjek's voice pulls me out of the memory—"when a girl offers tea to a boy, it means something more."

"Don't go getting any ideas." I blush. "In the tribal lands, tea is tea."

"Who said I had any ideas?" he asks as he comes to his feet again. "Tea is tea here too."

I don't answer as I turn back to the scroll. There's another awkward silence between us. Had it been another time, I would tease him to no end. I would ask if he wants an offer of tea to mean more than *just* tea. It isn't as if I've never thought about it too.

"I want to do this alone." I bite my lip. "I'll mess something up with you here."

"Why?" His voice drops low as he closes the space between us. He looks quite awful. "Am I distracting?" he adds in an innocent tone.

"In fact, you are." I squint at him. "You look like you're going to be sick."

"Arrah." He draws out my name and it's music to my ears. "I don't know what you're planning, but I can tell it's dangerous. I can't let you do it by yourself. If something were to go wrong—"

"Nothing will go wrong." I cut him off.

"Things have been different between us since you got back from the tribal lands." He searches my face for something, his dark eyes penetrating my cover of half-truths. "We used to tell each other everything."

"I've told you *almost* everything." The words slip out before I can catch myself.

"Almost everything," he repeats, taking a step closer.

"I know you want to help, Rudjek." I wince. "But I need to do this on my own."

He sighs, glancing away. "You're stubborn, you know that?"

More silence. There's been enough of that to make the shop feel too small. In the end, he's not feeling well, so I win out. We part ways with things left unsaid.

Once he leaves, I waste no time. For the hour of *ösana* waits for no one.

TWELVE

Several spells, incantations, and charms could help me find the demon. The problem is that most of them need some cherished possession to work. Oshhe has scrolls from all five tribes, and I find a Mulani ritual that doesn't need a personal item. The scroll promises to uncover something or someone hidden from plain sight. I wonder if my mother has been using a similar ritual at the Temple, or none at all. Those strongest in the gift don't always need rituals to focus their magic.

My hands shake as I untether the Mulani scroll and lay it on the table next to the one from the charlatan. First, I must enact the ritual to open a bridge between magic and myself during the hour of *ösana*. There's still time, yet the doubts start to creep in. For the ritual will bring me close to death. I have no reason to believe it will work either. I've never been good at magic, but that won't stop me from trying.

I cling to the hope that my natural gifts will come before it's too late. That if I do this one ritual, there's still a chance to break the connection. But what if my abilities to see magic and have it not affect my mind are the only gifts I will ever have? I bite the inside of my cheek, letting my doubts curl up next to my hope. One gives me the strength to keep pushing, and the other reminds me to never give up.

At night, sparks of magic flicker between the shelves of dried herbs, bones, and charms in my father's shop like moths drawn to flames. Shadows gather in corners and change into looming shapes that once terrified me as a child, and even now, set me on edge. The magic is aimless—lost without someone to wield it. There's something foreboding about being here without my father. I've never snuck into the shop before alone, and I can't shake the feeling that I'm invading his private space. That I shouldn't be here.

Oshhe stores his tools for brewing blood medicines in a small room at the back of the shop. Pots, shears, linens, knives, and needles to extract blood hang along the walls. Soil imported from the Aatiri lands covers the floor. He says it makes his magic stronger.

I should've sent word home that I would be staying with Essnai tonight to not draw attention to my absence, but it's too late for that. If Arti wants to find me, she will. When I step inside the storeroom, I close my eyes and curl my toes into the cool soil. I inhale a deep breath, anticipation and fear pulsing in my body. I can't fail again. Kofi needs me. But beneath the feeling of need is something else I can't deny. My motivations aren't pure. I want desperately to be able to call magic and control it like my parents, to catch it on my fingertips. And if I do the ritual and my own gifts never show, then this will be my only link to true magic.

I'm breaking my promise to my father. For that I'm sorry. I don't want to disappoint him, or endure the devastated look he gave me in the garden when he said that my magic may never come. Arti has always made me feel less for not possessing magic, even if she didn't do it on purpose. All my life I've watched the way she never doubted or second-guessed herself. The way her steps ring with pure, unchallenged confidence. I've always wanted to be powerful and sure like her—to have even a fraction of her gifts. For my father, my not having magic has never mattered. I wish it didn't matter to me either, but it's too late to wallow in my feelings about it now. I haven't the time.

I squat in front of a stack of wood and set a fire to make the blood medicine for the Mulani ritual. Once the herbs—bitter leaf, goat weed, and senna—start to boil there's nothing to do but wait. As I stare at the flames, I try to reconcile Grandmother's vision with Arti's. Tam all but confirmed that the green-eyed serpent was a demon. Demons need souls, and children's *kas* are the purest. Now there's no doubt left in my mind that seeking out the green-eyed serpent will lead me to the child snatcher.

When the herbs are ready, I mix them with ginger and eeru pepper paste and put the medicine in a vial. It's as thick as molasses and the smell is sharp enough to draw tears from my eyes. To seal the ritual, I must add blood infused with magic—magic that I'll have if the bargain to trade my years works. I'm nervous—more so than before the tests with Grandmother at the Blood Moon Festival. What will it be like when magic answers my call? When it becomes a part of me? Tonight, if all goes well, I'll know soon enough.

Something as simple as dyeing one's hair blue needs a bit of blood. My father's ritual to extend life needs much more. That is the true limitation of flesh magic. There's only so much blood a person can give over a short period of time. I've mixed countless medicines before on my own and with my father. None of them worked, but the action itself has always given me a sense of peace. This time my blood medicine has to work.

I work for hours, through the entire afternoon and late into the night. The first morning bells toll as I finish stringing a bone necklace. It's a charm for protection in case something goes wrong. As much as I'm willing to sacrifice, I want to come out of this ritual whole. It's foolish to think that a simple charm will protect me, but the necklace offers me the smallest solace. And right now, I'll take what little comfort I can get. Sweat drips down my forehead as I rush to tidy up Oshhe's shop. He might not notice the missing items, but if he asks, I won't hide the truth. Once he learns of what I've done, he'll see that I had no choice.

The moon bathes the cobblestones outside the shop. All the merchants have closed for the night, and most of the West Market is quiet. Fire lamps light my way through the darkened streets. I avoid the drunkards looking for *owahyats*, and the ones who lock arms with each other in song. As I enter quieter neighborhoods with the moonlight as my guide, every sound makes my heart jump.

It would've been safer to take the busier route through the East Market, but the hour is fast approaching. By the time I reach the sacred Gaer tree on the north edge of the city, I'm drenched in sweat. The bald tree is darker than the night itself. No leaves grow on its branches and no grass around its roots.

The first *Ka*-Priest of the Kingdom was buried here. It's said that his magic was so powerful that his *ka* took root and grew into a tree rather than ascend into death. Outside of the Temple, this is the most holy place in Tamar—and the most practical place to perform the ritual.

I settle into the cool embrace of soil as black and iridescent as obsidian glass. As the hour of *ösana* approaches, sparks of magic dance across the bruised sky. I wait for two gods to cross paths, wait for the world to wake and the magic to burrow into my veins. The moment languishes so long that my heartbeat fills my ears with a desperate plea.

This won't be easy. I'm not a fool, but I am a foolish girl doing a foolish thing. Magic has costs, even for those who make it look as effortless as kneading fufu.

First, the trade.

Magic will either obey or refuse me. It rejected me when I was a little girl at Imebyé and has forsaken me in all my years practicing with Grandmother. Now I have something to offer it.

Before I lose my nerve, I slam my hand into the sacred tree, and thorns pierce my flesh with the ease of a tobachi knife. The pain is hot and sharp, and I bite back a cry. One of the thorns cuts clear through to the back of my hand. I inhale a deep breath as my pulse throbs in my ears. The blood gathers at my wrist and drops down to feed the roots of the tree. It isn't so bad, I tell myself, but this is only the beginning. It'll be much worse before it gets better. The scroll had been clear about that.

I whisper the words to offer my life as payment for a taste of magic, and then I wait. I've been patient all these years; I can hold out a little longer. But the magic is impatient for once. Black vines sprout from the tree like weeds in a garden. They writhe and lash out at me. When I try to snatch my hand back, they burrow under my skin. I scream as the vines stretch up my arm, leaving a trail of excruciating pain in their wake. A new crop shoots from the tree and straight into my open mouth, cutting off my scream. I can't breathe. My first instinct is to pull the vines out, but I've lost control of my body. I can't lift my free arm. Fire burns down my throat, and I can't hold on much longer. Panic sets in. I want to call it off, but it's too late.

I can do this. The words taunt me as vines crawl behind my eyes and tighten around my organs. No, I can't. I'm going to die. It's the last thing that crosses my mind before everything blinks out and there's only darkness.

Then I'm gasping for air, my face half-buried in the dirt. My right hand almost gives out as I drag myself to sit up. It's crusted in blood, and the wound is raw. It takes a moment to gather my wits, and I lean against a place on the tree without thorns. I'm afraid the vines will come back, but I'm too weak to move, let alone stand up. I wipe away a sting of tears that turn out to be blood. Did it work? I can't tell. There's plenty of magic in the night sky, but it doesn't come to me.

My stomach clenches. I can't have failed again. Not after going through so much.

The bone charm rattles around my neck, reminding me of my father's warning. *When you barter your years for magic, it takes of you what it will. It could be five years, or your whole life as payment. It does not matter the complexity of the ritual, spell, or charm. There's no way to tell until it's too late.* I waste no time: after adding my blood, I drink the medicine to find the child snatcher. I gag on the foul taste and my pulse quickens. I should heed my father's words and stop before it's too late, but what then? I can't turn my back and pretend that everything's okay. Kofi needs me. I should've found a way to protect him when I saw the Familiars in the market.

"Heka, father and mother of magic, please let this work." The words taste rusty and bitter on my tongue. I wait for a sign, and a bird squawks above my head in the bald tree. My jaw hurts from clenching my teeth. I choose my next words with care. "Help me save Kofi."

The ground stirs around my legs. Bits of magic caught in the wind swirl in front of my face and mist collects at my feet, snaking across my legs. It's warm, and it makes my legs grow limp. Sweat trickles down my forehead. I wipe it away. My heartbeat thunders like drums in my ears. It's *really* working. A part of me didn't believe that it would. Magic is answering *my* call. I'm scared and thrilled at once after all these years of trying and failing.

The mist creeps up my thighs and torso, wrapping me in a cocoon as solid as stone. Cold stretches through my body, and ash coats my tongue as it leeches the years from my life. Years gone in a few breaths. Blisters crop up on my arms where the vines burrowed into my skin and the roots of my teeth ache. I bite the inside of my cheek to hold back the pain. It seems that magic would rather break me than heed my call.

Soil shifts beneath me as I slip into the space before unconsciousness. Neither here nor there. The place before dreams and nightmares, where darkness clings to my skin like beads of sweat. Anticipation and longing choke me as my mind splits in two.

Something or someone latches on to me, wrenching my split

mind from my body. I try to resist, but the pull isn't physical—it's spiritual and too strong. The same was true at the Blood Moon Festival when my *ka* almost untethered from my body.

Suns and moons race across the sky so fast that they become brilliant sparks of gold and silver. My *ka* stretches, leaving the broken shell of myself behind. Unfamiliar eyes bore into me, eyes that peer across time from some future place. Eyes that glow like the green fog that descends upon the city after a thunderstorm. The serpent eyes from Grandmother's vision. The demon. Had I been in my body, my heart would've quit that very moment.

"You don't belong here," the demon whispers in my ear.

The voice is that of a *child*. A very young one at that. Her magic pricks my skin. It rattles my bones like it's trying to tear me apart at the seams. I have enough sense to be more afraid than jealous. My consciousness stretches every which way. If it stretches any farther, there will be nothing left of me to return home. The child's magic slams into me so hard my spine stiffens against the tree—a reminder that my body awaits.

"Our time is yet to come," she adds, voice full of mischief. "Go back and find what you seek."

I seek the child snatcher, but if the demon's not the one stealing children, then who is? Could Arti have been right all this time about the craven bone, and the anti-magic? That someone in the Vizier's family was guilty?

My *ka* shrinks back into the night, but I don't return to my body. A single moon settles in the sky, and I am in the present again. My *ka* floats high above Tamar, even higher than the three giants that watch over the city: the Almighty Temple to the north, the Almighty

Palace to the west, and the Vizier's estate to the south. To the east, idle boats crowd the harbor on the Serpent River and the docks teem with people. I descend with my will alone and glide through the streets along the scholars' villas. Through the merchants' row houses and the mud-brick huts along the riverbanks. My path is not linear. My *ka* is a tapestry rippling in the wind.

This isn't at all what I expected from performing my very first ritual. Witchdoctors make it look so easy, but it's like wading through a forest of twisted branches that threaten to trap you in their snare. In this state, I'm a child learning to walk for the first time.

I'm aware of my body against the tree. The bark grows new thorns that sink into my back, and the pain shoots down the tether to my *ka* like lightning. Yes, magic abides in me, but it's killing me too. My *ka* lingers above the orphanage as if snagged on a clothesline.

"Twenty-gods, Majka," Rudjek tells him. "What happened to your face?"

Dread sweeps through my *ka* as I spot them. They are both dressed in black elaras with hoods shrouding their faces. For the second time tonight, my heart almost stops. What is Rudjek doing here at this forbidden hour? I refuse to believe the worst as my mind struggles to find a plausible explanation.

"Kira is what happened," Majka groans, rubbing his forehead.

"What did you do this time?" Rudjek laughs.

Majka shrugs. "I may have hit on her sister."

"Be glad Kira didn't break your arm for that." Rudjek wags his finger. "One would think you'd be smart enough not to annoy a girl who wears a dozen daggers on her person at any given time. She *has* beaten you several times in the arena."

"She's beaten you too!" Majka retorts, incredulous.

"She beat me once," Rudjek fires back, "and I was blindfolded."

"Liar," Majka hisses. "You were not blindfolded."

"With one hand tied behind my back," Rudjek insists.

"It's cold and I have to piss." Majka wraps his arms around his shoulders. "There's no one out here. This place is as silent as the dead."

"Stop your whining." Rudjek frowns, then startles. "Do you feel that?"

"Feel what?" Majka jerks his head like a scared bird. "What is it?"

Rudjek's palms slip to the hilts of his shotels. "I don't know."

The echo of my heart leaping in my chest travels down the tether to my *ka*.

Majka's gaze darts around, his voice low. "Could Arrah be wrong about this demon?"

"No, I don't think so." Rudjek draws his swords. "I trust her."

"I trust her too," Majka grumbles under his breath. "But if she's right, then we're the only two standing between the demon and the orphanage right now. That does not bode well for us."

Heat spreads through my body despite the pain of the thorns in my back. Foolish boy. Of course he would sneak out tonight to help. He's so ridiculous to think that he could—not that I'm any better. I feel a pang of relief seeing him here.

Something tugs at my *ka*, dragging me away from the orphanage. It's not the green-eyed serpent this time. I travel through the rainbow of canopies in the East Market. A grayness clings to the city, muting its bright colors. Even the drums, flutes, and harps from the street musicians sound dull. Brewed beer, pipe smoke, and spiced meats saturate the air. The sounds of unbridled laughter and conversations rush in at once. In dark alleys and corners, the market brims with those who trade in rawhide, ivory, and secrets. Night merchants who can read your heart's desire as well as a real witchdoctor who can read bones. Even with so much fear hanging over the city, there are people who refuse to let it change their routine. They keep hope alive.

My reflection stares up at me in a puddle of water. I'm almost transparent—a shadow of my true self. People pass through my form without pause. The split between my body and *ka* widens to a gaping wound. Should it feel like this, or have I traveled too far? I'm both lying on cool soil beside the tree and standing in the market. Confusion fogs my mind and some grave knowledge slips through my thoughts like a secret on the wind.

A brightness amidst so much gray catches my attention. It's amorphous, like me, but there's a solidity that I lack. Though the patrons do not sense me, they move around the brightness as if it's an orisha statue in their path. I follow, passing patrons gulping down mugs of beer and placing bets on cockfights. People spitting tobacco juice between their teeth and counting tallies. Children playing on the streets.

Kira and Essnai wade through the crowd, searching face after face. They walk so close that their hands brush, and their auras tangle in brilliant shades of blue. Essnai grips her staff while Kira fingers a blade sheathed against her thigh. From their body language the *amas* aren't only looking for the child snatcher, they're protecting each other too.

I'm relieved to see my friends helping. I know this is Rudjek's doing—he's always been good at taking charge. The market thrives with life, and the ebb and flow of the crowd puts me at ease. I could wander through the streets all night and never see the end. Not so different from the days I come here for hours to calm my restless mind.

When the brightness molds itself into a hooded figure that moves through the crowd, I freeze. My vision shrinks and there's only her. Everything else blurs and fades to the background. She wears a flowing green sheath that drags across the muddy ground; a matching shawl hides her identity. Her body glows with a soft light that at first glance is beautiful, but the edges are sharp as glass. If I come too close, her light will cut into my *ka*, and then nothing will be left of me. Yet I can't stay away. She is the reason I'm here. She is the child snatcher, and definitely different from the green-eyed serpent. The fog clouding my mind lifts, and my purpose comes into focus again. I know why I'm here.

The child snatcher's heavy steps vibrate in my *ka*, and draw sparks of magic from the sky. The woman darts this way and that. Soon it becomes clear that she's circling the children like a vulture above carrion. The echo of my heartbeat tugs at the tether to my body.

Gray mist creeps along the dirt paths in the market. It slows my progress, but I push harder. With each step the pain that rips through my body underneath the tree is sharper than the last. Is this the child snatcher's doing? Does she know someone's hunting her? Or is my *ka* too far from my body? My teeth grit so hard that my jaw aches, but I won't stop until I know the truth.

In this part of the market, people huddle together, and no one is without a weapon. They carry everything from shotels to butcher knives to staffs. The City Guard is out in full force too, along with a large contingent of gendars. They distract me until the woman's scent of honey and coconut cuts across my path. She smells *familiar*, and that confuses me.

I push my legs with all my might, but it's no good. My *ka* moves as if it's wading through a bog. Blood coats my tongue as the tether between my body and *ka* stretches taut, so close to snapping. No point of wondering what will happen if it breaks. Nothing good can come of it. I try to memorize everything about the woman. She's shorter than me, wide-hipped and fine-boned, a flash of golden eyes. My heart threatens to crack my chest open as she ducks into an alley.

Staying in the shadows, the woman follows a girl not much younger than me. The girl keeps glancing over her shoulder, as though she can sense the danger. When the moonlight catches the oval ring on the woman's left hand, I stop breathing. My body seizes. No, it can't be. This is a dream. *Wake up, Arrah. Wake up now.* The alley spins and my vision fades in and out. I'm in two places again, lying on the ground and in the market watching something horrible about to unfold. Watching the child snatcher, *watching* my mother.

My *ka* snaps back to my body. I lie in the soil beneath the bald tree, gasping for air, whole again, my bones threatening to snap in two. The moon curves into a wicked smile. What I saw can't be real. None of it makes sense. Hot tears slide down my face as I slip into darkness.

Time to pay magic's price.

KORÉ, ORISHA OF MOON, TWIN KING

Well, this is an interesting turn of events. I must admit that I didn't see this coming.

You have been busy, haven't you, old friend? Working your wicked magic right under my nose. We've been together a long time, you and I, and every day you grow stronger. It shouldn't be possible, yet here we are. My box won't hold your soul forever.

The War was long and bloody, and quite entertaining at times. But you couldn't leave well enough alone, could you? Our sister was gone, and all you had to do was stop eating souls, live out the rest of your unnatural life, and die. Was that so hard? Oh but no, that would be too easy. When she died, you showed your true face, the one you kept hidden beneath the surface. Perhaps it was she who suppressed your inner beast.

The two of you were always so synced in a way that I could never understand, your souls so intertwined. It was really quite lovely, had you both not been so naive. Had she not died, I do not *believe for one moment that the outcome would be different.*

You cannot change your nature. Even without souls, you were always destined to become a monster. Our sister only complicated matters. Looking back on it, we were fools for thinking you would just fade into the ether after she died.

It pains me that twenty of my brethren sacrificed themselves to chain you with their own kas. *It was only supposed to be a temporary solution until I could find another answer, but time is tricky, isn't it? Five thousand years is a blink of the eye in an orisha's life. That said, anyone would turn aloof chained that long, as they have grown.*

Do you think you're the only one who's been planning?

There is always a weakness in armor, old friend, no matter how strong.

I pledged my life to mortal kind, and I won't let you destroy it. It was a foolish promise at the time, but they are a reflection of me—a poor one, but a reflection no less.

Enough talk for now, old friend. I must sharpen my knives.

PART II

For where she walks death follows
Her heart is black and hollow
For her love is a dangerous thing
Full of heartache and pain.
—Song of the Unnamed

THIRTEEN

When I was little, my father told me lots of stories. Funny stories. Sad stories. Silly stories. But out of all his tales, he only told me one love story. The memory has always stayed with me and now it comes back in my dreams.

We're working in the courtyard on a lazy afternoon, the sun beating down our backs. Sweet honeysuckle lingers in the air. It's the start of Su'omi—the season of rebirth—right after I've turned eight. "The heart is a fickle thing, Little Priestess," my father remarks, pruning a shrub. "When magic is involved, it can grow as black as the hour of *ösana*. There are few things more powerful than the human heart."

I lie on my belly in the grass with my legs fanning in the air. "Do you love Arti?"

After a long silence, he warns me, "Love is a word that we must use with care."

Another long pause.

"Your mother . . . she is *Mulani*."

He says Mulani as if her tribe explains her coldness. She spends more time in the Almighty Temple than she does at home, and she never has a kind word for anyone. Especially me. I've met many from her tribe and none are like her. Other Mulani strike me as standoff-ish, temperamental even. But my mother's amber eyes have always been hollow when she looks at me, as though she's never satisfied with anything I do. The more I try to latch on to her, the more she pushes me away. I can't remember her ever smiling or being happy.

"What am I, Father?" I ask. "Am I a daughter of Tribe Aatiri or Tribe Mulani?"

"You are the daughter of my heart." Oshhe nudges my chin.

I laugh at that, delighted by his words.

"Do you want to hear a story about love, Little Priestess?" Oshhe asks.

I nod my excitement as my father puts aside his shears and settles on the grass beside me. The sunlight makes his ebony skin glisten and his brown eyes shine. He tucks his long legs beneath him and pulls a sachet from his pocket. "We can't have a story without candies."

He takes a handful and passes the bag to me. I inhale the sweet vanilla and nutmeg of the milk candy, and pop two in my mouth.

"Long ago an Aatiri boy attended the Blood Moon Festival at the Temple of Heka," Oshhe begins. "He saw a girl with the most beautiful golden eyes."

"It's about you and Arti?" I kick my feet faster. "It is, isn't it?"

"No, it's only a story." Oshhe shakes his head, his face a little sad.

"The Aatiri boy was very shy and the Mulani girl was so very beautiful," he continues. "Night after night the tribes gathered to celebrate the blood moon, and he wanted to ask the girl for a dance. But bigger boys would shove him aside and ask first.

"One morning when he was washing at the river, he saw the girl picking berries in the bushes. He thanked Heka for his good fortune and wasted no time approaching her. The girl was wary, but she did not run away. The boy struggled to find the right words. He wanted to make a good first impression. He thought about how the other boys called her Siren of the Valley behind her back. They said that she could steal your magic with one kiss, but he did not believe in such foolish things.

"'You don't look like a siren to me,' the boy had said. Not the best first words to any girl, but instead of shooing him away, she laughed. The girl asked if he wanted to help her pick berries. They became friends and spent much time together during the Blood Moon Festival. They learned about each other's hopes and dreams. The girl wanted to one day leave the tribal lands to see the world, while the boy loved his home with all his heart. Every year they would see each other at the festival, but the boy never told her of his feelings. Not for many years. When he finally worked up the courage, it was too late. The girl had fallen in love with a prince who could fulfill her dreams of seeing the world."

"This is a sad love story," I pout. "She's not supposed to fall in love with another boy."

"The story isn't over." Oshhe clucks his tongue. "The prince's best friend was a very powerful young man looking to make his mark, and he didn't like the girl very much. He commanded an evil witchdoctor to prove that the girl had bewitched the prince. But by the time the witchdoctor found this accusation to be false, he had stripped away her love for the prince. He didn't stop at that, though. He took away all that was pure and kind and good in the girl. In pursuing her dreams and imagining a different life for herself, the girl had been punished."

I stop swinging my legs and bite my lip to keep from interrupting my father again. This really was an awful story.

"When the boy did not see his love at the next Blood Moon Festival, he sought her out in a city far from the tribal lands. He found her broken and changed, but he held on to the memory of the sweet, kindhearted girl she used to be. He hoped that one day she could love him too, so when he became a man, he asked her to marry him. She agreed."

"For a brief time, they were happy together. They had a beautiful daughter. She looked so very much like her mother and had her courage and her spirit. The man vowed to love and protect his daughter so that she would always feel wanted and would never have to endure the suffering that befell her mother. He had finally found the love of his life. You see, Little Priestess, this isn't a love story between a boy and girl. This is a story about a father's love for his daughter."

My father has always kept me safe, and I desperately need him now.

My body is brittle and broken and pain. Black tendrils flow over me like cool water over a burn, lulling me deep into sleep. I'm walled away in some corner of my mind that's impenetrable—a place of solitude, secrets, and deceit. The echo of laughter and song pulls me back to the world of the living, but I'm met by only darkness.

I ache, but the pain is only a shadow now. Days have gone by. How many I can't say. My mouth is dry and my lips crack. The memory of Arti stalking the girl suffocates me. It bleeds into my every thought, twisting with the remembered story of the Aatiri boy and the Mulani girl.

Despite my wariness, the black tendrils drag me into sleep again. A flash of lightning wakes me—this time in the heart of night. My room is dark. Familiars flicker in and out of my line of sight, slinking around the floor and the walls like greedy pests. But it isn't the Familiars that draw my eye. My mother stands shrouded in shadows at the foot of my bed. I try to sit up, scramble away, but she moves with the grace of a cheetah. I croak out a scream that's nothing more than a soft cry. Arti settles at my side. Her hair hangs loose in soft, dark curls that promise kindness, but they're lullabies that end in nightmares.

Her amber eyes are brilliant in the moonlight, but so empty. Pain streaks through my belly. I ache for the girl whose innocence was snatched away, the one who won my father's heart at first sight. I ache for the mother I'll never know, and the husk of a person before me now.

"What have you done, foolish girl?" she hisses, her voice broken.

"Why?" The word scratches my dry throat and cuts off. For the briefest moment I'm lost in the anguish in her voice and feel ashamed, but no, I haven't done anything wrong. Foolish, yes, but not wrong. "I don't understand . . . *why*?" I manage to spit out.

"You're no better than a charlatan—giving up your years." She glares at the altar beside my bed, at the shrine of tribal trinkets, refusing to look at me. "It cannot be undone."

My mother has always kept me at a distance, never showered me with a tender embrace. She's never told me a story on a lazy afternoon in the garden. If I didn't look so much like her, I could be an orphan she plucked from the street out of pity and later regretted. Now her unshed tears and the pain threading her words cleave my heart in two. A part of me still clings to the hope that my mother cares for me. That she isn't a monster who snatches children in the night.

"Where's Kofi?" I demand, my voice hoarse. I fear the answer.

"The ritual took ten years of your life," Arti says, ignoring my questions.

"Answer me!" I scream, unable to hide my desperation. "Where are the children?"

"Do you think I wanted to take them?" Arti spits, seething. "I made a deal. One I could not break even if I wanted to." When our eyes meet again, hers are sharp edges, the tears gone, her emotions buried again. "Had I known the extent of the bargain, I would've refused, but it's too late for that now. It will be over soon."

Arti slips a dagger from her kaftan so fast that it's a flash of silver in the dark. My lips tremble, but only a soft moan comes from my throat. When I try to sit up again, her magic holds me in place. She presses the blade against my cheek. I expect it to be cold, but it's warm. It hums with magic. In my father's story, the evil witchdoctor had broken the Mulani girl beyond repair. Now she *is* the evil witchdoctor.

I can't pretend she'll go away. She means to do harm. "You foolish, foolish girl." She leans in close to me—so close that her saccharine smell of coconut and honey turns my stomach sour. "This wasn't a part of the deal. We are very upset, but this is your fault. I warned you."

I don't dare speak, and the pent-up breath in my chest aches.

"I can't let you ruin our plans." Arti digs the knife into the sheet. "Everything is in place. The time is near. The exact day and hour as *he* foretold."

She isn't looking at me when she speaks. She's staring at the altar again.

"Oshhe will know," she whispers, her face blank. "I'll have to deal with him too."

Magic floats in the room, but it doesn't come to me, no matter how hard I try to impose my will upon it.

Arti's gaze rakes over me, pity in her expression. "This is for the best."

Heka, please help me.

My only answer is the soft drumming of rain against the roof.

"Please don't," I beg.

"It will be quick." She grabs the neckline of my gown and rips the cloth. "I promise."

My mother's going to kill me. She's going to plunge the knife into my heart and get rid of my body before my father returns. What lie will she tell? Will she say I had an accident?

I struggle against the force of her magic holding me in place. Her dagger burns hot and the markings on the blade shimmer in the moonlight. The magic smells sharp and feral, nothing like the sparks of magic dancing in the air. There's something very wrong with it, something very different. It crawls across my skin, searching for all the ways it can invade my body. I push harder and harder, my pulse thudding in my ears, my heart beating too fast. But it's no use. Her magic keeps me in an iron grip. For all the resistance that's happening in my mind, my body hasn't moved the slightest.

Familiars stretch into long tendrils as they slink closer to me, but even they keep their distance from my mother. I scream when the knife tears into my chest. Pain winds through my belly and my limbs. My mother's voice breaks again as she chants a spell in a language that reminds me of birdsong. Her anguish is too much to bear, and I squeeze my eyes shut as tears streak down my cheeks. I can't trust anything she's said, and seeing her remorse makes it that much worse. All these years, she's been so cold, so distant, and now she pretends that she cares about me?

Arti carves symbols into my chest in long, slow strokes. After the first cut, the pain dulls with a touch of her magic. She's shown me some small grace, but I don't know why. She takes care with the knife, like an artist sculpting something beautiful. By the time she finishes, the magic in her blade has left a trail of heat in my body. It consumes me from the inside. So many regrets and missed opportunities race through my mind. I never told Rudjek how I want nothing more than to kiss him, if only once. I didn't spend enough time with Essnai and Sukar, or Grandmother. My father, oh *Heka*.

"Look at me, Arrah," Arti commands.

My eyelids tingle and snap open—forced by her magic.

"You are bound to me, your body and *ka*," she says. "You will never speak or act against me."

A dull ache settles in my chest. "What have you done?"

"I've made it so you can't ruin our plans"—Arti cracks a rare smile—"and I've given you a gift."

Before I can say more, my mother backs into the shadows and disappears. Soon after that the Familiars sweep from the room, too. I crawl out of bed once my legs stop shaking. Sweat soaks my gown and I hold on to the altar to keep from falling. The rain against the roof echoes in my head as I stumble to the mirror. I must see the damage.

Cool night air prickles against my chest, and the moonlight falls on smooth, brown skin. This can't be possible. No cuts. No welts. No burns. No scars at all. I stare into the mirror, and the tiniest spark of hope punctuates my shock. If I'd left it up to sight alone, I could brush tonight off as a bad dream, but my fingers tell another story. And so does the lingering heat pulsing beneath my skin.

I trace the invisible circles carved into my chest—circles that my mother made sure no one will ever see. In magic, circles unite, they bind, but these aren't quite circles. I drag my finger along the scars again, slower this time, winding my way from the thicker coils at the bottom to the crest. As I do, light glows in the wake of my touch—tracing a clear pattern. My initial shock turns into horror at what I find.

A serpent—Arti carved a serpent into my chest. The Zu are the most skilled scriveners, masters of written magic, but my mother has studied it too. I don't doubt that she's mastered the techniques of all five tribes. Now she's twisted that magic into something vile. The serpent she cut into my chest must have something to do with the child in my future—the demon. I'm sure of it. Arti said that the hour was near, as *he* foretold, which meant there was still time to stop their plans.

Sweat trickles down my back as I change into a tunic and

trousers and slip into sandals. I open the shutters on my window, letting in the smell of fresh rain. A few droplets blow into my face.

My mind is a slippery mess as I escape into the night. The rain is cool, but my skin still simmers with heat. One of my sandals falls into the puddle of mud beneath my window. I don't bother searching for it in the half light, knowing that if I bend over, sleep will drag me back into the abyss. How I wish it could wash away my memories too— that it could rewrite history, erase my mother's sins. But not even magic can undo her crimes and the pain of *knowing*. The hollowness, the raw grief. In a haze, I let my instincts guide me. I cross the garden, crushing irises underfoot. Behind me, our house is pitch-black and shrouded in an unnatural mist. Just like Arti, the mist is everywhere, all around me. Nothing happens without her knowing. If she wants to stop me, she will. I wrap my arms around my shoulders as I slip past Nezi's porter station. It's dark and empty.

I'm lost in the murkiness of my thoughts as I stumble across the cobbles, rain and tears clouding my vision. For every step forward, the wind howls back at me. Drunkards stagger on the streets; some pass out in alleys. My balance is off, and I fall so many times that my palms and knees are raw and bloody. A knot twists in my belly. The ritual took my years, but it's taken something else too, something more. I press forward as a new determination and purpose wakes inside me. I'm going to stop my mother.

There's still a chance. Arti said that the exact day and hour is approaching as *he* foretold. I don't know who *he is*, but I know who *he is not*. My father would never partake in something so despicable. Even if she hadn't been nervous about Oshhe finding out, I'd still know it wasn't him. Arti spends most of her time at the Temple.

Does she mean one of the seers? Sukar's uncle, Barasa, had been the one to suggest that the child snatcher was wearing craven bone at the assembly. But my mother could have planted that seed in his mind as easily as she can calm Ty during one of her episodes. It would've been the perfect ruse, especially since she hates the Vizier.

What do she and her accomplice want with the children? I have to believe they're still alive. They must be. Arti is cunning and patient. If there's a foretold day and hour that's yet to come, then they must be waiting to act. Performing a ritual during a solar eclipse or a new moon strengthens magic. Could that be it? My mouth fills with bile. She's planning a ritual involving *children* . . . I can't wrap my mind around the idea. At best my mother is unstable and at worst she's a dangerous beast prowling in the shadows.

The Almighty One's palace is a beacon in the night. Even in the storm, it looms in the sky, watching over the city. A great white mammoth with torches encased in glass, protected against the elements. Behind its walls is the man my mother once loved—when she was still capable of such things. I'm exhausted, but where I'm going, I won't have to climb so high.

When I reach the tan stone wall, I collapse against the iron bars and call for the porter. The wind swallows my voice, but he emerges bundled up against the downpour. It's the regular porter at the Vizier's estate, and he recognizes me.

"Twenty-gods, Arrah," he barks. "What are you doing about this time of night?"

My mother's magic boils in my belly. "I'm here to see the Vizier."

"The Vizier?" The porter frowns. "What business would you have with him?"

Blinking against a flash of lightning, I squint up at his narrow face. *The Vizier is not a kind man*, my father said. That's true, but he isn't a child snatcher, and he didn't carve a curse into his child's chest. The porter's eyebrows furrow as streaks of rain drop from his beard. I must look like a mess with my braids tangled and my clothes drenched, one shoe missing. *When did I lose that?* "We better get you to an attendant first. You can't see the Vizier in the middle of the night looking like a runt from the streets. He'll be right cranky that you've awakened him."

As we cross the courtyard, a hint of blood and vomit covered by hibiscus and lilac oils taints the air. It's coming from the arena nearby where Rudjek and his friends train. I trip over a loose cobble and the porter catches my arm, taking on some of my weight.

"The *Ka*-Priestess is going to skin your hide for coming to the Vizier," he grumbles.

"Skin my hide?" I laugh, my voice hoarse. "How quaint that sounds."

The porter side-eyes me and works his jaw. "We knew she'd be up to something with your father gone."

It doesn't surprise me that the Vizier keeps tabs on my family. Arti challenges him at every opportune moment. She questions his decrees, and rallies Temple loyalists against him.

"I swear your father's the only one keeping that woman in check," mutters the porter.

His words are hazy as my mother's magic drains the surge of energy from my body. It must know what I've come to do and is trying to stop me. I fight to keep my eyes open, but my legs give out.

"What's the matter with you, girl?" the porter demands, his voice distant and muffled.

Colors blur around the edges of the rain, and my vision fades as I'm lifted from the ground. I catch a glimpse of Rudjek soaked to the bone before the magic drags me back into darkness.

FOURTEEN

I awake to bright lights blinding me and an infuriating itch under my skin. When I try to sit up, the room spins so fast that bile burns my throat. Voices close in from all around me and nowhere at all. Ties on my wrists keep my arms pinned at my sides. Has Arti come back to do more harm? No, she wouldn't need restraints. Her magic locked me against the bed without her lifting a finger. Someone stands close and a wisp of lilac and wood smoke dances in the air— the scent familiar and comforting.

I blink until Rudjek comes into focus. His face is stark, his eyebrows drawn in a deep frown. He bites his lip and fidgets with his hands, not knowing what to do with himself. He is so *disheveled*. There's something endearing about seeing him this way. He's not the son of the mighty Vizier, second to the Almighty One. He's the boy who stayed out all night to guard the orphanage because he wanted to help.

I remember the little boy by the Serpent River fussing with his flustered attendants, men with shotels bigger than he was tall. He already had an air of authority about him. How could he not, raised in an estate that sat above the city like an ancient god? The place where I lie safe from my mother for the moment.

The boy standing before me now towers over his father, his frame no longer lanky. No more fishing pole jokes. When was the last time I'd teased him like that? Once, only his attendants had been cut from stone, but somewhere he had made that transition too. The drastic change hasn't gone unnoticed. Not by the girls in the market who smile and fan themselves when he passes them, nor by me. If he weren't an Omari, they would make bolder advances at him even with me around.

"Rudjek," I say, my throat raw.

It will be quick, Arti said. *I promise.* All the memories flood back and tears slip down my cheeks. It *was* quick, and although not painless, it could've been worse.

"Arrah, are you okay?" he asks, stepping closer.

"Twenty-gods, Rudjek." The Vizier grabs his arm. "Get out of the physician's way."

"I'm not in his way," Rudjek snaps at his father.

The Vizier's caterpillar eyebrows knit together as he gives his son a murderous glare. It's the same look that stopped me from going to see Rudjek compete in the arena. No matter where I sat in the crowd, the Vizier always made it a point to cast his disapproving frown my way. If only he knew how much time Rudjek and I spend together in the East Market. Or how often we meet in our private spot by the Serpent River to fish or lie in the grass and talk for hours. It dawns on me that he must know. He's the Vizier. Rudjek's his heir. The only one of his three sons who could take his place one day.

There must be nothing Rudjek does that the Vizier *doesn't* know about. Did I not see a larger number of gendars in the market in my *ka* form on the night of the ritual? Some must have been there to keep watch on Rudjek.

"Either get out of the physician's way," the Vizier orders in a voice like ice, "or leave."

"Son," comes the soft purr of his mother, Serre. "Let the physician do his job."

Rudjek groans in protest but doesn't argue as he steps back.

I've never seen his mother without the gossamer veil that protects her skin from the sun. She's a daughter of the North—a land of snow, ice, and white mist as thick as porridge. The North is not a kingdom, but a cluster of countries allied through a council much like the tribes. They don't worship the sun orisha Re'Mec, and he doesn't shine his glory upon them. They don't worship any god. The scribes say it's why they're cursed with skin as thin as paper and sensitive to sunlight. The veins stand out against the tawny skin along Serre's temples and beneath her flush of pale violet eyes. She isn't pretty in the traditional sense, yet no one could deny that she's striking.

A man dressed in simple blue linen thrusts a vial under my nose filled with a fume so strong it stings. When I jerk away, I end up face-to-face with the Vizier. It's the middle of the night, and he's dressed in his white-and-gold elara with a lion-head emblem pinned to his collar. He's wearing a craven-bone wristlet and pendant too, as though he has something to fear from *me*. Does he think that my mother sent me to do harm? He knows I have no magic—or at least I *didn't* before the ritual to trade my years.

I still don't possess magic of my own, but now I can coax it to answer my call. After the worst part of the ritual was over, the magic did come. It filled me with hope and possibilities. It showed me that there were so many tapestries to unravel in the world, so many layers to peel away. My mother ruined that; she's ruined everything. Thinking about her, I reel with shame and disgust.

Arti's magic still tingles in my chest. What has she done, binding my body and *ka* to hers? When I was little, Oshhe told me stories of powerful witchdoctors who could command the living or the recently departed to do their bidding. Would I become like those poor souls—the *ndzumbi*? I won't let myself become a monster like her. I'll fight, even if it means giving up more of my years to break her curse.

Staring at the lion-head emblem, I remember Rudjek saying that the craven bone only reacts when someone directs magic at him. That means that it won't register my mother's curse on me. I try to speak again, but my throat is too parched and I cough.

Rudjek launches forward and his mother grabs his arm. "Can't you see she needs water?"

"You are trying my patience tonight, boy," the Vizier barks. "Get out!"

I wince at the venom in his voice and give Rudjek a nod to let him know I'm okay. I can't help but feel guilty for not telling him the whole truth about the ritual. He's my best friend—I've never hidden anything like this from him. I should've trusted that he'd support me, even if he didn't approve of my decision. Serre glances between the two of us, her diaphanous face revealing nothing.

He relents and storms from the room with his mother on his heels.

More shuffling of feet, whispers, and then silence.

The physician presses two fingers against my wrist. "Pulse is steady."

"Release my arms," I groan.

"I bound your hands to keep you from scratching yourself to death," says the physician.

I don't remember scratching, but my skin itches all over. "What . . ."

"Do as the girl asks," the Vizier commands through gritted teeth.

The physician does as he's told, then the Vizier dismisses him.

After the man leaves, the Vizier pours me a cup of water from the pitcher beside the bed. I take a few sips and sort out where to start. First I have to tell him about the children. That's more important than what Arti's done to me. But when my mouth opens, my throat burns and my voice seizes. I cannot utter a single word. Arti's magic flares in my chest and heat spreads through me.

The Vizier's face is one of practiced indifference as he asks, "Is there something wrong with your tongue, girl?"

My heart races out of control. "I . . . I don't know."

"Why have you come to see me?" His voice thunders in my ears. "What is so important that you've come in torrential rain, no less?"

"I was coming to tell you . . ." My words cut off as if sliced by the serrated edge of a tobachi knife. I squeeze my hands into fists. My mother said that I would not be able to speak or move against her. I understand now what she meant. Her magic has bought my silence. In all my years reading through the scrolls in my father's shop, I've never come across one that could do such a thing. "My mother . . ." I grit my teeth when all I want to do is scream at the top of my lungs. There must be some way to fight this curse, some way to break it. My mother is powerful, yes, but no magic is infallible.

The Vizier sits in the chair next to my bed, his face blank of emotion. He adjusts his elara, ever the perfect dignitary. Silence stretches like a taut rope between us as he threads his fingers together. "I'm not in the business of wasting my time." He's dropped pretenses, any sign of kindness vanishing from his voice. "Nor wasting words."

"Nor am I." The magic tightens in my throat, preparing to stop me from speaking ill of Arti. My fists shake as tears slide down my cheeks. There has to be a way around her curse.

"Should your news strengthen my position, I could offer you my protection." The Vizier leans closer, his dark eyes gleaming with hunger. "Don't be afraid to talk, child."

I hate the thought that he could gain some small advantage over my mother. Their rivalry is a sick game, and he lusts for the next strike as much as she does.

"I'm not afraid." I test the words on my tongue. "I can't."

His face curls into a look of pure disdain. "What has she done now?"

My tongue stiffens and turns stone. The Vizier watches me open and close my mouth like it's a sheet flapping in the wind, until I give up, sighing in frustration. "I can't say."

"You can't say?" The Vizier cocks an eyebrow. "Not that you *won't*, but you can't."

I nod. "Yes . . ." My voice fades again and I dig my nails into my palms.

"One would almost think that your mother knew that you'd

come straight to Rudjek and, by extension, me," he says. "She wanted such a thing to happen. You show up at my home in a panic, feverish, covered in mud. Such an event may worry a lesser rival."

The Vizier's head snaps around at a soft tap on the door. One of his attendants brings news. The man bows, keeping his eyes on the floor. "The *Ka*-Priestess has sent her servants across Tamar looking for her ill daughter. Should we send word, sir?"

"No." The Vizier rubs his chin. "Send news tomorrow afternoon."

"As you wish, sir." The attendant bows again before leaving.

I catch sight of Rudjek in the corridor, peering into the room. His face is half smile, half question in the moment before the attendant pulls the door closed. I slump against the pillows in defeat. The Vizier *should* worry, but I have little faith in him. I'm the only one who knows the truth, and I'm the one who must stop my mother.

Rudjek sneaks into my room an hour after the Vizier leaves.

"Sorry it took so long," he whispers, gently shutting the door behind him. "I had to bribe a lot of people."

"I'm not impressed that you bribed people to see me," I retort as I sit up in bed.

"What happened with the ritual and the child snatcher?" Rudjek opens the curtains at the window to let in the moonlight, then he drops into the chair beside the bed. "Did you see anything?"

The magic swells again and chokes off my words. I sigh and shake my head. "I didn't see anything worth mentioning." The lie is bitter on my tongue.

"So the ritual *didn't* work?" Rudjek lets out a shaky breath. "I was worried when you didn't come to the market the next day. I sent word, but you never answered my letters. I stopped by, too. So did Essnai and Sukar. Nezi said that you'd come down with a fever and your mother had given strict instructions that you were not to be disturbed." He bites his lip. "I thought the ritual had hurt you."

As much as I'm tired and drained from fighting against Arti's magic, I'm also annoyed that he assumes I failed again. "I *said* I didn't see anything worth mentioning."

Rudjek grimaces, and his voice is accusatory. "So it *did* work."

"Yes, you could say that," I mumble under my breath.

"You think I don't know what you did?" Rudjek crosses his arms and looks away. "I asked around . . . talked to some of the other charlatans, since the one who gave you the scroll wouldn't tell me."

Seeing the look of betrayal on his face, I bite the inside of my cheek. I don't need to explain what I did to him or anyone else. It was my choice.

"You traded your years for magic." Rudjek's words teem with pain. When he finally meets my eye again, he adds, "Arrah, how could you do something so reckless? What if . . ."

I don't want to argue with him about this. What's done is done, and there's no point. Instead, I ask, "Did you know about what happened to my mother?"

Rudjek's face blanches, making the veins in his forehead stand out.

"You've known all this time." My voice crackles with rage that I can't—no—that I *won't* contain. "Haven't you?"

He threads his fingers together the same as the Vizier did earlier, which only irks me more. "My father told me a few months ago. I suppose even then he was preparing me to become his heir, but I didn't understand at the time. Before the Almighty One, Jerek, rose to the throne, he and my father were best friends. They met Arti when she came to Tamar with the trade council that represents the tribes. Jerek was immediately infatuated with Arti, to the point that my father suspected that she had bewitched him."

Bewitching a man would be the least of my mother's crimes now.

"They spent every waking moment together for months," Rudjek continues. "Jerek asked Arti to marry him during a public ceremony and started a flurry of gossip. My father told the Almighty One of his suspicions. The Almighty One took the accusation seriously and bid my father to deal with it. He called for the *Ka*-Priest at the time to interrogate Arti, and Ren Eké . . . he did horrible things to her."

People in the market always spoke well of *Ka*-Priest Ren Eké, said that he'd been kind and amenable, a peacekeeper. All lies.

I never understood how horrible my father's story had been until now—what it had truly meant. Dread sinks in my belly as I remember years of countless snide remarks and slights from my mother. The looks of disappointment, but also the vacant expressions, the weariness. The times she'd lose herself in thoughts. The quiet moments she sat in the salon drinking tea. The endless wishing, when I was younger, that things would get better between us. They never did. And now they never will.

It's hard to stomach my father's story and these missing pieces from Rudjek—that *his father* had been the one to give the order. What unspeakable things had the *Ka*-Priest done to Arti? What turned her from the sweet, innocent girl that my father loved in his youth to the monster in the alley? Whatever the answer, it won't excuse the awful thing she's done. . . .

At the Blood Moon Festival an aunt said that Arti could've married the Almighty One had she been clever enough. I didn't think much of it then. Everyone could see the way he leered at her at the assembly. The way he leered at many of the women in attendance. But what does her history with the Almighty One, the Vizier, and *Ka*-Priest Ren Eké have to do with taking the children? It doesn't make sense. There's something else at play here . . . *something more.*

I have no doubt that my mother is capable of revenge, but the *Ka*-Priest is dead. Could taking the children be a ploy at revenge against the Vizier and the Almighty One? With their anti-magic and guards, she wouldn't be able to strike at them directly. The disappearances have already caused outrage across the city, and this is only the beginning of whatever my mother is planning.

"I can't believe you knew about this and never told me." I can't meet his eye. It isn't only his secret I can't bear to face. I have one of my own. I've never told him that my mother has spies working in the Vizier's household. I can't stomach any more secrets, lies, and deceit. I'm drowning in them. Even if I want to be honest with him, I can't now because of this gods-awful curse.

"Arrah, I'm sorry," Rudjek says, his timbre low. "I thought that . . ."

"You thought what?" I snap, cutting my eyes at him.

"I thought you would hate me," he confesses.

Heat festers in my chest and stretches across my limbs like tendrils, but his words knock the fight out of me. Our parents' rivalry has always stood between us. We just try not to talk about it. "I don't hate you, but I *am* annoyed to no end that you didn't tell me before now."

After silence lingers between us a beat too long, Rudjek blurts out, "Your mother was innocent. The *Ka*-Priest said it himself after torturing her for weeks. And by having her questioned, my father put trade with the tribal lands at risk. The Mulani threatened to cut ties with the Kingdom. To preserve the alliance, the Almighty One named Arti the *Ka*-Priest's apprentice."

My breath catches in my throat. I can't wrap my head around this news. Whether in her right mind or not, Arti agreed to work for the man who tortured her. I dig my nails into my forearms and draw my knees to my chest to keep from trembling. I hate the Vizier for what he's done. He destroyed my mother, and now she's worse than him. "People say a fisherman found the *Ka*-Priest on a hook in the bay."

Rudjek swallows hard. "From what I've heard, *Ka*-Priest Ren Eké made many enemies doing the Kingdom's dirty work."

None more dangerous than Arti.

FIFTEEN

After I spend a full day at the Vizier's estate, one of his attendants takes me home. It's near sunset when Nezi hobbles to the gate and lets me inside. She shakes her head and returns to her station without a word. Where were they last night? Between Nezi, Ty, and Terra, one of them should've been home. Didn't they hear my cries? Was it one of them who gathered me from beneath the sacred Gaer tree after the ritual?

I stare at the villa, my teeth clenched. The tan brick walls, the earth-toned shutters, the white curtains drawn at the windows. The archway that leads into the inner courtyard where my father grows his medicinals. Every detail gives the impression of tranquility, but it's only more lies.

I round the villa on my way to the kitchen entrance and cross paths with Terra carrying a bucket of vegetables. She runs up to me, the sun shining against her loose golden curls. "We've been turning Tamar belly-up looking for you." She frowns. "Where—"

"Is my mother home?" I ask, interrupting her.

"Yes." Terra hugs the bucket to her chest. "She's in a mood and rightfully so."

I draw in a deep breath. I want to take the first ferry headed away from here, but I'm no fool. The curse wouldn't let me go far before it tore me apart. My mother would've made sure of that. "I'd best be getting inside."

I start to walk away when Terra whispers, "What happened to you?"

Her eyes dart across the flowers that have thrived in the downpour. The water lilies glisten with fat, bright leaves and the roses shimmer with raindrops. The irises that I crushed in my haste to cross the garden last night stand unscathed. My mouth pinches into a tight line to hold back my disbelief. Arti left no detail spared in tidying up her mess. "The *Ka*-Priestess gave us last night off and a few copper coins, but I saved mine. I went down to the cellar to read . . . I like to read when I have free time." Terra pales. "I was there when I heard your screams, but when I came up, your room was empty. I went to fetch your mother, but she was gone too."

I wish I *could* tell her the truth and not be so alone with this horrible secret. Unlike Ty and Nezi, who are close with my mother, Terra and I always confide in each other. She's been a good friend and never told anyone about me skipping lessons with my scribes. But I don't bother trying to explain; the magic will stop me anyway. "I had a bad dream."

"Was that all?" Terra raises one eyebrow. She doesn't believe me, but she doesn't pry.

When I nod, she spins on her heels, heading into the kitchen. Hoping to avoid my mother, I enter that way too, wearing the too-large silver slippers given to me by an attendant at the Omari estate. Arti is nowhere in sight as I creep to my room, and the dancers on the wall creep alongside me. Terra's brought in fresh water for my bath, but it's grown cold, likely having been there since daybreak. An ivory sheath lies on my bed.

Arti knew that I would return. She needn't worry with this curse in my blood. I grimace in the mirror at where the scar should be if not for my mother's magic. I want to throw something through the glass so it'll shatter into a thousand pieces, the way my mother shattered me. The way the *Ka*-Priest shattered her.

As the eye of Re'Mec settles over the Almighty Palace, I take my time getting dressed after washing. I trace the invisible serpent carved into my chest again. It doesn't glow at my touch this time, and even though my skin is smooth and unmarked, I remember the exact curve of it. I can't pretend the terrible things my mother's done never happened. She refused to answer my questions about Kofi, and that has me more worried than this wretched snake.

I dread going to the salon and eating with Arti, but her magic yanks me by an invisible leash. As soon as I walk into the room, I stop cold. My father sits on a cushion at the head of the table. He's drinking from a porcelain bowl, having his usual fill of beer before the evening meal. He'll know what to do. He'll be able to stop Arti. She sits to his right, nibbling on roasted figs and walnuts. Her magic brought me here, but she doesn't spare me a glance.

"You're back!" I exclaim.

My father flashes me a smile, his face opening up like the first rays of sunlight. Clearly, he hasn't gotten wind of my mysterious disappearance in the middle of the night. He sets his bowl aside and holds out his arms to welcome me. I almost collapse into him as he pulls me into a tight hug. I sink into the warmth of his embrace, knowing that he'll make things right again.

"I've missed you, daughter." He kisses the top of my head. "I have much to tell you."

Arti's mask is one of feigned disinterest as she lifts a cup of wine to her lips, but it doesn't hide the animosity in her eyes. Nor does it hide the way she shifts on the pillow as if unable to find comfort. She focuses her attention on a wall behind me instead of meeting my gaze. I should be glaring at her, cursing her in my mind, but despite myself I pity her. The news about the *Ka*-Priest is still fresh, seething and festering like bad blood.

Her amber eyes shine too bright, her raven hair too lustrous in the glow of the fire lamps. She is the opposite of Oshhe in every way. The light catches the angles of his ebony face, making his jaw more prominent, his nose more distinguishable, his forehead prouder. She is softness and curves and radiance even now. I catch my father stealing glances at her, his expression yearning, his smile small. After all this time, he's still so happy to see her.

The tribal boys had called her the Siren of the Valley.

They should've called her the Snake instead.

"Did you find the white ox, Father?" I shouldn't ask in front of Arti, but I'm desperate. Its bones may be strong enough to break her curse.

"Indeed, Little Priestess." Oshhe nods as I settle on the pillow to his left. "I spied the ox on the edge of the Dark Forest."

My father's voice vibrates in the room like a great song and wraps around me. He has to sense something wrong. At the very least he should be able to feel the tension between Arti and me that's thick enough to cut with a knife.

As Oshhe takes another gulp of beer, I wish I could gather up all the awful things in my mind and bury them someplace far away. I wish that I could burn the invisible cursed serpent from my chest. Why can't he feel something . . . *anything*? From the gleam in his eyes, he's on the verge of a story. I sigh in resignation, for it has been too long since my father told me a story and I need to feel safe.

When my father tells stories, I'm a little girl again, hanging on to his every word. "Did you see one?" I ask, my heart pounding against my chest. The twinkle of mischief in his eyes hints that something extraordinary must've happened. "Did you see a craven?"

"One does not see a craven, Little Priestess." Oshhe beams with pride. "For they are as elusive as they are dangerous. But if one has enough magic, one can sense their presence. It feels like a heavy cloak, like air that's too thick, like the sky is falling. It weighs upon your *ka* and makes you want to flee.

"As I said, I spied the white ox on the edge of the Dark Forest," my father continues. "As this was no ordinary ox, he knew why I had come and what I meant to do. He ran like the wind in a storm, wild, unbridled, and without caution. But I would not leave without his bones. I ran too—as fast as a gazelle—and caught him as he entered the forest. When I knelt to say a blessing for taking the beast's life, I felt them.

"Even in the heart of day, the Dark Forest is forever night," he tells me. "The trees are so tall and wide that they block out the sun. The cravens surrounded me in this twilight. I thought I was dead for sure, but they stayed in the shadows. How many I cannot say. Seeing that they did not attack, I used magic to lessen the weight of the ox to that of a child. It took much effort, for the cravens' presence had weakened my powers. The white ox bones contain powerful protective magic, but the cravens' anti-magic poisons it. It's a venom to which there is no antidote."

Oshhe pauses to refill his bowl with beer. "As you can imagine, I had no intention of lingering there for long. I carried the ox from the Dark Forest as fast as I could. It wasn't until I was far away that I stopped to rest."

"Thank you, white ox," I whisper. "I promise to honor your bones."

It's an Aatiri prayer, one to respect something taken. I hope his sacrifice can undo Arti's curse. "When will you make the charm, Father?" Again, my question is too eager in front of my mother, but I don't worry about that now.

"Wasting time with bone charms," Arti scoffs. "Such foolishness."

"Just because it is not your way does not make it foolish." Oshhe shakes his head at her, his look one of pity and disbelief. Then he reaches into a sachet near his side, grinning. "A gift for you, daughter."

He holds the charm out to me. It's a single curved horn, polished and hollowed out with a hole on either end. He's strung a silver chain through the holes so it can be worn around the neck. It's inlaid with gold and shimmers with his magic. Not just any magic—magic that will protect me from the green-eyed serpent, protect me from my mother.

But when I make to reach for it, the muscles in my arms tighten and I can't move. I raise my eyes to my father in desperation.

Oshhe's about to say something when Arti rings the bell for Ty to send our meals. She must know it won't be long before my father figures out the truth. She's trying to distract him. It won't work forever.

Terra slips in from the kitchen with a tray in her arms. She kneels between Arti and Oshhe, offering the food for their inspection. Peanut soup spiced with ginger and garlic, served with generous balls of fufu. Herb-crusted lamb garnished with mint leaves. Wagashi cheese and a warm loaf of bread. Oshhe gestures for Terra to set the platter down, but he hardly notices her or the food.

Arti dips her head to Terra. "Give Ty my compliments."

When we're again alone in the salon, my mother takes up the pitcher of beer and refills Oshhe's bowl. "We've missed you so very much," she remarks, her voice quiet and leading. "Haven't we, Arrah?"

I stare at the empty porcelain bowl in front of me. It's bone white. The air in the room shifts like the bubble the Litho boys created when I wandered into their camp. It's a shield so no one will hear or see what happens in the salon. I force myself to look at my mother. My eyes beg her to put an end to this, to confess, to tell us what she's done with the children. I'm losing hope that we'll find them alive—hope that there's a chance to make things right. If only I could reach the charm . . .

"Arti," Oshhe says, watching her intently. "What have you done?"

"I'm afraid that I have some bad news." Arti picks up a cloth from the table and dabs at the corners of her mouth. "I'm sorry for what I must do now."

My body stiffens as my father and I lock gazes again. His eyes are the shifting black of a night sky, a pool that reflects color with brilliant clarity. When he finds what he's looking for, his face shatters. The pain in his expression cracks me in two. His lips tremble as he opens his mouth to speak, but he doesn't. His words escape on a dead wind. Sparks of magic dust the room, passing through the ceiling to answer my father's silent call.

His skin takes on a white glow as he pushes away from the table, dropping the bone charm in his haste. I struggle against Arti's magic to get it, but the fight is only in my mind. The want, the need, the desperation balls up inside me like a storm. On the outside, I'm shaking but still seated on the pillow. I can't move, I can't speak, I can't act against Arti. The only things my mother doesn't control are my thoughts and feelings. Every curse word under the sun pops in my mind—and still it's meaningless.

Arti takes her time to come to her feet, her movements weary. Magic alights on both of my parents. It clings to their bodies. My father beckons for me. When I don't move, he tugs me behind him as if I'm still his little girl.

Their magic erupts in an explosion of bright lights and colors. It cracks through the room like thunder, swirling into clouds of mist. My father stumbles back a few steps as blood trickles from Arti's nose.

I throw my mind against the force binding me to my mother. My teeth tear into my cheek and my mouth fills with blood. I wiggle like a worm until my trembling hands brush against the bone charm on the floor. I clasp the horn in my fist, desperate to feel something—any hint that it's broken her curse. There's nothing, only a cold reality.

The white ox's bones, the strongest source of protection magic possible, fail to scratch the surface of my mother's curse, let alone break it.

Oshhe falls to his knees behind me, and I abandon the charm.

"Father, no!" I scream, crawling to him. "Let him be!"

Oshhe's jaw goes slack, and his arms hang limp at his sides. He tries to speak but the words come out in stops and starts, turned upside down and inside out. Tears cloud my vision, and I swipe them away.

"No, no, no," I whisper as I shake my father. "Heka, please."

Arti is half out of breath, her hair wild as she reaches down to pick up Oshhe's bowl. His whole body shudders, and his eyes roll into the back of his head. No matter how furious my cries for him to fight the curse, he doesn't answer. He can't.

"What have you done?" I want to claw out my mother's evil eyes, claw the vacant look from her face. Instead, I hold my father in my arms as his body falls completely still.

"You tried to reach the bone charm, even after I forbade it with my magic," Arti says, glaring at me. "How are you able to resist me?"

She's right. I resisted her magic for a moment, but my surge of defiance was for nothing. The charm didn't work, and I can't do anything to help my father.

When I don't answer, she shrugs, wiping the blood from her nose. "It doesn't matter."

Arti blows on the bowl, revealing fire script covering the white porcelain. Tears streak down my face as I cradle my father in my arms. His skin is so hot, *too* hot. He should've sensed the curse on the bowl upon touching it. If he had, he wouldn't have taken so long to feel the curse on me too. He only saw the sweet girl he once loved, just as I spent too long yearning for my mother's affection to suspect the truth. We had both been so blind.

"Why?" I hear myself ask over and over, the word tasting like bile on my tongue.

Arti stares at me across the bowl. "I need your help."

I blink back tears. The way she says "need" sends chills down my spine.

Arti glowers at the bowl again, her mouth set in a hard line, determined and unyielding. Her eyes rage with so many emotions that for a moment she looks confused. She balances the porcelain on the tips of her long fingernails. It wobbles as she rocks it back and forth—her attention never swaying, never faltering. Beer spills over the edges and runs down her hand. Mist creeps up from the rim and curls around her wrist. My mind races. I can't think straight. I've seen this script before at the Temple. In magic, script seals; like circles, it binds. If the bowl has captured something of my father, some part of him, and if it should drop and shatter, it will break him too. The bowl suddenly stills on her fingertips, and I inhale a sharp breath, daring to hope that she's changed her mind. Could there be something left of her heart after all? She blinks, her whole body rigid, then lets the bowl slip from her grasp. I lunge for it, but I'm too slow and can't untangle myself fast enough.

The bowl crashes against the table and shatters into a thousand pieces. Each shard lights up as bright as the sun. I shield my eyes as her magic scrapes my forearms. When the light dies, I pull my father closer as if I can somehow protect him against the impending firestorm.

I will find a way to free you, Father, I swear it on Heka.

SIXTEEN

I sit on the floor, cradling my father in my arms. The muscles in his neck jut out as he clenches his teeth. He fights the curse, but by the end of the night it takes control of him. Arti doesn't carve a symbol of a serpent into his chest. Lines of the fire script from his bowl crawl across his skin like centipedes and settle into tattoos.

Except for his face, which remains untouched, ink even darker than his skin covers most of his body. He's like Tribe Zu now, but instead of his tattoos protecting him, they bind him to Arti. Even tighter than the binding she inflicted on me. She asked how I was able to resist her, but have I done much? I couldn't tell Rudjek or the Vizier the truth. I couldn't warn my father.

Arti puts the salon back in order with her magic. A blinding light sweeps through the wreckage. It mends the broken table, rights the spilled food, makes shards of glass whole again. The bubble around the room flickers but remains intact. She doesn't so much as look at Oshhe as she sits back down at the table—as if nothing has happened. Anger flares in my chest. How can she completely dismiss him? The person who found her broken and tried to help her when she needed him the most.

Her hands shake as she pours herself more wine and lifts the glass to her lips. I want to shove it down her throat. The thought catches me off guard and dread pulses through my veins. Even if I *could* do it, there's no way to know for sure if her death would break our curses. My mother is powerful and she's no fool.

"This is your fault, charlatan," she spits after draining the glass. "Had you not poked your nose into my affairs, all would be well with you and your father."

She snatches up the wine jug again, spilling some on the table-cloth. "I had but one thing left to do," she hisses. "Do you think I would let you ruin my years of careful planning? Events have been set in motion that cannot be undone."

She speaks in riddles worse than the tribal elders. Let her keep talking so I can figure out a way to stop her. She snaps her fingers and Oshhe inhales a sharp breath. "Come sit, husband," Arti tells him, her singsong voice like poison, "and let's enjoy a nice meal together as a family."

Oshhe doesn't hesitate as he climbs to his feet, brushing me aside like a worrisome gnat. My tears choke me. This isn't my father. Oshhe's face is slack and gray, his eyes bright with admiration for Arti. My father is strong—he is a son of the Aatiri tribe, his mother not only a great witchdoctor but their chieftain. My father has a warm smile and a big heart. He's the ever-careful gardener with endless patience. He isn't afraid to stand up to Arti when she's wrong. This man is someone else wearing my father's skin.

"Come, Little Priestess." He pats the pillow next to him. "I have a story to tell you."

To anyone else's ears, there would be no difference in his deep timbre. But his spark is gone. The underlying promise that he'll always keep me safe is gone too. He sounds like a very talented stage actor performing as my father now, able to convince the masses of his sincerity. But not me. I won't play this game. I don't move even when he beckons me.

"Isn't it enough that you cursed him?" I glare at Arti, my hands balled into fists. "Did you have to make him your puppet too?"

Arti brushes off my words like specks of lint from her kaftan. "In binding his *ka*, I've made it so he will answer only to me. He will not have to suffer the truth," she explains, as if she's performed some small mercy. "In his mind, he will only know happiness. Isn't that enough for you?"

"Enough?" I shudder with disgust. "We should be basking in your mercy. Is that it?"

That gets her attention. She leans forward, her *Ka*-Priestess's ring flashing from sapphire to moonstone. Had the ring belonged to Ren Eké before? It's miserable to think that she'd wear his ring. That just as the first *Ka*-Priest had taken up root and grown into a tree to escape death, Ren Eké did the same with Arti. Did he carve out a place in her mind to live on? "Come sit, daughter," she orders.

My body trembles as I resist the pull of her magic. Then my muscles tense and force me to my feet. I grit my teeth as my legs drag me across the room and lower me to the pillow.

"All this time," she drawls, "we thought you didn't have any magic."

I don't speak. If I had any real magic, I wouldn't be in this situation. But that isn't true. My father has plenty of magic and he couldn't stop Arti either. What chance do I have?

"You shouldn't be able to resist my magic even the slightest," she says, her eyes gleaming. "I'm impressed."

The words are a slap in my face. How many years have I wanted an inkling of my mother's approval? Any little bit would do—and now this. She's impressed that I can sass her and struggle against her magic and fail. She's impressed that I had to crawl on my hands and knees for a charm that didn't even work. I can't help but wonder if I'd shown some aptitude for magic long before, if she wouldn't have become a monster. I know it doesn't make sense to feel this way, but I still do.

"There may be slack in the magic that binds you to me," she muses. "But make no mistake: you will not betray me, daughter. Try as you may, you'll still fail. It's—unfortunately—the one thing you're good at."

Better to fail at magic than to do something so evil with it. I don't speak my mind. No sense in antagonizing her. I need information about Kofi and the others. "I know what the *Ka*-Priest did to you . . . it wasn't right." I try another approach.

I half expect Arti to hide behind her vacant mask again, but she doesn't. Her eyes are hungry and dangerous, and I second-guess myself. "He deserved what he got," I add, and she cocks her head to the side. "But the children . . . why have you taken them? They're innocent—what harm could they've done to you?"

"Do you take me for a fool, girl?" Arti snaps. "I know the children are innocent."

There's no mistaking the regret threading through her shaky voice. She glances down. "I had to take them for that very reason."

"*Why?*" I burst out. "Wasn't killing the *Ka*-Priest enough? What purpose does taking the children serve?"

Oshhe cuts himself a piece of spiced lamb and herbed cheese. He's oblivious to our conversation as he eats his meal.

"You think I killed him?" Arti laughs.

"Didn't you?" I shoot back through gritted teeth.

Arti pours herself another glass of wine, her face flushed. "No," she answers, almost as an afterthought. "Killing him would have been too kind."

"Eat, Little Priestess," Oshhe coaxes me through a mouthful of food. "You don't look well."

Tears slide down my cheeks. He sounds so much himself.

"Do as your father says." Arti's voice is a low hiss. "Eat."

Her magic flares underneath my skin again and I eat. The food tastes like ash.

"There's much no one knows about the former *Ka*-Priest," she says. "Suran Omari has done an excellent job of keeping Ren's legacy intact by spreading lies. He does it to spite me, but also to keep his hands clean. The *Ka*-Priest suffered an unfortunate illness of the spirit." She scoops goat cheese onto her finger. "It kept him bedridden during his final years."

It doesn't escape my notice that she drops *Eké* from his name—a show of disrespect in the Litho tradition. Not that someone as vile as him deserves any honor even in death.

"That's a pity." Oshhe shrugs. "Had I been around, I could have healed him."

Arti scowls at him as she flicks the goat cheese away. "It's peculiar for an Eké not to have any family around, but Ren had none in Tamar and none willing to travel from Tribe Litho. I offered to care for him and take over his duties." Her words are devoid of emotions, as though she's recounting some mundane assembly matter. "I sought out girls whose minds he had violated. Most were street girls—the kind so-called men of status used and threw away. Most had perished or were beyond help. Ren never laid one hand on them; that wasn't his particular vice. What he did was worse.

"He'd reach inside your mind and twist your memories to suit his own perverse pleasures." Her gaze shifts to the wall behind me. "Then he would replace them with new, defiled memories, and those became the only memories you had. He violated hundreds of women before me, and Suran tidied it all up because Ren did his bidding too. He collected information to put the Kingdom at an advantage over its enemies. And the orishas . . . ," she spits out, "they knew the entire time and did nothing to stop him."

I stare at my mother, unblinking. As much as I want to deny it, my heart aches for her . . . for the girl she'd been before Ka-Priest Ren Eké. I never truly knew the depth of what he'd done to her. My father's story, and what Rudjek added, was the tale made pretty by smoothing over the details. Even the most horrible act isn't so bad if you skipped the devastating parts. And here they are, laid out before me. I don't know what's worse: hearing of the Ka-Priest's crimes, or hearing my mother's matter-of-fact tone as she recounts them.

"There was never much of a person's mind left once he'd finished playing in their heads . . . but some had withstood his worst. I hired two of them to take care of him when he grew . . . ill. It was quite remarkable they kept him alive as long as they did." Arti pauses, a shadow of a smile crossing her face. "I'm sure Nezi or Ty would love to share the details. They were with him in the end."

The fork slips from between my trembling fingers and crashes against my plate. I can't breathe, my mind racing to Nezi's limp and the scars on her hands, and Ty who never speaks. That bastard *Ka-Priest* did that to them. Arti helped them get revenge, but in the end, she's no better than him. He passed his depravity on to her like a disease spreads through tight quarters. I can't reconcile the two sides of my mother—the side that sheltered two women who suffered so much, and the side that snatches children in the night.

The next morning, I'm still dazed as Terra rifles through my clothes. She's prattling on about something, but I don't listen. All I can think about is my mother and father eating their meals last night as if nothing has changed. When Arti finished, she swept out of the salon with Oshhe trailing behind her like an obedient pet. Whatever the reason for my ability to resist her magic, I'm left with more control over myself than my father. My best chance to break the binding lies in his shop, among his hundreds of scrolls on tribal magic. There has to be some ritual or a powerful charm that can break my mother's curse, for no magic is infallible. I wait for Arti to leave for the Temple and Oshhe to set off to conduct business as usual, his patrons none the wiser.

Nezi is arguing with someone outside the gate of our villa. I'm halfway across the garden when Rudjek pokes his head around her, his forehead etched into a frown. When he spots me, his shoulders relax.

"Do I want to know what you're doing?" I groan, even if I'm glad to see him.

"Looking for you, of course." Rudjek squeezes the ribs of the gate. His dark gaze rakes over me, and whatever he finds bleeds the color from his face. "She wouldn't let me in."

Nezi straightens from her spot leaning against the porter's station and opens the gate. I stare at her scarred hands. They're covered in angry welts from scratching. When I was little, I never doubted her story about burning herself while plucking magic from the sky. Now, my throat bobs as a stone settles in my belly. If the *Ka*-Priest never touched the women, then did Nezi do that to herself?

After seeing my family struggle with pain my entire life, I'm filled with rage against the man who hurt them. If I were Ty, Nezi, or Arti, would I have done the same?

I push the thought away. "Why didn't you tell me Rudjek was here?" I ask her.

Rubbing the back of her hand, Nezi looks down her nose at him. "Your mother wouldn't approve of him coming here. The Omaris are nothing but trouble."

I grab Rudjek by the arm and drag him away from the villa as he opens his mouth to tell Nezi his mind. "Don't bother."

"Did she just insult me?" Rudjek glances over his shoulder at her. "I feel insulted."

"We need to go back to my father's shop," I say, releasing his arm.

My father's scrolls must have an answer. I remember the feel of their grainy texture against my fingers. Charms, rituals, and curses from the simple to the complex, from benign to ominous. I've rambled through them all out of curiosity at some point or another, but now they're my last and only hope. I take one step and my mother's magic blossoms in my chest. My legs come to a halt; my whole body seizes up. "Oh no," Rudjek protests. "Whatever you're thinking . . ."

"It's not your business," I cut him off before he can finish. I try to take another step, but the curse only tightens its hold. "Twenty-gods!" I blurt out in frustration.

The magic won't let me act against my mother, but there must be a way around it. She's manipulated my father's mind and likely intended the same for me, but a part of her curse had failed. All those years ago at Imebyé, Grandmother said my mind's ability to resist magic is my greatest gift. What good is it if I can't speak or act on any thoughts against Arti? The curse knows my intentions.

"You don't have to be so pissy about it," Rudjek grumbles.

"Don't be such a nag," I hiss at him.

Every time my thoughts flit too close to the truth, the magic surges underneath my skin. What would happen if I didn't focus on the *reason* for going to my father's shop? What if I can pretend my intentions lie elsewhere? Will the magic see through my deceit? There's only one way to find out. "I'm going to my father's shop to help him clean," I announce, more to myself than Rudjek. I let memories of me straightening the shelves and washing vials sweep through my mind. Today is no different from any other day. My father needs my help tidying up, nothing more. Rudjek stares at me, frowning, as if I've lost my mind. I take one step forward, my leg moving with ease again. A shiver of relief runs across my shoulders. It *actually* worked. I don't let my thoughts linger on this small concession so I don't get my hopes up. When I'm able to take another step, I say, "Are you coming or not?"

"I resent being called a nag." Rudjek looks me over again. This time his eyes linger long enough to make me uncomfortable. He takes hold of my arm, his fingers gliding down to my wrist. His touch is like sunshine kissing my skin. "It took something from you, Arrah. I can tell. The ritual, I mean. You must feel it."

There's no point in arguing or denying that my skin has lost some color. Even the fit of my clothes is a bit looser, though I was forced to eat my fill last night. If anything, I'm hungrier than usual, but eating didn't satisfy the feeling of emptiness inside me. "Yes, I know," I say before he can press the matter. "How many more have gone missing?"

Rudjek holds on to my wrist until I pull away. "Another girl."

When we're a few paces away from the villa, Kira and Majka fall into step with us, one ahead and one behind. I failed the children because I was too naive to see my mother for what she is. I failed Kofi—sweet, loquacious Kofi who always has a smile for everyone. A pang of guilt wrenches through my belly. Countless more children will go missing if I fail today. I can't let that happen.

Arti said that she *had* to take the children because they were innocent, but I'm no closer to finding out her reason. Whoever her accomplice is, she's turned against her family to protect him and carry out their plans.

Rudjek and I avoid the East Market altogether. There's too much yelling, cursing, and fighting on the streets. So many Familiars flit around that the air tastes bitter. We walk the rest of the way to my father's shop in silence. Rudjek doesn't have to tell me that the shotani haven't found any leads on the child snatcher. Now I know they never will. Arti and her seers trained the shotani. Their loyalty is to her.

"Even with all this chaos, my father refuses to postpone my Coming of Age Ceremony," Rudjek groans. "Please tell me you're attending . . . I need to see a friendly face."

"I don't know," I say, half listening. The magic stirs in my chest again, and I tell myself over and over that I'm only going to help my father.

Rudjek spots the smoke from behind Oshhe's shop first, and my heart skips a beat. I run around to the alley behind the shop. My legs almost collapse as I stumble toward my father. "What are you doing?" I yell, my vision blurring, the world spinning.

Oshhe tosses handfuls of scrolls into a barrel with fire raging inside. "Getting rid of some old things. I've been at it all morning—didn't realize how many of these useless scrolls I had lying around."

I run headlong to where my father is burning his magic scrolls and try to save the last one as it catches fire. I reach for it, but Rudjek grabs my waist and drags me from the barrel. I kick and fight to break free. His body is so hot against my back that my skin feels like it's on fire too.

Oshhe rushes over and they both keep asking the same question. "What's wrong? What's wrong? What's wrong?" My father's eyes bear no regret as he pulls me into his arms. Arti said that he will only know happiness, but the man holding me is a shell. I scream, my throat raw, my chest burning. I blink back tears as flames curl around the scroll. The smooth papyrus blackens and flakes away. The embers fade until there's only ashes left.

Arti has made my father destroy our last hope.

SEVENTEEN

The moon hangs fat and heavy in the night sky as my father and I make our rounds at Rudjek's Coming of Age Ceremony. It's been days since Oshhe burned his scrolls and I still can't get the image or the acrid odor out of my head. Now he's laughing with statesmen in the Vizier's courtyard and charming people with his stories. A warm breeze sweeps in from the garden, carrying hints of jasmine, lilac, and rose petals. The sweet smell only upsets my stomach. For the third time in less than an hour, an attendant offers me a glass of honeyed wine, and I wave them away.

Arti isn't here, and that worries me. This morning before leaving for the Temple, she said that Oshhe and I would attend. Her magic did the rest. Of course she'd known about the ceremony, likely from her spies. Or from all the gossip surrounding the important families who had come to the city for the event. No one comments on her absence because of her rivalry with the Vizier, but I have no doubt she's up to no good. I'm worried about Rudjek too. I wouldn't put it past her to move against him to strike at his father.

I crane my neck, looking for the other seers. I don't know if I'm more or *less* nervous when I don't spot any of them. It crosses my mind again that one might be her accomplice. Arti has no love for the orishas, that much is clear now, but do the other seers feel the same? Have they turned their backs on their faith, as they had on Heka when they gave up life in the tribal lands?

Oshhe is ever the perfect conversationalist, telling tales of magic. Many of the families of status in attendance are also patrons of his shop. Scholars, scribes, artisans, craftsmen. People with enough money to pay for youth and good health. People who would've died ten times over if not for his touch. Someone who's lived one hundred years, a great feat already, can live twice as long and not look a day over fifty. Such is his gift.

My father would still be in the desert had he not fallen in love with Arti. He'd be a healer in Tribe Aatiri, where no one wastes coins on changing their hair color or enhancing body parts. He'd be happy; he'd be whole.

In his love story, the boys said that the Mulani girl could steal your magic with one kiss.

Oshhe underestimated Arti. We both did.

I never will again.

"The *Ka*-Priestess let you come," muses Essnai, rustling at my side. "I didn't expect that."

I startle at my friend's sudden appearance. For a girl a head taller than most, she moves with the grace of a shadow. Her red dress shimmers with flecks of silver and matches the silver dusted on her ebony skin. She is, as always, radiant.

"It was kind of her," I say, my voice somber. I can't speak against my mother, but I can still control the temperament of my words. It's a small grace, but it hasn't done me any good.

"This ceremony is ill-timed." Essnai peers at the crowd, her hands on her hips. "The city mourns for the missing children."

"The Vizier doesn't care," I murmur under my breath. "He's a selfish bastard."

Essnai quirks an approving eyebrow at me. "Indeed."

Before my temper flares higher, I change the subject. "I'm surprised you came too."

"I made half the dresses here." Essnai shrugs. "Couldn't miss seeing them in the wild."

Of my friends, she is the most grounded. No matter the trouble, her serene demeanor always calms me. At Imebyé all those years ago, she helped me find my way back to the Aatiri camp. She'd been my beacon of light, guiding me in the dark. I wish she could show me the way now—that she'd tell me everything would be okay. "I'm glad you're here." I give her a small smile.

She turns her dark gaze fully on me, searching. "You haven't stopped by the shop lately."

"I know." She means I haven't visited her—never mind gawking over the gorgeous garb in her mother's shop. We've spent hardly any time together since getting back from the Blood Moon Festival. Essnai's never been one to pry, and instead of asking why, she waits for me to give a reason. "Things have been complicated."

Her eyes linger on my face a bit longer, and then she says, "I'm here if you need me."

When the doors of the estate open, the music falls silent and people stop talking to stare. Rudjek steps across the threshold, his expression blank. Underneath his mask of indifference, though, he clenches his jaw, his shoulders stiffen. He reminds me of the caged lions the Almighty One parades in the city at the start of Basi—the harvest season. Had this been a better time, better circumstances, with me in a better mood, I would tease him about it later. But no, I don't want to be here. I need to know what my mother is doing at the Temple.

The Vizier stands to Rudjek's right in a plain black elara, not his usual white silk embroidered with gold. All the men and boys attending the Coming of Age Ceremony wear black. Even my father wears a black kaftan. Rudjek's mother, Serre, flanks his left, every bit the Northern princess. Layers of lavender silk stretch behind her like the Great Sea. Her raven hair flows in waves down her back and she wears a crown of pearls. Powder gives color to her skin so that the veins beneath are invisible.

As lovely as Serre looks, all eyes are on Rudjek. Despite the fact that my mind feels trapped someplace far away, I can't stop staring at him either. I hold my breath. For the briefest moment, I let myself forget everything else, and take him in. Lush eyebrows crowning even darker eyes, full lips drawn tight. His sculpted jaw made more prominent in the flickering torchlight. His white elara stitched with gold thread, his sleeves inlaid with rubies. The craven-bone crest standing out as an understated prize against his rich ceremonial garb. Only the Vizier wears an elara of white and gold. He's making a bold statement about his son's future. I don't have to wonder if that's why Rudjek looks so uncomfortable standing on the steps.

The crowd parts to create a path down the middle of the courtyard. So many curious eyes watching him, so many shy smiles glowing beneath the soft firelight. But his gaze lands on me. His lips tug into a smile as his parents take each one of his hands.

"I present to you, Rudjek of House Omari, flesh of my flesh," the Vizier's voice carries over the crowd with ease.

"No longer a boy, but a man," adds Serre. "He shall present himself as such from this day forth."

"Heir to the Omari legacy," his father decrees, "and future Vizier of the Almighty Kingdom."

"Let it be known," Rudjek speaks for the first time, his voice flat. "I have stepped out of my father's shadow and into my own."

The crowd acknowledges his declaration with a simple nod, and the flutes and harps cue up. Three dancers in sheer shifts that leave nothing to the imagination sashay down the aisle. One is tall, all legs, with skin a rich brown that turns heads. The second dancer has lips the color of fire and bright ribbons coil around her long braids. The third woman is all curves and bats her lashes at Rudjek as if they are the only two people in the entire courtyard. A warm blush creeps up his neck and sets his cheeks aflame. He takes a step back as all three women converge on him, and his father nudges him forward. Some of the men in the crowd whistle. Some laugh.

Foolish tradition.

Instead of sulking at the women slithering against Rudjek like gnats stuck in honey, I turn away. Kira slips out of the crowd with a glass of honeyed wine. "Do you mind if I steal away my *ama*?" She reaches for Essnai's hand and plants a kiss on her palm. Essnai smiles, her dark eyes bewitched. "She's been a wayward bird all night." A pang of longing twists in my chest as I dip my head, my fingers sweeping my brow, and the two disappear in the throng of people.

When the crowd gasps, I snap my head back around. The dancers twist and contort their lithe bodies to the call of the flutes and harps. The way some of these *supposed* people of status gawk at them makes my flesh crawl. The vile *Ka*-Priest may have once leered at Ty and Nezi the same way, itching to do his worst. And he had: Arti is proof of that.

Once the dance is over, Rudjek bends to one knee and, one after another, the women kiss his forehead. He stands again and the crowd breaks into cheers and slaps him on the back. Guildmaster Ohakim, a tall, gaunt-faced man who heads the laborers' guild, says, "I couldn't have controlled myself that well if *those* dancers had been at my ceremony." Ohakim seemed more interested in the dance than when Arti told the assembly about the missing children.

Majka slips up beside me, nudging my arm. "He hated that, you know?"

His left cheek is swollen and bruised dark purple.

I cast a seething look at Rudjek. "Yes, I can see how much he's suffering right now."

Several people surround him, and he keeps glancing in our direction. His face begs for someone to come save him, but he'll get no sympathy from me. Majka bites his lip, watching the curvy dancer as she flounces through the crowd. He isn't the only one.

"The two of you are ridiculous," Majka huffs, and turns his attention back to me. "Carrying on as you do."

"Like you can talk." I cross my arms. "Did Kira hit you again for flirting with her sister?"

Majka shrugs and straightens his elara. "That wouldn't be proper, would it?"

I cluck my tongue. "When have you ever been proper?"

"Don't you ever tire?" Sukar rolls his eyes, stepping out of the crowd.

Majka presses his right palm to his heart. "Well, if it isn't my favorite Zu boy."

Sukar returns the Zu gesture of greeting, his hand to his chest. A latticework of tattoos loops around his fingers. He's gotten new ones on his cheeks too—raised scars like tiger stripes. "What happened to your face this time?" He grimaces at Majka.

Majka adjusts the collar of his elara. "One match in the arena or another."

I grab Sukar by the arm and drag him off before he can pester Majka more. "Don't you have Temple duty tonight?"

Arti had hurried off in her *Ka*-Priestess kaftan long before Oshhe and I left for Rudjek's ceremony. Now that I see Sukar here, the ache in my belly grows. It was too much to hope that my mother had rushed to the Temple this morning only to keep up her ruse. She's planning something. Tonight.

Sukar frowns at me, the tattoos on his forehead creasing. "No, why?"

"I thought Arti . . ." My throat tightens and my voice fades. Damn this curse. "I thought the other seers would be with my mother at the Temple."

Sukar nods in the direction of his uncle. Barasa and the Litho seer are the only men aside from Rudjek not dressed in black. Even Sukar wears a black tunic and trousers. His uncle wears the seer's pale yellow kaftan, lighter in color than the rich gold of Arti's. The other two seers wade through the throng, also in their traditional kaftans.

The serpent tingles and I press a hand to my heart. The magic stretches through my body, setting every nerve on fire. I'm out of time.

"Are you okay?" Sukar touches my shoulder.

Head spinning, I lean against his arm. "I need to sit down."

Sukar looks around, but people fill the benches in the court-yard. The magic isn't just causing me pain; it's calling to me. We walk into the gardens next to the courtyard where it's quieter and sit on a bench. A chill runs across my arms.

"Was that what it felt like?" Sukar questions, his eyebrows shooting up.

My tongue won't let me say anything that points to Arti. I try, but I can't even say *magic*. His tattoos don't shimmer as they did when he broke through the Litho bubble in the tribal lands, as they usually do in the presence of magic. He looks confused as he reaches to touch my arm again, then stops himself.

"May I?" he asks, and I nod even as the magic tightens its grasp on my throat, not enough to hurt me, but to silence my words.

When Sukar rests his hand on my arm, the magic hums. "Do you feel that, too?" he asks.

I struggle to find the right words. "What do you feel?"

Sukar smirks. "That you might not be a *ben'ik* after all."

I sink so deep on the bench that my sheath drags on the ground. Sukar lets go of my arm and does the same. He *knows* me. He should sense the difference between me having magic and being afflicted by it. My mood is much worse, knowing that he's mistaken my mother's curse for something good. I lay my head on his shoulder as we stare across the gardens into the courtyard. I miss spending time with him and Essnai, without a real care in the world.

Two of the dancers saunter through the crowd, the curvy one absent. Majka is missing as expected. Kira and Essnai have slipped away for a private moment of their own. Rudjek stands in a circle of scholars and statesmen while his father introduces him. Their pretty daughters squeeze in the circle, waiting for their turn to meet him too. I don't have the energy to be jealous, yet I can't deny the heat rushing up my neck.

Sukar and I sit in silence for a moment, and the magic grows stronger. It prickles like needles against my skin. When I can't sit any longer, I jump to my feet.

"When were you going to tell me your secret?" Sukar teases, his eyes amused.

"What secret?" Rudjek asks from behind.

I whirl around and he's standing there scratching his head as he looks between Sukar and me. He doesn't seem to know where to put his hands, which he usually rests on the hilts of his shotels. No fancy swords tonight, but fancy everything else.

I cough. "I'm surprised you were able to tear yourself away from your adoring fans."

"I'm not the only one with adoring fans," Rudjek says.

His accusation makes me blush, but before I can protest, he turns his winning smile on Sukar. "I want to know this secret too."

Oh, there's a secret, but it's not what either of them might think. I blow out a loud breath, annoyed by this whole conversation. "There is no secret," I lie, exhausted.

Rudjek clears his throat. "I need to talk to Arrah alone."

Sukar remains slouched on the bench to spite him.

Rudjek gestures for me to follow him instead. We go deeper into the gardens, stopping beside a pond of blue fish that glow in the dark. "I thought I'd never get away." He rubs the back of his neck. "Be glad girls don't have to go through that."

I cross my arms. "Such a hardship, I'm sure."

"You're mad at me." Rudjek glances to his hands. "I'm sorry. I couldn't talk my father out of the dancers. He insisted it was tradition."

I step back from him when I want nothing more than to sink into his arms. I need him to quell my growing sense that something bad is about to happen. "It's a ridiculous tradition." My voice falters as the magic tingles in my chest again.

"I know." Rudjek steps closer and his sweet scent tangles in my nose.

"You didn't have to look like you were enjoying it so much," I say, even though he had looked no such thing.

He moves closer and I hold my ground. "Are you jealous?"

I shake my head and purse my lips, my mind everywhere but where I am now. I can't give in to my mother's magic. If I keep resisting it, I can at least postpone her plans until I find a way around the curse. "Why would I be jealous?"

"What if I told you that I was jealous when I saw you with Sukar?"

Another step closer and warmth spreads through my chest—not the curse, but something else. Something that feels nice amidst so much uncertainty. "But you weren't jealous when I was talking to Majka?"

"You wouldn't offer Majka tea," Rudjek says, his words a low hum that snap my attention back to the moment, back to him.

I cock my head. "How can you be so sure?"

"Would you offer me tea?" Rudjek asks, a sly grin on his lips, his perfect lips. Have they always been so beautiful? How can I be thinking about him like this, right now? I know it's because I don't want to think about my mother and all the awful things she's done. I want to lose myself in the depths of his dark eyes and pretend everything is okay.

"Yes," I answer, my heart fluttering like butterfly wings. "I would."

"Arrah." Rudjek breathes my name and it's music to my ears. We're far from the celebration. Far from prying eyes. No better than Majka and his dancer. "I should've told you a long time ago how I felt."

I close the small gap left between us. "I could've said something too."

Rudjek reaches up to caress my cheek and I lean closer, staring into eyes that mirror the ache inside me. A feeling of foreboding shadows the moment. There's still so much uncertainty between us, so much left unsaid. So many secrets and missed opportunities and wasted time. Had we been braver before now, put our families' feud aside and let our hearts decide, where would that have led? It's a question that I'm finally ready to lay to rest.

After tonight, there may not be another chance, so I let myself fall into his bewitching gaze. He lowers his face to mine and I press mine up to his. Our breaths intertwine as we lean in for a kiss. The kiss I've dreamed about a thousand times. Sparks of warmth set my body aflame. But just as his lips are about to brush mine, his scent pulling at my heartstrings, he jerks away.

"Have you lost your mind, boy?" the Vizier hisses, his hand clutching Rudjek's shoulder.

"Twenty-gods." Rudjek pulls away from his father. "Are you spying on me?"

The Vizier is even more imposing in a black elara than in his usual white, and twice as menacing. "I've invited important families from across the Kingdom here to meet you tonight." He cuts his eyes at me. "And you're hiding in the gardens, taking liberties with a girl."

Rudjek frowns. "In case you haven't realized it yet, Arrah is—"

"She is my enemy's daughter," the Vizier barks at him, "and off-limits to you."

I ball my hands into fists as anger prickles across my skin. I can't stand to look at the Vizier after the awful things he's done to my mother and let happen under his watch. I may not be able to talk ill of Arti, but her curse won't mind if I give *him* a piece of my mind. "How dare you—" I start to say, when a hand clamps down on my shoulder too. It's my father.

"It's time to go," Oshhe announces, his face blank. "We're needed."

The words echo in my mind as the magic wakes. This time the call is stronger—much stronger than it's been all night. I dig my heels in to resist, trying to root myself in the gardens. I grit my teeth until my jaw aches, but none of it does any good. In the end, I can't resist my mother's call. Even if I could, Oshhe would drag me away kicking and screaming. I look to Rudjek, helpless, as he and his father glare at each other. "You have no say in my affairs." He spits on the ground.

"Don't I?" the Vizier bites back.

Arrogance twists the Vizier's face into a conniving smile. I want to shake some sense into him, but it's useless. The bad blood between the Vizier and my family is too great to overcome. When he sees me, he must remember the girl he accused of bewitching his best friend. A girl robbed of her innocence. If only he knew the true monster she's become—and his part in helping to create her.

I back away, the curse's invisible chains drawing me to Arti. I fight it every step, pushing my will against it, but my legs don't falter. The magic wears me down and fatigue washes out the last of my resistance.

"Arrah, wait!" Rudjek calls as I turn my back to him.

A flicker of defiance sweeps across my shoulders, but I keep walking.

Arti's plan is unfolding tonight and the worst is yet to come.

EIGHTEEN

Oshhe and I trudge up the precipice slick with dew toward the Almighty Temple. The first morning bells toll, the chimes vibrating in my bones. We'd been at Rudjek's ceremony all night, and now it's near the hour of *ösana*—when magic is at its most potent. My father hasn't said a word since we left the Vizier's estate. Once Arti summoned us, the little that remained of him faded away. He's like the stories of the *ndzumbi*, no control over himself, no agency. He lives and breathes for her.

"There has to be a way to break our curses." I wrap my fingers around my father's. His hand is cold. "You'd know how if you had your right mind."

I imagine my father nodding, but in truth his face is completely blank.

Some of the other tribal people in Tamar must have records too. The seers would have scrolls but gaining access to those would be too risky. The charlatan who gave me the ritual to trade my years had other tribal texts in his sack. I'll ask him tomorrow, if I can get the words out of my mouth. The magic winds tight around my body, and I march onward against my will. Dread creeps deeper into my bones and my stomach churns. The farther we climb, the tighter my mother's hold over me becomes.

Oshhe moves up the slope with the determination of a mule on a lead rope, his eyes never veering from the Temple. Whatever Arti wants help with, it can't be good. At least if she's at the Temple, she's not on the streets looking for more children to steal. They'll be safe for now.

The morning Tam told me the origin story, when he confirmed the connection between the green-eyed serpent and demons, feels like a lifetime ago. I came looking for answers then, and now everything that's happened makes even less sense. When we reach the Temple, the gates are open and there are no attendants on duty. It's uncanny seeing it so quiet and empty when during the day it's always bustling with people. The stark, gray buildings remind me of the tales of how the people in the North erect towering mausoleums carved out of ice to bury their dead.

Torchlight pushes back the darkness around the courtyard, leaving the rest of the Temple grounds in shadows. None of the shotani are around—if they were, I would feel their magic drifting on the breeze. We enter the long ingress lit by more torches, our steps echoing against the stone floor.

Through the ingress, we slip into the Hall of Orishas. Constellations spark across the darkness that molds the gods and their thrones. When you look straight at them or touch them, they are as solid as marble. But out of the corner of your eye, their shapes shift and pulse, ever restless, ever watching.

Even during the day, shadows shroud the Unnamed orisha's statue, but her rough-cut face is far more eerie at night. It's become something twisted and ugly and unbearable. When Essnai, Sukar, and I were young and still taking regular lessons at the Temple, we made up stories about her. Essnai said the Unnamed had reached her arms into a serpent's den and died from snakebites. The question of why she had done such a thing started a debate between the three of us. Sukar said the Unnamed had done it on a dare, and Essnai said she wanted to test the limits of her immortality. I thought that maybe she was looking for something she lost. Staring at her now and knowing about the demons, I have a different theory.

Her name is absent among all the scripts about the war between the orishas and the Demon King. There's no mention of her in any form, which is why the scribes call her the "Unnamed." Is it possible that the other orishas had struck her name from history because of some egregious wrong she'd done? Her posture is relaxed, at ease, and the snakes look like they could be her pets. Had she sided with the demons in the war? Why?

I want to look away, but she pins me in place. The magic coiled in my chest draws me closer, and I sink into the bottomless pit of her eyes. Eyes that are a gateway into a forbidden place and a forgotten time. I blink, and the feeling vanishes, chills creeping across my shoulders.

"The time is near," Arti whispers from the shadows in front of us.

I suck in a deep breath that catches in my throat. My mother doesn't wait for a response as she starts down a half-lit corridor. Her gold kaftan flaps against her ankles. Oshhe moves to follow, and so do I. We have no choice; her magic is a leash around our necks.

We trail behind Arti through a maze of narrow halls, then down two sets of dark stone stairs. As we descend, the air grows thick with dust, and the temperature drops. Prayers to the orisha decorate the Temple walls, but there's no mention of Heka among these artifacts. The Kingdom doesn't worship him.

The stairs end in a chamber with a low stone ceiling filled with shelves of empty glass jars. Eyes closed, Arti presses her hand against the wall at the back of the room. She whispers in that same ancient songbird language that sealed my curse. The wall protests as it slides open, like a great mammoth waking from its slumber. By my estimation we've arrived somewhere underneath the courtyard or the gardens.

"The *Ka*-Priest brought the girls whose minds he violated here." Arti pauses at the threshold between the two rooms, one hand braced against the stone. "And in the end, this is where they took his life. Fitting, don't you think?"

Our porter, Nezi, with her burnt hands and ever-present limp. Ty, who never speaks to anyone. Two women who could be ill-tempered at times, but never cruel. Ty who baked my favorite sweets on my birth days, and Nezi who taught me how to play jackals and hounds. Both women helped raise me. I can hardly believe that they dragged the old *Ka*-Priest down these stairs and tortured him to death. How can two people I've known my entire life be murderers?

Arti enters the dark chamber with Oshhe on her heels. Cold radiates from the walls like it's a living, breathing thing. I want to run away, to see how far the curse will let me go, but I can't leave my father behind. He wouldn't be in this mess if it wasn't for me. My hand slides to my belly as I step into the room and the door closes behind me with a heavy thump of finality. A soft light illuminates the chamber. Not chamber: tomb.

I back against the wall, my fingers searching for purchase on the slick grime. The air squeezes from my lungs, the room spinning. My eyes burn at the sight of the children before me. I step toward them, but Arti lifts one hand to stop me. I strain against her magic, my teeth clattering, fists at my sides. I scream, but she stops my voice too.

Arti has arranged the children in a single line at the base of an altar. Seven of them lie on makeshift pallets, a jar of gray mist above each of their heads. Their chests rise and fall as their soft snores fill the chamber. It's freezing here, but she's tucked them beneath blankets. It takes only a moment to realize what the gray mist is. It's their *kas*. Arti stole their souls and *trapped them in jars*.

The room smells damp and musty as my nails dig into the stone wall. She hasn't stopped me from doing that. My nails break and my warm blood mixes with the grime. I need the pain to keep from collapsing to my knees. I need it to keep from dying inside. I need it to give me strength.

I struggle to speak, but my words jumble like a babe trying her tongue for the first time. *There won't be peace for you in this life or the next. I'll make sure of it.* I scream the promise in my head, but I mean every single word. I will find a way to end my mother.

Arti stares at the children for a long time and whispers something under her breath. A single tear slips down her cheek. It's a slap in the face to me, to their families, to the people who mourn them. Anguish and sadness brim in her bloodshot eyes, but the emotions flit away as she turns to the altar. Any illusion of regret is just that—an illusion.

Instead of prayers to the orishas, spells written in blood cover the walls here. The words have odd edges and curves, and unabashed boldness in their strokes. A coiled serpent threads through the script like a great sea monster. Inside the snake's body, she's drawn two interlinked spheres, the symbol for binding. There are other symbols too: vines, eyes, and beasts with teeth sharp enough to cut stone. Symbols I've never seen before.

Oshhe waits in a corner for her next command. I look at his shaved head, the gold rings that line his ears, and I can't see my father. So much of what makes a person is in their *ka*, and his is imprisoned somewhere deep inside him. He doesn't deserve this. He's always been so kind to Arti, even in the face of her indifference.

"Why do you hate us so much?" I spit.

"Hate you?" Arti frowns. "Don't be foolish. I don't hate you."

I'm left speechless at her perplexed expression after all her crimes.

"I'm disappointed in you, yes." She wrinkles her nose. "You should be stronger."

"Disappointed?" The word tastes bitter as I stare at my friend. The horror of what my mother's done outweighs my relief in finding him. He's in a deep sleep, and there's a crooked smile on his lips. Kofi, my friend. The boy who goes out of his way to annoy Rudjek and make me laugh. The boy with a thousand and one fishing tales. I hope he's dreaming about a wild adventure on the Great Sea— anything but this nightmare. I have to convince Arti to let him go. There must be some good beneath the black ice covering her heart. I want to save them all, but if I can save only one . . . I swallow the bile burning up my throat. I'm awful for thinking it, but if I can only save Kofi, I will.

"He's at peace," Arti comments, peering at him too. "They all are. I made sure of it."

"He's my friend," I whisper.

"I know." Darkness stirs behind her eyes. "You will lose many friends before the end."

"Please let him go." I hold her cold gaze.

"I will not have you beg!" Arti snaps, and her magic stills my tongue. "This world is a cruel place, and only the most brutal thrive," she hisses, glancing to Oshhe. "Between the both of us you should've inherited an exceptional talent for magic, but instead . . . you're weak. You need to be strong to survive what's to come."

My mother's words cut me so deep that the wounds seethe and I know they will never heal. There's no getting through to her, no changing her mind. She lays a dagger across the top of the altar. It isn't a stretch to believe that she'll kill the children with that very knife. I imagine plunging it into her belly instead. My body feels heavy at the thought of killing my mother, but if she won't see reason, there's no other way.

"Before," Arti says, voice as sweet as honeyed wine, "you asked me why children."

She busies herself at the altar, as if it's a routine night at the Temple. Now that I know her secret, it stands to reason that this *is* normal for her. From the looks of the chamber and the way she moves around it, she's spent much time here. All these years my father and I thought she'd been with the other seers, she's been in this gods-awful place instead.

She puts a straw doll next to the knife and a bowl of dried herbs and oil—all things used in traditional Mulani rituals. "Do you still want to know why?"

I struggle to speak, but the curse keeps my tongue still. She glances up when I don't answer, and her magic loosens. I try to make sense of the spells on the walls again and the great serpent. I wipe sweat from my forehead so hard that it leaves a trail of heat across my face. But I can't wipe away the truth as the pieces fall into place and my mother's plans become clear. The interlinked spheres, the symbol for binding. Not so different from symbols on the trinkets the charlatans peddle in the market. Powerful Zu symbols, coupled with my mother's magic and her ironclad will. The serpent, the same as the one carved into my chest. No more guessing. "You're trying to summon a demon," I blurt out, hardly able to believe it. "You're summoning *her*—the green-eyed serpent from Grandmother's vision. But why?"

"When *Ka*-Priest Ren invaded my mind, he saw the entirety of my life." Arti uses a quill dipped in blood to draw symbols on the doll. "Except my most private memories. At first he found it to be a welcome challenge, but by the end, it frustrated him that he couldn't see that part of my mind." She looks up at me again, her eyes absent. "Those memories are the only ones I know to be real. Every other memory before my encounter with Ren reeks of his twisted perversions.

"Do you know what he would've learned, had he been able to steal those memories too?" She marks the doll's forehead in blood. When I don't answer, she offers, "He would've found out that my first memory is of the Demon King whispering in my ear. That when I was a young child, he showed me what the orishas did to him and why. You won't find that history within these Temple walls." Arti glances at the ceiling, her voice brittle. "Even so, I was too young to understand. When I left the tribal lands for the Kingdom, I left him behind too. I wanted to experience everything . . . see the entirety of the world. Not only through magic—through my other senses too.

"After Suran's accusation, Ren brought me to a chamber like this one." Arti's eyes hollow out, her words barely audible. "That's when I truly understood the Demon King's warning about the orishas. While the *Ka*-Priest was in the middle of stealing my memories, Re'Mec appeared to demand another Rite of Passage. I begged the sun god for help. I offered him my eternal servitude. But no, he didn't even spare me a glance.

"Do you think I don't feel Heka's presence every blood moon, that I do not hear his call? I choose not to answer. When I needed help, it wasn't Heka or the orishas who answered me. The Demon King did. Still in his prison, he poured a part of himself into my mind—and that is the only reason I survived Ren.

"Why did I take the children?" Arti stares at them. "I took them out of necessity . . . to give back what the orishas stole from my master and to punish them." She jerks her face away and turns to Oshhe. "Come, husband. It's time."

I glare at my mother so long that my eyes ache. Her words crash against my mind, shattering the fragment of hope that I can somehow get through to her. No, it's too late for that, too late for reason, too late for pleading. All these years, my mother's had a connection with the Demon King. I can only guess it's because of her extraordinary gifts . . . she *talks* to him, she *serves* him. He's in her mind.

My mother's accomplice . . . is . . . the greatest threat to mortal kind. Could she be wrong about *Ka*-Priest Ren Eké? Did he plant this fantastical story in her mind? How can she be so sure? It would be better if she is delusional, easier to stomach, but no, my mother is anything but . . . Her ideas of right and wrong are as twisted as her memories.

My father climbs onto the altar and lies flat on his back. Tears slip from the corners of his eyes and hope flares in my chest. He's still fighting her curse. If he breaks free, he can put an end to Arti—but he doesn't move a muscle. His tears keep coming as she raises the bowl above his chest and it erupts into flames. His *ka* may be locked deep inside him, but he hasn't given up.

"I give these innocents to the Devourer of Souls, Executioner of Orishas," Arti recites. "Demon King, accept these offerings."

My mother has turned her back on the orishas and Heka, on her tribe, on the Kingdom. Children's souls are pure, which makes them powerful. That's why she needed their *kas*—to feed them to the worst demon of all. But if the Demon King is still trapped in Koré's box, then how?

Once the fire dies in the bowl, Arti lifts Oshhe's chin and pours the thick black remnants down his throat. "I await your grace," she bows her head. "Send me your servant."

A strong wind blows my braids across my face. As a foul odor overwhelms the air, I slide to the floor and wrap my arms around my knees. My head swims as a sensation of prying eyes overcomes me. The hot breath of the unseen demon touches my lips. I recoil against the stone wall until it digs into my flesh.

Oshhe's back arches, almost as if it'll crack in two. Then he collapses and moves in fits and jerks. Tar foams from his lips; his face twists in pain. When he screams, two voices come from his mouth. One that is my father's and one that is primordial and dark like the belly of a murky well. He struggles to sit up, his breathing labored. His spine curves so much that his head hangs limp between his shoulders. "The souls . . ."

His voice splits again, both tones grating against my ears. "Give them to me."

"Take them yourself, Shezmu," Arti spits. "I don't answer to you."

Shezmu lifts his face, my father's face. "A tribal witch . . . how interesting."

His eyes glow sickly green. The demon from my vision—her eyes were the same.

Sweat drips down Shezmu's forehead as he turns to the children and their *kas*. He reaches his hand to them and the tops of the jars fall away. I scream as their *kas* drift to the demon's open mouth—a mouth wider than should be possible.

Like a great serpent, Shezmu eats the children's souls. I want to look away, but I can't. I can't stop staring, tears lapping down my cheeks. Kofi still has that crooked grin on his lips as his *ka* flows up from the jar. *He doesn't feel it. He's at peace.* The thought stabs me in my heart. His *ka* funnels to Shezmu, and Kofi's smile fades. The lines of his forehead smooth until all the muscles in his face fall completely still. I beat my fists against the stone, wishing it was the demon instead. Kofi's chest rises and falls and . . . *stops.*

I can't breathe. The room tilts. He's gone. My pretend-brother is gone. I couldn't save him.

Sweat glistens upon Arti's brow, her face blanched. She is a blur of shadows through my tears. "You will grant me a favor in return for this small gift."

Shezmu's spine cracks as he straightens up. "Unless you've found a way to give me a permanent body, I have no use for you." He scowls at her, then with a look of indignation, he adds, "I'm not strong enough to expel the soul from this one."

I release the air aching in my lungs. My father will be okay; he'll come back to me.

Arti clucks her tongue. "I can set the Demon King free."

"Tell us how," Shezmu commands, his voices both a high-pitched screech and my father's deep tenor.

"If it were as easy as that, I wouldn't need you." Arti grimaces and looks down her nose at him. "We need magic that is more powerful than you or I have. Only demon magic and Heka's combined is strong enough. I'm in a position to collect a debt on behalf of the tribes who share their souls with Heka in return for the gift of his magic. I am the true Mulani chieftain. Heka will answer my call."

A sharp pain cuts across my head. Each year at the Blood Moon Festival, the Mulani chieftain calls Heka down from the sky to the tribal lands. No other person, not even the other *edam*, can call upon him. For Heka first bestowed his gift upon a Mulani woman a millennium ago—and the Mulani became his emissary. Why would he answer Arti now when she begged him for help before and he didn't come? She's been gone from the tribal lands a long time, but could it be that when she left, she never stopped being the Mulani's true chieftain?

Heka can't answer her now—a traitor to his name, to her people, a servant of the Demon King. But Heka isn't an orisha, and he doesn't have a reason to despise the demons. He came to our world and gave us magic four thousand years after the war. He can't help her if he knows what she intends and the consequences of releasing the Demon King's *ka*. I don't understand why she wants to do this. As a seer at the Almighty Temple—the orishas' temple—she knows the history of the war better than anyone. She knows the devastation the Demon King will wreak upon the world. But if the Demon King has been her confidant all these years, she doesn't believe it.

"I'm listening, tribal witch." Shezmu narrows his eyes at her. "What do you propose?"

"While you inhabit my husband's body, you will give me a daughter."

I cover my mouth to cut off another scream, and my pulse thunders in my ears. Arti can't be asking something so vile, something impossible. She shouldn't be able to conjure a demon if the orishas killed the entire race. But the scripts in the Hall of Orishas got it very wrong. That much is obvious now. I shake my head, but denying the truth won't make it go away.

"You know that I can't." Shezmu grumbles between gritted teeth. "None of us are strong enough in this state."

Arti steps closer to him. "With the full glory of Heka's magic you can."

Shezmu breaks into a cold, unfeeling smile.

Conjuring the demon has stretched Arti's magic too thin, and there's slack in the rope that tethers me to her. Freedom taunts me like a mirage shifting in desert haze. "Don't do it. She'll find a way to cross you too." I spit out the words against an unwilling tongue.

"She's a curious one," Shezmu says. "She hides her secrets. I want her soul too."

"Out of the question!" Arti snaps, her magic sparking in flashes of lightning.

Shezmu laughs. "Touchy, touchy, tribal witch."

What he says doesn't make sense—but I think of my own gifts, the ones that I've brushed off as weak and unhelpful. My mind resists the influence of magic, and for once I'm relieved that it does.

I don't know why my mother cares about my soul, when I'm so much of a disappointment, so much that she wants another daughter. Shame simmers in my belly as I push back more tears.

"I've been told you haven't the sense to honor a deal unless you're bound," Arti tells the demon.

Shezmu's green eyes brighten with amusement. "You *have* spoken to my master."

Arti snaps her fingers, and another flutter of her magic brushes against my skin. "Then I bind you to Arrah. Trick me and be forever trapped in her shadow."

"I have terms," Shezmu counters. "Should you fail, I will consume your *ka* and hers too."

"I agree to your terms," Arti answers without hesitation. "I will not fail."

The demon smiles again, knowing that either way he has won. Arti smiles too. She'll have no intention of honoring her promise should she fail; she would've planned for that contingency, too. But I don't care about my *ka* right now . . . Let the demon have it if it means stopping my mother.

Arti raises her arms to the ceiling and speaks in a terrible voice that quakes through my body. "I call upon the son of he who gave birth to the stars. He who was born before his mother yet existed. He who belonged to the universe before orishas had yet come into being. Descend upon us, Heka. Come so you might pay your debt to the tribal people, who share their souls with you so that you may reveal your magic. I compel you on the pact you made. Create for me your prestige. I am the rightful Mulani chieftain; you must heed my words."

The entire chamber shakes until the ceiling cracks and peels back like flesh skinned from bones. Clumps of wet soil rain down, and a warm breeze sweeps through the tomb. We're beneath one of the gardens. The moon fills the sky with a soft glow, and the stars move together. A blinding white light descends.

Heka's presence sucks up all the space in the tomb.

I sit very still for fear that his *ka* will crush every bone in my body. Heka sees inside my mind. He knows me and I know him. I yearn for his comfort, his closeness. His magic hums in my blood, and invisible tentacles allow me to taste the world for the second time. It's only in his presence that a sliver of true magic stirs deep inside me, like it did at the Blood Moon Festival. My mind stretches beyond my body, this tomb, this world, time and space. The magic is that of possibilities, of seeking, of knowing the unknowable. I am one with the universe. It's nothing like my mother's curse, which aches to strike at the smallest provocation. But I know this feeling won't last. Heka has already denied me his gift once—deemed me unworthy—and even if I am, I hope that he'll listen to my plea. He mustn't help my mother.

Heka, please. Stop her now before it's too late.

He floats above our heads. His physical form is ever-shifting ribbons of light. My body pulses like a drum, and my *ka* speaks to Heka. It speaks of suffering, it speaks of endurance. It speaks of hope, it speaks of rebirth.

Stop her, please.

"As the rightful heir to your temple in the tribal lands, I'm the only one who can ask that your debt be repaid in full." Arti humbles her voice. "In return for sharing our souls, you promised us the full glory of your magic. I, Arti, of Tribe Mulani, hold you to your pact bound by your magic. It's time for you to keep your promise."

He must say no. He can't do anything that she asks. If he sees inside me, then he sees inside her too and knows that her heart is rotten and twisted.

Heka answers in images: a bull-headed man with blood running down his bare chest, his hands bound in chains, his feet aflame. *What you want is against the natural order of this world. The consequences will be unimaginable.*

Arti raises her voice, undeterred. "It's my wish to have a child who will be both human and demon, and possess the full glory of your magic. This is what I demand and you cannot refuse."

A picture of a woman kneeling before an altar appears in my head, her hands chopped off at the wrists. *This deed I do unto you will pay my debt, and I will not return when you call. The tribes will be forever lost to me. For what I've given of myself, I will not take back, but after this night, I will not give more. We are repaid.* The last bit of my hope flees. He's not going to stop her and, even worse, he's helping her.

"Good riddance," groans Shezmu.

This can't be happening. If Heka will not return to the tribal lands for the blood moon, then he won't gift magic to future generations. What does this mean for the tribal people? Will the magic they have continue to pass down through the bloodlines or will there be more *ben'iks* like me? Will mortal kind's magic become a relic of the past? How can Arti be so selfish to ask such a thing, to make such a sacrifice? And all to release the Demon King, who has no regard for life. The scripts said so . . . but the *scripts* also said the demons were dead.

"So be it." Arti speaks with no emotion in her words, no remorse that she's taken Heka from the tribal people. He could refuse, but he doesn't. He answers my mother's whim like an obedient dog. He's no better than Re'Mec and his Rite of Passage.

A piece of Heka, a ribbon of white light, separates from him and floats down to Arti. I close my eyes, unable to watch this act of desecration. In my mind, Heka shows me lily petals showering down on a sunny day as I lie on the grass along the Serpent River. Rudjek lies beside me and we stare at the brilliant blue sky.

"Be brave, Arrah," Heka tells me in Rudjek's voice.

"You could've refused her!" I scream. "You're the only one who can stop her."

"It is not my place," he says, his words a soft purr. "My time is over. Now *be brave*."

There's such command in his words, such weight. "I don't know how to be brave."

"You must. If you fail," he whispers, "no one will survive."

The scene changes to a mountain of broken bodies piled so high that they reach the edge of the sky. Blood rains down on the Kingdom. Puddles of it turn into lakes and lakes into raging rivers.

The green-eyed serpent—my sister—will be the death of us all.

FRAM, ORISHA OF LIFE AND DEATH

I love my sister. We all love her. Our love for her should never be questioned.

I don't regret killing her. Perhaps I should have left well enough alone.

But I'm the orisha of life and death.

I give life.

I take it away.

And sometimes I give it back.

Now that bastard has found her.

The others do not know my secret. They cannot know what I've done.

The decision to kill our sister wasn't easy. We lamented over it for decades until we all agreed that she must die. Re'Mec and Koré were the ones to suggest it. They wanted revenge, but it was also a necessity, the lesser of two undesirable choices.

When we took our sister from him, the Demon King unleashed his rage. He loved her. Perhaps too much. She's the reason he's immortal. She gave him our gift, but it was not meant for his kind. Immortality changed him.

I remember the boy he was before. When our sister found him dying by the frozen lake. He was such a scrawny thing. Abandoned by his people. She nursed him back to health and fell in love with him.

Love is a dangerous thing, especially among our kind.

Our love is boundless, endless, all-consuming.

But I digress.

Let me start at the beginning.

I killed my sister.

I reached into her chest and snatched her soul from her vessel.

While Koré and Re'Mec and the others battled the Demon King, I found my sister seated upon her throne. When she sensed my presence, she smiled and leaned forward. She knew why I had come. She accepted death. But as I held her beautiful ka in my hands, I couldn't bring myself to crush it. She always had a kind soul, be it misguided.

I stood with her empty vessel before me. Indecision is my nature, so if I happen upon that state, I pay close attention. Instead of destroying my sister's ka, I put it in my pocket and told the others that I had ended her. Every now and then I would reach into my pocket and feel the essence of her soul. She's a thing of firestorms and ashes and lava. How could I let her die when I love her so much?

When I was walking among the humans, I decided to release her ka back into the world without the burden of the past. I did it *so she could atone for the suffering her gift to the Demon King has caused. I have watched her reborn over more generations than I can remember. Making a little progress every time.*

But now the Demon King has ruined everything. My sister has been asleep for a very long time. When she finally wakes, her wrath will be the death of us.

NINETEEN

Arti blames the ground caving in at the Almighty Temple on the people for angering the orishas. She and the seers call for more tithes to restore the beauty of the Kingdom's most sacred temple. It's been a full month since then, and rumors have spread through the East Market like wildfire. People say the collapse is a horrible omen. They claim the orisha Kiva is angry at the Kingdom for letting the children go missing. Some even allege to have seen the children's restless *kas* roaming the alleys at night. The farmers say the tortured souls have driven their livestock mad. The fishermen blame them for their meager hauls.

Still, there are some who hold out hope that the Guard will find the children alive, but I know the truth. The shotani removed the bodies after Arti's ritual. They washed the blood from the walls and got rid of the evidence from the chamber beneath the gardens.

At night, sleep taunts me and becomes as elusive as the white ox. I dream about the children . . . *about Kofi* . . . lying on the floor in the tomb. Shezmu's mouth stretches wide to eat their *kas*. My father's mouth. Sometimes he has teeth sharpened to fine points. Sometimes blood stains his lips and runs down his chin. Sometimes he's smiling at me with my father's kind eyes before his two voices split into a piercing scream.

During the day, I wander through the market to lose myself in the crowd. I pretend for a brief respite that I'm someone else, hiding my pain beneath the noise. I don't know how to stop my mother, and I'm seething with anger. Where are the orishas that they let this happen? *And Heka* . . . I can't believe he agreed to help her, and then left this burden to me. Now I'm on my own with no clue what to do next. I haven't been able to approach any of the charlatans about their scrolls. Whenever my eyes land on one, my mother's curse takes my voice.

After Rudjek's Coming of Age Ceremony, the Vizier sequestered him at their estate. With all that's happened, I haven't had time to think about the almost kiss, and we haven't seen each other since that night. Every day either Majka or Kira find me in the market and deliver a message from him.

"Rudjek says not to worry. He'll handle his father." Majka stifled a laugh. One does not handle the Vizier of the Kingdom. One obeys him. "He also says that you were the most beautiful girl at his ceremony." Majka pulled at his collar, the slightest flush showing on his rich brown skin. "And it's the memory of your smile that keeps him sane in these trying times. He's very melodramatic, isn't he?" That last part Majka added with a crooked grin.

Majka was right. He's the most melodramatic boy I know. Rudjek could've sent a letter rather than have his friends relay his messages. Each exchange has been quite uncomfortable for both them and me.

Today the message was: "I've seen the reports about the mood in the markets. The Guard expects a full riot any day now. You should stop going for a while, until things calm down."

To which I answered: "The market isn't the problem. You know that as well as I."

That was as much as the curse let me say.

After the evening meal Arti tells Terra to go fetch her some palm bark tea and strong wine. I corner Terra in the kitchen and ask to tag along. I need to get out. I can't stand another moment listening to Oshhe's stories, his voice as dry as someone reading a market list. And to make matters worse, Ty, Nezi, and Terra seem none the wiser about what happened at the Temple or to my father. They go about their daily lives the same as always—and it infuriates me to no end. Arti is close with Ty and Nezi, and it's hard to believe they don't know. I can't help but wonder if they not only know but support what she's done.

Every time I look at my father, I see Shezmu's sickly green glow in his eyes. But the demon fled my father's body that same night, his exit as awful as his arrival. Oshhe remained bedridden for days after that, and to my surprise, Arti stayed at his side. She fed him when he wasn't strong enough to hold a spoon. These two warring sides of my mother paint conflicting visions of her. But no matter how hard I try, I can only see the darkness now.

Terra and I arrive in the East Market to mobs gathered on corners, whispering of betrayal and vengeance. If only I could tell them about Arti instead of standing around with my tongue caught in a flytrap. The Guard marches down the streets in its gray uniforms, breaking up crowds.

"Are you okay?" Terra asks, her voice timid. "You haven't been yourself lately."

The pain of my secret eats at me. I want to fall to my knees, to tear out my hair, but instead I push back the tears yearning to burst free. "I don't think any of us are okay."

"It's awful, isn't it?" Terra shudders at my side. "Some people say the children are dead."

My nerves flutter, and I look everywhere but at her. Arti's sins are my sins, too. To serve as witness to a ritual is to be a part of it. "I hope . . ." The curse stops me from finishing my sentence. *I hope they make Arti pay.* "I hope the city will have its answer soon." The words sour on my tongue.

As we search for an apothecary still open at this late hour, a somber mood hangs over the market. No Familiars slither across people's backs, feeding off their sorrow and hate. None flicker in and out of the shadows, which would be a relief if it wasn't so unusual. If they aren't here, then there must be trouble brewing somewhere else. We left Arti heaving into a bucket at the villa, so chances are she's not the source. But even with her sick, the shotani could be up to something on her behalf.

"Your mother asked for palm bark tea. Is she . . ." Terra swallows. "Pregnant?"

When I don't answer, Terra adds, "The tea helps with the sickness."

"Yes." I let out a shaky breath. "I know."

"You'll love having a sister or a brother." Terra flashes me a smile. "I have five myself. Three sisters and two brothers."

Yes, but none of *your* siblings were green-eyed serpents with both demon's and Heka's magic. Magic so powerful that she pushed her way through time, into my vision, into Grandmother's, blocking her sight.

Grandmother.

I should've thought of her before. Would have, if my mind hadn't been reeling ever since that night at the Temple. What if I could get a letter to Tribe Aatiri? Would the curse let me? If I write something that has nothing to do with Arti, but still convince Grandmother to come to the Kingdom at once—could that be the answer? She wouldn't fall for Arti's tricks, and she'd be able to put an end to this nightmare. If tonight's plan doesn't work, I'll try it first thing in the morning.

"I ran into one of the Vizier's attendants this morning." Terra brushes her hand across a bright roll of silk as we pass through a busier part of the market. "She overheard what happened in the gardens the night of the Omari heir's Coming of Age Ceremony."

"Terra." A flush of heat creeps around my collar. "I'm not about to gossip with you."

"Well . . ." She shrugs, her face reddening. "If you ever do want to talk . . ."

"I won't."

While Terra ducks into the only open apothecary, I slip away. It's busy inside and that should give me the time I need. I haven't come to find medicine to soothe Arti's sickness. I've come for something else. I can't let my mind settle on the reason, for if I do, her magic will stop me. I need poison, yes, but it doesn't matter for what. As long as the magic doesn't know, no harm done. Not yet.

I cut a path through the street musicians to reach the seedier, quieter parts of the East Market. On the surface the streets look deserted, but pockets of people linger in the shadows. I circle toward the vendors who sell poisons, but my path takes me away from them. No matter how much I try to cover up my intentions, I can't get any closer.

"You look like you're up to no good," a woman leaning against the wall of a closed shop says. She's small and slight and wears a dirty shift. Her eyes are so light that they glow in the dark. It's the woman who offered to read my fortune before Kofi disappeared—*before* my mother took him. A bowl with a few coins sits atop a tarnished metal box covered in fire script at her feet. There's something familiar about the words, the way they loop and curve and end in sharp edges.

I should keep walking. I don't have much time, but a charge in the air makes my forearms tingle—the way they do when there's an abundance of magic near. The woman's braids writhe around her face as if they have a life of their own. A sense of danger pricks the hairs on my neck. I back away, but her next words root me in place. "What's a girl like you doing about at this hour?"

The moonlight reflects off her dark skin in an iridescent glow.

"Who are you?" An eerie stillness comes over me and I can't move or stop gawking at her. Unseen magic flows against her body in rushing waves. It's not the magic that dances in the night sky; it's boundless and unbridled and invisible even to my eyes.

She bows in greeting like Tribe Kes, but she doesn't have their diaphanous skin. "A concerned friend who knows that you're hunting for something."

"How—how do you know that?" I stutter.

She shrugs, a crooked grin on her lips. "I know a lot of things."

One of her braids strikes out at me like a venomous snake and I stumble back, tripping over my own feet. I stare at the box. It's almost identical to the one on Koré's lap in the Almighty Temple. The fire script shimmers in the moonlight as the pieces fall into place.

Re'Mec and Koré are the most powerful of the orishas, the sun and the moon gods. Koré forged the box with her own hands, and Re'Mec carved the *kas* of their brethren into the sides. Their very souls became chains to hold the Demon King in his prison. Now Koré stands before me, the air splitting around her. Her magic isn't the feather touch of Heka, or the prying eyes of demons. Her magic feels like clinging to the edge of a cliff in a raging storm.

My eyes sting as I gape at the box again, unable to breathe. He's in there. *The Demon King.* It isn't my imagination that the box quakes, that it hums with magic, that it wants me to open it. I wipe my hands on my trousers and swallow the acid on my tongue. He's the reason my mother took the children—the reason my friend . . . *is dead.* I'm so angry that my head swims and I can't see straight.

"You're Koré, one of the Twin Kings," I hear myself utter, not quite believing it.

I should be afraid, but I'm not. I've seen too many awful things, and if an orisha is here, she means to do something about my mother. That can be the only reason why she's revealed herself.

She wags her finger at me. "I know what you're thinking."

"You could stop her," I say. "You have the power."

Koré flips over the bowl of coins with her bare foot and they clank to the ground. She puts her foot on the box and it stops quaking. I blow out a breath, relieved that it's not moving anymore. "I can't . . . I've got my hands full already."

"I don't understand." I flinch in disbelief. "You know what she's planning . . . what she's already done."

"The beast stirs." Koré's tone is serious now. "I must keep him asleep."

My mother's curse surges at the mention of her master.

"You're using all your magic to keep the Demon King imprisoned."

Braids still writhing, she smiles. "I wouldn't say all."

"Can Arti bring him back?" I swallow hard. "Is it truly possible?"

"He never left, Arrah," Koré answers, her words sharp with hate.

It shouldn't surprise me that she knows my name. She's an orisha, but what else does she know about me? How long have they known about Arti and done nothing?

"Had my brother and I been able to kill him," Koré hisses, "we wouldn't be in this situation."

The serpent constricts beneath my skin. I cross my arms to keep from shaking and draw back from Koré. She'll kill me if she can. She'll strangle me with her bare hands.

No—it's the demon magic in my body responding to her.

"That's an unfortunate scar you have there." Koré nods at my chest as though she can see the serpent through my tunic. "Interesting that the *Ka*-Priestess chose that particular mark." She sticks out her tongue, nose wrinkled. "To answer your question, none of us can get close enough to kill your mother. She's protected by demon magic that extends to those who surround her. She's even put a nasty obedience spell over the other seers so they don't suspect a thing. Many serve her willingly, and bear marks of protection."

"But if her magic is that strong . . ." I lean against a barrel to catch my breath. "How are you able to talk to me now?"

"The binding she placed on you has a very specific set of rules," Koré explains, sounding annoyed. "For the others, if they try hard enough to betray her, the magic will stop their hearts. But she bound you with a demon curse that could never hurt you . . . in fact, it's made to keep you safe. She knows us well; we would have killed you if given the chance to strike at her."

I wipe beads of sweat from my forehead. My mother said her curse was a gift; now I understand what she meant. Although I don't understand *why*. Everything my mother does is a contradiction, and I don't know what to make of it. Is there a chance to convince her to stop searching for a way to release the Demon King? He saved her life, and even before that, he's always been in a corner of her mind. I remember the countless times she slipped into that vacant expression. Was he talking to her then? "Why are you here now if you can't do anything?" I scoff, my patience worn thin. I'm foolish to yell at an orisha, I know, but I haven't much else to lose.

Koré blinks her long lashes while studying my face. "I *am* helping, silly girl. Don't you feel the *Ka*-Priestess's magic wavering this very moment?" She has a sly gleam in her eyes. "I've been watching you, and if you're up to what I think, now is the time to act."

I sense the change too—and a brief feeling of disorientation.

My mind settles on the poison, but the curse doesn't stir. I imagine myself pouring it into Arti's wine. Still nothing. I meet Koré's gaze again, my heart racing. "I'm going to kill her."

Koré picks up the tarnished box and the script glows brighter, then she turns to leave. "In truth, it could be too late, but I thought I'd try to help anyway."

"Wait, I need your help for my father!" I dart after her, but she dissolves into mist.

Frustrated, I storm out of the alley and run straight into Terra. She clutches a small pouch in her hands—the palm bark. "Who was that?"

I already know that the shotani can't be trusted, but Koré said that others serve my mother by choice. Could Terra, Nezi, and Ty be among them? Even if Terra isn't in league with my mother, Arti could've put a curse on her too. If so, she may try to stop me. I can't risk it. "I'll take the wine and tea home." I clutch the jug so hard that my fingers ache. "I need you to carry a message to Rudjek."

"A message to the Vizier's son at this hour?" Terra protests, loud enough to draw attention. "That's a bad idea after what happened at his ceremony. Give it some time and his father—"

"I need you to tell him that . . ." I bite my lip. "Tell him that I miss him."

She frowns. "Arrah . . ."

"Terra, please," I beg. "What harm could it do to try?"

In the end, she works for our household, and for me—so she relents. Shame washes over me for ordering her on a fool's errand. The trip to and from the Vizier's estate will take at least an hour— more than enough time to find poison.

I wade back through the shadowy parts of the market, shooing off drunkards and night traders. One merchant claims that his concoction is strong enough to kill ten cows. To prove that it works, he pours a bit of the clear liquid on an apple peel and feeds it to a caged rat. As soon as the rodent eats the offering, it drops dead.

I wince, staring at its lifeless body, and the merchant gives me a look.

The man asks no questions as he sells me a vial the size of my thumb. I pour most of the poison into the wine and soak the palm bark with the rest. Once I'm back home, I brew the tea myself and pour a cup of wine. I'm doing this for Kofi, for the other children, for my father, for all the people my mother hurt. There's no other choice. I have to stop Arti before she succeeds in releasing the Demon King's *ka*. By doing this I may forfeit my own life, my father's, but I know he'll understand. He'd do the same.

I focus on everything but the reason so I don't tempt the curse. For now I still have control over my actions. I don't think about the consequences or about the darkness growing in my heart. Instead my mind turns to one of my fondest memories of my mother. It was an afternoon in Su'omi—the season of renewal, of rebirth. I couldn't have been more than seven or eight years old. I was crying because Nezi and Ty had forced me into a frilly sheath to attend a ceremony at the Almighty Palace. I caused such a ruckus that my mother came to see what was the matter. Before she could ask, I buried my face into her golden kaftan and cried even harder. She'd hugged me tight against her waist, and I'd inhaled her sweet smell of honey and coconut oil. The moment didn't last long, but it's stayed with me all these years.

I replay the memory over and over in my head as I prepare the tray of tea and wine, and take it to the salon. Arti sits there alone, half stretched out on the pillows, her face stark, with the bucket beside her. The sharp odor in the room turns my stomach.

Her magic presses around me like feather strokes. My hands shake as I squat before her with the tray. Her hold over me is growing stronger again. "Your palm bark tea and wine." I keep my voice as unfeeling as her own.

"What took so long?" Arti struggles to sit up. "Where's Terra?"

"She's still out." I answer with a half truth.

Arti's hand shakes when she reaches for the tea. The cup overturns. Sweat drips down her forehead. Something deep inside me hates seeing her this way, but I'm glad she must suffer too.

I rush to collect the cup to keep from meeting her eyes. "I can make you more."

"Don't bother." She grimaces and takes the wine with steadier hands. "This will do."

I stand still in front of my mother while she drinks the poison, holding my breath. She's about to say something, remind me how clumsy I am or how much I disappoint her, but instead she mouths a quiet "Thank you."

My knees almost give out as I take the tray to the low table and pretend to be straightening the dishes to stall for time. I can't leave until I know the poison is working. I bite the inside of my cheek while she drinks her fill of it. The coughing starts and doesn't stop even when blood coats her lips. I stumble back, not quite comprehending what I've done, that the nightmare may be over. But instead of loosening, her noose tightens around my chest—my freedom vanishing.

Leaning forward, Arti cradles her belly. My teeth clench as her bloodshot eyes find mine. Does she know? Let her strike me down if so. Arti throws up at my feet. Poisoned wine and what's left of her evening meal splatters to the floor and sloshes between my toes.

She wipes her mouth with the back of her hand. "Did you poison my wine?"

Her voice cuts into me like a tobachi blade. Long, slow strokes.

My mother can sniff out deception without so much as trying. Perhaps it's because she's so good at being deceitful herself. Had I told Terra, all it would take is one glance for Arti to suspect something. She'd read it in Terra's eyes or a slight shift in her posture, or take notice of the smallest gleam of sweat on her brow. Her magic would skim around the edges of Terra's mind, a trick she learned from her tormentor. But my mind is my own. It's the one thing that even her magic—the demon magic—couldn't take from me.

"Of course not," I lie, my voice smooth. Too calm. Too even. I step back from the mess at my feet. "Terra and I bought the wine from a merchant in the East Market." I frown a little. "I haven't seen him around before, but he had the best prices."

Arti shows no sign that she suspects I'm lying. I tried to kill her. Tried to kill *my mother*. Moths settle in my stomach, but I'm not sorry. I tell myself that my only regret is that it didn't work. "You have many . . . many enemies," I stutter, making up an excuse. "It could be that one of them recognized I was your daughter and tried to strike at you."

"A likely story had my true enemies not tried before and failed." Arti smiles and a bit of the color comes back to her face. "The blood that runs in my veins is deadlier than any poison."

She glances away, done with me, but as I start to leave, her sing-song voice catches me off guard. "You're more like me than you realize, daughter."

Her accusation freezes me in place and I almost spit out a retort but hold my tongue. She wants to get under my skin. I won't give her the satisfaction. I failed this time, but I won't give up. I'll keep trying until I take my last breath. Her eyes bore into my back as I remind her, "I am your daughter, after all."

TWENTY

Familiars sweep through the East Market again like gnats, drawn to death. The sting of rotten meat and rank fish drowns out the usual smells of peanut oil, spices, and fried plantains. Although the bright colors of the market haven't changed, a grayness seeps into the cracks. It cloaks everything in shadows and mist.

It's only midday and sadness and anger thread through the crowd. People push and shove and curse at each other. Patrons shout obscenities at merchants over prices instead of just haggling. Merchants yell back and fights break out. The Guard in its drab uniforms is as bad as the Familiars, the way it clings to the market. They rough people up without rhyme or reason. The whole city feels like my mother's curse is destroying everything it touches.

I couldn't sleep last night—after trying and failing to poison my mother. When she said that failure was the only thing I'm good at, she was right. I've proven that. She found my attempt at murder amusing and simply dismissed me from the salon. Her arrogance, added to everything else, might as well be salt poured into an open wound. Although she made it seem like she didn't care, I've sensed the curse's keen presence all day. I couldn't write to Grandmother when I sat down this morning and tried.

I push and shove through the crowd too, my irritation growing. I yank at my collar as sweat glides down my back. It isn't hotter than any given Tamaran day—which is to say it's blistering hot. But the market is so packed that it's hard to breathe, let alone move. Every third person is looking for a fight, or fresh out of one. I search for Majka or Kira to hear what message Rudjek sends.

It's the memory of your smile that keeps me sane in these trying times. So melodramatic. Majka blushed delivering the message, but he'll get no pity from me. As much as Majka and Kira complain about Rudjek's behavior, they're every bit as insolent as him. Yet his messages bring me comfort when I lie awake in bed at night, reliving those awful moments at the Temple.

When I'm not thinking about the Temple, I dwell on another fear—a fear that the almost kiss unlocked. A part of me worries that Rudjek's mother will want him paired with a Northern princess like her. All the beautiful girls at his Coming of Age Ceremony weren't there by accident. Their families brought them to meet the future Vizier. Whenever his father introduced him to someone, they introduced him to their daughters. Girls of sweeping grace who could charm snakes with their sweet words.

But in the gardens, there was only us. His scent of wood smoke and lilac tangling my senses, his lips so close to mine. Heat awakened in me, and my thoughts had little to do with meeting in the market or fishing at the river. How long has this thing between us been boiling beneath the surface?

I shouldn't think about him, not with all that's happened. I'm betraying the memory of Kofi and the children by having even the smallest moment of joy. Why should I be happy while their parents suffer and grieve? It's not fair. But my friendship with Rudjek is the only thing my mother hasn't taken. It keeps me from falling to pieces. Hope is daunting in the face of desperation, yet I cling to it, no matter how withered and how small. It's foolish to believe someone like me can stop my mother when even the orishas have failed, but I won't give up. I've failed at magic so much that I know how to lock the pain away and keep trying.

"I've missed you too."

I stop in my tracks, my heart racing and warmth flooding through my body. Rudjek's voice is deep, low and playful, punctuated by the longing dancing in my chest. It has none of the arrogance and bravado of when he talks about the arena. I turn to find him by my side in the sway of the crowd, and despite myself, my breath hitches a little. I'm surprised he's come himself; I expected another message through Majka or Kira. He beams at me with twinkles in his midnight eyes, another foolish grin on his face as if he's bewitched.

Bewitched by *me*.

I'm bewitched by *him*.

Rudjek, my best friend.

Rudjek, something more.

We stop in the middle of the crowded market, people flowing around us like a rushing river. The throng hums with noise, but it fades to the background as I take a step closer to him. He does the same. Now there's very little space between us, like in the gardens, and a flush of anticipation flutters in my belly.

"Your father let you leave?" My words come out husky.

Rudjek scratches his head. "He finally saw the error of his ways."

I spot Majka and Kira nearby, scanning the crowds. "I doubt that."

Rudjek's eyes land somewhere on my body that makes his cheeks burn, and then he glances away. "I'm sorry you had to see that. My father is a selfish ass."

I laugh not because it's true or funny. I laugh because if we are competing for who has the most awful parent, I would win that honor a thousand times over. "He could be much worse."

"My mother took my side, and we wore him down," he says as two patrons sidestep us, one cursing under his breath.

"Wore the Vizier down?" I laugh again. "I can't imagine that."

"We reminded him that I'm his only viable heir."

I cock my head and purse my lips at him. "A threat, then."

"If I'm so disagreeable"—Rudjek shrugs—"he can always choose Jemi or Uran."

I take a deep breath. "I never meant to cause strife between you and your father."

Rudjek leans closer. He's going to kiss me. I want him to, but instead he runs a teasing finger down one of my braids. "You can't imagine how long I've wanted to do that."

Heat creeps up my neck. "You used to pull my hair all the time when we were little."

"Can we get out of here?" Rudjek shifts his hands to his hips. "Go to our fishing spot?"

I arch an eyebrow and cluck my tongue at him.

"With Majka and Kira, of course." Rudjek winks. "I promise to behave."

I don't want him to behave. I want the kiss his father interrupted—a kiss to forget the bad, a kiss to bury the pain. Heka's vision showed me a bleak future, but at least I can have this one thing, while the Kingdom is still in one piece.

The muted sounds of the market rush back in.

They never left, did they?

When a troupe of paid mourners cuts through the crowd, we split apart. Rudjek steps to one side and me to the other. Women tear at their already tattered clothes, kohl streaking down their cheeks. They pray to Kiva, the orisha of children, to save the souls of the fallen. A chill runs up my spine as Familiars fan through the mourners, feeding off their emotions.

They know.

"They've found the children!" someone screams.

Guards shove through the market.

"Below the cliffs near the Temple," yells another.

By the time the mourners pass, I wonder if Koré or another orisha has seen to it that someone found the children. The shotani would've hidden the bodies well, so this can be no accident.

"The Temple is on fire!" comes a third shout.

It's true.

Black smoke swells atop the cliffs above the city, obscuring the Temple from sight.

I grab Rudjek's arm and push against the flow of the crowd. People elbow their way toward the Temple, but another path will get us to the bottom of the precipice faster. By the time we clear the throng and land by the sacred Gaer tree, we're both soaked in sweat and panting. Somewhere in the fray we've lost Majka and Kira. Rudjek stares at me, his mouth open, his earlier flirtation replaced by grim realization. Neither of us can speak. My mind slips back to the nightmare of Arti's ritual and the demon eating the children's souls. My father eating their souls.

"We tried, Arrah," Rudjek says.

He doesn't know how wrong he is, or the depths of my involvement. What would he think of me if he did? I watched the children's lives snatched away so that the monster in my mother's belly could exist. Rudjek shudders, seeing the guilt in my eyes. *Put the pieces together! They found the children near the Temple.* My thoughts scream what my tongue won't allow me to speak.

"It isn't your fault," he reassures me. "You gave so much with that ritual."

The plume of smoke above the Temple has doubled in size. Good. Let the vile place burn to ashes and my mother along with it. Let the fire destroy her the way she's destroyed me. "This isn't about me, Rudjek." I wince. "You don't understand."

I strain against Arti's magic, the demon magic, but it tightens around my body and *ka*. Sharp pain cuts across my ribs and spreads to my belly. Koré said that the curse wouldn't kill me. So I'll keep pushing until either it cracks, or it tears me apart. My legs are the first to give. Rudjek launches forward, and as he grabs my arm, the magic relents. Relief floods through me, and the curse uncoils in my limbs, as though testing to see if it hurt me. It reaches for my mind, tickling at the base of my neck, and stops there.

Rudjek glances down at his craven-bone emblem. "Arrah . . ."

"You felt that too?" I ask, hopeful.

It wasn't the same as with Sukar at his Coming of Age Ceremony. That had been like the sting of fire ants. This feels like a simmering fire pressing against a cold night, the crash of waves against a rocky shore.

Still entangled with me, Rudjek looks at me with flushed cheeks. "That felt . . . nice."

The Gaer tree nudges against my back. No thorns this time. Rudjek's hands are warm on my forearms, and he's so near that his chest almost brushes mine. He realizes how close we are and makes to pull away, but I hold on to him. I need him to make the connection between the children and the Temple, but he mistakes my intentions.

"Arrah." He recites my name in his throaty timbre—drawing it out like a song.

There it is.

My undoing.

Rudjek beams at me with that *look* again, but I tense at the five men lurking behind him. I don't recognize any of them—and they're not City Guard or wearing fancy elaras. Rudjek gives me a knowing nod, and turns on his heels, his hands on the hilts of his shotels as the men draw closer. Their faces are hard, with deep lines etched into their skin. Smut and dirt stain their threadbare tunics. But it isn't their appearance that sets me on edge, it's the glint of trouble brewing in their eyes. "The orishas have answered our prayers," one of the men muses. His voice is low and seething like stone grating against stone. "They have delivered the son of the

Vizier and daughter of the *Ka*-Priestess. If we punish you, they will forgive Tamar for the tragedy that has befallen the Kingdom."

The tragedy that is my mother.

Rudjek draws his shotels before the man finishes speaking. I can tell there will be no negotiating. No talking them off this path. People want answers, and men like these speak with their swords first. The Vizier doesn't let Rudjek leave their estate without attendants for a reason. Majka and Kira aren't servants who fetch his slippers or pin his cloak about his shoulders. They aren't just his friends. They've been arena-trained for most of their lives before passing a rigid test to become gendars.

The Omari family has enemies. They've held the Vizier title for generations and no shortage of people want to unseat them. My mother chief among them. What of the enemies *she's* gathered over the years? The families of the children she claimed for Shezmu.

The men pull their shotels, the curved blades like crescent moons. Although they each have one to Rudjek's two, their blades are no less sharp. It's not like at the Blood Moon Festival where the Litho boys had been all talk. These men advance without warning and Rudjek rushes forward to meet their steel. I grit my teeth— desperately searching for anything to use as a weapon. If only I had my staff, or even a halfway decent stick, but there's only the tree and the soil shifting beneath my feet.

Rudjek clashes swords with two of them, and spins to stop another headed straight for me. His steel is a flash of brilliance as he becomes one with his weapons, stalking and leaping like a great leopard. The men aim their shotels for his throat, his heart, and his stomach. All the spots to kill, but he bats them away with finesse and ease. He always brags that he's one of the best swordsmen outside of the gendars. It may be true, though he'll never get me to admit it.

Spinning on his heels, Rudjek slices through one of the men's shoulders and cuts another across his side. Tension stiffens his neck as he strikes and draws back. He wants them to relent, but they keep coming. Another cut. This one across a forearm.

Bile creeps up my throat as blood pours from the men's wounds, and my thoughts drift to the Temple. To the children. The magic in my chest flares and I grab fists of dirt and throw it at the two men closest to me. At least I can slow them down.

They drop their shotels and claw at their faces.

Dirty swine.

Serves them right for attacking us. Let the dirt burn their eyes.

I scoop up two more fistfuls and gasp. The other three attackers stumble back, their wide eyes pinned on their friends. I back against the bald tree too, my hands trembling. I only meant to stop them.

The men's screams ring in my ears as the soil burns through their flesh and blood runs down their cheeks. They fall to their knees, their skin blistering and cracking. I can't breathe as the demon magic coils around my heart like a protective cocoon. This is my mother's doing. This is her cursed gift.

TWENTY-ONE

I'm still shaking when we reach the bottom of the precipice that leads up to the Almighty Temple. Black smoke billows from the cliffs in earnest now; it's hard to tell how much of the Temple has burned. As we shove our way through the crowd, I see flashes of our attackers' faces. Their skin melted like churned butter in the heat. I keep wiping my hands against my tunic, desperate to wash away the horrible thing that I've done.

I'm not like her. I mouth the words as Rudjek pulls me along behind him. The crowd pushes against the line of City Guards blocking the path. They shout that Re'Mec sent a firestorm to strike down the Temple for allowing such desecration. They whisper that the seers are dead. I hope it's true—at least of my mother. That would mean this nightmare is finally over. If Arti is dead, I will spit on her body for the wrong she's done and what she's made me do. Even then, it won't absolve me of my part in the ritual, or my crime today at the sacred Gaer tree. The orishas should strike me down, too.

Rudjek and I are so close that his breath is on my face, and I can almost taste his fear. There are shotani in the crowd, hiding in plain sight, dressed as commoners or posing as City Guard. The echo of their magic dances across my forearms. I used to think of their magic as taunting, beyond my grasp. But no more. Now that I've seen a glimpse of what this curse is capable of.

A guard steps in my path. The man is twice my height and glares down at me with hazel eyes sharp enough to cut stone. Behind him people pass buckets of water up the steep precipice. They have wet cloth tied around their mouths and noses to fight off the smoke. "We need to get to the Temple," I shout over the noise of the crowd, an ache growing in my belly.

"No one gets through!" the guard yells, spit spraying my face. "Orders from the Vizier."

"But . . ." I try to push around him.

"You heard me, girl," the man barks as he tightens his grasp on his shotel.

"Step aside," Rudjek demands, authority threading through his words. Disheveled after the fight, he wears an expression as unwavering as his father's. "Don't make me repeat myself."

The guard spots the lion-head crest pinned to Rudjek's elara. His face turns grim, and he curses under his breath before moving. The panic in my belly eases a little, but it doesn't go away.

Once we're through the line, Rudjek touches my shoulder and we stop. His hand is ice-cold and my legs tremble beneath the weight of his searching eyes. Though I don't want to talk about the awful thing I've done, I can't avoid the subject forever. Behind him a man with a braided beard and sun-blistered skin pushes his way up to the same guard who let us pass.

"That was magic, Arrah," Rudjek says. "I thought that . . ."

"I can't explain . . ." The curse clamps down on my words.

"How long have you known?"

"Not long," I answer. Damn this curse. Damn it for what it did to those men and for holding me hostage. Koré had said that the demon magic would keep me safe. I didn't expect anything like what happened beneath the sacred Gaer tree. This curse is a sick, twisted joke.

All my life I've longed to have magic like my father, like my mother. I wanted to make Grandmother, the great Aatiri chieftain, proud. Years toiling over blood medicines in Oshhe's shop. Years undertaking the tests at the Blood Moon Festival. The anticipation that I might one day reach into the sky and pluck up a spark of magic. The frustration of constantly failing. Then giving up my years for enough magic to see the child snatcher—to see *my mother*. I don't want this . . . *gift*. If I could, I'd claw it from my chest.

"Let me through!" the man with the braided beard yells. "My boy's up there."

My heart sinks as I think of Kofi's father. The families deserve to know what happened to their children, even if it won't ease their suffering.

"Same as I told you last—"

Before the guard can finish, the bearded man punches him in the face.

All it takes is one person unable to hold back his rage, and fighting erupts in earnest. Fists swing, followed by flashes of silver. Within moments the crowd overruns the guards. Some abandon the water chain to help restore order, but no one bothers us as we climb the cliff.

Halfway up, we slow to catch our breath. Rudjek's eyes are bloodshot, his skin smut-stained. The smoke draws tears from my eyes and soot coats my tongue, too. Choking back a fit of coughing, Rudjek offers me his hand and I take it. We stare at each other in silence, our fingers intertwined in an unbreakable bond. A bond that started all those years ago over a fishing pole beside the Serpent River. We don't need words for this moment. This small gesture is a declaration of all the things we've never said.

The second afternoon bells toll as we reach the summit and pass through the Temple gates. My chest hurts from breathing in smoke. People scatter across the courtyard and gardens in disarray. Some shout out orders, some look dazed and confused. Smut and grime cover everyone and everything. Of the five buildings once linked by the half-moon ingress, three stand unscathed. The fire is under control and the last tendrils of smoke drift up from the desecrated Hall of Orishas. The building next to it, where I attend lessons, is nothing but cinder and charred stone too.

Free from their shadowy home, the orisha statues remain untouched by the fire. They towered in the hall, but that was nothing compared to their magnificence beneath the open sky. Even the Unnamed one looks ethereal. Sunlight bends around their eternal darkness, the effect breathtaking and surreal. Where each statue sits, a patch of forever night persists in the heart of day. Beyond them, the rocky cliffs sketch a line against the horizon.

Three bodies lie on the ground near the part of the gardens that collapsed during Arti's vile ritual. Their faces are covered, but one wears a kaftan blackened by smut. My muscles seize and I stop. It's not my mother. That would be too easy. No simple fire could put an end to her.

The Vizier appears from one of the buildings the fire spared, a dozen gendars on his heels. They're in full battle armament, their red tunics beneath silver breastplates. The poor bastards must be sweating rivers. They wear two shotels on either side of their hips in leather scabbards. The Vizier raises one hand to stop them in their tracks. His white elara is pristine amidst so much devastation.

He advances on us alone, his hands on the hilts of the polished swords sheathed at his side. His gaze rakes over me like I'm nothing more than a gnat for him to swat. Then he takes in Rudjek's dirty elara. The smut and bloodstains. His eyes shift from annoyance to disgust.

"I see you haven't learned your lesson," the Vizier snaps at him. Rudjek crosses his arms by way of a response.

A stitch catches in my side from the climb. "Is my mother . . ."

"Dead?" the Vizier spits, seething. "Unfortunately, no."

I can't look at him without remembering that he accused Arti of bewitching the Almighty One. Does he think that I've bewitched his son, too? His accusation set her upon this path. He isn't to blame for her actions, but his hands are dirty too.

"Must you always be so crass?" Rudjek frowns at his father. "What happened?"

"I'd think that would be obvious by now," he answers. "Someone set fire to the Temple."

"The children." The curse tightens in my chest. "Is it true?" I work out what the magic will let me say. "Is it true about the children?"

The Vizier grits his teeth. "Yes."

I choose my next words with care. "Two tragedies befall the Temple, and . . ."

I let the statement trail off, leading. I need them to figure out the truth.

Rudjek grimaces. "You think that someone in the Temple killed them?"

Yes. I struggle to get the word out, even to nod, and they both notice.

Now put the rest together, Rudjek, I beg with my eyes, with my heart. *It's Arti.*

"I don't like you one bit." The Vizier glares at me. "And I'm sick of your riddles."

"Nor do I like you," I shoot back, "but I'm trying to help."

"Mind your tongue or lose it." The Vizier's tone is the calm before a storm. It's not an empty threat.

The demon magic seethes underneath my skin, like a taut cord aching to snap. I take a step forward so I stand toe to toe with him. This is a mistake. I should stop before things get worse, but I hate the way his lips curl into a mocking smile. A not-so-subtle challenge. How dare he threaten me when he had the *Ka*-Priest break my mother's mind beyond repair? He should pay for his crimes and right now, I'm of a mind to make him.

Another force pushes against me; its sharp fangs prick my neck in warning. My eyes land on the craven-bone pendant on the Vizier's elara and his smile turns darker. Dirty, cheating swine. He'd be nothing without those bones to protect him.

Rudjek steps between his father and me. He shifts his stance wide and reaches for the hilts of his shotels to rest his hands. The two face each other, mirror images, both unyielding. "Leave her alone." Rudjek squeezes the hilts so hard that the color bleeds from his knuckles. "You've done enough damage already."

"I haven't the time for this foolishness." The Vizier walks a few paces away and waves for his gendars. "I have the Kingdom to run."

The soldiers lead the seers from the part of the Temple that hasn't burned. Smut spoils their tattered robes. It's obvious why the Vizier doesn't want more people here. In this state, the seers look worse than the charlatans on the streets peddling good luck charms. The attendants come out next and I let out a sigh of relief. Sukar is among them. He's busy helping another attendant who's been badly burned and doesn't see us across the courtyard.

Another set of gendars march Arti out last. To my disappointment, she's unscathed—no sign that the fire has touched her. Her growing belly doesn't show yet underneath her gold kaftan. Even in the midst of all this damage and chaos, my mother is radiant and composed. More so than the Vizier himself. The gendars give her a wide berth; they dare not touch the *Ka*-Priestess, lest she damns them. They march her to the Vizier, who stands flanked by two guards. He would have more if he knew the true reach of my mother's powers, the devastation she's capable of.

"By decree of the Almighty One," the Vizier announces, "I hereby remove you from your position as *Ka*-Priestess of the

Kingdom." His impassive expression doesn't match the satisfaction brimming in his voice. "The defiling of the Temple and the murder of innocents happened under your nose. You alone are responsible and hereby banished from the Kingdom."

My breath catches in my throat. *Banishment.* It pales in the face of what she deserves, but this could be a chance. If she's gone, the distance between us may weaken her curse and I can try again to send a message to Grandmother. But before my thoughts settle into any sign of hope, a sense of dread comes to roost in my chest.

My mother returns his arrogant smile with one of her own. "I accept my punishment without argument, Vizier," she answers, as if he's said nothing of consequence to her.

"If it were up to me," he barks, "I'd have your head, but Jerek is a fool."

Arti wrinkles her nose at the mention of the Almighty One by name. "I'm grateful for your mercy."

"Should you set one foot on Kingdom soil again"—the Vizier leans closer to her, his eyes menacing—"I will have you executed on sight."

Arti's look of indifference doesn't falter, nor does she lower her head in submission. The hairs on the back of my neck stand up as a hint of magic licks the air. The Vizier turns a little gray, and he takes a half step back from my mother. If not for his craven bone to block her magic, she could kill him with the snap of her fingers.

The Vizier cuts his eyes at me, then back to Arti. "I banish your *whole family* from the Kingdom from this day forth."

"No," Rudjek whispers, his body tensing next to me.

A trickle of sweat glides down my forehead, and my pulse drums in my ears. He . . . he can't do this. Where would I go? Tamar is my home. My friends are here. My *life* is here.

The demon magic roars, and I curl my hands into fists. It wants to strike at the Vizier, but I fight to get control over it. Attacking him would only make matters worse. I was so close to making that mistake only moments ago. Now I must be smarter. Compared to the Demon King, the Vizier is of little consequence. Perhaps Arti thought the same.

Rudjek, though, storms toward his father, his face flushed with heat. Two gendars grab him from behind. He elbows one in the stomach and twists out of the other's grasp. Another two disarm him, and as he fights to free himself, more come to stop him. "Don't do this, Father!" Rudjek screams. "Arrah's done nothing wrong!"

"Come, daughter." Arti beckons me. "The Vizier's word is law . . ." She pauses, and her callous, matter-of-fact tone cracks me in two. "For now."

If the Vizier hears her slight, he doesn't respond as he watches Rudjek fight against his gendars. They have him pinned to the ground. I want to go to him, but the magic responds to Arti. Tears cloud my eyes as I walk to her side. *Is this it, then?* The last I'll see of Rudjek, my friends, my home. An eerie numbness settles in my body and mind as I stare in disbelief. This whole day has been a waking nightmare from which there is no escape.

"Let me go," Rudjek yells. "Release me!"

He kicks and screams and punches. It takes a dozen gendars to hold him, and they're beaten and battered and bloodied in the exchange.

"This is for your own good," the Vizier calls out to his son. "You'll come to realize that soon."

Arti rests a hand on my shoulder. There's calculation in her cold eyes, and I realize what she's done. The orishas didn't strike the Temple, nor did the people rise up and burn it for revenge. Arti set the fire. She could never give birth so close to the Temple, lest the other seers sense the child's demon magic and wake from her curse. Now she's free from the watchful eyes of the Kingdom. Free to wreak havoc on those who stand in her way. Free to give birth to a child who will bring the world to its knees.

"I will find you!" Rudjek shouts. "I promise."

His words echo in my ears and I cling to his voice, wondering if it will be the last time we set eyes on each other. If Arti wants to disappear, she will make sure no one can find us. I cling to hope too. I'm the only one who can stop my mother before it's too late.

FRAM, ORISHA OF LIFE AND DEATH

You should not have interfered without consensus from the rest of us!

I did not say you needed our permission, Re'Mec. But it would have been nice if the two of you thought to include us. You never think ahead. It's no different from when you waged war against the Demon King. Selfishness is your nature.

Save your profanities for someone who cares. Let's discuss the matter at hand.

You made a mockery of those children and now the Kingdom is in chaos.

Are these not the people we swore to let live by their own accord? Are these not the people we fought for?

You never could leave well enough alone. Always one scheme after another, or a war when you're bored. Are you bored now? Is that ridiculous Rite of Passage not enough to entertain you anymore?

If you let your serpents bite me again, Koré, I swear I will strike you down myself.

You take me to be too gentle, but recall I'm the only one of us who's killed our kind before. I'm not opposed to doing it again.

You misunderstand my intent. I'm not against action, but the Demon King is still in his prison and the child has yet to be born. We do not know if she will have the strength to release him. We cannot see her future.

We know the girl will be powerful, but we cannot act without facts.

What do you expect us to do, Koré? There's so few of us left.

In all this time, we haven't found a way to free our brethren. They suffer even now. Those who have chained the Demon King, and those who sealed the gateway between this world and the abandoned realm we left behind. They're as good as dead. They deserve better.

The Supreme Cataclysm knows best. It mothered this universe like many before it. We should go back into the womb to be unmade and emerge born anew after this world has destroyed itself.

You don't have to state the obvious, Re'Mec. I know that the Supreme Cataclysm didn't create the Demon King. Our sister did.

No, I will not say her name. She is gone. Leave it be.

Must we always fight? We weren't like this before.

Yes, I'm an old, nostalgic fool. I yearn for a time when life was simple.

I don't want to fight anymore. The others are arriving. Essi, Nana, Mouran, Sisi, Yookulu, Kiva, Oma, Kekiyé, Ugeniou, and Fayouma. We are the last orishas. There will be no more after we're gone.

TWENTY-TWO

Rudjek will find me. He means it. My fingers are ice-cold and a shudder wracks my body. He will come. I swallow and a knot settles in my belly. He will come and Arti will have no qualms with killing him. She hates the Vizier so much that it would be a pleasure for her.

Two dozen gendars march us from the Almighty Temple. The mob at the bottom of the precipice quiets upon our approach and parts to form a path down the middle. The crowd hums like angry bees. At first no one speaks, and then a woman spits on the path. More people step up and spit too.

I know some of them from the markets. Jelan, who bakes the best sweets in the whole city. Ralia, whose patrons line up at dawn to get measured for her extravagant shoes. Chima, a friend of my father who stops by the shop for tea once a week. They don't know that Arti took the children, but it doesn't matter. They need someone to blame, and they bare their teeth, like we're the dirt beneath their feet . . . like *we're worse*. A tremor winds through my body as their pain and hatred and anger pour out in sick waves.

I try to ignore them, but their glares bore into me. Their animosity is so thick that it chokes the air. Someone flings a headless chicken in our path and blood splashes on my cheek. I cringe, swiping at my face as though the blood will burn through my skin. The mob laughs and the demon magic uncurls, ready to strike. I ball my hands into fists to calm it. I can't let the curse loose, but it's so easy. It begs to answer to me. I can feel it stretching into my limbs. It does that when I'm afraid, but never when I want to act against Arti. A cursed gift indeed.

"Do nothing." Arti's singsong voice knocks the fight out of me, but her magic doesn't clamp down on my will. She *asked* me to do nothing, leaving me freedom to choose. The magic wants to lash out—to slice and burn and suffocate the hatred in their eyes.

Blood splashed on her gold kaftan too, but she doesn't bother with it. Sweat drenches my tunic, but my mother never loses the proud tilt of her head. Her fearless steps only make the mob angrier.

A scribe rears back his arm to throw a rock, but before he can let go, his fingers snap like twigs underfoot. He screams and falls to his knees, cradling his hand.

"She did that," some whisper. "She cursed him."

"Dirty *owahyats*!" several more people yell at once.

My body shakes as I clench my teeth to hold the magic inside. I don't want to hurt these people, but I won't let them hurt me either.

The first would-be rock thrower emboldens the others. Three people—two women with tobachi knives and a man with a shotel—step into our path.

Arti's magic wafts through the crowd as gentle as the brush of feathers, and one by one the mob falls to its knees. It starts with the three would-be attackers, who have to drag themselves off the path. The rest of the way, we pass bent heads and trembling hands. Tamar bows at my mother's feet.

The gendars march us to the docks, where another two dozen await. My father is there with Nezi, Ty, and Terra, and a few crates of our possessions. The Vizier arranged our banishment with quickness and precision. I don't doubt that he's always planned for this outcome or worse.

A green fog settles on the bay, and the boats moan like giant sea monsters skimming the surface of the water. Before we board, Majka slips through the gendar ranks. "Send a message to my father's estate with your whereabouts," he tells me. "I'll make sure Rudjek gets it and we'll come find you."

I don't answer; I stare at him in shock until a gendar orders me to keep moving. I'm leaving my home. I'm leaving my friends, Rudjek, everything I know. My mother has taken them from me too. She's taken everything. I'm in a daze as I set foot on the ship. Arti talks to the captain in hushed whispers about our destination, but I don't bother to eavesdrop. It doesn't matter. Wherever we're going, it's not Tamar. It's not home.

The day goes by in a blurry haze. The captain refuses to navigate at night for fear of sandbars that can trap a ship in their grasp like prey in a spider's web. We dock in a small port town where the Serpent River splits into two heads. One riverhead continues along the Kingdom into the neighboring land of Estheria. The other veers into the Great Sea toward the North and the nations between.

Oshhe once told me stories of the dead wandering the night with their faces turned backward. Dead who were out to steal the life from babies as they suckled at their mothers' breasts. But it isn't the dead I fear. It's the child in Arti's womb. A sense of doom lingers in the stifling heat as water rocks the ship to and fro. I squeeze the railing harder to keep myself steady. Every so often I hear a heavy splash, a low growl, and then a hippopotamus pokes its head out of the dark water. The other animals that stalk the river shy away from the lights of the docks and the other idle boats.

I could jump into the river.

Take my chances with the hippopotamuses and crocodiles.

Swim until my arms and legs cramp up.

Drift into the sea.

My spine stiffens as the curse stirs. Arti climbs from below deck with Oshhe at her heels. Most of the crew disembarked hours ago, running after the promise of a good time for a few copper coins.

Arti's presence brushes against my senses before she reaches me, and I resist the urge to shiver. "I should have put a stop to you spending time with Suran's son in the beginning." She leans back against the rail beside me and her saccharine perfume drowns out the river rot on the breeze. "But I enjoyed how much it infuriated him to know that his son favored my daughter."

I swallow my tears and stare at the inky belly of the bay again, not giving her the satisfaction of an answer. Rudjek and I tried to be discreet, although we could sometimes be careless in the markets. It was hard not to be, with so many people around that you could lose yourself in the crowds. I always thought that either Arti hadn't taken notice of our friendship or she didn't care. She never brought it up, but I was naive to think that. Of course she noticed, and she's kept watch on us the whole time. I want to push her over the side of the ship so that a crocodile will eat her. My fingertips tingle, and I can almost lift my hands to try. *Almost.* I dig my nails into the wood to channel my frustration.

"I will tell you a secret that no one knows outside of the seers," Arti says, absently peering across the ship. "When each of the Vizier's sons was born, his wife brought the child to the Temple. The people of the North don't worship the orishas, but she wanted to see their futures. I told her that the Rite of Passage would break the first two. Never mind that Re'Mec hadn't visited the Temple in twenty years to demand a Rite . . . not since *Ka*-Priest Ren."

All this time Rudjek blamed the orishas for what happened to Jemi and Uran, but Arti schemed the whole thing. She knew that the Vizier's sons would volunteer, if only to prove her wrong. How could they not, living up to the legacy of the Omari name? Arti set Jemi and Uran up to fail for revenge.

"Have the orishas *ever* spoken to you?" I spit, my words like lava.

Arti smiles at me. "Never."

My father stands haplessly at the bow of the ship. His expression is blank. My throat bobs as my mother waits for me to ask the one question burning on my lips. I don't want the answer but must know the truth. "What did you see in Rudjek's future?"

When she finally turns to me, her amber eyes are flat and cold— lifeless as smoldering ashes from a dying fire. "He will die in the Dark Forest."

The Dark Forest. The place where Rudjek's ancestor, Oshin Omari, defeated the cravens and took their bones. The place where my father hunted and killed the white ox. I can't breathe as the gentle sway of the ship makes my head spin. It can't be true, but my words tighten in my throat as I ask, "Why would he be there?"

Arti scowls, her lips drawn tight. "Because he is not who he thinks he is."

"What does that mean?" I snap, reeling from the news.

"Nothing that concerns you." She lets out a huff of breath—and glances away. "He will go into the Dark Forest and die. That's the end of it. His future is set in stone."

"I don't believe you." A half-forgotten dream of Rudjek standing at the edge of a forest of endless night skims the edges of my mind. *Just a dream.* It didn't mean anything. She's lying because she hates the Vizier, and she wants me to think that my friend won't come after me like he promised. "Keep your lies for someone else."

Arti doesn't let surprise paint her face for more than a moment. "It will devastate Suran," she presses, her voice seething with scorn. "I only wish I could be there to see the great Vizier's legacy falter."

"The *Ka*-Priest should've killed you when he had the chance." My words are full of all the spite I can muster, and I mean them.

Arti laughs. A genuine laugh I haven't heard from her in a long time. But it's short-lived as her mouth turns into a grimace. She hunches over, cradling her belly. The tethers of her curse loosen a fraction, and there's slack in the cord that binds us. Before, Koré countered Arti's magic enough for me to act. Could it be the child or the sickness that comes with pregnancy weakening her now? It might lessen the curse the further along she gets, giving me an opportunity to try again. I cling to hope. After so much failure, it's the only thing I have.

I don't dare test my freedom in front of her, lest she finds a way to tighten the noose again. My father startles, his back rigid. Does he sense the curse waning too? His shoulders heave up and down, and my hope soars. *Fight it, Father. You're stronger than her.*

"Have Ty make more tea." Arti winces, sweat beading on her forehead. "Try not to poison it this time."

I can't stand to look at her, not after the wine and tea, and the awful thing I said about the *Ka*-Priest. Nor after all the things she's done.

A war wages in my father's eyes, yet he remains in her trap and some of my hope fades. Koré said my mother's curse could never hurt me, but the rest she cursed would die if they tried to strike against her. If my father has his right mind even for a moment, he'll know this too.

I set off without a word. Let my mother wonder about that. Ty and Terra are in the galley below deck, gutting fish and shucking mussels for supper. Nezi must be off by herself as usual.

Ty wipes her hands on her apron and clears her throat. She and Nezi are loyal to my mother, but do they know the true extent of Arti's deeds? Could I convince them to reason with her? I don't know who to trust anymore, especially in my household. I miss my friends, and I miss when my only worry was if I would ever have the gift. Now that I'm below deck, Arti's tether slips further. It feels like peeling off a heavy cloak for the first time in days. While there's still slack in the curse, I'll write to Grandmother. I'll do it tonight.

"Hello, Ty." Heat floods my cheeks.

Our matron shakes her head. Of course she heard the awful thing I said about the *Ka*-Priest. Terra keeps eyes on her work—her hands wrist-deep in fish guts. After Ty's made me wait a beat too long, she lifts her eyebrows to ask, *What do you want?*

"Arti wants palm bark tea," I answer.

Ty scratches her chin and shakes her head again to say, *We're out.*

"I'll go find some ashore." Terra rises to her feet. "It shouldn't be too hard."

"I'll come too," I offer, eager to get off the ship. "I could use some fresh air."

"Next time," Terra mumbles under her breath, still refusing to meet my eye. "It isn't safe at night for a proper girl."

I start to protest, but Ty pushes aside her bowl of fish guts and stands up to make it clear that she'll go with Terra. She sheathes a knife in her apron, and my heart lurches. It takes everything in me to hold my ground. Now that I know the truth, it's hard to look at Ty and Nezi the same way. Sensing my apprehension, Ty rolls her eyes and sighs. Between this and my comment about the *Ka*-Priest, I've worn out my welcome in the galley.

"I'm sorry," I blurt out and rush from the galley in haste.

I stumble down the passageway, bumping into walls that reek of mildew. I don't need to go with Terra. I'll write the letter on my own and sneak ashore while the curse wanes. Between the ship rocking to and fro and my mother's news about Rudjek, I can't think straight. His voice shatters like glass over and over in my mind. *I will find you! I promise.* Even if Arti is lying, how will he find me when we're headed to some unknown place beyond the Kingdom?

The lanterns bolted to the bulkheads push back the shadows but not by much. On my way to my cabin, I run into one of the crew. The man passes so close that his sour breath brushes my ear. He leers at me, his greedy eyes crawling over the length of my body. The demon magic hums like a pet viper beneath my skin, begging me to wield it. The man steps closer. I take a step back. I know what the magic is capable of. I have only to want it, to command it, to guide it. That's what I hadn't understood at the sacred tree. There, I'd let it command me, now I command it . . . and *it feels good*.

The magic laps around the man and his jaw goes slack. He turns away from me, his legs stiff, and takes the hatch to another deck. He'll go straight to his bunk and fall asleep soon. When he's gone, I let out a heavy sigh and wipe sweat from my brow.

Once I'm in my cabin, I waste no time. The room is the size of my closet at home—the home I may never see again. There's a bunk bed with a musky quilt and a lumpy mattress, and a desk next to it. I rummage through the desk drawer for papyrus and a stylus. When I find them, I wipe my palms on my trousers. My previous failure edges at the back of my mind, but I don't think; I let the words flow. When stylus meets paper, the sudden freedom fills me with renewed hope.

I wonder how Grandmother will react to my letter, when I must dance around the topic. She knows me. She'll see that something is wrong. With her ability to travel great distances through the spirit world, she'll be able to find us and see for herself.

"What are you doing?" someone demands, startling me.

I let the papyrus roll shut, hiding my message from view. I whirl around to see Nezi standing with her back pressed against the door. She crosses her arms and clasps her elbows. I didn't hear her knock or enter the room. "Nezi?" I clear my throat as a fog lifts from my mind. I'm out of breath and irritated that she's disturbed me. "I was writing down my thoughts." I shove aside my annoyance and choose my next words carefully so she doesn't suspect my motives. "These are trying times."

"Do you despise your mother so much that you'd say such horrible things?" Nezi asks. There's no spite in her question, only curiosity and *surprise*. When I don't answer, she adds, "I talked to Ty and Terra."

The curse has loosened its hold on my tongue, and it's my first chance to speak my mind since meeting Koré in the alley. "Does *she* hate the Vizier so much that she's willing to *do* such horrible things?" I retort. "Or is she only doing *his* bidding?"

Nezi doesn't blink. I try not to think about the Demon King, let alone say his name. Even now his magic burrows deeper inside me, stretching into my limbs and settling in like an old friend. Magic so dangerous that it destroyed two men with mere soil. I can't lose myself to it and become like my mother.

"You truly do not understand." Nezi frowns. "The Demon King is not our enemy."

"What?" I hiss, not quite shocked that she already knows. Of course she does. She, Ty, and Arti are too close for her to not know. "He eats souls. He almost destroyed the world, and you stand there telling me he's not our enemy. Can you not see the destruction that releasing his *ka* will bring? We all know what the holy scripts say!"

"The holy scripts are only stories, Arrah." Nezi sighs. "By now you should've realized that not all is as it seems. The orishas are not what they seem either. I had a daughter once, and she wanted a better life than I could give her, so she volunteered for the Rite of

Passage. Like so many others, she never returned home, thanks to your orishas. And Ty . . ." Pain flares in Nezi's eyes as she lets her sentence trail off.

The demon magic breathes against my neck, and I squeeze my hands into fists. *Go away.*

"We want the orishas to pay for their crimes," Nezi tells me, her tone matter-of-fact. "And the crimes that happen under their noses to those who can't protect themselves."

We. Here I'd thought that I could talk Nezi and Ty into helping me.

"I don't pretend that the orishas are wholesome or good." I grit my teeth—my vision red with anger. "But what my mother's done to help the Demon King is wrong. There's nothing you can say to convince me otherwise."

"You'll come around." Nezi turns to leave. "It's only a matter of time."

At that, she slips out of the room as quietly as she came. I rush to the door and bolt it shut this time, my hands shaking. She can't believe that I'll support what my mother's doing, that I'll stand aside and let her. *Twenty-gods.* Has everyone on this ship lost their good sense?

I storm back to the desk to finish my letter while the curse is still weak. When I unroll the papyrus, my head swims and my heartbeat quickens. This can't be right. I stare at the grim reality of what I've done. On the paper there are circles drawn upon circles upon circles. Circles that bind, circles that connect. The serpent tattoo aches as the demon magic curls tighter around my heart.

TWENTY-THREE

After ten days of drifting on the river, we leave the ship for Kefu, a free trade territory that borders the north edge of Estheria. Magic flutters across my forearms like velvety moth wings, but I can't *see* it. It makes no sense when it feels as thick as in the tribal lands. Even if magic is less visible during the day, usually it looks like flecks of lint on the wind, but here it's almost imperceptible. The eye of Rc'Mec hides behind a cloud that casts the docks in shifting shadows. It's midday, but it sits too low in the sky.

Arti hires laborers to carry a litter big enough for Oshhe and me, but I refuse to ride with them. My father objects until Arti tells him to leave me be. I walk with the rest of our household, leading the donkeys packed with our things.

Dust coats everything in Kefu, from the people to the squat buildings. Gaunt faces and hollow eyes stare at us as we make our way through the town. Kefu lacks the spark that radiates from the people in Tamar, especially in the East Market. The merchants have no heart as they sell their wares, and the patrons are downtrodden.

There's no boasting on the corners. No gambling in the alleyways. No melody of flutes or djembe drums. Most of all, no song or laughter. There's something very wrong with this place.

Sweat trickles down my forehead as I shoo away flies. I linger far behind the caravan, until it disappears in a cloud of dust at the edge of town. I'm sick of walking in my mother's shadow, and it's nice to have a little space for myself after the tight quarters on the ship. I pull my donkey along, dragging my feet as much as it does.

"Can you spare some bread?" asks a little girl rushing to match our pace.

She blinks at me with sad violet eyes, and skin so ashen it's hard to believe the sun has ever touched her. Though, she doesn't have visible veins like the Northerners do, no matter their shade of color. "Can you help me, please?"

The magic in Kefu shifts around the girl, leaving a pocket of air that keeps it away from her. Her own magic feels like being on the edge of a storm. This little girl isn't who, or what, she appears to be. "You again?"

"Aren't you happy to see me?" Koré pipes up in a high-pitched version of herself—strange coming from the mouth of a child. In her presence, the curse loosens on my tongue again.

"If you don't have a way to kill my mother," I reply, "then no."

"Are you always so sour?" The little girl Koré pouts.

She sniffs around the saddle on the donkey until she finds the salted fish and bread from the night before. She acts like a real child. Without the touch of her magic, I would've been none the wiser. She lifts the sack without asking. "What does food taste like these days?"

Seeing Koré pretend to be a precocious child reminds me of Kofi, and shame tingles in my belly. I couldn't protect him, and I can't help but wonder if he'd still be alive had he never met me. My heart sinks.

Little-girl Koré smiles at the contents of the sack. "As much as I would love to sample your delicacies, I've come with a purpose, or several for that matter. There are things you need to know."

My belly clenches in anticipation. Whatever she's come to tell me can't be good.

"You must have noticed that Kefu is not what it seems." She adjusts the straps of an old leather bag across her shoulders. "The city is like the space between time that the tribal people call the *void*. We . . . my brethren and I . . . travel vast distances in the matter of moments through it. But this place is a different kind of void. It's where the demons coalesced after the war."

"Coalesced?" I wrap my arms around my shoulders. "You mean they didn't die? None of them? But . . ." I inhale sharply, remembering Shezmu's gaping mouth, his horrible piercing scream, and what Nezi said about the holy scripts in the Temple. *Only stories.* "You . . ." I can hardly speak. "You lied to everyone."

"We stretched the truth, yes." Koré shrugs. "When we destroyed the demon race, they found a way to keep their souls from ascending. We all must return to the Supreme Cataclysm in death. It made orisha, and we made everything else. But the demons found a way to cheat."

I stare at her in shock as the scribes' lessons about the orishas—about her—unravel in my mind. "What else did you *stretch the truth* about?"

Koré glares at me through narrow slits. "The point is . . . we couldn't force the demons to ascend, so we had to contain their souls to keep them from taking new bodies. This place is a prison, and like the void, time is fickle here. It moves at a whim and cannot be trusted. Sometimes the hours in a day stretch on too long, and sometimes in the blink of an eye years go by." She glances at a group of patrons who've stopped to stare at us. They whisper to each other. "The people who live in the physical space of Kefu are none the wiser, while the demons cling to life by siphoning off bits and pieces of their souls. A rather harmless exchange . . . until your mother arrived."

"Harmless?" I hiss. "Can't you see that these people are miserable?"

"This is not my domain!" Koré bares her teeth at me. "Another orisha keeps watch here."

"Keeps watch while doing nothing," I spit.

"Something you know much about," she bites back.

I swallow my retort. "I'm doing what I can."

"That brings me to the second reason I'm here." Koré shifts her bag in front of her. She removes a box and hugs it under her arm— keeping it safe. The wooden box is nothing like the one with the Demon King's *ka*, which I only now realize isn't with her.

I rock on my heels as the demon magic stirs in my chest, reminding me that though it may be dormant, it's not asleep. "Is his soul . . . ," I gasp, my throat parched.

"It's safe from your mother for now." Koré scowls. "I've hidden it." She opens the box, revealing scrolls and bones. "I can do nothing about the *Ka*-Priestess, but I come bearing gifts. Do you want to get rid of that nasty curse?"

I'll do anything to break the curse on my father and me. "Yes."

"It requires a steep price," Koré warns. "The demon magic will not leave you willingly."

After the last ritual left me bedridden and took years from my life, I know the risk.

I know the price.

My years in exchange for freedom.

I don't hesitate to take the box. My fingers tremble as they brush hers, which feel surprisingly *human*. She glances away, but not before I see the profound sadness in her eyes. "Can you do me a favor?" I swallow the knot in my throat. I'm not afraid to perform the ritual, but I am afraid of failing again. "Can you tell my Grandmother . . . the chieftain of Tribe Aatiri . . . what's happened? Tell her that I need help."

"She already knows, Arrah," Koré says, meeting my gaze again. "She called for me after her first vision of the green-eyed serpent at the Blood Moon Festival."

When Grandmother mentioned an old friend, I'd never have guessed an orisha. The orishas are not the gods of the tribal lands, but for better or worse, they're still gods. Once more I'm left reeling.

"The *edam* will help you, but their time is yet to come," Koré adds, speaking in riddles again. "You must do whatever you can to delay your mother until they are ready to act."

"I don't understand," I murmur, but by then Koré has faded into the crowd. Grandmother can see across time and space, so has she discovered the right moment to strike? I think of all the times she read the bones and hid their meaning from me. She'd always answer my questions with: *The time is not yet right for me to say.*

Did Grandmother know this would happen and still left me in the dark? If she had and couldn't stop Arti, what good would it have done to tell me? Some of my frustration deflates. I don't understand why, no, but I trust Grandmother and I'm relieved that she and the *edam* have a plan.

When I catch the tail end of the caravan on the outskirts of town, no one seems to have noticed my absence. Sweat pours from my body beneath the oppressive heat and shallow air. Our caravan kicks up so much dust that even my shawl can't block it. Our trek is silent for hours, save for the donkeys' mournful brays.

In the far west, crimson mountains press against the horizon. Behind us, a thick haze gathers around Kefu. It forms a near perfect sphere that renders the town invisible. It's nothing like the green fog that settles in Tamar after a hard rain. The haze wraps around Kefu like a snake curled about its prey. Something tells me that it's always like that, day or night, no matter the weather. Is it the manifestation of the coalesced demons? We don't know much about demons, as the orishas intended, and now it makes sense why. The orishas never killed the demon race; they only trapped their *kas*. And some, like Shezmu, it seems, remain at large in the spirit world, still dangerous.

The laborers stop for a respite, and Oshhe steps outside to stretch his legs. Arti leans over the side of the litter and whispers something to him. Her lips brush his ear, and I cringe inside. Seeing such a rare moment of affection between my parents used to warm my heart. Once, I craved my mother's attention, and would do anything to win her favor. Now it turns my stomach to even look at her. Someone should wrench her out of her litter and stomp a mud hole in her. As soon as we're settled in our new home, I'll find a way to do this ritual and break the wretched bond between us.

I want to believe that my father's pride allows him to stand up to Arti in small ways. His eyes twitch sometimes. His hands, too. Sometimes he's so still that I touch his arm to make sure he's okay. Sometimes he paces. When Arti leans back into the litter, my father tells the laborers that we're ready to go again. He walks over to Nezi and takes the extra bag she's been carrying. Then instead of climbing back into the litter, he falls into step with her and she gives him a playful nudge. It all seems so normal on the surface.

No bells signal the passage of time, and the eye of Re'Mec still sits in the same place in the sky. We've been walking for at least three or four hours, and the caravan's pace begins to slow the farther we go. The desert beyond Kefu stretches as far as the eye can see. The sand is endless, and the shifting heat makes it impossible to tell how close we are to the mountains to the west.

Walking beside her donkey, Terra slows until I catch up with her. We're far enough behind the others that we can talk without being overheard.

"This place feels cursed." She reaches for the Kiva pendant around her neck.

She's right. The tribal lands are lush with feather touch magic. Here the magic is heavy. It settles in your bones. A thought strikes me and I stop. Has Arti found a way to tap into the orisha magic that binds the demons?

Terra shields her eyes as she glances at the sky. "My family traveled through deserts, crossed wild lands, and voyaged across the sea. I've never seen the sun not move."

"It's not the sun," I realize, finally understanding Koré's warning. "Time is wrong here."

To prove my point, when we look behind us again, the sky turns from high noon to purple to pitch-black. It happens in a matter of moments. It should be impossible, but time moves in Kefu at its own pace. After all the hours we've been traveling, the town still looks to be a short walk away. I almost think the heat is playing a trick on my mind, but there's still the smell of fresh water and fish on the air.

"Please tell me you're seeing this too." Terra stands completely still, her body rigid. "Tell me that I haven't lost my mind." Ahead where the caravan trots forward, the sun is still high noon, and no one else sees the broken sky.

I put a hand on her shoulder. There's nothing reassuring I can say. "I see it."

Terra mumbles a desperate plea. "Gods help us."

When I was little, my father and I prayed together before bedtime. *Heka, protect me. Conceal me. Keep me safe.* He said that Heka favored those who prayed to him. Now that I've seen Heka, heard his words in my mind, watched him turn his back on the tribes, I know it isn't true. Any prayer that crosses my lips is out of habit and has no real meaning.

Koré gave no sign that the other orishas are doing anything to help. The sun orisha Re'Mec with his ostrich feathers, ram horns, and eyes made of fire. Essi, the sky god. Nana, the world shaper. Mouran, the roar of the sea. Sisi, the breath of fire. Yookulu, the weaver of seasons. Kiva, the protector. Oma, the dreamer. Kekiyé, the shadow of gratitude. Ugeniou, the harvester. Fayouma, the mother. Fram, the balancer.

I imagine they look like their statues, but no, that must be only one of their endless manifestations. Koré appeared to me in two forms, neither exactly like her statue. I hope that they're doing something to help the *edam*, for with each moment that passes, I doubt myself more.

Blisters cover my feet by the time we reach the sand-swept villa that is to be our new home. Terra's face is scarlet from the sun. The others haven't fared any better. There is magic here too, and as soon as we're inside the granite wall, time shifts, and we're in the early evening hours. Terra gasps, and Nezi whispers something to Ty. I press my lips together. My mother will not have the satisfaction of any reaction from me.

Inside the wall, ducks float among lily pads and lotus blossoms in the middle of a pond. Palm and nehet trees glisten in the moonlight, healthier than any tree ought to be in the desert. Beds of lilies, daisies, and roses fill the garden. Birdsong breaks the silence.

When Arti climbs from the litter, we stop cold, unable to trust our own eyes. Terra clutches her donkey's lead rope so hard that her knuckles turn white. Nezi and Ty busy their eyes elsewhere. I cradle my belly as a whimper escapes my lips. Had they not understood before, they understand now. There's no going back. No return to normal, or in our lives what passed as normal. My father doesn't react to the change in Arti, and the laborers seem to not notice or care.

Koré's message from earlier taunts me. *You must do whatever you can to delay your mother.* It plays in my mind like a broken harmony as bile burns a trail up my throat. Under better circumstances, I'd laugh at the irony, but I can't even breathe as I stare at my mother's belly. It's thrice the size it was when we left Tamar. Growing so fast. The child will soon be born.

PART III

She tastes of firestorms and ashes,
Of new beginnings and endings.
She is the monster stalking the dark,
The savior guarding the light.
She sleeps in a pit of vipers and fire,
And awakes in a windstorm of fury.
—Song of the Unnamed

TWENTY-FOUR

The donkeys stamp their hooves and back away from my mother. Her gaze sweeps over the lot of us, her forehead slicked with sweat. She takes one step and falters. My heart lurches as the curse relents again. My father, Ty, and Nezi rush to Arti's side.

Terra stares at me with eyes stretched wide, the lead rope wound tight around her hand. She opens her mouth to speak, and I shake my head. I realize now that like me, she had no idea what was going on in our household.

"I need rest," Arti grunts, still hunched over. "The child stirs."

Oshhe and Ty walk with her across the courtyard and gardens to the arched entrance of the two-story villa. Nezi stays behind to oversee the laborers unloading the donkeys. I slip the box of scrolls into a sack and throw the strap across my shoulder. I can't risk someone discovering them.

The laborers spend hours carrying our possessions into the villa. Like earlier when the day stretched on far too long, night is never-ending. Perpetual darkness blankets the sky, and all the lights in the villa come to life on their own. The magic is simple, but here I don't trust it. I stay with Terra in the kitchen, so neither of us is ever alone, although that won't last beyond tonight.

"How . . ." She lets her question hang in the air between us.

With the tethers of the curse slack, I could reveal the truth about Arti, but I don't want to drag Terra any deeper into my family's troubles. There's still a chance that she's under my mother's influence too, whether she knows it or not.

Two of the laborers pass by the kitchen, heaving a large crate down the hall. "Ty likes you." I bite the inside of my cheek. "Get her to convince my mother to release your contract. Tell her you're homesick, that you miss your family. Say whatever it takes."

Terra hugs an arm around her stomach. "I've been thinking about some things since the banishment . . ."

I cut her off. "If Arti won't release your contract, do your work, keep to yourself, be invisible. As soon as you get the chance, run away and don't look back."

Tears streak through the dust on her cheeks from the trek across the desert, and my heart aches for her. "I'm scared, Arrah."

I clasp her shoulder, remembering all the times she bustled around my room in the mornings. Her plopping down on my bed to dish out the latest gossip, or sharing news of her family. She doesn't deserve to be stuck in this gods-awful place. "I'm afraid too," I admit as Ty sweeps into the kitchen. Both Terra and I startle, and Ty raises her eyebrows to ask what's wrong. The answer should be obvious.

"I'm going to rest." I cast Terra a look that I hope she understands. *Be invisible.* "You should get some rest too. We have plenty of time to unpack." Or no time at all—it doesn't matter in this place where time is so fickle.

My new room—unfortunately—is down the hall from my parents' on the second level. My legs tremble as I climb the steps, and my feet are on fire from walking all day. Once I'm inside the room, jars of oil on a table flare to life. I sense greedy eyes on me, demons' eyes, like the moment before Shezmu possessed my father. Except more intense this time. It's hard to breathe, knowing that the demons are here too, outside my perception. I try to ignore the panic racing through my body, but it's impossible.

There had been a heavy curtain around my bed at our old villa, one of the many Mulani touches, but not here. There are no dancers on the hallway wall, leaping and twisting to unknowable songs. No salon with a low table and colorful pillows to sit upon. No courtyard teeming with medicinals for my father's shop. No sneaking off to meet Rudjek by the Serpent River. No visiting Essnai at her mother's dress shop or Sukar teasing me to no end. No more witty banter between Majka and Kira. The villa is sparse and cold, filled with stiff high-back chairs, rough stone columns, and vaulted ceilings. It's nothing like home.

I wash before climbing into bed with the box of scrolls and bones. I'm reluctant to open it here, but I'm desperate and don't think there will be anywhere else more private in the villa. My hands shake as I remove the two scrolls and spread the bones on the bed. The rituals are written in Aatiri, and it takes me a moment to fall into the rhythm of the language again. The first scroll has instructions on breaking bindings and curses. The second one calls upon the ancestors for help.

As I reread the first scroll—more carefully this time—demon magic washes over me like a cool spring. I can't lose myself, not like on the ship. I can't let it lure me away from the task at hand. Not again. How easy it would be to embrace it, to give in, to let it merge with my soul. That's what it wants. It's not satisfied with Arti's curse. It wants all of me. I close my eyes, falling a little deeper. It's hard to resist the temptation. The magic feels like a part of myself that I hadn't known was missing until now. I want to let go, to sink into the promise that it will always protect me. No. I can't fall into this trap.

The magic is more powerful here in Kefu. It redoubles its effort, tugging harder. The echo of my heartbeat drums in my ears as I fight to keep from slipping away. It's trying to stop me from . . . from doing *something*. The way it brushes my lips reminds me of the almost kiss in the garden with Rudjek.

Twenty-gods. I wish he were here. He'd at least have something foolish to say to ease my worry. He'd crack a silly joke or proclaim his prowess in the arena. I miss him so much that it hurts. I miss his midnight eyes and the way they sparkle when he looks at me. The prick of fine hair on his skin—skin that I could traverse to no end— and his sweet scent of lilac and wood smoke. I inhale and can almost smell him, the way I did the night of the almost kiss.

Without warning, the magic falls silent and I snap out of the memory. A fog lifts from my mind. Is it that simple, then? If I focus on something else hard enough, it keeps the demon magic in check? With Rudjek in my thoughts, I return to reading the scroll, deter- mined to learn the ritual to break my curse by heart.

I should write to him, but I can't bring myself to do it after Arti's declaration that he will die in the Dark Forest. What if I think I'm writing one thing and the demon magic writes another? It could make me tell Rudjek to go there. I can't risk it.

I study the scroll late into the night. Although it's written in Aatiri, there are elements of the ritual that remind me of the other tribes. If the last ritual was any sign, I'll need a few days to recover once it's over, but it's worth the price. The incantation promises to rid my body of the demon magic and rebound any attempt to curse me again.

Tomorrow I will trade my years again and break my mother's curse.

Tomorrow I'll be closer to death.

The core of the ritual involves Arti's hair and an object she cherishes. The next morning while she's taking a bath and my father is downstairs, I sneak into their room. I expect to crawl the floor looking for stray hairs, only to find her brush ripe. She's either grown careless, or too cocky. Witchdoctors burn their hair so no one can use it in magic against them. I find the ring that once marked her *Ka-*Priestess of the Kingdom sitting at the bottom of a chest of trinkets. She's taken care to wrap it in the finest scarlet silk, so it must still mean something to her.

Since we set foot in Kefu, the curse has been much less constraining. The farther along Arti gets in her pregnancy, the more freedom I've had, but I'm sure it won't last much longer. I pack her artifacts in a burlap sack with the other items needed for the ritual. I bury the ancestor bones for the second ritual in the gardens. Before I can slip into the desert, Terra catches me near the empty porter's station.

"Are you running away?" Terra stares at my sack, her eyes round with surprise. It's not like I haven't thought about it. But Koré gave me a simple task: delay my mother until the *edam* can act. If I can't stop her, this is the least I can do.

"No." I glance over my shoulder at the villa. "I have this . . . *thing* I must do. I'll be back."

Terra kneads her fingers together against her thighs. "What if someone asks about you?"

"Tell the truth." I clutch the bag tight to my side. "You saw me leave, nothing more."

"Be careful." She rubs her fingers across her Kiva pendant. "And you better come back."

I flash her a smile. "I will."

As soon as I'm out of sight of the villa, a nighthawk appears in the sky. Its expansive black wings cast shadows upon the sand, and I freeze in place. When something to the south catches its attention, I breathe a sigh of relief.

I walk until the weight of the sack becomes too much to carry and settle in the middle of the desert. The eye of Re'Mec is so bright that it almost washes out my vision. I draw a circle of animal bones and sit cross-legged in the middle of it. I hold the straw doll I made last night after reading the scroll. She's as crooked and broken inside as me. Using a chicken feather, I write script on the doll in my blood, naming my mother and myself. The endless night served as the perfect cover to gather the things I needed for the ritual.

Once the blood dries, I wrap the doll in linen and put her aside. My hands are steady as the pestle grinds against the herbs, reminding me of the lazy days helping in my father's shop. The way he told stories as we worked, eating so many milk candies our bellies ached.

The cries of the nighthawk rise from a distance as the sun's path across the sky leaves a trail of heat haze. I wipe my forehead, the small cut on my palm stinging from the sweat. Thankfully, this blood medicine doesn't need to rest. I drink my fill, and it burns my throat. It tastes of ginger, mint, castor, and sulfur, and boils in my belly.

I dip my fingers in the rest and flick it on the bones in front of me. Another sip, then I flick some on the bones to my left. The sun beats down my back and blisters my skin. It matches the heat pulsing in my veins. I perform the sequence twice more: once for the bones at my back and once for the bones to my right. My body throbs like a toothache and my sight blurs.

My pulse vibrates in my ears as the nighthawk's shrieks grow closer. I place the doll in the empty bowl, the remnants of the medicine soiling her tan shift. Inhaling a shaky breath, I douse her in palm oil. She ignites without kindle, and the flames burn bright green when I add my mother's ring and hair.

"Charlatan," a gruff voice taunts. "Don't dabble in things you don't understand."

I startle and look around, but there's no one here. At first I think the voice is inside me, but it travels on the stiff wind in the desert. It must be one of the demons trapped in Kefu, still strong enough to communicate without a body. That's how the Demon King was able to reach my mother.

I ignore it and concentrate on the bowl, letting the flames lull me. A low humming drones in my ears like bees. Sweat drenches my body and the hum vibrates in my throat, growing louder.

"She's got a nasty curse on her," a second voice says. This one sounds old and shrill.

"She smells like death," muses the gruff voice.

"Go away, demons," I snap.

The one with the old voice taunts, "Let us split her open and see if she's stuffed with straw too."

They want me to fail. I can smell their bitter intentions. If they could stop me, they would've already. I won't waste time on them.

"I give my life to break the curse and free my *ka*," I recite.

"Are you sure you want to be doing that?" the old one asks. "That's bad business."

"I have a better deal for you," the gruff voice lowers into a menacing tone. "Better than giving away your years."

I should pay them no mind, but if there's another way . . . "I'm listening."

"This place is very old," the gruff voice replies. "It needs fresh blood."

"People don't trade their souls like they used to," adds the voice of the old one. "But you can convince them with your pretty little face."

I spit, disgusted. "You want me to get people to trade their souls for trinkets?" I could never be a part of something so vile. I already have enough to atone for.

"I give my life to break the curse and—"

"Consider our offer, girl," the gruff one snaps. "Don't be foolish."

"We should know better than try to deal with an Aatiri," the old voice hisses. "They're self-sacrificing to a fault."

"—free my *ka*." The final words cross my lips.

Purple ink bleeds across the sky, and the clouds part to reveal a black tunnel stretching toward me. My heart thunders. It aches.

"You've done it now, charlatan," jeers the old voice. "Too late to change your mind."

I'm frozen in place, my head tilted to the sky. A scream aches in my throat. It feels like someone's yanking my teeth out one by one. I want to call it off, but my tongue doesn't obey me. The tunnel will devour my body and soul. There will be nothing left.

"Do not falter, Little Priestess." Koré appears as shimmering mist in front of me with an arrow notched in her bow.

The name brings tears to my eyes. My father calls me that. I miss hearing it from his lips. I miss his smile and his laugh, and sipping mint tea together. I miss all the quiet times we spent in his shop sorting and drying herbs. Had I not been so consumed with wanting magic, I would've appreciated those moments more. Moments that I'd give up all the magic in the world to have back.

The bird plummets through the black tunnel, its sharp talons angled for me.

Koré lets her arrow soar and it slices through the nighthawk. "I'll be having a delicious stew tonight."

"The orisha doesn't belong here," the old voice cries, the indignation in it unmistakable.

"She will lead you astray," the gruff voice warns.

"Why must you demons always be so petty?" Koré spits in the sand. "Can you not see the girl is busy? Do not disturb her."

The black tunnel stretches closer, profound and infinite and cold. Its long mouth extends like a pit of tar. When it finally touches the top of my forehead, it pushes fire and ice inside me. I hear Koré's last word: *breathe*, before it devours me. I'm breathing, but my chest doesn't rise or fall. I'm at once hollow and full. The weight of my *ka* is as heavy as ten stones, and it shines a brilliant silvery white that rivals Heka's radiance. Where his light is as clear as fine crystals, mine is opaque and sparkles.

My eyes feel heavy. My tongue. My neck and back. The beast suckles my life as a babe does its mother's milk. My mind becomes a bottomless pit. Much time passes and no time at all. When my eyes flit open again, my face half-buried in sand, there's no sign of Koré or the nighthawk, or that they were ever here.

I'm on the edge of losing consciousness when the old voice sneers at me. "We tried to warn you."

The mirages of the demons shift into focus in the desert heat, their expansive wings made of shadows. I lie in the sand so long that the sky turns overcast and nighthawks circle. They are frantic as they crisscross each other, their feathers showering down. The voices tell me what I already know.

"The child is coming," boasts the old one.

The demon with the gruff voice laughs, and the sound is so wicked and terrible that it curdles my blood. "She's going to make you pay, charlatan."

TWENTY-FIVE

Rudjek carries me from the desert cradled in his arms. I curl against his warmth, knowing that I'm safe. The way the sunlight hits the angles of his face makes him even more beautiful. His bewitching dark eyes, his chiseled jaw, the large, proud nose. Even those caterpillar eyebrows. I try to laugh, but it comes out as a grunt. Every bone in my body aches.

He came for me just like he promised.

Rudjek strokes my cheek, and his hand feels like polished stone, cold and soothing against my hot skin. "Arrah . . ." My name rolls off his tongue in his deep timbre and sends thrills through me. "You're going to be okay."

He says it with a kind of reverie and nostalgia that fills me with longing and regret. How long did I spend wanting him and hiding from my feelings? So much time wasted, and so little of it left with my life slipping away.

I settle into a place of darkness and sleep for a long time. There are no dreams. Only silence and a cold that becomes a part of me and I a part of it. It soothes me like one of my father's stories and pieces of sweet milk candy. I'm never hungry here. I do not fret. I'm not dead, but I'm not alive either. I'm protected. There's something familiar about this place, like I've been here before. No. Like I've always been here. I belong here.

Rudjek and I sit along the Serpent River in our secret place. He wears a simple gray tunic and trousers instead of his usual fancy elara. He's taller than I remember, broader too. How much time did I lose in Kefu?

No. I'm still there. This is a dream—none of this is real. Rudjek didn't rescue me after the ritual because I never sent him a message. Dream Rudjek casts his fishing line into the river while Majka and Kira sleep under a tree nearby.

"It's your dream." Rudjek laughs. "You can wake them if you want."

"I prefer not to," I grumble as Majka lets out an awful snore. "They nag like two old hens."

"They *are* old hens." He shakes his head at them. "Only they don't know it."

"Why are we here?" I ask.

The Serpent River is vast and wild, and we're upwind from the docks. Far enough that we don't hear the noise from the harbor and far away from our responsibilities, too. Our secret place is near a crook in the river too small for even a reed boat.

"I'm hiding from my scribes." He ducks his head, pretending that one is nearby. "I'm too smart for them anyway."

"Too smart?" I scoff. "Says who?"

He slips into his smug voice, one eyebrow arched, melting my insides. "Every scribe I've ever snuck a silver coin to who has let me out of my lessons. I'm going to be Vizier one day no matter how much I study, and I'll do a better job than my ass of a father, that's for sure."

"If the Vizier hears you talk like that, he'll skin your hide." I stifle a giggle. "Although I can't argue with that last part—you'll definitely be better than him."

Rudjek winks at me. "Now it's your turn to answer. Tell me why *you're* here?"

I shrug as a warm breeze sweeps in from the river and stirs up the minty scent of the grass. He's asking for the real answer, not something made up to suit this dream. "I'm dying."

His forehead wrinkles in question. "Are you?"

"I don't know anymore." I frown. "I thought I was."

He stares at me, his lips parted. There's hunger in his gaze, lust, desperation. "You look very much alive to me."

The heat rushing through my veins pushes aside all doubts. I am still alive.

The colors around me change. The river becomes a deeper blue. The grass a richer green. My sheath a brighter yellow. Rudjek's tunic a gray as sharp as rainbow granite.

I rub my fingers across my chest, feeling for the serpent. My skin is smooth and unscathed. The scar's gone. The ritual worked.

"You're free, Arrah." Rudjek beams at me. "You can run away."

I swallow hard—fear edging into my mind. "Not without my father."

Oshhe sits on the grass beneath the tree where Majka and Kira were only moments ago—a pile of milk candies on his lap. "You will know when the right time comes."

I'm relieved that my father is here. There's a promise beneath his words—that one day, we'll return to lazy afternoons in the gardens. One day, things will be normal again. He'll go back to running his shop, and I'll come to help him.

I can't hide in this dream any longer. I must find my way out of the darkness. The dream sputters and groans, pushing me into another illusion, trying to chain me here. I'm in the desert, following a trail of dead nighthawks. Their broken wings and split bones flow like a river up to the gates of the villa.

Magic coats me with an oily residue that clings to my flesh. I've wished for magic all my life and once I had a taste, I couldn't wait to rid myself of it. The irony of it twists in my belly. Grandmother once told me that our greatest power lies not in our magic, but in our hearts. I thought she was trying to placate me, but no, she understood the importance of knowing one's strength. With or without magic, my power lies in my mind, my decisions, even in my mistakes.

Once I take two steps into the garden, it plunges into darkness. I force myself to keep going. Beyond the gate, it's still midday. Beyond the gate is the place of dreams. This place is something else. It's a manifestation of where the orishas imprisoned the demons. My unconscious mind clings to it, stuck between life and death.

I trudge forward, every step labored. I'm unable to see the villa, only unending darkness that bleeds into my eyes. A weight presses against my skin to keep me from returning home. The darkness means to keep my *ka* here—lost like a leaf on the wind.

The darkness is something else too. It manifests into endless people crowded around me like a pit of writhing serpents. Men, women, and children covered in white ash like Tribe Litho.

They screech in agitation and the sound scrapes against my mind. I cover my ears, but it does no good. Their screams are inside my head. I'm in this place, and this place is in me.

The villa is my body—the brown stone, the asymmetrical shape, the arched entranceway. They're all pieces of me.

With my teeth gritted, I wade through the bodies and dozens of hands reach for me—smearing their hot ash everywhere they touch. My racing heartbeat echoes in the darkness, but I keep my focus. In this place, my mind is all I have.

I push and shove.

They clasp my shoulders and arms.

"Don't go," they whisper.

I elbow and duck.

They block my path.

"Stay with us," they plead.

A woman with braids stacked atop her head like a crown beckons to me from the door to the villa. It isn't Grandmother; she's much taller and not quite as slight. Arti is shorter, her form fuller like all Tribe Mulani women. It's not Terra or Essnai or Kira either. The woman is my guide. She's my cord to the living. She's my path back to my body.

I won't let this be the end of me.

Sweat pours from my forehead by the time I'm through the tribe. It isn't until we're standing close to each other that the shadows lift from the woman's form, and I realize: she is me. I'm her.

Although she is young, she looks tired and worn, and her skin is sallow. But she smiles. A weary smile. A warm smile. I shake off the last hands holding me back and reach for her. When we touch, she inhales a sharp breath.

I stand in her place now, looking upon the people in the dark with their hollow cheeks and sunken shoulders. They stare at me with sad eyes that glow with the mark of demons. They open their arms to invite me back into their fold, their collective plea a chorus on a dead wind. Koré told me that the demons here take bits and pieces of your soul, but these demons are different from the depraved ones that taunted me in the desert. I almost pity them, until I remind myself why the orishas trapped them here.

"You will not have my soul," I say to the demons. "I promise you that."

When I awake from that place of dreams and nightmares, Arti is at my bedside. She's nursing a baby and startles when I move. The child looks to be six months or more. The ritual shouldn't have knocked me out more than a few days, but it's hard to tell how much time has passed when time has no meaning here.

Arti is gaunt with dark circles under her eyes. She sighs and the tension melts from her shoulders. There's no mistaking her relief at seeing me alive. "I keep underestimating you, daughter," she says, drawing her lips tight. "I won't do that again."

My mouth is too dry to answer, my tongue too tired to move, and I can't stop staring at the child. She has our mother's golden honey complexion and wild black curls. Her green eyes shine with an insatiable appetite that rivals our mother's too. She gurgles.

Actually gurgles like a normal baby. Had I not seen the deeds that brought her into existence, I'd think that she's like every other six-month-old. I'd cradle her in my arms, glad to have a little sister.

Efiya, Efiya, Efiya. The invisible demons crowding the room sing her name.

I'm weak for now. It'll take time to build up my strength again.

But when I do, I will kill my sister.

TWENTY-SIX

Efiya's wistful cries drift into my room as Arti paces the hallway to calm her. She's been like this the whole day, and no amount of walking or cuddling seems to help. I don't know what's wrong with her, but I'm grateful that she's keeping our mother busy. Even the demons in the walls fall silent in the wake of her despair. As far as I can tell, Arti has done nothing save for answer to Efiya's every whim. Her plan to unleash the Demon King's *ka* is on hold for now, and I intend to make sure it stays that way.

My head throbs, and I want to escape to the gardens to think. But though it's been days since I woke from the ritual, I'm still too weak to get out of bed. I strain to move my legs again and spasms tear through my spine. I slump against the pillows. Outside my window the sun is overcast; the clouds ripe for a storm. In Tamar, the sky is like this during Osesé—when cool winds wrap around the city and rain floods the Serpent River. We left the Kingdom in the middle of Ooruni, which means that I've missed a whole season between the two. Koré warned me about Kefu, but nothing could have prepared me for *this*.

Not for the first time, my mind falls on Grandmother and the other *edam*. I don't know if a day or a year has passed for the rest of the world, but I wonder why they haven't come yet. Koré can't expect me to delay Arti for long, not with how fast Efiya is growing. Not that I've been able to distract my mother when she's so preoccupied with . . . *my sister*.

At nightfall, Ty sweeps into my room with a tray in her arms, and I resist the urge to wrinkle my nose. I hope it isn't lukewarm broth or tepid water again. I peer past her into the hall as Arti rocks Efiya against her chest, stroking her curly hair. A pang of longing moves through me, and I bite my tongue. Ty smiles. She's been in a good mood since the ritual. Having a new baby in the house has lifted her spirits.

"Hello Ty." I return her smile. Despite everything that's happened, I'm glad that she's well. I straighten my back against the headboard before I catch one of her disapproving hisses. At least I can do that on my own now. It was worse the first days after the ritual when Ty and Terra had to prop me upright and feed me because I couldn't move. Neither complained, and I was grateful for that too.

Ty sets the tray on the table beside the bed, and a delightful smell whiffs up my nose. Peanuts, roasted tomatoes, and ginger. It reminds me of home, of the East Market, *of Rudjek*. Another pang. This one is a different kind of longing, an ache stirring in my heart. He'll be mad that I haven't written, but whenever I leave this godsawful place, I'll make him understand.

My stomach growls and Ty's smile widens. She's brought two bowls of soup and a ball of seeded bread to split between us. For a while we eat in silence, Efiya's cries tempering the mood. The soup is the most delicious thing I've eaten in days.

"Why does she cry all the time?" I ask Ty, who looks up from her bowl at my question.

Ty points to her mouth and when I don't understand, she taps one of her teeth.

"She's teething?" I grimace. Even with the evidence in front of my face, I never thought of Efiya as going through the normal stages of childhood. Koré said that time was finicky in Kefu, but Arti and Efiya must somehow be manipulating it.

Ty nods as she takes a stylus and paper from the pocket of her apron and writes a message. "Reminds me of you. You were a fussy baby."

"Don't compare me to that *thing*." I drop my spoon against the porcelain bowl and the clank echoes between us. "She's nothing like me. She's hardly even human."

Ty shakes her head and puts the note in her pocket. We pass the rest of our dinner in silence, and after she's gone, I spend my evening reciting the two rituals in my mind. The box of scrolls had been missing from underneath my bed when I checked after waking up. I should've hidden them, but it doesn't matter. I had enough sense to bury the ancestor bones before I went into the desert. I still need to break the curse on my father. With his curse broken, he'll be able to help me slow Arti down until the *edam* can come.

I fall asleep with rituals teeming around the edges of my mind and the sound of Efiya crying in the background. In the twilight hours, I'm startled awake by a sudden presence. Someone curls against my back and buries their face in my hair. The touch is so comforting that sleep almost lulls me back into its grasp.

My breath catches in my throat as I turn over, moaning from the pain ripping through my muscles. A girl peers at me with pale green eyes full of curiosity. Her wiry hair sticks up every which way. *Efiya.* She's grown again—a child of six or seven now.

"I saw you before." Efiya climbs to her knees, then feet. She bounces around the bed, her hands balled into little fists as she jumps higher and higher. "You were some place you weren't supposed to be."

She must be talking about the vision, when she traveled into the past, long ago—when I first sold my years. The magic that clings to her now is even stronger than it had been then.

"You . . ." The word grinds against my raw throat.

Efiya blinks at me, then reaches down to touch my neck. "Is that better?"

The pain fades, leaving the taste of blood in my mouth. "How much time has passed?"

"Time?" She puts her hands on her hips. "Time isn't important here, silly."

"How are you aging so much," I ask, frowning, "when I am not?"

"Because I want to," Efiya answers. "Mother doesn't let you and the others succumb to the whims of time."

"So you really are *six*?" I ask, hesitant.

"Seven!" She grins. "Since I woke you up a year has passed for me while it's only been moments for you."

I can't wrap my mind around it, but it's true. She's a little taller, her cheeks a little less round. The change happened in the blink of an eye.

I try to sit up, but my body doesn't cooperate. It never does at first. It takes a while for the stiffness to leave my bones.

"I don't know anything about you." She points at my forehead. "I can't see inside your mind, not like the others. I know their spoken and unspoken words, but you . . . you're different. Why?"

"Go ask Arti," I spit, "and leave me alone."

"Mother doesn't know," Efiya says. "I can see everything in her mind."

"Does it matter, then?" I snap.

"I don't know yet." She frowns. "Do you want to play in the gardens?"

"Does it look like I can play right now?" I glare at her. Only this evening she was a baby still in Arti's arms and now she's a little girl. A little girl with endless questions like any other child. Eyes as bright as lightning bugs. A smile so . . . *so* pure that my mind struggles to connect her to the horrible ritual in the Temple—to *her making*. A child, but for how long?

At the pace she's growing, I won't be able to do anything to stop her. For now she hasn't harmed anyone. I want to believe that Heka's vision was wrong, that there's another way, another possibility, but I'm not a fool either.

"I can fix you!" Excited again, she bounces on the bed. "I know how."

Every bounce sends a shock of pain as her magic slams into my spine. "Stop," I yelp. "Please!"

The room door flies open and Arti rushes across the space. She grabs Efiya from behind—the girl kicks and screams in protest. "I was fixing her!" she says. "Let me fix her."

"Stop it!" Arti's tone is sharp, and Efiya ceases her hissy fit at once.

Arti puts her down. "I told you not to use magic on her. Why did you disobey me?"

"She needed fixing." Efiya furiously twirls her trousers' string around her finger. "I only wanted to help."

Arti's magic crackles in the room and she cuts a look so dangerous that Efiya falls still. "Never go against what I say, do you understand me?"

"Yes, Mother," she answers, her bottom lip trembling.

"Good girl." Arti pats her shoulder, and Efiya offers a shy smile in return. "We have work to do."

"Get her out of my room!" I manage to croak, tears masking my rage.

I've failed again. I fail at everything. I can't stand the sight of either of them.

Arti raises an eyebrow at me and holds my gaze a beat too long. She looks like she's going to say something; instead she puts a hand on Efiya's back and walks her from the room.

I'm so angry that my whole body shakes. I can't keep lying around doing nothing. I can't keep hoping that the *edam* will save me, and stop my mother and Efiya. I grit my teeth and sweep my legs over the side of the bed. A dull ache spreads down my spine, but the pain is bearable for the first time since breaking my mother's curse. I take a step, stumble, and catch myself against the wall. Sweat streaks down my forehead as I try again and again and again.

I keep trying as time in Kefu flashes from night to day to night in a matter of moments. In that time, walking becomes natural again. For what it's worth, Efiya's magic did help, but I don't know why she even bothered.

I stare at my gaunt face in the mirror. I have dark circles and lines that weren't there before. My skin is ashen, and there are still scabs on the bridge of my nose, healing over from sunburn. Bruises cover my arms and from my aches, they must cover the rest of my body too. I look like one of the charlatans in the market. *I am a charlatan.* What will it cost when I do the ritual again to free my father? How soon before there will be nothing left to pay?

I open the door to my room and step into the hallway. The demons in the walls seem to hold their breath. I'm thankful that they don't talk to me like the two in the desert. I have to force myself to not think about the demon magic. How without it, it feels like someone's stolen one of my vital organs, and I'm surviving off a phantasm, a memory, a dream. Still, I'm relieved the ritual worked. I have full control over my actions again without the curse curling in my chest, enforcing its will on me.

Arti's and Efiya's matching singsong voices drift from the room across the hall. Efiya's room. I step close to eavesdrop. I expect to hear Arti telling Efiya how proud she is of her, how she's the daughter of her dreams. How she's so very gifted, or so very pretty, but their conversation isn't about anything so benign.

"He's in a very dark place," Efiya blurts out, her little voice shaking. "Very dark."

"Describe what you see," Arti presses. "What else is around the box?"

After a long pause, Efiya answers, "I . . . I only see darkness."

"You're not trying hard enough," Arti hisses, her desperation almost palpable.

"But I *am* trying, Mother," Efiya whines. "My head hurts again."

"Once more," Arti commands, dismissing Efiya's complaints. "Close your eyes and seek out his *ka*. Let your mind reach beyond your body, beyond the villa, beyond this world. Search in every crevasse, every space, follow the lines that connect everything in our universe. Find where the orisha has hidden it."

"I see too many lines, too many possibilities, too many futures." Efiya sounds near the verge of crying, and I can't help but feel sorry for her. I know what it's like to disappoint our mother. "I can't follow them all. *They are endless . . .* can I stop now? I'm tired."

She is the daughter my mother always wanted, but Arti treats her no better than she treats me. She is everything that I could never be. I should be glad that our mother is disappointed in her too, but I'm not.

Arti inhales a sharp breath. "We will rest for now, but you must practice on your own."

"Can I go back to see Arrah?" asks the little girl.

The question catches me off guard, and it must do the same to Arti because there's a long silence before she speaks. "If you want to see your sister, then you must try harder to find the Demon King's *ka*."

"Yes, Mother," Efiya says as sweet as milk candy. "I will, I promise."

Efiya is part demon, but she's also part human. Perhaps I can use that to my advantage, if she's taken an interest in me. She is only a child, full of wonder. Arti needs her to release the Demon King, that much is clear, but two can play my mother's game. The object of jackals and hounds is to outwit your opponent. Now I have a strategy of my own. I've seen that my sister is capable of empathy despite all that my mother's done to mold her into a pawn. Children are innocent, and I intend to keep Efiya that way.

TWENTY-SEVEN

The sound of Arti's footfalls echoes beneath my door as she returns to her room after lessons with Efiya. Wasting no time, I pad across the hall. Hushed whispers drift from Efiya's room. Her voice is too low to hear, so I invite myself in, like she did when she snuck into my room.

Efiya stands on her bed, facing the wall. There are no candles or lit jars of oil in the room, yet an iridescent light fills the space. The furniture is sparse. Aside from the bed, there's a dresser with a full-length mirror and a lounge chair. There are toys scattered everywhere—dolls, balls, and blocks to build things.

As I step farther into the room, the floor moans underneath my feet. Efiya doesn't notice me as she whispers to the wall behind her bed. At first I think she's playing make-believe, then my eyes adjust to the soft light. Hundreds of faces with hollow eyes and mouths of tar stretch from the wall in silent screams. Writhing tendrils twine around the bed and snake toward me. I stumble back, and almost lose my footing.

"No, you can't have her," Efiya yells at the wall. "She's my sister."

I can't bring myself to speak, and I don't trust my legs. I stand still, clenching my stomach. The darkness is an echo of all the demons' *kas* trapped in Kefu, unable to ascend, unable to rest, coalesced in a prison of the orishas' making.

Efiya turns around and breaks into a conspiratorial smile. "Arrah." On her lips, my name is a sweet, menacing lullaby. "You've come to play!"

This is a mistake. It's too late. I trip over my feet as I back away from her. Efiya frowns and her attention snaps to the wall again. "Go away! You're scaring my sister."

My sister. Her declaration is so full of pride that she reminds me of Kofi, and how much I miss him. When I was younger, I always wanted a sister. Someone to trade secrets with. Someone to understand how hard it is to grow up without magic in a gifted family. Efiya can never replace Kofi. She can never be the sister I dreamed of, but she's the one I'm stuck with now.

Efiya has only to give the command once in her high-pitched child-voice, and the demons melt back into the wall. It's impossible to tell that they were ever there. Her control over the demons is absolute, nothing like when Arti had struck a deal with Shezmu. I won't let myself forget that.

"I've . . . I've come to ask if you want to play in the gardens tomorrow." The words tumble from my lips, my throat tight. "*With me.*"

"Can we play hide-and-seek?" Efiya pipes up. "Terra taught me how."

I press a finger to my lips. "Shhh, you don't want to wake Arti."

"She's no fun!" Efiya whispers with her hands clasped around her mouth.

I'm foolish for trying, but Efiya is still a child. I hope that my mother hasn't poisoned her mind yet. Since breaking Arti's curse, there's no magic stirring in my chest, waiting to snatch away my freedom. I'm free to speak for the first time in what feels like an eternity. "You can't help Arti release the Demon King's *ka*."

"I only want to play, but she doesn't like it," Efiya whines.

"You're a child," I say, my heart pounding. "You should be playing all the time."

Efiya pokes out her lips. "But the Demon King needs fixing like you."

I cringe, wondering what Arti has told her. "If you fix the Demon King, we can't play."

She crosses her arms. "You said children are supposed to play!"

"That's right." I force myself to step closer to her. "But if you release the Demon King, no one can ever play again."

Tears spring to her eyes and she stands there sobbing. I try not to feel pity for her, but it's impossible. She's at once a little girl, innocent and impressionable. She's also Shezmu's daughter—born from the death of others. In the end, it's the little girl who wins out. I open my arms, and she climbs from the bed and hugs my waist. This isn't permanent, or normal, but when Efiya asks to sleep in my room, I say yes. She tucks herself against my side, and it feels like we've slept like this our entire lives. I fall asleep with her in my arms.

The morning is slow to come, but when it does, I awake excited about spending time in the gardens. I haven't rested this well since

Grandmother's vision, when my trouble began. Efiya is gone. My first thought is that she's in her room, but I don't find her there. Now that I can move with ease again, I make my way to the first level. I pass the salon where Arti, Oshhe, and Ty sit in high-back chairs, eating their morning meals. Nezi is milling around the porter's station and Terra is in the gardens. She's facing a shade tree and counting to ten.

"Where's Efiya?" I ask. Last night as she slept in my arms, I managed to convince myself that if I keep eyes on her, she'll stay out of trouble.

Terra startles and sighs when she sees it's only me. "Hiding in the gardens." She wipes her hands on her green shift as Efiya ducks from behind a tree. I bite back a curse. My sister's grown again. Now she looks like a child of ten, with twiggy legs and even wilder hair.

"I have a new game." Efiya runs across the grass barefoot. "I have a new game."

Before I can ask what game, Terra taps my shoulder and points to the gate separating the villa from the desert. Two dozen sand-swept faces stare through the wrought-iron bars. Nezi emerges from her porter's station and tries to shoo them away. That is, until they start to chant my sister's name, and Nezi smiles. "Efiya . . . ," I choke, breath trapped in my lungs.

This is my fault. My foolish wishful thinking led my sister to seek out these children. She wasn't interested in playing with other children until I gave her the idea. I had her undivided attention before then. My broken body and impenetrable mind fascinated her, but like with all toys, my sister has grown bored. Now she's turned the children of Kefu into *ndzumbi*.

"Efiya," I say again, louder this time. "Why are these children here?"

"To play with us, silly!" She beams up at me and bounces on her toes.

Standing impossibly still, Terra pales and looks on the verge of passing out from shock.

"We don't need them to play." I wave my arm dismissively, trying and failing to sound unfazed. "Let them go home."

"They're here already!" Efiya skips to the courtyard to greet them. A mangy ginger cat that's come with the children sweeps around Efiya's ankles. She giggles as she bends down to hug it. The cat tries to slip from her arms, but she scoops it up. With the children on her heels, she walks back into the gardens. My sister has too much power—too much magic and no one to teach her right from wrong. She couldn't have known this was bad. I bite the inside of my cheek, hoping that I can teach her better.

The children run themselves ragged playing all day. When I tell Efiya that they need to eat, drink, and rest to be well, she frowns and plops down under a tree. The other children sit too. If I'm miserable in the midday heat, they must be too, but they don't complain. They look upon Efiya like she's a god and hang on her every word.

Terra runs to the kitchen to get food and drink as I settle on the grass. I have to convince my sister to send the children home after their midday meal. But I'm unable to get a word in as Efiya asks the children endless questions about their lives. Even if she can read minds, she seems to delight in hearing them tell their stories. Soon Terra and Ty return with trays of sliced fruit, almond paste, bread, and pitchers of water. Ty gasps when she sees the children with their blank stares. Unlike Nezi, she doesn't smile at my sister's perverse game. Now she sees the truth for the first time. I warned her, but she wouldn't listen.

Once Ty retreats back to the villa, Terra sits beside me. The nehet tree's dense leaves cast much-needed shade upon us, and clusters of figs hang fat above our heads. The stray cat's tail slaps against my hand as he slinks through the throng of children. He's slept underneath a tree most of the morning, and now he's stalking a bird foraging near the duck pond.

Efiya makes us all play a game in which she pretends to be the Almighty One of the Kingdom. Her magic sticks to my skin worse than the sweat.

"Boy," Efiya drawls. "What can you offer to entertain me?"

I don't like the gleam in her eyes and the sudden shift in her mood. Her attention is on the boy at her feet. He sits on his knees with his hands on his thighs, gazing at her with reverence. Arti is the strongest witchdoctor in all the lands, and even she has to perform rituals to bend people to her will. Efiya needs no such thing. She *is* magic.

"Anything, Almighty One," the boy says. "What will please you the most?"

"*Almighty One.*" The words taste as bitter on my tongue as blood medicine. "Shouldn't you tell us who will be in your court? Who will be your Vizier? Your *Ka*-Priestess? Your seers? Your scholars?" I keep rambling to draw her attention, but she only spares me a knowing smile. My stomach sinks to my knees.

Her eyes bear none of the innocence of a child anymore. None of the innocence of the little girl who climbed into bed beside me. They shine with hunger—the mark of her demon blood. She stares at me as she gives the boy her next command. "Cut off your thumb."

The boy doesn't hesitate as he picks up a knife from one of the trays.

"No!" I snatch the knife from his grasp. "Children don't play like that, Efiya."

"Why not?" She pouts. "They will play whatever way I wish."

"Let us play!" the children chant together. "Let us play!"

If only I could shake some sense into her. I can't give up. "Other people are not like you," I tell her, my voice riddled with false calm. "Our bodies are fragile, and things that wouldn't hurt you would cause us great harm, or even death. Do you understand what death is? People go away and never come back. You wouldn't want to hurt your friends, would you?"

"That's not how death works, silly." Efiya plucks up blades of grass, then one by one, lets them slip through her fingers. "Do you want me to show you?"

A sharp pain knots in my belly. "Efiya, don't do this."

"Why not?" she asks. "Don't *you* want to play with me?"

"A good queen doesn't harm her court," I croak.

"Good?" She muses over the word, toying with it on her tongue. "*Goooood.*"

In that moment I truly understand that my sister has no concept of good or bad. It was cruelty and hatred that brought her into the world.

The pain in my belly cuts like a tobachi knife and I double over. "Please, Efiya."

"No!" She slams her fist against the ground. "I've listened enough; I want to play."

Her magic sends a second wave of pain through my entire body, and I ball up on the grass, unable to move. It isn't like Arti's curse that sought to control. This is something different, something that will only go away if Efiya chooses to make it stop. The boy pries the knife from my hand while the other children stare at me, their faces blank. Terra covers her mouth and sobs.

I beg and scream and cry, but my sister doesn't spare me another glance. The boy squats, spreading his fingers wide on the ground, and does as Efiya asks. He smiles through the tears that run down his cheeks. I bury my face against the grass for the worst of it. She could take away his pain, but that isn't the point. She wants him to suffer.

I catch a glimpse of Arti on the second-level balcony, looking down on the gardens. From here I can't see her expression, but she clutches the guardrails. When Efiya asks another child to give her a gift, Arti shifts into white mist. The same shape she used when she snatched children in the market in Tamar. I wriggle, desperate to get to my feet. I have to do something, anything, to stop Efiya, but with the pain, I'm useless. The mist—Arti—snakes down from the balcony to the garden like a raging storm cloud.

Arti appears in her physical form, standing in front of Efiya with her hands on her hips. Her eyes are vicious and red-rimmed with fire. "I've been patient long enough." She bares her teeth at the children. "We have no time for these foolish games. There is much to do."

The boy picks up his severed thumb, his hands trembling. "Does this please you, Almighty One?"

"I want to play!" Efiya shouts, ignoring him. "Arrah says that children should play."

"Fix his hand," Arti demands, her voice menacing. "*Now.*"

Efiya crosses her arms. "You can't make me."

There it is.

Arti's magic sweeps through me, gentle as wingbeats, and brushes away the pain. Every muscle goes slack and I roll onto my side, panting, sweat stinging a cut on my lip. I dare not move as mother and daughter cast dagger-eyes at each other. When Arti reaches for the boy, she yelps and cradles her hand against her belly. The hand blackens and turns as hard as charred wood.

"I said no!" Efiya screams and a flock of birds flee from the nearest tree.

She let Arti take away my pain, when she could've stopped her from doing that too. She does care about me—and for better or worse, I do care about her. I can't stop clinging to the idea that there's some chance, no matter how small, that Efiya can help me turn this around.

"You're such a disappointment." Arti flexes her fingers so that the ashes fall away and the color in her hand fades back to normal.

Efiya's eyes fill with fat tears, and against all logic I pity her. If only I hadn't been asleep for so long after the ritual, I could have been there. I could have taught her the difference between right and wrong, good and bad. "Using magic for petty parlor tricks," Arti snaps at her.

The children boo and bare their teeth at Arti, but she pays them no mind. "Your sister gave her years for magic to get what she wanted. Although I detest her foolishness, she has conviction.

You, Efiya, have none. You have no focus and no direction. You have everything that she doesn't, but no sense."

"Stop it," I spit. "Stop trying to manipulate her into doing your bidding. You're the reason she's like this."

"It's your fault!" Arti whirls on me and points her finger. "You've poisoned her, and now she's weak like you."

I tell myself that my mother can't cut me any deeper, but she always finds a way to twist the blade. It isn't Arti accusing me of being weak again that hurts. She's accusing me of influencing Efiya, when I've done nothing but fail. I haven't swayed my sister from her deadly course, only served as the smallest of distractions. My attempts have been futile, and deep down I knew they would be.

"What of your other friends, Efiya?" Arti asks. "Will you ever let them out to play too?"

My heart lurches in my chest as my mind falls on the demons in the wall behind Efiya's bed. My sister grins as the mangy cat saunters up to her. She reaches her palm to the sky, and the fabric of the world splits like torn paper. From it, a gray mist emerges and lands in her hand. A *ka*.

The cat doesn't have time to sense the danger before the demon's soul flies down its throat. The choking that follows is too much to bear, but the sight of the cat twitching on the ground is even worse. When the cat opens its eyes again, the color has changed from yellow to green. It stretches its limbs and snatches the boy's severed thumb from his hand in one swipe of his claw.

With the thumb between its jaws, the cat jumps into Efiya's lap and curls up, a soft purr coming from its throat. Efiya pats the cat on the back.

"His name is Merka." Efiya kisses the top of the cat's head. "He wanted a human body, but he has to earn it first."

Arti crosses her arms and smiles. "Well, that's better."

The children cheer. As Merka picks at the bloody thumb, my last hope that there's any good in my sister fades away.

EFIYA

I've grown weary of Mother's little game of house, and my pets no longer amuse me. Once it suits me, I give my favorite pet, Merka, a new vessel—the body of a man from Kefu. A fisherman with calloused hands and skin like rawhide. Merka isn't at all pleased. He murmurs his complaints when he thinks I'm not paying attention, but I'm always listening.

I hear every sound in the villa. Arrah weeping in her bed. Arti's feverish whispering to her master. Oshhe screaming inside his head, cursing Heka and the orishas. The mice's claws as they scurry across the stone floors. The greedy thoughts of all the demons who beg for me to unleash them upon Kefu. They promise to serve me. Still, I'm unsatisfied. I'm meant for more than silly games.

In the mirror, I admire the lean lines of my arms, the curve of my waist and hips. My hair flows in wild curls, even prettier than Mother's. My face is soft like the morning dew, and my eyes are gems that shine with eagerness. I'm the most luminescent shade of golden brown like Arrah, and I'm as tall as her now. Although I *have no age, I make myself appear to be the same as her. So that when she looks upon me, I remind her of the perfect daughter she can never be.*

I hate the way she presses her lips into a tight line and tilts her chin up when she talks to me. All the little ways she is insolent because she knows I can't see inside her mind. The mirror shatters into a fine powder that I suspend in the air with a thought. Such things are simple, but seeing inside of one pathetic girl's mind is not. Nor can I find the Demon King's ka.

Mother says I must learn to channel my anger—that if I don't, our enemies will use it against me. When she says "our enemies," she's thinking of hers—the Almighty One and the Vizier. Her hatred for Suran Omari is pure, visceral, and tastes sweet on my tongue.

Her feelings for Jerek Sukkara are peculiar, and ever changing. I see into her past. Her love affair with him, what the Ka-Priest stole from her. The bitterness that festered into seething hate. The time when they desecrated the altar at the Temple. How she still hates herself for being so weak but relishes the feeling of his hands on her bare flesh. The spark that still lingers between them. How she doesn't want him now—instead she wants everything he has. She wants the Demon King to secure the Kingdom for her, but I can do that on my own.

As I flick my hand to restore the mirror, I decide that I will destroy Jerek. It will free Mother from this burden that she calls love. Love, such a peculiar thing. Oshhe loves her, I see it in his mind, even if it's buried beneath layers of hate. These emotions feel so frivolous and malleable that I'm not sure I want to experience them. I smile in the mirror as I fold myself into the space between time, the corridor the orishas use to travel great distances with one step.

There's no air in the void, but I don't need to breathe. There are only the countless threads that connect everything like an intricate tapestry. At once I'm in my dark room in the villa and on the edge of a precipice where Tyrek, the Almighty One's youngest son, sits overlooking the sea. I take one step forward and my sandal lands on rocky terrain.

The wind blows against my back, threatening to push me over the edge of the cliff. It would be interesting to fall and break every bone. One day I'll try it, but today I have work to do. I could kill Jerek myself—rip off his little protection trinkets and shove them down his throat—but there's no fun in that . . . no finesse. I will make his own son kill him.

One day I'll kill my sister too and that makes me sad.

TWENTY-EIGHT

Efiya is missing. It's hard to tell how long she's been gone, with the way time passes in Kefu. It could be days, or it could be much longer. Even in her absence, she leaves a piece of herself behind. It's nothing I can see, only feel. A chill that creeps down my back in the heart of day, or a breeze so sweet that it makes my stomach ache.

I pace around the gardens to calm my nerves, but it doesn't help. I keep expecting to see her little face poke from behind a tree. I wish things could be different. But I can't forget that she turned children into *ndzumbi* and released a demon from its prison. The mangy ginger cat is gone too. Terra and I have searched up and down for him.

I pass by Nezi tilling the soil in the vegetable garden. She's been at it all day without rest. Even though she's covered in dirt, I still see the red welts on the back of her hands. I keep walking. I haven't been able to face her since the first time the children came to the villa. Ty has been avoiding her too. I find our matron standing in the kitchen door, staring at the wall that surrounds the outer edge of the gardens. She wrings a dirty dishrag in her hands. Terra is next to the well, washing clothes in a barrel, scrubbing so hard that her fingers must be raw. She doesn't talk either. None of us do. We wait.

At least Efiya released her control over the children. One day in the middle of running in the gardens with them, she said she didn't want to play anymore. On her command they snapped out of their trances. The younger ones began to cry. Terra and I took them home to parents who hadn't even known they were missing, because of Efiya's magic.

The children who came from the streets, I put on a barge headed for Tamar with a letter addressed to the orphanage. I stopped myself again from sending a letter to Rudjek. It was harder the second time. I can't say how long we've been in Kefu. Sometimes it seems like years have passed and sometimes mere bells. Sometimes the sky doesn't change for days. The eye of Re'Mec tilts at an angle like it's about to spill lava from its mouth. The thought of years passing in the rest of the world makes me anxious. Rudjek could be fully grown by now. Essnai and Sukar, Majka and Kira too. Would they forget me, or hate me because I haven't written? Either way, now that I've seen Efiya's powers, I know that I can never ask my friends to come here. I couldn't live with knowing what would happen.

And the *edam*. What's become of them and their plan? Something must have gone wrong, otherwise Grandmother would be here by now. Oshhe sits cross-legged on the second-level wraparound balcony with his eyes closed. Even though I would give more of my years without regret to free my father, the risk is too great. If I fall into another deep sleep, Efiya could release the Demon King and I would've done nothing to stop her. I bite back my tears and they ball up inside me, brewing and swelling like tides, aching to break free.

Heka showed me a mountain of broken bodies piled so high that they reached the edge of the sky. Blood rained down on the Kingdom. Puddles turned into lakes and lakes into raging rivers. I can't let that happen.

"I'm sorry, Father." I press my hand to my heart. "I'm breaking my promise again."

Arti paces back and forth on the balcony. At night, she stalks up and down the hall, waiting for Efiya to come home. She's been more agitated than usual, so Efiya must've left without telling her either. If so, then what new perverse thing has captured my sister's attention? After she turned children into *ndzumbi*, I can't fathom what else she's capable of. I'm worried that she'll do something even worse.

I stop turning in circles and sit with my back against the nehet tree closest to the pond, alone save for the ducks. I'm waiting for a good moment to dig up the ancestor bones I buried here before the ritual. No telling how many years this next ritual will take from me, and no guarantee that it'll work, but it's worth a try. The ancestors are our link between the living and the ascended, and we call upon them for help and guidance. Before, Oshhe often called them through dream visions and Grandmother read their bones to see the future. I will use their bones in a different way. I'll use them to call my ancestors across time to join with me if they choose to answer. Now I wait for Efiya. My plan depends upon her presence.

Since she's been gone, the demons in the walls whisper in my ear at night, calling me *ndzumbi* because I've given up so many of my years to magic. They say that I don't have enough life to give for another ritual. They say that I'm as good as dead, but I don't care. I don't want to die, but if trading my years means I can stop Arti and Efiya, then I'll do it again.

I convince myself that I'll know if she releases the Demon King because I've felt his magic before. It was at once a calming force and a raging fire inside me; it protected me, it almost seduced me. His magic gave me the one thing that I've always wanted. No longer was I the charlatan daughter born of two powerful witchdoctors, desperate for magic. Arti had in fact given me a gift in her own twisted way—magic that answered to me without question, and without having to trade my years. It's gone now, and I miss it.

Efiya's presence pricks against my skin, and she steps out of thin air in front of me. I jump to my feet, refusing to believe my own eyes. My sister . . . she's . . . My mind tries to make sense of the girl standing face-to-face with me, no longer a child. She's the very spitting image of our mother, but even more beautiful. She's like the orisha statues at the Temple—hard to look at too long. If the Unnamed orisha was unremarkable, then Efiya is on the other end of the spectrum. She's as old as me now.

I drop down on the grass again, breathless. "You're back."

"Did you miss me?" Efiya's words flow like the sweetest song, her voice all grown-up.

I tighten my arms around my knees but don't give her the satisfaction of an answer. She smiles at my clenched fists. She knows that I fear her whims. It was only a little while ago that she delivered her first nasty surprise.

"Are you well, Arrah?" she asks, sitting down across from me. "You look a little ill."

Her magic scrapes my mind like cat claws against stone. She

doesn't let her frustration show when she's met with a barrier that she cannot penetrate. I allow myself the smallest smile. My mind is still my own. Even if it's nothing compared to the demon magic or my sister's, it's something that will always be my one advantage over her. Something that will always be truly *mine*. "Quite well," I grumble.

"You are an enigma." Efiya takes one of my braids into her hand. She runs her fingers down the length of it. "One day I'll see inside your mind and know your secrets."

I blink at her. "Why does it bother you so much that you can't see in my mind?"

"I see all the possibilities of what can and will be." Efiya twirls my hair around her finger. "I see across time with little effort, but when I focus on you, the future is blank. I can't see the consequences of any action I take against you or any action of yours. Why is that, dear sister?"

For all the magic she has, she lacks common sense. The answer is obvious, isn't it? I swallow hard, but it doesn't soothe my parched throat. I haven't been the same since the first ritual, and the second one took a little more from me. I've walked the plane between life and death. The demons caught my soul and almost wove me into the tapestry of Kefu. Even with most of my strength back, there's a part of me missing.

I'm already dead in her future. That's the answer. I've traded enough years that I ought to be. "You're giving me a headache asking questions I can't answer."

Efiya tugs at my braid so hard that my scalp screams. I reach up and pull one of her loose curls back. She seems delighted by this exchange and laughs. In this way, she isn't the sixteen-year-old girl she appears to be. She still marvels at the oddest of things because she's never experienced them before.

I snatch my hand away and press my fists against my legs again. I can't forget who she is, what she is, the things she's done. She plucked a demon's *ka* from thin air. "Where have you been?"

"Hunting," Efiya whispers like she's sharing her most sacred secret. "I killed an orisha today."

My mind reels with a thousand horrible thoughts. "You what?" I say, my head pounding.

Efiya frowns. "He wouldn't tell me where Koré hid the Demon King's *ka*."

I shake my head, my whole body trembling. "Efiya, you must stop. Can't you see what will happen if you release the Demon King? The world will bleed."

"Yes." She leans closer to me, her eyes bright. "And I have seen the afterworld too. It's beautiful, sister."

I wipe away tears as a lanky middle-aged man with pockmarked, suntanned skin steps into the garden. Nezi is with him. Nezi's limp is gone, and she walks with a newfound confidence. At first I'm confused, and think that Efiya has healed her. That is, until I see that both her eyes and the man's are shades of green with a spark of light that isn't natural. The man runs his fingers through his greasy hair and winks at me. He has the same mangy hair as the ginger cat—but I can't stop gaping at Nezi. She's never walked straight in all my years of knowing her, and there's nothing left of her in these cold eyes.

"Nezi?" I stutter.

The thing pretending to be our porter smiles.

"She's wanted to die since *Ka*-Priest Ren Eké hurt her," Efiya says. "Mother should've done it a long time ago, but she's too sentimental."

I'm stunned into silence. My heart aches for Nezi—the *real* Nezi. I'd seen her only moments ago in the vegetable garden, or was it already the demon I saw then? I hadn't known she felt that way; I hadn't even suspected it. Ty, maybe, because of her outbursts, but never Nezi.

"Do you like my new vessel, Arrah?" muses the ginger-haired Merka. "It's rather plain, but better than the cat, isn't it?"

"I will speak to you now, Efiya," Arti calls down from the balcony, her voice tight.

"Coming, Mother!" Efiya calls back, not even bothering to look Arti's way.

"I took your advice, sister." She climbs to her feet. I watch as beyond her, a horde of demons—too many to count—enters through the gates of our villa, and I can't hide from the truth. My sister has released hundreds of demons to feast upon the *kas* of unsuspecting people. She's killed an orisha without a second thought. All this time, I was worried about the Demon King, but Heka's warning had been about her too. "I'm building my court. Don't worry, I'll leave Ty and Oshhe for Mother, and Terra for you. It's only fair that you have playthings too."

She arches an eyebrow like she's expecting me to thank her.

"Do you like my subjects?" Efiya beams. "I'll make you one too if you want."

I say nothing, clutching strands of her hair in my fist while she slips back into the void.

Ancestor bones.

Bitter iboga bark.

Mint and ginger.

Palm oil.

Hair.

Ancestor bones.

Bitter iboga bark.

Mint and ginger.

Palm oil.

Hair.

I mean to kill my sister tonight.

TWENTY-NINE

When evening settles upon the villa, Efiya steps into the void and vanishes. A weight lifts from my shoulders. She's left none of herself behind to watch. With her gone, the villa is more spacious, the air cleaner. Her magic, along with Arti's, had felt like a thousand beating wings bearing down on me.

Arms crossed, I lean against the porter's house as Merka marches the other demons toward Keſu. There are at least two hundred of them, if not more. My sister hasn't raised that many demons as a simple game. She's raised an army. She means to bring the Kingdom to its knees. Rudjek, Sukar, Essnai, Majka, Kira—everyone—will be in danger if I can't stop her.

Once the demons are gone, I walk to the nehet tree near the pond, careful to keep my steps unhurried in case Arti is watching. I wait until nightfall to search for the bones. My fingers meet nothing but the cool underbelly of the soil beneath the warm top layer. They're not here.

Sweat glides down my forehead and my back. Did I bury the

bones under another tree? Did Arti find them? A white haze of confusion clouds my thoughts. Where are they? The grave was shallow. It shouldn't take this long to find.

Oshhe clears his throat behind me. "You never listen to my stories anymore, Little Priestess."

I pivot around on my heels, my heart pounding against my ribs. My father stands tall and still like one of the stone monuments in Tamar. He's always been a lean man, but he's too thin now, his cheeks and shoulders bony, his features sharp. Shame washes over me and I look away. I haven't given up hope for him, but for now, stopping Efiya is more important.

"You haven't told any stories in a long time," I remind him. "I miss hearing them." What I don't say is that right after the curse when he still told stories—it wasn't the same without his *heart* in them.

My father frowns as his attention shifts to the holes. "What are you doing?"

I suck in a deep breath through my teeth. "I'm digging holes."

Oshhe stares at me, his eyes sharp for once. It's the magic inside him on alert. If he thinks that I'm acting against Arti, he'll try to stop me, but my mother is the least of my concerns now. She said that she wouldn't underestimate me again, but behind her cold words there was a spark of pride—a spark of respect. Of course I almost had to die to win my mother's approval.

"I'm going to plant rain daisies in the morning." I bite my lip. "Like back home."

When I say *back home*, my father's face lights up. There's nostalgia in his eyes, and a longing that breaks my heart. "They should do well here if we keep them watered." I brush my fingers across the soil, remembering another garden and another time. "Even if the air's dry."

My father rubs his chin. "Yes, I think so . . ."

"Under the nehet tree will make a good spot." I bite the inside of my cheek.

Some part of him must know that something—everything—is wrong, but he can't make sense of his thoughts. Since we've been in Kefu, he's less and less himself. He rarely tries to make conversation, let alone tell stories. Arti is always too busy scheming with Efiya to notice. "They would do better by the pond, where they can get more sunlight. You should know that, Little Priestess."

"You're right," I admit after an exaggerated sigh. "I'll dig new holes tomorrow. I'm tired."

"I'll go to the market in the morning and get some milk candy." His voice is full of excitement. "We'll work in the gardens together, like we used to. It's been far too long, and I miss spending time with you. You're growing up so fast."

I smile, my heart collapsing in my chest. I want so badly to go back to those times. "What do you think of your other daughter? Has she not grown up even faster?"

Oshhe never talks to Efiya. With the way time passes in Kefu, he hasn't gotten the chance to know her. She doesn't share the bond that I have with him. I can't help but think if our father had been himself, he could've helped me sway her.

"She has." Oshhe smiles. "You both have grown up so fast. My two little priestesses."

"She's not a little priestess." I grit my teeth. "She's a damn demon."

"Would you like to hear a story now?" Oshhe asks, not listening to me.

"Not now, Father." I cringe. "Tomorrow when we're planting the daisies."

"Good." Oshhe claps once. "I'll tell you a story about one of my ancestors."

He smiles, but he doesn't tarry much longer. I turn the ground belly-up beneath three separate nehet trees before I find the bones. Sweat trickles down my back, and my fingertips are raw from digging. The moonlight shimmers in the soil and my mind turns to Koré. I haven't seen her since the day I broke Arti's curse.

Once I have the bones, I steep half the iboga bark in mint and ginger tea and wedge the other piece under my tongue. It tastes nutty at first but turns sour after a while. By the time the brew is ready, my mouth is numb and my tongue feels fat and useless. Once Efiya's presence wafts around the villa again, I go back to my room to begin the final stages of the ritual.

I sit in front of the mirror in my room, threading Efiya's hair around the bones. Every nerve in my body pushes me to hurry, but rituals take time, even in this place where time has no meaning. I must be patient. Ancestor magic demands respect. It's the same as respecting one's elders. The bones are so small it takes me several tries to get it right. Finally, I grease the bones with palm oil and secure them to my left hand with a piece of cloth. I drink the mint and ginger tea and wait.

I am Arrah.

Hear my voice, great ancestors.

Hear my plea.

Answer my need.

Bless me with your presence.

With my Tamaran accent the Aatiri words are rough on my tongue—I've been practicing them only in my head for so long. Now the wait begins. Time passes with the drumming of my heartbeat, the rise and fall of my breaths. So much time that doubt crawls into my mind. The demons in the walls whisper that I won't have enough years to trade for another ritual. The longer I wait for the magic to come, the more I fear they're right. I repeat the words again, slower, drawing out each syllable. This time, sparks of magic drift through the walls and the ceiling. I hold my breath as it floats in the air, still deciding if it wants to answer my call. Instead of lighting on my skin, it forms a circle around me.

Fire tears through my muscles. I clench my jaw tight to keep from passing out, and soon the pain fades—quicker than it has before. My gums ache, and when I poke around my mouth with my tongue, one of my back teeth shakes free. I reach up with a trembling hand, desperate to put it back in place, foolish to think that I can. When I finally give up, I hold the tooth in my palm—it's riddled with black rot. Magic takes of you what it will, my father said. It could take a little or all your years. By some small grace, this time, it hasn't crippled me. A tooth is a small price to pay.

Fog creeps from the bones and obscures my view, but only in the mirror. My bedroom remains unchanged. My eyes ache from staring too long and I blink. In my reflection, three women appear behind me. My heart races against my chest. Even though I hoped that the ritual would work, it still catches me off guard.

When I look over my shoulder, there's no one. The three great

Aatiri ancestors are with me only in spirit. Their eyes are white and their faces blank. I go to my knees and rest my hands flat on my thighs to show respect.

I'm not to speak before they do, so I wait again. They blink and their eyes change from all white to all black. The one in the middle, who reminds me of Grandmother, speaks first. Her voice is hoarse and commanding.

"Who are you to call upon us?" she asks.

For the magic to work, I must convince them of my worth and learn their names. "I'm Arrah," I answer, "daughter of Oshhe, who is son of Mnekka, the great Aatiri chieftain."

The woman smiles. "Mnekka was my favorite granddaughter."

"And I'm her favorite." At least I hope I am.

The woman nods. "I'm Nyarri."

I wait again.

The other two women seem inclined to make me wait longer.

I itch to say something first, but still my tongue.

My fists clenched against my lap begin to tremble. Please. Please. Please. I need them to concede their names and agree to help me kill Efiya. I can't do it on my own. "Please," I whisper.

"Begging will not work," hisses the woman to Nyarri's right. "You're not a true Aatiri, girl. Mulani blood runs through your veins."

"You do not speak our language well," adds the woman to Nyarri's left, her voice cold. "How dare you call upon us if you do not know our customs?"

I squeeze my fists so hard that my fingernails dig into my flesh. "I have Mulani blood, yes. Yet I'm still of you, too. Am I not worthy of your help because I'm different? Am I not worthy because I didn't grow up in Tribe Aatiri and I don't speak your language? Judge my worth on who I am, not what I'm not. I'm still of your flesh. Answer my call, ancestors, and hear my plea. I need your help."

"Spoken like a true Aatiri." The ancestor on the left nods approvingly. "I'm Ouula."

The ancestor on the right scoffs at me and waves her hand. She acts like I've done some trick to win over the other two. She doesn't wear her hair in the braids that are common among the Aatiri. Her coils are loose about her head and stick up every which way, like my hair when I don't braid it. Even though I look like my mother, I have this ancestor's deep-set eyes.

Since she's already spoken, I ask, "Can you deny that I am of you, ancestor?"

She crosses her arms. She is stubborn like me too.

"If you can deny that I am your blood," I press, "then I will beg your forgiveness."

The woman's frown softens, even if she still looks at me sideways.

"I'm Arra." She sighs and rolls her eyes. "I suppose you are my namesake."

I inhale and blow out a shaky breath. Now that that's over, I can give the ancestors my request. I don't explain all the details, but what I do share leaves them seething. They argue among themselves about how typical it is of a Mulani to be so shortsighted. I hate to cut them off, but I remind them that time is of the essence.

"Carry us inside you to the green-eyed serpent," Nyarri says, "and we'll do the rest."

This has to work. Without help from the *edam* or Koré, it's my best and last chance. "I'm ready." I struggle to my feet and my legs tremble from the burden of what I must do.

Arra clucks her tongue. "Let's go, girl. You're not strong enough to hold us for long."

When I leave the mirror, they walk in my wake, silent and invisible. We reach the salon where Efiya is with Merka and the demon who's taken Nezi's body and name. My sister sits on a pedestal upon a throne inlaid with jewels and gold. It's an exact replica of the throne in the Almighty Palace—of which I've only seen a few times. That means that Efiya must've gone to the Kingdom. My pulse throbs so hard that my eardrums vibrate. My mind immediately falls on my friends, and I don't so much as walk as stumble closer to my sister.

Merka is complaining about something, as usual, but Efiya isn't listening anymore. She rises from her chair—her smile growing bigger each step she takes toward me. She knows. Of course she does.

"Bring us closer," Ouula whispers.

Excitement gleams in Efiya's eyes as I close the space between us. My sister wants this challenge; she expected it. I haven't fooled her with my act. She's too smart for that, too clever to fall into my trap. No one would dare stand against a girl who can pluck demon souls from thin air like plucking apples from a tree. A girl who can step into the space between time to travel great distances. A girl who can turn children into *ndzumbi*. My sister is every scary story my father ever told about evil witchdoctors—only she's so much worse. But I'm not a child anymore, and even if my knees shake beneath her wicked glare, I will not relent.

Efiya glances over my shoulder—her smile growing bigger. "You are full of surprises, sister."

Merka and Nezi remain on the pedestal, looking cross that Efiya isn't paying attention to them anymore. Not seeing the ancestors, they carry on their conversation without her.

"Well?" Efiya arches one eyebrow in anticipation.

I've tried to imagine what my sister would be like had she not been born under such horrible circumstances. Would she be sweet and playful? Would she be bold and headstrong? How different would she be if not for the demon magic and Arti guiding her every move? She'd be a baby to cuddle in my arms, then a little girl to trail behind me in the market. She'd want to go fishing with Rudjek and me, and although I'd complain about it, I wouldn't dream of leaving her behind. The thought of that version of Efiya sends a pang of longing in my belly. Longing for something that will never be. We will never be real sisters. We will never be anything but enemies. Our mother has made sure of that.

"Now, girl," Nyarri hisses in my ear. "Release us."

When the ancestors leave my shadow, Merka and Nezi startle, but Efiya does not. The force of the ancestors' *kas* hits her so hard that it knocks me backward. I crash into a wall, but leap to my feet again, head spinning, chest on fire. They converge upon Efiya like a raging storm, and something inside me aches. A part of me wishes they could rip the demon magic from her soul and leave the girl behind. The girl who could be so much more. Slashes appear across Efiya's throat, arms, and chest as wind hollers in the room like a wild beast. But the cuts heal almost immediately, which forces me out of my useless reverie. My sister is exactly who she is meant to be and that will never change.

Efiya bursts into flames as another ancestor unleashes her magic. The fire burns stark white, and my sister's skin blisters and cracks, then it flakes away in heavy ashes. She doesn't make so much as a sound as the fire consumes her, as she becomes a thing made of flames—a girl-shaped fire. When she retakes human form, she begins to shrivel up, wrinkling like leather left in the sun too long. That doesn't work either. Everything the ancestors throw at Efiya only slows her down for a moment.

I take the knife hidden beneath my sleeve and run at my sister. Merka steps in front of me at the last moment, and my knife plunges into his heart. Blood covers my trembling hand as I wrench the knife from his chest. He stumbles back, and Efiya grabs his shoulder. The wound closes before my eyes. Merka straightens himself up as Nezi steps to Efiya's other side.

It's too late. I can't hold the ancestors' *kas* any longer. They untether from me with a snap that leaves me breathless. Efiya smiles as pain slices through my spine and I drop to my knees. She catches the knife as it falls from my hand. "Give me one reason I shouldn't kill you, dear sister." She presses the blade against my throat. Her eyes gleam with excitement again. This is a game to her, no different from when she made the boy cut off his thumb to give as a gift. "If I like the reason, then I will spare your life. If I don't . . ." She shrugs.

I'm working my mouth to spit in her face when Arti steps to my side, her magic wrapping around me. Our mother's expression is as emotionless as always. Maybe she'll tell Efiya to do it, to finally put an end to me. I don't know why she's let me live this long now that she has the daughter she always wanted. Instead Arti crosses her arms, her eyes hard. "I'll give you the only reason that matters."

Merka and Nezi glare at her, but Efiya only tilts her head to the side to let our mother know that she's listening.

"You can't foresee the consequences of killing her." Arti lets out a sigh—one that's guttural and brimming with frustration. "It could be that nothing will happen, or it could be that you'll ruin everything. Are you willing to take that chance?" Efiya looks at me again, the knife digging a little deeper into my flesh. Her eyes shift out of focus for the briefest moment. Is she looking into the future again? Does she see me? She blinks and lowers the knife.

Arti narrows her eyes at Efiya, her voice just as bitter as when she's scorned me in the past. "Stop this foolish game and focus on the task at hand."

"You would stand against me for her?" Efiya asks, her face screwed up into a frown.

"You tell me, Efiya." Arti squints, her look reproachful. "You can see inside my mind."

Efiya pouts like a spoiled child and stomps back to her throne, Merka and Nezi on her heels. The pain disappears and I gasp. It's not my imagination that Arti's hand is shaking when she clasps my shoulder and tells me to go back to my room. There's relief in her cold eyes, and she keeps her magic wrapped around me like a shield. My mother saved my life.

THIRTY

Grandmother has been on my mind all night. I miss our times together at the Blood Moon Festival, when my only worry was failing at magic. How frivolous that seems now. I've done everything to delay my mother and sister until the *edam* could act. When that didn't work, I tried to sway my sister, then tried to kill her three days ago. There's nothing more I can do on my own. I need help. Grandmother wouldn't abandon me, but I'm resigned to believe that either the *edam* can't or won't come. So I'll go to them.

I plan to escape tonight. If Efiya can kill an orisha and raise a demon army, I'm not sure the *edam* will be able to stand against her. But I can't think about the what-ifs now. There's no other way. I need Grandmother's ironclad strength. And if decades have passed outside Kefu and there's a new generation of *edam*, I will appeal to them.

I lie in bed fully clothed in a tunic and trousers with a sack of provisions tucked under the sheet beside me. I keep still, my muscles wound tight. I've been waiting hours for Efiya to leave, and once she does, I wait a little longer to be sure. I can't stop thinking about the Almighty One's throne in the salon and what it means. Efiya has been to Tamar and not only that, she's been in the Almighty Palace. I tell myself that my friends are okay. She has no reason to go after them, yet Arti's voice rings in my head too. Her horrible decree from the night she summoned Shezmu at the Temple. The awful night that brought Efiya into existence.

You will lose many friends before the end.

A pang twists through me, and no amount of deep breaths calms my nerves.

My mouth parches as I think about my mother. She saved me from Efiya, though she gave no sign that it meant anything to her. Except that she'd squeezed my shoulder after, her hand ice cold and shaking. She'd offered vague comfort in that moment. Does she have a shred of regret for what she's done? I don't know, and I don't have time to consider it. I can't risk her finding out about my plan either.

I'm halfway out of bed when a splitting pain shoots across my forehead, and I collapse against the pillow. Whispers prick at my mind like sharp needles. Even though the air is as hot as a brazier in my room, chills snake down my back. I wrap my arms around my shoulders to ward off the cold and panic. The whispers are different from the demons in the walls, who do nothing but taunt me. This is something new. They buzz like a hive of angry bees who have lost their queen. I cover my ears and grit my teeth, but the sound vibrates in my scalp. Dread courses through my body. What horrible thing has my sister done now?

Soon the whispers fade to the back of my head. Now isn't the time to wonder what this means—I have to leave before Efiya returns.

Without allowing fear to settle in, I slip into my shoes and grab my provisions. My feet slap against the floor as I rush from my room and the darkness drinks the sound of my steps. That shouldn't be possible, but I'm relieved as I descend the stairs to the first level. Familiars flicker in and out of the moonlight beaming in the open windows, but they don't notice me.

I don't want to leave my father at the mercy of Arti and my sister. He's done the things my mother wanted, but after all this time, she doesn't have the decency to let him go. He won't come without her. A knot hardens in my belly at what I must do. There's no other choice. I feel like the most awful daughter in the world for leaving without him. But if I can get to Grandmother, she and the other *edam* can free him. I have to believe that. The alternative is unbearable.

I slip into Terra's room. Ty's too; she moved in after the demon took Nezi. "Wake up." My voice vibrates like a low hum.

Ty wakes first and lights a jar of oil beside her bed. The light makes the space too bright. The room is windowless, I realize, with no moonlight to be had. I shouldn't have been able to see them to start.

"We have to leave," I insist. "We have to go while Efiya is away."

If we are to escape, it has to be now, while she's gone and before Arti figures out what's happening. Terra stares at me instead of moving. Ty crosses her arms.

"Go where?" Terra asks. "She'll find us."

"I know a place." I don't, but there's no time to convince them to come.

Ty shakes her head. She's still loyal to my mother, even after all that Arti's done.

Terra knots her blanket in her hands. "You shouldn't be here, Arrah."

"I'm leaving," I say, stubborn. "You can either take a chance at freedom or stay a slave to Efiya's whims. How long do you think it'll be before she gives your bodies to demons too?"

Ty presses her palm against her heart in a gesture of love, and slumps back on her pillow. Her eyes are glassy, like freedom is some childhood treat that she's outgrown. She's not coming. I blink back tears as I return her gesture. Biting her lip, Terra climbs from her bed and starts to dress. Ty grunts as if to say Terra's a fool, but then, Terra has a family waiting for her. A father whose gambling debt she's more than thrice paid off, and a mother caring for her siblings.

Terra and I say nothing as we sneak out of the villa and cross the darkness that surrounds it. It's infinite and heavy against our skin like molasses. There's a restlessness within it that claws at my mind. But this time the darkness doesn't suffocate me. I don't know how, but I see a clear path through it, a crossroads of sorts. I point out the faded white lines, but Terra doesn't see them. The demons are one shapeless form, but their individual minds whisper to me. I clench my teeth, trying to ignore them.

She will find you.

She will consume you.

You're as good as dead already.

You can't run, little charlatan.

The voices speak of suffering, of desire, of intense hunger. The other voices—the ones from my room, the ones in my head—all spoke at once and I couldn't understand their words. Terra touches my arm. I can't see her in the unyielding darkness, but her worry pulses in her fingertips. None of this makes sense, that I can see these white lines. That I can see the shape of the demons' souls and the impression of their wings. That they had wings was one of many details the orishas kept for themselves.

"Are you okay?" Terra asks.

I'm not okay, but one way or another I will leave Kefu tonight. Outside the gate, nighthawks lay siege to the desert, their screeching frantic. Whatever has the demons flustered, it's done the same to the birds. My stomach sinks when my gaze lands on Arti's back. She stands in our path, her sleeping gown flapping in the stiff breeze. Terra tenses at my side and shrinks behind me. I should've known that my mother would try to stop us—nothing slips her notice.

I stand a little taller, take Terra's hand, and trudge forward. I will no longer cower before my mother. Let her do her worst. If it comes to it, I'll appeal to the side of her that saved my life.

"She's ruining everything," Arti says, her voice so meek that it surprises me. "All my careful planning for this . . . ?" My mother turns around, and I stop cold at the sight of her gaunt, tired face. Her red-rimmed eyes. She lets her words trail off like she expects me to console her.

I won't allow myself to pity Arti. She knew the consequences— she was too obsessed with releasing the Demon King to care. "Heka warned you," I say, shaking with rage, "but you didn't listen either. Now you can't control her." As much as I want to rub it in her face, my satisfaction is bittersweet.

Arti lifts her chin; her lips draw tight. "I can fix this."

"*Can you?*" I yell. "Can you bring back Kofi and the other children? Can you undo all the harm that you and Efiya have caused?"

A flutter of Arti's magic brushes against my forearms as she narrows her eyes. "What are you doing here?" I'm bewildered that it took her this long to ask, but like me, she must sense that Efiya's committed some new gods-awful crime.

I cross my arms. "There's no place for me here."

"You're leaving?" Arti asks, her expression blank.

"I am," I reply. *Don't try to stop me.*

"Perhaps it's for the best." My mother turns her back to me again. "Efiya is unpredictable."

I glare at her, half in shock that that's all she has to say. I almost spit at her feet, but no, it's not worth it. Let her suffer here with Efiya. It's the fate she deserves.

With so much left unsaid, there is no true goodbye between my mother and me. Terra and I continue for Kefu as Arti's last words and blank stare taunt me. Perhaps it *is* for the best.

We walk for what feels like too long, and Kefu is still a glimmer in the distance. The nighthawks begin to circle us, their cries louder with every step we take. Terra keeps cursing at them, but I don't waste my energy. It's the sting of demon magic that worries me. Wherever my sister has gone, she's left some of her army behind to keep watch. I haven't seen any demons in human form outside of Merka and Nezi since the rest marched into the desert. I hadn't expected that some would be following us now—keeping to the shadows.

I clutch the strap across my shoulder so hard that my hand aches. I should've come up with a real plan, but I'm here now and I have no intention of going back. Why don't they attack? Whatever their reason, I don't fear them as much as before. Something has changed, something new has awakened within me. It runs hot in my blood.

"What are we going to do when Efiya comes after us?" Terra asks.

"I don't know yet." It's the most honest answer I can give her.

It's still night when we finally reach Kefu. The port city is quiet and the streets dim. The air is wound tight with tension. Do the residents also feel the restlessness of the demons? I stare at face after face, looking for unnatural green eyes, my heart racing. There's demon magic here too—faint on the breeze. We head for the docks. It's our only way out of this miserable town. Men haul crates of supplies from boats with ropes and pulleys. Fishermen, laborers, merchants of all walks of life move about their business in a slumber.

Three fishermen step in our path. Not fishermen—demons. Their magic crawls up my arms, chilling me to the bone.

"No." Terra shakes her head. "I won't go back!" In a panic, she ducks into an alley.

"Terra, no!" I run after her.

I'm halfway down the alley when I catch up with her and realize we're trapped. Tears stream down Terra's cheeks as two sets of demons close in on us—five on either side. I search for something, anything to fight with, but there's nothing but barrels of garbage that reek of fish guts. Not for the first time, I miss *my* demon magic, but would it work against them? I reach for Terra's hand, and we hold on tight to each other. This is it, then. I can't believe it's going to end like this after everything that's happened.

The air shifts around us, and Koré steps out of the void. I sigh, letting go a pent-up breath. Part of me thought she and the *edam* had given up. She's dressed in a captain's black trousers and a vest with a white blouse underneath. Her long braids are in a ponytail, not writhing about her head for once. She flashes me a wide smile, and it's good to see a friendly face after my mother's cold gaze. "You brought your little friend."

Terra startles at my side and backs against the alley wall.

"It's okay." I hold up my hands to calm her. "Koré's here to help."

Terra frowns, but she doesn't protest.

"Where have you been?" I ask Koré. "Where are the *edam*?"

She regards me with sad eyes. "They'll be here soon enough."

Relief floods my body. Grandmother and the other witchdoctors are coming. They'll finally put an end to my sister's reign of terror.

"Filthy beasts." Koré spits on the ground and makes a show of wiping her mouth. Now that she's here, the demons turn their attention on her. Their green eyes glow brighter, their teeth bared. Her hair begins to wriggle as she stretches her neck to one side, then the other. "This is going to be fun."

She's the reason they didn't attack in the desert. They wanted to get close to her first, to steal their master's *ka*, which must mean that Efiya hasn't found it yet.

Koré flourishes a bow at the demons. "To what do I owe the pleasure?"

They hiss at her, their voices like twisted birdsong. "Give us the box."

"What box?" She shrugs, feigning ignorance.

"Do not toy with us, false god."

"False god?" She grimaces. "You wound me."

"She's coming for you," warns another.

Koré raises an eyebrow, her interest piqued. "You'll be dead before she arrives."

"What are they saying?" Terra whispers as she slips close to me.

"What . . ." I frown, realizing that both Koré and the demons are speaking a language that I shouldn't understand. The language that Arti used in that awful summoning ritual. First the whispers and sudden sharp pain in my room, now this. There's something very wrong. I can feel it. "They're posturing . . . ," I mumble, lost in my thoughts.

The demons draw their swords, but they do not advance. They must be waiting for my sister to arrive. Two phantom daggers appear in Koré's hands. The handles shimmer, the blades glow. A demon eases up behind her. When he gets too close, one of her braids strikes his throat and a bolt of lightning cuts through him. His *ka* escapes his vessel and disappears into the night.

The nine remaining demons charge at Koré. Her daggers soar through the air and cleave two clean through their hearts. I snatch up a fallen sword and step in front of Terra, the blade heavy in my hands. It's nothing like a nimble staff, but I'll make do.

Koré sprints and leaps against buildings. Her body is horizontal to the ground as she propels herself through the air. The demons launch too, their claws, teeth, and swords aimed for her small frame. She crouches midair when her daggers reappear in her hands. She strikes again. Her aim is true. My heart soars with hope that we'll survive this night. That there's still a chance to stop my sister from breaking the world.

Then another sharp pain slices through my head and brings me to my knees. The sword lands with a heavy thud on the ground. Magic whirls around me in a cloud of sparkling dust, settling on my skin before shrinking inside me. The magic is like feather strokes, wingbeats, and fills me with longing. It's the magic of the tribal lands, the magic of Heka. When I open my eyes, everything appears sharper, crisper, like a fog lifted from my mind. I sway as the world tilts around me.

Hurry, whispers a voice in my head. Grandmother's voice.

"Where are you?" I choke back tears. When Grandmother doesn't answer, I turn to Koré. "Where are the *edam*?"

Koré stands in the alley covered in blood with ten broken bodies at her feet. "What's left of them is with you, Arrah."

Her voice is a soft coo, but her words don't make sense.

The blood in my veins turns to ice. "What do you mean *what's left of them*?"

I wrap my arm around my belly, thinking of the last time I saw Grandmother, at the Blood Moon Festival. The endless colorful tents and sparks of magic dancing in the air. The beat of the djembe drums and the witchdoctors' chants. Grandmother's silver locs reaching her waist as she sat cross-legged in front of me. Her gap-toothed smile. *The bones don't lie*, she said. But they hadn't warned her either.

Koré pats me on the shoulder. Her touch slows my heartbeat, quells my stomach. Her magic commands me to be calm, and the more I struggle against it, the deeper it draws me into its embrace.

"Wait at the Almighty Temple until I arrive," Koré says. "There's still a chance to stop your sister."

I nod, but it's only a reflex. "Is my grandmother dead?" I know the answer.

Koré casts a glance behind us. "Mouran, take them."

A tall man—no, not a man, an orisha—steps out of the shadows. His eyes are ice and stand out against his black skin and woolly hair. Mouran, the orisha of the sea, here in the flesh, his barbed tail curled at his feet. He flashes his teeth and moonlight shines off their sharp points.

"Go now!" Koré shouts, and Mouran wraps his magic around Terra and me. He drags us away, but I don't want to go. I need to know what happened to my grandmother. I grit my teeth and the tribal magic thrums inside me. It roots me in the empty space between the alley and the sea, but my mind—my consciousness—stays with Koré.

In the alley, the air shifts as my sister steps out of the void in front of Koré. Efiya wears a white flowing sheath, her black hair in a crown of braids—like when I put my hair up. In this state, I can see her true form. Her eyes are pale emeralds—lacking the intensity of a full-blooded demon. Ribbons of Heka's light thread through her *ka*.

"You have something I want." Efiya breaks into a smile that cuts like shards of glass. "And I haven't the time for your games."

Her voice is a sweet song that breaks me. There's nothing left of the little girl in her.

"I don't think we've met." Koré dips her head. "Hello. I'm the moon orisha, I'm eternal."

Efiya laughs, and Koré crashes to her knees, her whole body shaking under the weight of my sister's magic. For once her braids fall still. "I'm your god now, orisha. Give me what I want."

My sister's magic buzzes in the air as Mouran whispers, "Time to let go."

His magic tugs at my mind, drawing me deeper into the void. The scent of salt water fills my nose. My body is already on the deck of a massive black ship. Slow to follow, my consciousness moves farther from the alley, still watching the scene play out.

"I should warn you." Koré coughs up blood. "I've always been bad at losing."

"Is that so?" Efiya bends down and grabs the Twin King's chin. "I can fix that."

Koré's neck snaps.

EFIYA

I bend time so I can relive the memory. I must know where I went wrong so that I will never fail again. I stand on the edge of the valley overlooking Heka's temple. The edam *waste their time performing rituals for a god who has abandoned them. Fools.*

In the valley, 114 ripe kas *hum in tune with the djembe drums. They are the witchdoctors. The strongest among all the tribes. Their magic vibrates against my skin. Once I consume their* kas, *that magic will belong to me. Sensing my presence, the witchdoctors stop their dance to stare up at me. The drums fall silent and there's nothing left except the hum of magic and the whisper of wind in the grass. They've been waiting for me.*

I take another step in the void and land in front of the chieftains. My grandmother, head of Tribe Aatiri, steps forward. Silver locs snake down her back, and a bone charm rattles around her neck. A fool's artifact. The other chieftains step forward too. These five are the strongest of the edam, *and more powerful than the rest of the witchdoctors. Their magic crackles in my ears like thunder.*

Grandmother is hiding something. They all are. They're using their combined magic to conceal a shared secret . . . a secret that will be mine once I consume their kas. They can't hide their anguish, their fear, or their knowledge that their lives are forfeit. I grow sick of their emotions. I close their windpipes as my demons descend upon the valley to begin their siege. The witchdoctors fight with magic and weapons alike, but they are no match for the demons. Every time one of them dies, I absorb their ka. My body tingles as I grow stronger. It pulses.

Grandmother falls to her knees, along with the other chieftains. They claw at their throats, but she laughs. I search her mind for their shared secret. I see a hundred images, a thousand, a million. Endless flashes into her past, her birth, her childhood, her marriage, her children's births. She's trying to distract me from seeing the truth. I press harder, until her nose bleeds. I see them together now—the chieftains, making a pact. They perform a ritual to bind themselves to another.

I grab the old Aatiri by the chin and lift her face up. I'm out of breath, my body trembling. I need their kas. I crave them. I must have them. I force life back into her body. Fix her crushed throat. I will have my answer.

In my moment of lapse she plunges a dagger into her heart. The knife weeps with a curse, and I don't realize before her ka slips through my fingers. It's icy in my hand, and I'm empty, even with all the other kas I've consumed. I've allowed them to trick me. I must know where their kas have gone. I must take back what belongs to me.

I replay the moment again and again until I see one face—one I know like my own.

The chieftains bound their kas to Arrah.

I move forward through time, past the moment I killed the orisha Koré in the alley. She was nothing more than a nuisance. She had removed her memory of hiding the Demon King's ka; a neat trick, but it made her of no use to me. I step into the courtyard at the villa, into the darkness of the demons who still wait for me to free them.

I've taken only a step or two when Mother bursts through the double doors of the villa and storms into the courtyard. Anger rolls off her in waves. I'm in no mood to deal with her. I need time to myself to look at all the possibilities.

The tears streaking down Mother's face give me pause. I've never seen her cry save for in her memories. She's crying because of what I've done. I didn't need the witchdoctors' kas, but I wanted them anyway.

I've seen this outcome a thousand times, yet I want to step back into the void and disappear. I can't stand the look of disappointment and disgust in her eyes. In this moment she hates me; she despises me; she wishes I was never born. It isn't the first time and it won't be the last. I've never been able to do anything to please her. She always reminds me of what a failure I am for not finding and releasing the Demon King. He's all she cares about, but I'll release him in my own time.

There were always many possibilities of how she'd take this news, from silence to raging anger. In some futures, she'd wept on the ground. In others the news gutted her, leaving her completely incapable of emotions. The worst scenarios were when she attacked me, and I had to kill her. I don't want to kill my mother. She's all that I have now that Arrah has betrayed me.

I didn't foresee this outcome because my sister blocks me from prying into her mind. It's infuriating at times, but not now. My sister wants to play a game of hide-and-seek, the same way we used to play in the gardens. She'll hide. And I'll seek.

THIRTY-ONE

My sobs ball up in my belly, aching for release, but nothing feels quite real anymore. Koré's calming magic deserts me as the alley in Kefu fades away, and I'm left with the numbing truth. She's dead. Grandmother and the other witchdoctors are dead. Efiya killed them too. No magic in the world will bring them back. It must have been desperation that made the chieftains tie their *kas* to mine. They were the strongest witchdoctors in the tribal lands and couldn't defeat my sister.

I've been a fool to think I, a charlatan, could stop my sister. Heka told me to be brave, but what good has that done? In the end, Efiya will destroy everything in her path, just as he foretold. She'll come for me soon enough.

Grandmother and the chieftains' *kas* are with me now, and so is their magic, humming beneath my skin. One of *her* memories crawls to the surface of my mind. She cradles a baby—*me*—in her arms, smiling down with pride in her eyes. My father never told me that she traveled all the way from the Aatiri lands to Tamar for my birth.

I miss you, Grandmother.

She answers with another memory. This one of Imebyé. She sits across from me and offers me her bones. She's given this honor to me alone, for no one else has ever laid hands on them since her grandmother gifted them to her. In her memories, there's an underlying message that she'll always be with me, a small sense of closure. I take solace in that.

Mouran's ship is a massive vessel cut from dark wood with ribbons of black silk trailing in the wind. He stands at the helm with his arms at his sides, and there's no crew to be seen. Fog swivels in the orisha's eyes as his invisible magic buzzes in the air. The ship navigates away from the port and parts the river so fast that wind whips my braids across my face. It's dizzying at first, but the ride is smooth. I hold my hand up, studying the way my fingers glow. So this is what it feels like for magic to belong to you. To know that when you call for more, it will abide without question. It feels nothing like the demon magic that tried to lure me into a false sense of peace.

Now I understand why the holy scripts say that the orishas wanted to keep magic out of the hands of mortal kind. Magic isn't good or bad. It's people who make it dangerous. We've done nothing but use it to destroy each other. My mother let herself become a pawn. And for what . . . to exact revenge against the Vizier? She played right into the Demon King's hands. Maybe he saved her life once, but he did it for his own selfish reasons.

With Mouran's magic, the ship traverses the Serpent River in a matter of moments. The fog in his eyes clears as we arrive at the harbor in Tamar. Terra wraps an arm around her waist and peers across the docks to the East Market in the distance. She isn't coming back to the city. Mouran will take her to find her family.

She leans her shoulder against mine—and I do the same. "Be careful, Arrah."

I smile weakly, sad to part ways but happy that she can finally go home. "You too."

Once we've said our goodbyes, I rush through the busy docks and the mud-brick houses in a daze. Grim faces, none of whom I recognize, stare at me as I stumble into the market. I search for signs of how much time has passed. Everyone and everything looks rundown. I don't know any of the merchants or the patrons perusing their wares. The night chill rips across my shoulders and makes me shiver as I keep moving.

More so than anywhere else in Tamar, the East Market never closes and never slows. Its patrons never sleep. People are still about doing business that calls to them in the twilight. But in these early hours between night and morn, there's no laughter, no boasting. No people betting on cockfights or standing around playing jackals and hounds. No roasting chestnuts in firepits or plantains fried in peanut oil to mask the decay that clings to the air.

A tremble creeps down my spine as I think about how my mother set this decay in motion. It started within her and spread like a blight across the land. There's been much recent death here. With the new magic inside me, it tastes bitter on my tongue. Have I come all this way for nothing? No one will be able to stop my sister. She's too strong.

The Vizier's estate stands out against the night, looming atop its precipice at the south edge of the city. I remember the last time I watched Rudjek compete in his father's arena. His broad shoulders glistening with sweat. His confident stance against an opponent twice his size. I miss him so much that my heart aches. I can't imagine that he might be older—*a grown man*. I can't allow myself to stop believing that there's still a chance . . . that my friend will be waiting for me.

I'm nervous about seeing him after all this time. It *feels* like years. In truth it could be only a few weeks, or two decades. He could be Vizier now. He could have married and started a family of his own. Knots twist in my stomach. I don't like that thought at all—Rudjek with a wife. Outside of my father, he's all I have left. I need to lose myself in his obsidian eyes, if they can make me forget for even the briefest moment.

As I reach the Vizier's estate, sunlight stretches across the sky, pushing the last of night away. A chill creeps up my spine when I don't recognize the guards, or the porter leaning against his station. I'm exhausted and dirty but force myself to stand tall. I can't think the worst—not yet. There could be any number of reasons the Vizier replaced his staff. Maybe he found out that Arti had spies in his household. "Good morning." I clear my throat. "I'm sorry to bother you, but—"

"This isn't a charity house." One of the guards frowns. "Go beg somewhere else."

I bite back my annoyance that he should assume me a beggar, even if I look the part. The regular porter knows me. He wouldn't be so rude and I'm in no mood for this foolishness. "I'm a friend of Rudjek. Apologies for calling at this early hour, but it's an important matter."

The two guards flash each other a look that I don't very much like.

The porter steps closer and grips the gate. "If you were a friend, you'd know that he left for the North months ago to meet his betrothed."

My breath catches in my throat. *"His betrothed?"*

The words crash against my ears. They dig into my flesh. They punch me in my gut.

His betrothed.

How long was I gone? I was a fool to think Rudjek would wait for me, especially after I never sent him a message. He would have come to Kefu, if he'd known, if I'd sent the *damn* letter. He would've come like he promised. I swallow hard and square my shoulders to show them that I don't care, but my head feels airy. I need to sit down. The energy that kept me going all night flees, and exhaustion settles in my bones.

"Oh, are you sad?" The porter spits on the ground. "Did you think someone of your low status would have a chance with the Vizier's son?"

My best friend is gone—Rudjek's gone to be with another girl.

The guards laugh and hot anger fills my chest. I have the urge to snap both of their necks. Now that I have magic, *real* magic, I could wipe the smile from their faces without so much as lifting a finger. The temptation is so strong that it pulses in my every pore. They must see murder in my eyes because they stiffen, their hands slipping to the shotels at their sides. I stumble back and almost lose my balance. Even with their taunts, my own reaction confuses me. They've torn my heart in two and I want to break them. *I'm not like her. I'm not my mother.*

I peer into the courtyard behind the gates once more, remembering our last day together. He wielded his shotels with cool efficiency against the men who attacked us near the sacred tree. Then he tried to fend off a dozen elite gendars to get to me. Now he's traveling to the edge of the world, to a land of ice and snow, for another girl.

I remember the times we sat in our secret spot by the Serpent River, fishing rods in hand. His wide smile, him stealing glances at me when he thought I wasn't paying attention. I stole glances too and inhaled his sweet scent. How can I face the Vizier to tell him about my sister? How can I meet his dark eyes without dissolving into sobs? He wouldn't believe me anyway. To hell with him too. He's as bad as my mother.

I'm numb inside as I wander through the streets of Tamar in a daze on my way to the Kelu estate—Majka's family home. If anyone knows Rudjek's mind, it's him. I want him to tell me that Rudjek searched for me. That he didn't give up easily, that he tried to find me like he promised.

Majka stands with his arms crossed in the courtyard and my heart leaps. Near him, Kira sits on a bench with Essnai curled against her side. The two speak in hushed whispers. Sukar paces back and forth, cursing under his breath. They look as grim as the patrons in the market—but they also haven't aged. Then that means Rudjek . . . *that he didn't wait for me.*

Majka catches sight of me first. "Arrah?"

Essnai bolts upright. Both she and Sukar sprint across the courtyard and open the gate. Kira follows close behind them.

My quiet, brooding, beautiful friend Essnai smiles through her tears. "Is it really you?"

I nod, too choked up to speak.

Sukar scratches his shaved head. "Not bad for a ghost."

I press my hand to my heart in the Zu greeting, pushing back tears of my own.

"You know what happened?" asks Sukar, sucking in a deep breath.

"Are they . . ." I struggle to get the question out. "Are they all really gone?"

"Everyone in Tamar with a drop of magic felt their deaths," Essnai answers for him.

The three of us huddle together in a circle—Essnai, Sukar, and me—our arms draped across each other's shoulders. Sukar's tattoos pulse with soft light. We stay that way for a long time, and neither Majka nor Kira interrupts our silence. As the eighth morning bells toll, Essnai recites an Aatiri burial rite and Sukar chants a Zu farewell. I'm the first to pull away, thinking about Koré's final words to me.

"We need to go to the Temple," I say. "I'll explain on the way."

Essnai looks from Sukar to me. "You have magic now?"

I wince, aching for the tribal people, aching for Rudjek. "It's a long story. I'll tell you later."

"Then you're the last one." Sukar gawks at me in shock.

"The last what?" My heart pounds against my chest.

Sukar's protection tattoos shimmer in the morning sunlight. They've been glowing this whole time. I've only seen them like that in the tribal lands around a lot of magic. "The last witchdoctor."

I rub my throbbing head. Everything is such a complete mess. In both Grandmother's and *my* own memories, I see her reading the bones. At every Blood Moon Festival before the last, the bones always landed in the same way. Now I understand the grim truth: in her vision she saw me standing in the valley outside Heka's Temple alone. She didn't know exactly what it meant, but she knew that a great tragedy would befall us all.

"Did you hear from Rudjek?" asks Majka, cutting through the noise in my head. I notice for the first time that neither he nor Kira are in their red gendar uniforms.

"I guess the Vizier got what he wanted." I shrug to pretend that I don't care, when it's eating me alive. "I heard he's betrothed to a Northern girl now."

"Twenty-gods," Majka curses. "They're still spreading that lie?"

I frown. "What do you mean, lie?"

"Rudjek went looking for you." Majka shifts on his heels. "He wouldn't let us come."

"What?" I whisper. "How long ago?"

"Right after you left," Kira adds, breaking her silence. "Three months ago."

"I didn't see which way your ship headed." Majka grimaces, his expression riddled with dread. "There were too many ships and the fog, but Tam told Rudjek that he'd overheard the *Ka*-Priestess say at the Temple that your family would go to the Aloo Valley." Majka rocks on his heels and glances away. "Rudjek went to look for you . . . and no one's heard from him since. The Vizier sent shotani and gendars, but they weren't able to find him."

His words ring in my ears. Rudjek would have to go through the

Aloo Valley to get to the Dark Forest. *He will die in the Dark Forest.*
Arti warned me on the ship to Kefu. I didn't believe her. Rudjek had
no reason to be there. Except he had. He'd been searching for me.

That weasel Tam—it's his fault. He lied to Rudjek. I lean against
the gate, my legs weak. This can't be real. None of this. It's all a
nightmare. My mother, Efiya, Rudjek, the tribes. So much destruction. He's dead, then. Like she said.

Now Essnai and Sukar stare at me like I'm some kind of savior,
when all I am and will ever be is a charlatan.

THIRTY-TWO

In the heart of day, Tamar's wounds are visible beneath a bruised sky of violet and gray clouds. Trash litters the streets and orisha statues lie smashed to pieces in the usually pristine West Market. Essnai, Sukar, and I walk through row after row of boarded-up shops. The place is all but abandoned, and there's more windswept garbage than people on the streets. Chains bar the mammoth doors to the coliseum where Arti butted heads with the Vizier for years.

I pause in front of my father's shop. It's much the same, except for a few scratches to the yellow paint on the door. Thanks to the protection spell that Oshhe cast years ago, no one can enter the shop without one of us present. I want to go inside and curl up on the pillows in the back and cry myself to sleep. I could pretend that these last few months have all been a dream. I'd wake to the smell of mint tea and milk candy, the sound of my father telling another story.

"We should keep moving," urges Sukar. "The West Market isn't safe these days."

Thieves have kicked in some of the shops' doors and stolen the wares inside. Although it's never been my favorite of the two markets, I can hardly believe what's become of it.

I step around a broken cart left in the middle of the street. "Where is the City Guard?"

Sukar watches everyone we pass and they do the same to us. "Most fled after the deaths."

I stop cold. "More children?"

"Children, adults," he answers, his shoulders tense. "People from every age and status."

"Whole families," adds Essnai, shaking.

I bite the inside of my cheek hard enough to draw blood. Tamar has become a city of death and despair. Soon my sister will lay siege to it with the full weight of her army, but not yet; no, that wouldn't be any fun. She wants to toy with them first. This is another one of her games.

The witchdoctors' whispers seep into the edges of my mind, faint this time. When they all speak at once, it's hard to understand them, but a sense of urgency pulses through me.

"Heka cursed Tamar," Sukar says, his usual playfulness gone, "as punishment for what the new Almighty One did to my uncle and the other seers."

He peers west toward the royal palace, a shining beacon above the decaying city. There's darkness in my friend's eyes that wasn't there before—a coldness. "The new Almighty One?"

"Tyrek." Essnai clasps her staff so hard that her hand trembles. She spits on the cobbles and lets out a slew of Aatiri curses. Sukar has his sickles too. As a Temple attendant, he never used to carry them in the open while in the Kingdom. I didn't notice earlier that they both had weapons.

Tyrek was a prince, but not the Crown Prince. I last saw him at the coliseum in the skybox with his father and his brother. He'd been watching the political games play out between the Vizier and Arti with keen interest. He wasn't destined to become king, but now his fortune has changed. This must be another one of Arti's schemes since Efiya hasn't found the Demon King's *ka*. But to what end? I can't ignore the sinking feeling in my chest.

"He became the new heir after Crown Prince Darnek died in an *accident*," Sukar explains.

A hunting accident, Sukar and Essnai tell me. Tyrek claimed that their guards ignored his brother's cries for help. Upon hearing this story, the Almighty One ordered the guards be put to death. Not one full moon later, an attendant found the Almighty One murdered in his bathhouse. Tyrek accused his mother and the seers of conspiring to take his crown. He imprisoned his mother and had the seers executed. Now a sixteen-year-old boy runs the Kingdom.

Sukar hides his pain behind a hard face, but anguish shines in his soft brown eyes. My heart breaks too. His uncle is dead. Barasa had always been kind to me, and he and Sukar were close. "His *ka* is at peace, my friend." I recite a tribal blessing, knowing that no words will be enough. "May he join with the mother and father, may he become one with the kingdom of souls."

Sukar nods, glancing away.

"That little runt Tyrek has a price on his head," Essnai bemoans, as if she's so much older than him. "He moved gendars to the palace grounds for protection and sent the rest on some secret mission.

Rumor is he tasked the shotani with infiltrating rival nations. He says that he will unite the world under one god."

"He calls this god *Efiya*," Sukar spits out my sister's name. "No one has ever heard of her. Some believe that she is the Unnamed orisha come back to reclaim her name and glory."

My sister raised a demon army, destroyed the tribes, and left Tamar in ruins in three months? All those times she slipped into the void, I thought she was searching for the Demon King's *ka*. And she was—along with killing orishas and seeding chaos in Tamar too.

Efiya will leave nothing of the world when she's done.

My stomach sinks as I recall the serpents coiled around the Unnamed's arms. The thought that my sister could be *her* would be preposterous had I not seen Efiya's powers. The Unnamed's anonymity isn't by accident, I realize, now that I know the truth about the demons.

But as I see my friends' grief, guilt wrenches my thoughts back to the here and now. They want answers, and I'm the only one who can give them. Now it's my turn to speak the truth, and I find it difficult to get the words out. I can't bear my friends' shock as I tell them who Efiya is—that she is my sister. A demon, not an orisha. I expect a weight to lift from my chest, but the terrible news about the tribes and the Kingdom gnaws at my bones.

Essnai and Sukar stop in their tracks—both speechless as a pair of robed scholars skirt around us. Unable to hold their intense stares, I look away. Shame settles in my limbs.

"She's your sister?" Essnai hisses, her face twisted in disgust.

I duck my head, heat creeping up my neck.

Sukar laughs. "Talk about plot twist."

Usually Essnai or I would scorn him for his ill-timed jokes, but right now, it's good to see my friend's sense of humor back. As we continue toward the Temple, they ask me endless questions and I answer what I can. We pass a shadowed alley, and the hairs on the back of my neck prickle. The magic warms in my veins. Sukar's tattoos shift like puzzle pieces sliding into a new configuration. A spiked circle covers most of his forehead; more complex Zu symbols settle on his cheeks.

Catching me staring, he shrugs. "A gift from my uncle before his death."

We turn our attention to the mouth of the alley, but I already know what's in there. The sting of demon magic taints the air. Sukar draws his sickles, and Essnai readies her staff. This time we won't be fighting tribal boys with the barest grasp on their magic; we'll be fighting demons. The chieftains' magic gives me confidence, but I'm no fool to rely on that alone, or let it lull me into false security. Yet, I would be lying if I said I wasn't glad to have it.

When we stalk into the alley, I startle. It's the old scholar woman who came to my father's shop to extend her life. She squats over a man slumped against a wall and pries his lips apart. Her mouth opens like a gaping hole—like my father's the night Shezmu consumed the children's *kas*. I can't move. I can't breathe. She sucks the man's *ka* out of his jerking body. His soul is a gray mist that seeps from his lips. Essnai curses under her breath and Sukar clucks his tongue. The demon swings her head around and smiles.

"What a fortunate day," she says, her voice as slick as ice.

She wipes her mouth as she rises from the ground, her moves slow and deliberate. There's nothing left of the scholar in the demon's eyes, only greed and insatiable hunger. With the powerful witchdoctors' *kas* inside me, I have more magic than I could've ever imagined. Magic to see across time, to call firestorms, to travel the spirit world, to manipulate *kas*, to heal. So many gifts that my mind spins as I search for one to strike down the demon. Before I can decide, a curved blade pierces the center of her chest. Someone steps out of the shadows behind the demon, shoving the sword farther through her heart. The demon stares at us, slack-jawed, as the blade shimmers with her blood.

"*One more demon on my sword*," Tam sings. "*Another one dead and I'm so bored.*"

Tam rips the sword from the demon's back, and she crumples to the ground. Without thinking, I rush across the space between us and shove him hard in the chest. "You told Rudjek I went to the Aloo Valley!" I scream. "You bastard."

Tam squints like he doesn't recognize me at first. I poke my tongue against the hollow place where the missing tooth should be, feeling a flush of heat creep up my neck. "I was at the Temple the day of the fire." He frowns. "When it was clear the Vizier was going to exile your mother, I heard the *Ka*-Priestess say she'd go to the Aloo Valley."

I push back my tears. I don't know if it's true, but I can't put it past my mother. She must've known the news would make it to Rudjek's ears one way or another. "Either she was lying," I spit. "Or you're lying now."

"I'm sorry." Tam shakes blood from his sword, but he doesn't sound sorry.

"As much as it pains me to admit it, he's been helpful." Sukar wrinkles his nose. "He warned us that it was demons stalking the city and killing people before anyone else had a clue."

"And how would you know?" I say, itching to let my new magic burn Tam.

Tam cocks his head. "You said it yourself, that day in the Temple when you asked about the green-eyed serpent. I told you that was what the orishas called demons."

Magic stirs around the dead scholar woman at our feet—it lifts from her skin in wafts of smoke. The sight of my father's magic guts me—and I stumble back. With her death, the woman turns wrinkled and old as the magic leaves to rejoin the sky. "If demons are this easy to kill, then why did the orishas have such a hard time stopping them before?"

"They're in a weakened state right now." Tam sheaths his shotel. "Ask again once one has consumed a hundred or a thousand souls."

"Why are you here, Tam?" Essnai demands, her tongue sharp.

"Same as you." He grins. "I stumbled upon this little grub fest and meant to stop it."

I storm out of the alley, unable to stomach Tam any longer. Rudjek was his friend, but he doesn't even care that he sent him to the Aloo Valley to die. He's too damn selfish and happy playing hero on the city streets, basking in his moment of glory.

"What happened to *her*?" I hear him ask Sukar before I'm out of earshot. "A bit rough around the edges now, eh?"

Essnai catches up with me. "I would've broken his legs."

"I should've done worse," I say, still seething.

Sukar slips up beside me as we pass the first *Ka*-Priest's tomb. A stump with jagged splinters is all that's left of the sacred Gaer tree where I first saw an inkling of the future. Where I saw Efiya's serpent eyes. Where I made my first kills.

The path to the Temple is overgrown with weeds and littered with offerings to the orishas. Withered flowers and fruit picked clean by birds, clay dolls carved in the orishas' likeness. Re'Mec with his ram horns, Koré with her writhing hair, Kiva with his lopsided eyes. Two-headed Fram. How could they do nothing? They've failed Tamar and the Kingdom much the same as Heka failed the tribal people. What's the point of gods if they turn their backs when we need them the most? But I'm not being fair: they haven't all turned their backs. Koré helped me break Arti's curse, and she sacrificed herself to save me—a charlatan.

Halfway up to the Temple, I stop to catch my breath, my gut twisting. We've climbed high enough that we have a view of the entire city. Tamar lies in waste. Whole neighborhoods flattened to rubble. Others scarred by fire. Essnai and Sukar tell me that the new Almighty One purged any citizens loyal to the Temple. Had I seen this in a vision, I would've dismissed it as a dream.

Still staring at the city, I say, "I need to tell you something." Again I can't meet my friends' eyes as I speak. They rustle at my side, both waiting for me to work up my courage. "When the witchdoctors died, the chieftains bound their *kas* to mine . . . they are with me now."

"Twenty-gods, Arrah," gasps Essnai. "That explains your magic."

"Well, twenty-one-gods, if you count Efiya," Sukar muses.

"Not the time, Sukar," Essnai warns.

Despite myself, I crack the tiniest smile. I've missed them so much. There were times in Kefu when I didn't know if I would ever see my friends again.

We arrive at the Almighty Temple—where it all started. Where Arti performed her egregious act of desecration. There's no one here now, not a soul in sight. No shotani lurking in the shadows. "The Vizier had guards up here until the Almighty One relieved him of his position," Sukar says.

I grit my teeth upon hearing his title and feel a little satisfaction in knowing that he's fallen too. "There's something here." A flutter of magic that's so faint I almost miss it hums in the air.

"We've been up here a dozen times." Sukar shakes his head. "There's not much left. The seers destroyed their records before Tyrek had them arrested."

The Temple looks much the same as before it burned. A half-moon ingress connects the five buildings again. The orishas have returned to their shadowy home beneath a new Hall of Orishas. But the parts still under construction stand out in sharp contrast against the old stone.

The last time I saw Rudjek, we were here. I'd stood by while he fought off gendars—I'd stood by and done nothing while the Vizier banished my family. Yes, Arti deserved it. She deserved worse. But the Vizier banished me out of spite. He did it to keep Rudjek and me apart.

"Call to him." Sukar snaps me out of my daze.

"What?"

"You have the *kas* of the five chieftains inside you." Sukar points at my chest. "They each possessed great power—with that, you should be able to see across time and space to find Rudjek." His voice drops. "Or at the very least you'll see what happened to him."

"After she's rested." Essnai takes hold of my arm and leads me across the courtyard. Sukar trails behind and I don't argue because I'm bone-tired. At first I mistake Essnai to mean that I need to sit down, but she walks me to Sukar's room in the attendants' barracks.

"Sleep," Essnai issues a gentle command before she and Sukar leave me alone.

I lean against the door and blow out a shaky breath. There are Zu masks of people and animals, and some in combinations of the two, painted in bold colors on the walls. His room is simple with a bed, desk, basin, and dresser. It smells of ink and sweet perfume.

Where are you, Rudjek? I need you. I miss you.

Sensing my want, the magic rises to the surface. I could calm it, but I don't. I don't want to sleep. I want my best friend back, and now I have magic to answer my call and do my bidding. I command it to take me to Rudjek, and as sparks of magic light on me, the sound of water sloshing around the bow of a boat fills my ears. Suns and moons travel in a reverse course in my mind, and my *ka* leaves my body like it's a discarded husk. This time I don't feel pain at the separation. I'm moving so fast that I can't make sense of the blur of images flashing before my eyes. But a force pushes against me, shoving me back, trying to keep me from reaching my destination.

I won't let it stop me. I push harder. I break through an invisible barrier and my *ka* lands in a clearing in the heart of the Dark Forest. Rudjek stands face-to-face with a thing of nightmares. The creature has tree-bark skin, a horned nose, and claws. Long, curved, razor-sharp claws. Claws soaked in blood. *No, no, no.* My mind reels and

I stretch myself to descend closer, but the craven's anti-magic keeps me at bay—anti-magic, and the fabric of time. This moment is in the past.

Rudjek's shotels slip from his hands in a silent thud as he drops to his knees.

I scream in my *ka* and the trees in the forest tremble, and I scream in the room and Sukar's masks crack in two. *Rudjek, oh gods, no.*

I blink, and he's lying in a pool of blood. The craven crouches over him, its black eyes examining Rudjek like he's some curious thing. It dangles his family crest on one of its claws.

"Here lies Rudjek Omari." He coughs up blood. "The one to put an end to the Omari legacy."

My foolish, foolish Rudjek. Only he would make jokes on the edge of death.

He falls still.

I lash out at the craven, but even with all this power, I can't reach the past. A veil separates me from it. I push my *ka* so hard that my tether starts to tear from my body and pierce the veil—pierce time itself. I don't care what will happen if it breaks. I'll lose myself in the spirit world forever, or I'll die, but not before I rip out the craven's throat.

I'm almost free when a dozen cravens step into the clearing. They peer up to where I'm floating above the tree line, and their anti-magic sends me back to the present. I land inside my body so hard that my back slams against the door. Chest burning, I lie on the cold floor, weeping for my friend.

PART IV

For her story begins at the end,
Full of pain and sweet revenge.
For she shall not rest in this life,
For she must suffer for her sins.
—Song of the Unnamed

RE'MEC, ORISHA OF SUN, TWIN KING

I want to tell you a story about a Tamaran man who walked into a forest and died.

No, this story isn't about you. Yes, you're dying and yes, you're in the Dark Forest, but this is about another man. Are you always this insufferable, Rudjek?

Where was I? Yes. The man lived in a time when a single king thought himself the lord of all the lands. He sent his army into places that did not belong to him and took things that were not meant for him. When he finished warring with the people of the North, he turned to the tribes. But the tribes were clever. They offered him magic and he took them into his council.

The king had riches beyond his wildest dreams, but he still wanted more. He heard of the fertile lands beyond the southernmost valley bordering his kingdom. The witchdoctors warned him that an orisha protected that land. The fool did not listen, of course. Fools never do.

Who am I? I'm Re'Mec. The cravens are my wards.

You noticed! Yes, I'm Tam too. It's short for Tamar, which is another of my names.

The cravens gave you that nasty wound, but they had good reason. You'll see.

On with the story.

The king commanded his cousin, Oshin Omari, to take the land by force. Oshin and his army arrived in the valley at sunset. His men retired for the night to rest before battle. Half kept watch while the others slept. When the second shift woke to relieve their comrades, they found their heads on stakes. No one had heard a thing. Not even a whisper.

Oshin, having had too much to drink and too little sleep, decided to charge into the forest on his own. By now you already know he's a fool, so that shouldn't come as a surprise.

Yes, I know he's your ancestor. Why do you think I'm telling you this story? I know who you are, Rudjek Omari. Better than you know yourself.

Here's the version of the story that you've accepted as true. Though if you take half a mind to think about it, you'd know it couldn't be.

Oshin Omari marched into the Dark Forest alone to find the cravens unawares. Like the honorable warrior he claimed to be, he made his presence known. The cravens wanted to tear away his flesh with their teeth and claws, but their elder was so impressed by his courage that she challenged him to a fight to the death.

As the story goes, Oshin Omari bested the elder with his shotels.

Seeing that a mere human had beaten the strongest of them, the cravens conceded to his prowess. They vowed never to attack the

Kingdom so long as the army stayed away from the Dark Forest. Oshin agreed to these terms.

This next part is debatable. Some claim he made it up to win his cousin's favor.

When Oshin left the forest, he took the elder's body as a souvenir. He used her bones to make trinkets that his family passed down from generation to generation. The bones protect their wearers from the influence of magic.

Most of that story isn't true. Except the part about the bones.

Cravens are anti-magic. I made them that way.

Do you want the truth, Rudjek? Not the story?

I promise you the truth is much more interesting than the lie.

THIRTY-THREE

Between sobs, I tell Essnai and Sukar what I saw in the vision of Rudjek. The room trembles, more masks falling and cracking as the magic responds to my anguish. Essnai forces me to drink red bush tea spiced with snakeweed to calm me. It's effective, but my father would have steeped a matay leaf in the tea so sleep would come faster. Thinking of him makes me that much more miserable. My mind drifts in and out of sleep the whole day and half the night. I dream of Rudjek stretched out on a blanket by the Serpent River. Him palming his shotels with a foolish grin. Me in a panic, searching for him in the East Market. Him lying still in a clearing in a forest of forever night, a pool of blood spreading from his wounds.

"Let me go," Rudjek's deep timbre echoes in my dream.

"Arrah," another voice purrs, one that is warm air on a perfect day and wraps around me.

The chieftains' memories tangle in my head, too. They tell me their stories.

The Litho chieftain, a man of many vices and an affinity for taking lives.

The Mulani chieftain, Arti's cousin, who served her people faithfully.

The Zu chieftain, the greatest scrivener of his people, lover of men and wine.

The Kes chieftain, a man who lived most of his life traveling the spirit world.

The Aatiri chieftain—Grandmother—who loved deeply and led with an iron fist.

They're a part of me. Their memories, their hopes and dreams. Their secrets, truths, and lies twist in my head until they ring in my ears as loud as morning bells. I bolt upright in bed, their voices teeming on the edge of my mind. I'm drowsy from the tea, but it hasn't dulled the pain—nothing will do that. Rudjek is gone, and there's a hole in my heart that throbs like a toothache. Some part of me would be content to stay in this room while the rest of the world burns, but no, I can't do that. I couldn't live with myself. With the chieftains' magic, I have a chance to do something useful for once. There has to be a reason that Koré sent me to the Temple. It must have something to do with the low hum of magic in the courtyard.

I climb out of Sukar's bed and go to the basin to splash water on my face, but it's empty. I avoid the mirror—afraid of what I'll see. Sukar and Essnai have lit the torches down the hallway outside the room. I pad down the long ingress, and peek into the communal barracks. Favorite attendants like Sukar got their own rooms, but most of them shared quarters. My friends aren't there. I try to reach out with my mind, but I'm too tired and the magic fizzles.

Sukar pokes his head from the kitchen down the hallway. "I thought that was you."

He leans against the doorway. His tattoos have rearranged themselves back into their original position. Raised tiger claws settle on his cheeks and bars stretch across his forehead again. "It was getting late, so we didn't want to wake you." He pushes away from the wall. "You okay?"

I shrug because it's better than a lie. I catch the scent of something burning in the kitchen. "What is that awful smell?"

"Whole bird stew," calls Essnai. "My mother's special recipe."

Sukar pitches his voice low, "It tastes worse than it smells."

"I heard that," shouts Essnai.

"It's time, Arrah," Grandmother whispers in my mind. "Go."

I don't question her. My legs move before I can process what I'm doing.

"Hey, where are you going?" Sukar runs to catch up with me. "It isn't that bad."

I don't stop until I'm standing in the middle of the courtyard and the night breeze cuts through me. Save for the moonlight, shifting shadows shroud most of the courtyard. "Someone is coming."

Essnai catches up too, and they both look toward the gate. A ripple of magic sparks from my skin, reaching out, searching. It latches on to something. Sukar startles at my side and pulls out his sickles in one breath. His tattoos burn so bright that I cover my eyes. I groan as a gust of wind hits me so hard that I almost lose my footing. We all do. I don't have time to wonder what's happened as the light from Sukar's tattoos fades and the magic settles inside me.

Someone lies curled on the ground not ten paces from us, in a

tattered, bloodstained elara. Not someone. I half run, half stumble.
The whispers reach a fever pitch and drown out my screams. I collapse at Rudjek's side. Tears blur my vision and choke in my throat.
There's so much blood. Too much blood, and dirt like he's been
dug up from a grave. My magic reaches out to feel for his *ka*, but it
rebounds and dissipates in the air. I push thoughts of healing toward
him, but that magic flickers away too. The Litho chieftain within
me has an intimate knowledge of death and he's brought many back
from the brink. But no matter how hard I push, the magic bounces
off Rudjek's broken body.

Gods, no. How could he come to be here after the gruesome
scene in the Dark Forest, and be too far gone to save? There has to
be a way. It can't be too late.

"Arrah." Essnai squats beside me. "He's ascended."

"No, no, no," I whisper. "He's going to be all right."

Both Sukar and Essnai pull me away, and I don't have the
strength to fight them. He's dead and the cursed cravens sent his
corpse to taunt me. There can be no other answer.

Silence stretches the moment out, dragging my anguish with it,
but then he moves.

"Twenty-gods." Rudjek coughs. "Am I dreaming again?"

Something inside me collapses, and I reach for him.

"Am I?" I ask through tears. "Are you real?"

Rudjek rolls on his side, his obsidian eyes tired and bewitched.
"You're a hard girl to find."

The words vibrate in his chest—a chest cut from stone and
warmer than a thousand suns. Bits of his smooth brown skin show
through his shredded elara. I run my fingers across his tattered

clothes to make sure he's not an apparition—to make sure he's real. My skin tingles with the first inkling of heat. The way it always does when we touch. There's no wound on his belly, unlike in my vision when the craven almost cut him in two. So much blood, and no sign of where it came from. I don't care. He's alive and he's here with me. Sukar clears his throat from behind us, and I jerk my hands away.

"How did you get here?" I ask as he sits up. "How did you know to come?"

"Re'Mec sent me back," Rudjek answers as Sukar and I help him to his feet.

Sukar crosses his arms. "How did you get mixed up with an orisha?"

"Long story," Rudjek says, taking in the empty Temple grounds.

He kept his promise. He looked for me.

I search him thrice over for injuries, while he stares down at me like I'm some spirit conjured from thin air. His gaze is of longing and pain and regret. Except for the fact that he smells atrocious, he's okay. He's more than okay. He's alive.

"I saw you . . . die in the Dark Forest." The scene of Rudjek lying in the clearing replays in my mind.

"I did die in the Dark Forest."

"Another long story?" Essnai sighs.

He inhales a ragged breath. "Even longer."

As Rudjek searches my face a wave of heat burns up my neck. I have no doubt that like Tam, he sees what the rituals took from me. His eyes beg for an answer to a question he doesn't ask. "Re'Mec told me everything." He doesn't elaborate. He doesn't have to. The silence between us is deafening.

"Good—we've all finally arrived," comes a voice like crumpled scrolls.

We turn and Sukar stutters, "Uncle?"

Barasa stands in the courtyard, his yellow kaftan tattered and dirty. "Who else would trap his *ka* in this gods-awful place?"

Sukar laughs—tears swimming in his eyes. "Only a fool."

The seer appears to be flesh and blood, but as I stare at him, he becomes mist shaped into a man. The way Arti had been in my vision before she took form. It was his magic humming on the wind when we first reached the Temple. The magic of a dead man.

"A fool who needs to deliver a message." Barasa waves for us to follow him. "The wind tells secrets."

Sukar and Essnai do so without question. Rudjek raises an eyebrow at me, and I shrug. We're so close that our fingers brush against each other as we follow too. We rush into the vestibule and pour into the Hall of Orishas. Thinking of what Sukar said earlier, I try to imagine Efiya in the Unnamed's place. *Could* my sister somehow be her? The magic inside me reaches out to the statue, seeking answers, but Barasa breaks my focus.

"There isn't much time," he explains. "I must deliver the message that binds my *ka* to this place before the magic fails." His voice falters, then he frowns. "I am aware of recent events . . . of the *tragedy* that has befallen our people."

I glance down to hide from the pain in his eyes—pain that's like a rancid wound growing worse. "Does Efiya know that I'm here?" My question echoes in the hall, and we all seem to hold our breath.

Barasa nods, his face pinched. "Yes, but she's too busy killing orishas to care at the moment."

I grit my teeth, remembering how Koré fell at my sister's feet. "How many?"

"Along with the Twin King . . . Ugeniou, the harvester, and Fayouma, the mother of beast and fowl," Barasa says.

I lean against an orisha statue, not even seeing which one as I absorb this new information. "Eleven left if we count the Unnamed."

Barasa snaps his fingers and the torches along the walls flare to life. "The Temple is safe for now." He shuffles across the floor, half floating, half walking. His pale yellow kaftan rustles in his wake. "It's warded against demon magic."

"Why didn't you appear before now?" Sukar crosses his arms and glares at his uncle. "I've been up here more times than I can count and you never showed yourself to me. I'm your *nephew*. I performed your burial rite, for Heka's sake."

"Always so fussy! Pipe down, boy." Barasa pats Sukar on the shoulder. "Don't you think I would have shown myself if I could? The orishas had a hand in the magic binding my *ka* to the Temple, and they wouldn't let me appear until both of *them* were here." The seer juts a crooked finger at me, not meeting my eye, then at Rudjek.

Rudjek and I exchange a look, not understanding.

Chills creep down my arms. "Why us?"

"You two must kill the serpent." Barasa threads his fingers together. When he finally meets my gaze, he gives me an apologetic look. "Before she finds the Demon King's *ka*."

I hug my shoulders. "I've already tried that. I failed."

Rudjek rests his palms on the hilts of his shotels. "I'll do it."

Same old Rudjek, as brash as always. I bite back a smile.

"If just anyone could do it, boy"—Barasa throws up his hands—"then we wouldn't be having this conversation. While the orishas keep Efiya busy, they want Arrah to take the Demon King's dagger. Only someone touched by his magic can wield the blade. *You* are to help her."

"What's so special about a knife?" Essnai leans against Re'Mec's statue, arms crossed. It's so large that her head rests against his knee.

"The Demon King used the dagger to trap the souls of his enemies," Barasa says. "The orishas used a similar magic to trap his *ka*."

Koré knew about my curse all along and how she could use it to her advantage. Rudjek steps closer to me, his stance protective. He doesn't know. Now is a good time to tell him. I keep it short. I can't admit to him the worst of it. The thing that I haven't wanted to admit to myself—that the Demon King's magic burrowed deep inside me. It coiled around my heart and touched my *ka*. It felt familiar in a way I couldn't explain. I tell him about Efiya too—about the children she turned into *ndzumbi*.

When the seer opens his mouth to speak again, Rudjek lifts a hand to shut him up. "Twenty-gods, I can't believe we're wasting our time listening to this," he says, voice shrill. "The orishas and the seers are the ones who cooked up the Rite of Passage. How many families have they destroyed with their little games? This is another game for them. They don't care what happens to any of us."

Essnai and Sukar look away from Rudjek's shattered face. His pain for his brothers swells in his midnight eyes like the first raindrops of an impending flood. No one in Tamar can claim the Rite hasn't touched them in some way.

"Didn't Re'Mec send you back, boy?" Barasa demands. "He helped *you*."

"He helped me after he got me killed," Rudjek retorts.   .

I startle at the coolness in his tone—the resignation. We'll have to talk about this whole dying and coming back business. At the first opportune moment.

I think of my mother's hands, curled around the dagger that carved the serpent into my chest. "I'll do it," I say, and Rudjek falls silent. "I'm not going to stand by while Efiya destroys the rest of the world. I've stood by long enough. I won't anymore."

He opens his mouth to argue and I give him a look.

"I agree with Rudjek for once." Sukar clears his throat. "If Efiya can kill orishas, what chance does anyone have against her? She killed the witchdoctors too, and even with the chieftains' combined magic it will be near impossible."

"She has a chance." Barasa cuts his eyes at me again. "She alone."

"I'm the only one touched by demon magic," I mumble to myself.

"I thought the Demon King ate *kas*?" Rudjek asks, still seething.

"He ate the *kas* he wanted"—Barasa's voice is impatient—"but every *ka* he consumed became a part of him. The rest he imprisoned in the dagger."

"The orishas used his own trick to trap him," I whisper, thinking of Koré's box.

"What's to stop Efiya from killing Arrah before she's close enough to use the dagger?" Rudjek asks.

"I can stay alive long enough to do it." I cross my arms. I almost got to Efiya before, when Merka stepped in my way. I can again.

Essnai pushes off from Re'Mec's statue and stands up straight. "I don't like it."

"Finally, someone else has come to their senses!" Rudjek's voice peaks again. "It's a bad plan! It doesn't account for the fact that Efiya has a demon *army*. It's not like we can walk up to her and stab her in the heart."

As soon as I decided to do it, it became *we*. Rudjek wouldn't let me go alone.

"When you say *we*"—Sukar steps forward—"I hope you're including us all."

Rudjek shrugs. "I volunteer myself to help."

"I volunteer as well," says Essnai.

If Essnai helps, Kira will be at her *ama*'s side. Majka will want to help too—if not for me, so that he can pester Rudjek. But I dread my friends anywhere near my sister, knowing what she's capable of.

I sigh, head and heart heavy. "Where's the dagger?"

"Hidden in a vault beneath the Temple of Heka," the seer answers.

"How come the orishas didn't think of this before, when Efiya wasn't as strong?" Rudjek asks.

"Arrah had to break the *Ka*-Priestess's curse first," Barasa explains, his tone sharp, "then the chieftains had to die . . ." He meets my eyes again. "As your Grandmother foresaw."

I'm left speechless as Rudjek tenses at my side. *Grandmother knew.* Her vision at the last Blood Moon Festival surfaces in my mind. In all her previous visions, she had seen me standing alone in front of the Temple of Heka. In her last vision, she saw the shadows of the five chieftains standing behind me, each with a hand on my shoulder. Dread sinks in my belly, knowing how horrible it had been for her to live with that knowledge.

Sukar narrows his eyes at his uncle. "What aren't you telling us?"

Barasa's phantom body twitches as he turns to me again. "Wielding the dagger will kill you, too."

THIRTY-FOUR

Had the seer not already been dead, Rudjek would have driven his shotels through his heart. Chills scrape down my back as their raised voices echo in my ears. My heartbeat pulses so loud that pain shoots along my temples. I don't want to die, but the truth is I already have one foot in death. Even the chieftains' magic won't bring back the years I've traded off my life. The demons in the desert called me walking *ndzumbi*. I *am* a walking corpse, and to stop my sister, my life is a small price to pay.

"Enough," I say, putting an end to their argument. My vision blurs as I rub my forehead. "It's my choice, and I've already made up my mind."

A shadow falls across Rudjek's face, but it doesn't mask his tears. His hands slip from the hilts of his shotels and go slack at his sides. He doesn't challenge my decision; he knows it's pointless.

With him quiet, I ask, "Why will the dagger kill me?"

"The orisha who forged the blade made it that way," the Zu

seer spits, disgusted. "She gave him and him alone the ability to trap souls, and the magic only answers to his touch."

I've known Barasa most of my life, and I've never seen such darkness, such pure hate, as he regards the Unnamed's statue. The orishas stripped away her name. They erased her from history. If Koré is any example—a petulant child one moment, a dangerous assassin the next—then the orishas are volatile. The Unnamed must've made his dagger. She *did* side with the Demon King during the war—she betrayed her brethren for him.

"Anyone else would die if they touched the knife, but you can trick it," the seer tells me. "A residue of the Demon King's magic still lives within you. The dagger is powerful enough to kill both mortal and immortal kind . . . It'll be enough to do the deed, but not enough to keep you alive."

Barasa's form begins to fade around the edges. "If you have more questions, now is the time to ask."

I have none.

We decide to stay at the Temple until we're ready to set out on the eight-day trip to the tribal lands. Barasa spends his final moments alone with his nephew before the magic binding his *ka* fades. Afterward, Sukar and Essnai leave to buy supplies for the journey, fetch Kira and Majka. Rudjek and I wash in the barracks, then ramble through the bunks looking for a change of clothes. We both end up in the black tunics and close-fitted trousers worn by Temple attendants. The clothes smell as musty as the halls.

Sukar's uncle had searched my mother's quarters and found nothing of interest. He'd searched the catacombs beneath the Temple too. He told us that there are three levels underneath the

Temple—two he discovered only after death. Most of the chambers remained untouched, but it was clear that my mother had used some to perform rituals. I decide that I will search them, too, and use my magic to see if there are any clues to her next move.

My mind is uneasy as Rudjek and I cross the dark antechamber on the way to my mother's apartment. I'll start there and depending on how that goes, then I'll try the catacombs. Though I'm afraid if I go beneath the Temple, the memories from that night with Arti and Shezmu will rush back in.

As we make our way through her apartment, I want to ask Rudjek about the Dark Forest. But it's nice being together like this without talking, so I hold my tongue. In contrast with the stone corridors outside, Arti's chamber is lavish in a way that I've never seen at home. It reminds me of props on a stage—like she was in front of the assembly, grander than life itself. Wisps of my mother's honey and coconut scent perfume the air—and conflicting emotions twist in my belly. It's a smell of home, and a smell laced with bad memories.

Gossamer curtains hang around a bed large enough to sleep a giant. Gold-plated finery and trinkets of all sorts litter her sitting room. During vigils, the seers would sequester themselves at the Temple. I always looked forward to those times because Arti stayed away, working, for days. No one guessed that she was plotting the destruction of the world. Yet there's nothing more than a faint echo of her magic here, and I'm relieved when we leave.

The firelight in the antechamber holds the shadows at bay. I close my eyes and in my mind, I see a shotani in every corner. Where has the new Almighty One sent them and the rest of the gendars?

Essnai said that no one knew for sure, but I can't help but question the timing. If he doesn't care about the demons pillaging the Kingdom and killing his people, then what *does* he care about? I run my hand across the damp wall, feeling the seers' sharp-edged script carved into the stone. It swirls in my mind. The whispers of the Zu chieftain—the master scrivener—grow louder than the others. Since the witchdoctors' *kas* joined with me, my perceptions have changed. I sense a deeper connection to the world—that there's so much more that I can't quite wrap my head around.

I stare at the mural of the Supreme Cataclysm, the orishas' creation story, on the opposite wall. Storm clouds spew from the mouth of a volcano. According to the seers, the Supreme Cataclysm existed before all. Before the orishas, it created order and chaos. From order came time, and from chaos came life and death. The whispers in my head are so feverish that they make me feel like I'm falling into the Supreme Cataclysm too. Tam told me a more colorful version of the creation story. The more I learn of the orishas, the more his version sounds closest to the truth.

I've walked through these halls countless times, but now I see them through the chieftains' eyes, too. I catch impressions of past seers performing rituals. A brush of very old magic. The faintest lines that connect everything in the universe. The chieftains' thoughts jostle beneath my own. It's dizzying to keep mine separate from theirs. To keep my memories whole.

Rudjek touches my hand. "Are you okay?"

I blink and his face comes into focus. "Turns out the five chieftains are high-maintenance. They like to talk over each other." I'm aware of how close Rudjek is to me and a flush of warmth creeps up my neck. I clear my throat. "Were you with Re'Mec this whole time?"

"So to speak, yes. After I escaped from my rooms, I ran into *Tam* on the way to the East Market." Rudjek sneers when he says his name. "By 'ran into him,' I mean, he stepped into my path and we collided." Rudjek pauses and takes a breath to gather himself. "Arrah . . . How well do you know Tam?"

"I know he's a selfish bastard." I wrinkle my nose. "He didn't care after he sent you on a false trail."

"Indeed." Rudjek's brows shoot up in surprise. "I've known Tam all my life. We grew up competing in my father's arena and took private lessons together for years. I didn't question his word when he said he overheard the *Ka*-Priestess ordering an attendant to secure passage to the Aloo Valley."

Twenty-gods. I should've known it was a mistake not to burn Tam to a crisp in the alley. He had single-handedly delivered Rudjek to the cravens. "I don't know if he was working with my mother or . . ."

"Tam isn't who we thought he was," Rudjek says quietly.

Tam with his Yöome bronze complexion set upon bold, Tamaran features, hair the color of sunlight, and azure eyes. Before he became a scribe, I hadn't seen much of him in either of the markets. I'd thought nothing of it, since many families of high status didn't frequent the heart of the city. They sent their servants for that.

Tam told the orishas' origin story with such nostalgia that one would think he saw it firsthand. And the thing he said in the alley about the demons when I pondered why one was so easy to kill. *Ask again once one has consumed a hundred or a thousand souls.* The truth dawns on me.

"Tam is Re'Mec."

Rudjek nods. He's been right all along about the orishas. They like to play games. The hot lash of the truth burns—we're no more than rag dolls to them. The first time I met Koré in the alley, she appeared human by all accounts. Her magic and writhing hair and the box had given her away, but only because she chose to let me see those things. I've never felt a hint of magic from Tam, but he's always been a chameleon. The whole time that Koré was helping me, he must have been with Rudjek. But there's more to it: Re'Mec has been watching him since childhood.

After years of lessons with the scribes, my mind still can't wrap around the idea that the orishas walk among us. To them, we're no more than pieces in their game of jackals and hounds. Arti and Efiya are the Demon King's pieces, and Rudjek and I are the orishas' counterparts. I trusted Koré even after discovering that the orishas lied about the demons. Now I realize she'd known the chieftains' plan all along and kept me in the dark. It frustrates me to no end that without them we would already be dead.

Rudjek studies my face again. "You look like you've just seen the end of the world."

"Old news," I sigh, waving my hand, "I saw that months ago."

We stand so close that the heat from his body rolls off him in waves. I can't stop staring at his long, dark lashes, and the hall feels much smaller, and more private than it ought to. With our families scattered and our friends away, there's no one to interrupt this moment. No one to snatch us apart now.

"A few days after I crossed into the Aloo Valley, I found an abandoned camp." Rudjek clears his throat and continues his story.

"I can't explain it, but . . . the camp smelled of you." He ducks his head to hide his blush. "Like you smell right now. Sweet and intoxicating. Like something forbidden—"

"Rudjek!" My cheeks warm too. "We're talking about the Aloo Valley, *remember*?"

"Sorry." He runs his fingers through his messy black curls. "You're very distracting."

"And you're not?" I retort.

Rudjek grins and I cluck my tongue at him. "Where was I?"

"The abandoned camp."

"Someone had ravaged the camp." He swallows hard, shifting on his heels. "I thought of the Dark Forest and the cravens. About the stories we were told as children . . ."

One does not see a craven, my father said. *One feels its presence.* They chose not to reveal themselves to Oshhe the day he hunted the white ox, but Rudjek hadn't been so lucky. His family crest is gone; the craven that killed him in my vision took it. "I get the feeling there's more to the cravens than the stories led us to believe."

"The stories don't do justice to what *they* are." His voice shakes. There's so much pain brimming in that simple declaration that I reach up to stroke his cheek. He turns his face against my hand, his lips brushing my palm, and inhales. His skin is so hot. "They can do things that I've never seen before . . ." He stares at me with eyes full of a desperate longing that tears into my heart. "I don't know if I can trust my own memories."

"Rudjek," I whisper. "What happened to you?"

"I fought a craven who damn near cleaved me in two," he says, weariness punctuating his every word. Then he adds, "I died."

Silence stretches between us as he lifts the black tunic to show me his smooth, unmarked belly. "The craven's claws cut me here." He moves his hand from left to right across his middle, and I trace the same path. Warmth spreads through my body and goose bumps prick his flesh beneath my touch. The invisible cut ends above his hip bone, and my hand lingers there for a moment too long. I can almost feel the anticipation pulsing in his veins, same as my own.

"But Re'Mec brought you back?" I ask, pulling my hand away and glancing up at him.

"No, he didn't," Rudjek says, his cheeks flushed. "I healed myself."

My mouth drops open, ready to ask more, when a familiar tingling rises across my forearms. Rudjek must feel it too for he spins around, his shotels ready. We both stare into the bleeding darkness.

"Well, isn't this a lovely reunion," purrs a familiar voice that sends ice down my veins. "It took time to take down the orishas' wards on this place." Merka steps into the torchlight. He's still in the fisherman's body—lanky with pockmarked cheeks, with the mangy ginger hair he had in cat form. But he moves with a strange new grace. "Your sister's worried sick about you, Arrah. She would've come herself, but she's quite . . . busy."

The chieftains' whispers start again, so loud that my head feels like it will crack open.

Rudjek and I back away from him, but something in the darkness shifts behind us.

"Looks like this is my lucky night," Rudjek growls. "I get to kill my very first demon."

Dread fills my belly. Rudjek doesn't know what he's up against. His shotels will be useless if what Tam said in the alley is true. The more souls they consume, the more powerful demons become. Four more demons step out of the shadows behind Merka.

If they're here, then Efiya is close and so is her army.

"It's going to be a pleasure to kill your kind." Merka grins, and the other demons charge. As Rudjek raises his shotels, someone grabs me from behind. I kick and scream and punch, but something slams into my head so hard that my legs falter, my vision fades in and out. Rudjek tries to reach me, but he's surrounded by a horde of demons now—more than I can count.

"Did you miss me?" Merka whispers in my ear, his voice slick as honeyed wine. He drags me into a room and slams a heavy door behind us, then shoves me forward. I almost stumble and fall. He's stronger than before, faster too; it shines in his glowing eyes.

We're in a small study with no windows and no escape save for the door behind him. Lit jars of oil line the floor along the walls. A single chair and a table sit in the corner. I back toward the table while Merka closes the space between us.

He smiles. "I thought we could use some privacy."

"Where is my sister?" I ask to distract him.

"Waging war on her enemies." Merka shrugs. "She sent me to deal with you."

It's not hard to figure out what he wants—what Efiya wants. She's never been able to see inside my mind. She's sent Merka to get information—does she know that the chieftains' *kas* are with me?

His eyes shimmer from jade to sea green to emerald to jade

again. My heart drums against my chest as his gaze lulls me into calm. I'm sinking into warm quicksand. It draws me into its belly, and the deeper my descent, the more I bask in its sea of tranquility. My worries slip away; Efiya no longer matters, and neither does Rudjek nor my father. All that matters is that I go deeper inside Merka's eyes, travel to his soul.

"Do you know why your sister chose to remake me *first*?" Merka asks.

I'm sitting in the chair now and he kneels before me. My lips move to speak, but I'm too tired, so I shake my head.

"She brought me back because of you," he says, amusement lacing his words. "She thought my particular talents would be useful. It is much the same as the old *Ka*-Priest's, but unlike him . . . I can make it very pleasurable."

I blink and I'm alone on an empty plane in Merka's mind. Soft light glows around me, but his perverse darkness crawls across my skin, invading every inch of my body. There is nothing good inside this creature—only sweet illusions. I can see his true face. He's taller than should be possible and misshapen, two-headed with a mouth of blood and no eyes.

"Let me know your mind, Arrah." Hearing my name again snaps me out of his trance and I am back in the half-lit room, back in the chair. "Tell me your secrets."

"Tell me yours first," I croak out, barely able to breathe. "Are you nothing more than my sister's chained dog?"

Merka slaps me. My jaw cracks and the pain that follows would've brought me to my knees had I not already been sitting.

The blood in my mouth tastes of wet soil, but it clears away the last of the fog. The magic inside me mends my jaw, and the pain is nothing more than a fading memory. My mind is sharp as it vibrates under my skin.

"I admire your spirit." He grits his teeth. "It will be a pleasure to break it."

From the gap beneath the door, I see dark shadows flitter across the room as the battle rages on in the antechamber. If there's still fighting, then Rudjek's alive. There's still hope.

Sweat trickles down the small of my back as Merka grabs my chin, forcing me to look at him again. But I'm ready for him this time; the Mulani chieftain tells me what to do. Her magic digs into the deepest corners of his mind. He is a creature of vices, and beyond that he is a withered-up thing of no substance. Power surges through me as I twist him to my will as easily as crushing herbs. His eyes go wide with surprise, then fear.

In an echo of the Mulani chieftain's commanding voice, I say, "Let me go."

Merka nods, his jaw and arms falling slack. My palms glow white and I press them to his cheeks. His jade eyes turn almost translucent. He struggles to speak as cracks stretch across his face, but I hold him still. His skin begins to flake away like burned paper. His flesh blackens and sloughs off his bones. Our eyes lock one last time, and he curses before the transformation spreads to his entire body.

My fury has no limits, and when I'm done, there's nothing left of him.

THIRTY-FIVE

Fury still running hot in my blood, I can't stop staring at my hands, thinking of what they did to Merka. What I did of my own free will. I killed him. I can't blame the tribal magic like before when the demon magic killed those men at the sacred tree. Now I understand that the fire raging inside me is mine alone. I control it. Even then the demon magic answered to me, it enacted my wishes, however devastating. I've dreamed my whole life of having magic. Now that I have it, I can't help but wonder if this is why Heka had refused me his gifts at the Blood Moon Festival. He knew what I was capable of.

The magic cools inside me and my rage ebbs away as Rudjek bursts into the room, throwing the door back on its hinges. He's covered in blood, and he lets out a long whistle. I sigh with relief. He's okay.

"Twenty-gods—did *you* do that?" He looks to the pile of ashes—the only thing left of Merka. Awe and disbelief lace his next words. "I guess I'm not the only one with a secret."

The next hour is a blur of action. We can't wait for our friends.

There's no time, and the truth is, they aren't safe with me. Efiya will send more demons or she'll come herself. I don't trust the orishas or their plan, but I have to do something.

I try to convince Rudjek to stay behind too, but my heart isn't in it. He refuses to even listen to my protests. It isn't like leaving him behind after the Vizier banished my family worked out so great for either of us. Barasa said that Rudjek and I together could stop my sister—and Rudjek makes it plain that he's coming. I'm relieved that he'll be at my side at the end.

We leave the Temple, descending into the heart of Tamar. At the western edge of the city, we see the distant outline of the Barat Mountains. To my relief, no one recognizes us when we stop to buy supplies and horses and a staff for me. People are too busy with making ends meet and surviving another day. Seeing the glimmer of defiance in their eyes in the face of so much destruction fills me with hope. I can't save myself, but maybe I can save them.

Rudjek doesn't say much, but he watches me when he thinks I'm not paying attention. I do the same. At times he turns inward, his eyes distant, his expression guarded. I've seen his face become a mask before, but never a fortress like this. I've changed too, for there are moments that take me back to Kefu and quicken my pulse. Moments when I break into a cold sweat upon hearing the crack of a twig beneath the horses' hooves. Moments I see my father's sad, silent face, begging me to set him free.

We ride most of the day, pushing the horses more than we should. Both of us trained to ride at a very young age for fun—a popular activity among people with coins to spare. Although it's hardly a thing you see in practice within the city limits. As the sun starts to wane, my legs and back ache from spending so long in the saddle. Neither of us is very good at riding, but Rudjek seems to be faring better than me.

After a short respite at dusk, we're back on the dirt road traveling the farmlands on the Kingdom's west flank. Rudjek keeps biting his lower lip as he works up to ask me something. The way his teeth pinch into his soft, supple skin sends my mind reeling and a flush of heat down my neck. The only sounds are the wistful neighs of the horses and the crunch of their hooves on the dirt. All at once, after hours on the road, the strangeness of our silence becomes too much.

"It's not like you to hold your tongue," I say to distract myself from my thoughts.

"How did you kill that demon?" he counters, fast as a whip.

"One of the chieftains told me how," I answer after a pause. "I don't understand the mechanics of it exactly, but their magic answers when I call." I shrug. "It seems to know what I want even if I don't quite know myself—at least it does most of the time."

"And it's not taking your years?" he asks, his gaze sweeping over me. "Like before?"

I look away, unable to hold his intense stare. He doesn't know that I traded more of my years in Kefu. "No . . . it isn't." I force a smile. "No thanks to the orishas, or Heka for that matter."

The rest of the day, the conversation is awkward, spotted with bouts of nervous laughter, anticipation, and longing. We find a place to settle for the night not far from a stream, where we replenish our water skins. The valley is quiet save for the owls and the occasional trees whispering in the wind. Sheep roam free in the grassy hills nearby, and the smell of their dung coats the air.

For supper, we nibble on stone bread and cheese, but we're both too nervous to eat much. Rudjek flashes a smile that causes me to straighten my back. Am I reading too much into that wicked gleam in his eyes, or how he doesn't know what to do with his hands? He washed at the stream using soap that's left him smelling like perfect skies. *Heka, save me.* I can't control how my body reacts to the sight of him, not when he looks at me like that. We sit close enough that our arms touch, neither of us daring to retire to the tent.

"I can sleep out here." Rudjek scratches the back of his neck. "There's plenty of space."

"You don't have to do that," I say. "I promise I won't bite."

Rudjek laughs. "I'm not so sure."

I'm not misreading his glances, nor is he misreading mine. I wasn't expecting anything like *this*. If this is what I think it is, I will have my kiss by the end of the night. I need some air. I stand and Rudjek jumps to his feet too.

His eyes flit from me to the fire, his face flushed. "Re'Mec told me many things when I was in the Dark Forest. I don't know if I believe everything he said. I need to tell you something, and I can't figure out how to say it."

"Tell me when I get back." I glance in the direction of the stream, then cast Rudjek what I hope is an inviting smile—a promise.

He frowns up at the sky as night cloaks the valley. "Don't stay away too long . . . I might get lonely."

I hadn't planned to, but I need a moment to myself to think.

As I walk through the trees to the stream, I spin through the possibilities of how the rest of the night will go. How far do I want to take things? I splash cool water on my neck, but it does nothing to douse the yearning burning through me. Before I forget, I swallow some powdered cohosh root mixed with herbs. Not that I expect things to go that far, but I'm prepared in case they do. The tincture will ensure I don't become with child.

Something pricks the back of my neck. I slap my hand across it and stare at the smear of blood on my palm and the crushed mosquito. If Efiya releases the Demon King, will humans be nothing more than mosquitos to swat? A bout of dizziness overcomes me as the witchdoctors' voices start again. They whisper of their hopes, dreams, and fears, as if confessing to me will give them another chance at life.

There's not much time left for me. How many years did the magic take to break my mother's curse? Too many. How does one tell their best friend that they will be dead soon? Dread sinks in my belly, knowing how it will devastate Rudjek when the dagger finishes the deed. This night will be one of our last together.

As I'm washing up, the moon and stars disappear. A knot tightens in my stomach. Koré, the moon orisha, is gone because of me. She sacrificed herself for a charlatan because she wagered that I could stop Efiya. I hope she's right.

Without the moonlight, I stumble through the trees along the path to camp. I've walked for too long and see no sign of fire. Have I gone in the wrong direction? Chills rake down my back as Familiars flit in and out of the trees and across my path like a pack of wild dogs. My heart slams against my chest. Wherever they go, trouble follows.

Efiya.

I break into a run, bushes cutting across my feet and ankles. The camp is nowhere in sight. No matter which direction I go or how far, the path takes me back to the stream. Sweat streaks down my forehead as I stop with my hands on my knees, panting. My chest burns. I'm trapped in a maze.

She has him.

I should've known better than to let Rudjek come with me, no matter what the orishas say. Efiya is more terrible than our mother. A girl with almost limitless power, who can't even tell the difference between right and wrong.

"Rudjek!" My voice echoes in the dead of night.

The silence that answers is vast and impenetrable.

Tears cloud my eyes as tingles crawl up my arms like an army of spiders. I imagine the worst. She's torturing him. She'll make it slow and painful if she's in the right mood. I should've sent him away the moment he appeared at the Temple.

Oh Heka, please, no.

I can't lose Rudjek too—not when I've only just gotten him back after all this time. It's foolish to pray to a god who has turned his back on his people—a god who let Efiya slaughter the tribes like cattle—but I pray anyway.

"I will find my way out of this maze," I shout into the darkness, through gritted teeth, "and I will find Rudjek!"

Deafening silence rings in my ears like bitter laughter. The chieftains helped me before, but they don't speak now, when I need them the most. There must be another way. I wrack my memory for a ritual that can help. Efiya can't affect my mind, so the maze must be only a trick of the eye. I only need to see the right path, like I did escaping the villa in Kefu. At the water's edge, I pick up several stones and throw them into the trees. Some travel far, but some disappear into thin air only to land at my feet. I could throw rocks all night and pick my way through, but by that time Rudjek could be . . .

The witchdoctors' whispers finally come. One voice stands out above the rest—a man with a tone that flows like a gentle river. I focus on only him—his words. I can see him in my mind. He's tall with semi-translucent brown skin. The Kes chieftain. I don't let my fear push aside his voice. I sink into it, let it flow through me, and it invades every space in my mind until his is the only one I hear.

I am not alone.

I can show you the way.

"Show me," I whisper to the darkness.

The Kes chieftain appears at the edge of the tree line. He shifts in and out of focus. He only stands there, waiting. His eyes, white speckled with gray. His cheeks twitch like he wants to speak but can't. It could be that the energy to create this fragile physical form leaves him too weak. He looks down at me, then beyond the trees to tell me to hurry. I step aside and he begins to wade through the trees, twisting and turning, walking in circles. I can no longer hear the gentle flow of the stream, even though it appears to be within an arm's length.

Instead I hear laughter. Rudjek's laughter. I let out my pent-up breath. If he's laughing, then he's okay. But why is he laughing? The witchdoctor in my mind fades to nothingness, and I lurch forward, shoved through an invisible door.

I'm back at the stream again. *No, no, no.* I ball my hands into fists. But the moon has returned and the stars too. If they're back, then I must be out of the maze. I run through the trees and this time I can see the campfire in the distance. As I grow closer, I slow my pace, legs threatening to collapse.

Rudjek's bare back is to me, facing the fire. He shifts his position and—someone else is buried beneath him in the furs. Her sweet laughter drifts from the covers like birdsong. I move closer, so close that I stop on the opposite side of the fire and smell her cloying scent mingled with his lilac and woodsmoke. Flashes of her honey-brown skin and her ruffled black tunic burn into my eyes as his fingers traverse the peaks and valleys of her body. He cradles her in his arms, holding her like she means everything in the world to him. No, like she *is* his world.

My presence, or maybe the tickle of wind against Rudjek's back, causes him to glance over his shoulder. When our eyes meet, his go wide and he climbs out of the tangle of furs clumsily. He jerks his head back and forth between the girl still lying in the furs and me, an expression of shock on his face. When she sits up, I stumble back.

I can't breathe. I can't fathom what I'm seeing—*who* I'm seeing. I clasp my arm around my waist.

Efiya smiles.

"Arrah?" Rudjek gapes at Efiya, then at me.

He acts like he cannot tell us apart. Efiya and I look like sisters, yes, but she's taller, more feline, more beautiful. Even in the night we could not pass for each other. Even if she did not have green eyes when mine are the color of sunset. Are we that interchangeable in his mind? "I don't understand . . ."

"You don't understand?" I say, magic raging inside me. "You attempt to bed my sister and now you seek understanding?"

His mouth drops, his face almost as diaphanous as his mother's. He draws farther away from Efiya. "*Your sister?*"

"Aren't you glad," Efiya says, lying back again, gazing up at the stars, her voice slick with seduction, "I protected your virtue from this pathetic creature?"

Rudjek shakes his head. His whole body shakes. Did he *really* think that she was me? But Efiya can kill gods—changing her appearance has always been child's play. I don't ask why she's done this. She wants to punish me, to make me suffer, to destroy what little joy I have left in this world. I thought that she would torture Rudjek to get back at me, but it never crossed my mind that she would do something like *this*. That she would use him to torture *me*.

"Arrah . . . I . . . I didn't know," Rudjek stutters. "I thought . . ."

Efiya stands. "No need to thank me."

I cannot tell if she's talking to him or me. Rudjek lunges at her, but Efiya's magic latches on to me and we disappear into a storm of wind and rain.

The world washes away—the valley, Rudjek, the tent, the campfire, all gone. Thunder cracks in my ears and lightning strikes so close that it singes the hairs on my arms. Rain beats against my body in a constant assault and clouds wrap around our feet. We stand on top of a mountain peak, and the cold chills me to the bone.

"You disappoint me, sister." Efiya's voice is howling wind. "I thought you wiser than to run away to be with a boy, but I see that you're no different from the others. You are all such emotional creatures. Although, I do admit he was very delicious—the taste of his skin is *inspiring* and the things he can do with his—"

"Shut up!" I roar like a cornered animal ready to leap. The

whispers are quiet, but their magic pools in my fingertips, lurking in my veins. They've waited for their moment of revenge. I want to give it to them. I want revenge too. "You are nothing, Efiya. You're less than nothing."

She tilts her head to the side, considering me, her smile turning into a scowl.

"The only reason you're alive is to free our mother's master," I say. "Do you know how pathetic that is?"

She blinks against the rain. Her hair is slick and falls in tangles. I see a bit of the little girl she'd been only months ago, her eyes shining with the curiosity and wonderment of a child. The little girl who tried to take away my pain one moment and crippled me with her magic the next.

"The chieftains' magic has made you bold." She brushes off my insults.

I say nothing, and the wind pushes us a step closer.

She laughs, glancing me over. "I should've known they would bind themselves to you—use you to hide from me, because I can't see your mind. That was very clever of them, but it won't work. I will have what belongs to me."

A pang tears through my belly as Grandmother's face flashes in my head. Her white braids had cascaded down her shoulders as we sat cross-legged in her tent. She'd seen Efiya for what she was even then—a green-eyed serpent, a demon. Still she couldn't do anything to stop her. None of us could. My sister is too strong.

The magic roaring inside me now is my grandmother's last act of defiance. For she and the other chieftains knew my sister would come for them. Grandmother foresaw it in a vision. I don't have to ask to know what happened to the *kas* of the rest of the witch-doctors. Efiya must have eaten them to grow more powerful.

"You're nothing but a disease," I say as I call down the wind.

I barrel into Efiya and we fall and fall and fall. The ground races up to meet us. We are a mess of tangled arms and legs, both kicking and screaming. As Efiya tries to enter the void—the space between time—I grab her wrist, my touch like a pit of writhing vipers that sink fangs into her. She yelps, flustered for the first time ever, but I can't hold her. She wrenches out of my grasp and disappears.

When I hit the ground, my world shatters into a thousand pieces.

THIRTY-SIX

I climb from the cracked ground beneath my feet. I cannot undo what's done. I cannot look at Rudjek as I stalk over to the tent and change into dry clothes. Even though I sit close to the fire, a deep chill takes hold of me and won't let go. He goes to the stream to wash twice, but Efiya's saccharine scent lingers on him like a dog's marked territory. The rest of the night is long and insufferable, and I lose track of time waiting for daybreak.

"Arrah, I'm sorry," he says for the hundredth time. "I didn't know."

"You've said that already," I groan, staring into the fire.

"Will you at least talk to me?" His deep timbre cracks on every other word.

"Can you give me some space?" I huff, exasperated. "I have a lot to think about."

And it's true. I need to forget about what happened between Efiya and him and focus on the fact that I hurt my sister tonight. The moment before she entered the void, my gifted magic tore through her and she fled from it. I tried to kill my sister the same way I burned Merka, but the magic's effect on her paled in comparison to what it did to him. He was only a demon. Efiya is both demon and Heka—much stronger. But tonight gives me hope. If I'm able to hurt her with just the chieftains' magic, then when I have the Demon King's dagger, I can end her.

As much as I try to keep my mind on the task at hand, my heart burns with jealousy.

I picture Efiya wrapped in Rudjek's arms.

My sister has everything: magic, my mother's love, and now Rudjek. I've longed for magic my whole life, prayed to Heka for it. She was born overflowing with it while I traded my years for scraps. I tried to earn my mother's love—while Efiya does nothing but rebel and our mother still hasn't given up on her. Now that I know Arti's history, I realize that nothing I could've ever done would have changed her. She loves me in her own tortured way. But even under normal circumstances, that love wouldn't have been enough for me.

And Rudjek. Twenty-gods.

He paces back and forth. I hate the way he's looking at me, his face riddled with regret and pain. It's so easy to place the blame on Efiya, but he should've known she wasn't me. How much time have we spent together? The lazy afternoons prattling on about whatever silly thing crossed our minds. Something about Efiya—*however small*—should've made him realize. How could he be such a fool?

My ears perk up when the air shifts and blades of grass rustle in the field. Rudjek stops pacing and reaches for his shotels. Soft footfalls grow closer—the sound so subtle that I almost miss it. I come to my feet with the staff in my hand. Magic tingles beneath my skin. I'm ready too.

Rudjek stomps out the fire and we crouch in the high grass. There's movement in the forest to the east. My heart leaps against my ribs. We've seen no signs of my sister's army, but they will come soon. There's magic wafting on the wind.

"I don't see how *no one* in that dank town had a few horses to spare," says a voice that's high-pitched and bratty. It's *Majka* and I don't think I've ever been gladder to hear him whining about something as I am now. I sigh, tension easing from my chest.

Essnai steps into the clearing, the moonlight reflecting against a yellow swipe of paint from her forehead to the bridge of her nose. Sukar is on her heels, his tattoos shimmering with the faintest light. Kira trails behind him. I don't know how they've come to be here, but I'm thankful to see our friends.

"We shouldn't have run down our mares in the first place," Kira grumbles.

"They offered donkeys." Sukar shrugs. "You turned them down, Majka."

"Did you see those donkeys?" Majka waves his arm. "They looked half-dead already."

"You four are as noisy as a pack of hyenas," I say, straightening myself up.

Kira clutches two daggers, poised to strike before her sharp eyes land on us, then relaxes.

Essnai clucks her tongue. "Still always wandering off, I see."

"Twenty-gods." Majka grins upon seeing Rudjek. "It's true, you're alive."

Rudjek rubs the back of his neck. "I've seen better days."

"So I've heard." Majka clasps his friend's shoulder. "By the way, your aunt dismissed us from the gendars because of your stunt. I'm itching to kick your butt for it."

Rudjek winks at his friend. "Get in line."

Sukar greets me with a hand to his brow and a slight bow. I return the gesture. "Did you think you could sneak out without us?" he asks. "You know I can never turn down the chance for a good fight."

I shrug. "I didn't want to drag you into this."

Essnai frowns, searching me up and down. "We saw the carnage at the Temple."

"We were worried about you," Sukar adds, scornful.

The three of us press our foreheads together, our arms draped across each other's shoulders once more. I let myself forget about Kefu and Efiya and my mother for the briefest moment. My friends are glad I'm okay, but their fear is palpable too. They know what will happen soon. That our time together will not last. I'm going to miss them.

"I can't believe the so-called great orisha Re'Mec is Tam." Majka grimaces. "I fought him in the arena many times, you know. He's awful with shotels and not that much better with knives, either."

Rudjek glances everywhere to keep from meeting anyone's eye. He squeezes the handles of his shotels so hard that the blood drains from his knuckles. "He wanted us to think that."

Kira roams over to the crater in the ground where I landed after falling from the sky. She fingers a blade with an intricate carved handle made of bone. They're different from her usual daggers. "Well, this is interesting."

"I see you have new daggers," I interject so I don't have to explain the hole.

"Tam—um, Re'Mec—gave us some new toys to stand against the demons." Sukar holds up a shiny new pair of sickles; the blades catch the moonlight. Even in the dark, the script carved into the weapons glows. "He's still a lying weasel, though."

Is that how Rudjek killed all those demons at the Almighty Temple? Did Re'Mec enhance his shotels with magic too? I burn to ask, but rage and hurt still my tongue.

Dozens of shadows suddenly flit in and out of the moonlight, and Rudjek reaches for his shotels. Kira sends a knife sailing into the dark. It goes through a shadow that disappears along with the blade. Kira gasps and I turn to see her staring down at the knife, which has returned to the sheath at her hip. She looks at me, wide-eyed. "Hello, orisha magic."

There's no time for a witty retort as a small army marches on our position; no mistaking who they are. Their magic charges the night air, and they move like still wind in plain black uniforms.

"Shotani," I whisper. If my sister controls the new Almighty One, then she has the Kingdom's armies at her disposal too. Who better to send after us than the elite Temple-trained soldiers? They could kill a man in a crowd without anyone noticing.

"Form a circle," Rudjek barks, slipping into the role of leader without pause. A natural fit for a boy groomed to be the next Vizier of the Kingdom. And if I'm being honest, it suits him well. "The shotani's greatest strength is stealth. They're good at killing in close quarters, but not in the open like this."

Rudjek speaks like he's fought them before. Not for the first time I wonder what he's gone through since setting off for the Aloo Valley, and notice the change in him. I grip my staff as we follow his orders. He stands to my left and Sukar to my right.

"The weapons Re'Mec gave you will negate the shotani's magic," he tells us. "They'll try to break the circle. Don't let them."

"Are you sure about the weapons?" I ask. "Arti and Efiya would've anticipated that."

Rudjek has that twinkle in his eyes again. My chest throbs with longing and a familiar warmth spreads through me. His look reminds me of the almost kiss in the garden when his scent toyed with my senses. Even with so much uncertainty between us and the looming battle, I can't deny the part of me that still aches for him. "You're talking to me again," he observes, his voice low and raspy. "That's good at least."

His eyes linger long enough to make me glance away.

"Pine for each other later," Majka moans. "We're busy at the moment."

The shotani slink into the valley as silent as Familiars. There are at least fifty of the elite assassins, and six of us.

"Twenty-gods. I take that back." Majka rolls his eyes. "Do all the pining you want since we're screwed anyway."

Sukar rotates his wrists, his blades ready. "I'm not going down without a fight."

Half of the shotani charge at once while the others stand back.

They dart through the field like gazelles. Kira launches her daggers, and when the shotani drop, the blades reappear at her waist in a shimmer of gold light.

Despite our efforts, they manage to separate us with ease. Essnai and Sukar fight back to back—taking on five shotani who move like slippery snakes. Majka and Rudjek are back to back too, and most of the shotani have come for them. They dance around us like wisps of wind, landing cuts and blows.

Rudjek breaks away from Majka to run down any shotani who come after me, but he can't stop them all. I bat them back with my staff, landing blows in the soft spots that my father taught me. While I push them back, Essnai takes out eyes and teeth and breaks bones. Her staff is a flash of brilliance that moves in time with her body. Kira runs back and forth through the field, dipping in and out of shadows. Her blades soar through the air, sometimes connecting, sometimes not.

Rudjek plunges his blade into a shotani's belly and slashes another across her chest. He ducks, but not fast enough. A third shotani's blade bites into his shoulder. My pulse throbs in my ears as the shotani rips the sword from Rudjek's shoulder and he yelps in pain.

So much pain.

So much blood.

So much death.

A tang of iron coats my tongue as I block another shotani's blade with my staff. My arms tremble against his brute strength. Magic flares beneath my skin, but I don't need it. I duck right and sweep the staff in an arc to cut the shotani's legs from beneath him. When he hits the ground, I slam the staff into his temple. None of the shotani have tried to kill me. Efiya must want to do the deed herself, so she can take the *kas* of the chieftains.

While Rudjek holds off two shotani, a third one sneaks up behind him. He pivots right and ducks. Not fast enough. The third shotani rams a sword through Rudjek's shoulder. The blade shimmers with magic that crawls up his neck and down his back before dissipating into thin air. Rudjek shrieks at the pain and his right shotel crashes to the ground. Like at the Almighty Temple, the magic rebounds off him, even without his craven-bone pendant. Before I can wonder how he's repelling magic, he spins his remaining shotel across his body and cuts the shotani down. With his attention split, the other two shotani seize their opportunity to strike.

I dart across the space between us and ram my staff into the shotani's belly, and he goes hurtling backward. No, *he flies*. The magic did that. I crouch and spin, cracking the second one across the knees. His bones shatter and his screams cut through me. Once he's on the ground, I deal the killing blow.

"Thank you." Rudjek winces, reaching for his sword.

His shoulder knits itself back together and I stop, my mouth agape. There's blood and dirt and smooth skin where the wound had been only moments ago.

The clang of metal against metal echoes in my ears.

Rudjek shrugs. "There might be more to my Dark Forest story."

"There always is with you," I say, shaking my head.

He winks at me.

White light flashes among the shotani holding the line and they scatter. They clash swords with newcomers who move as well if not better than the elite assassins. The newcomers cut down the shotani like they're untrained recruits in the City Guard. I slam my staff into more heads, bellies, and vital organs. My shoulders ache and sweat streaks down my forehead. I'm exhausted. We all are.

When the white-robed saviors cut through the wall of shotani, they race across the field to help us. There are only five of them—I'm astounded that they've killed so many so fast.

Yet every time we kill a shotani, more join the fight. Majka favors his right side, and blood runs down Sukar's face. I fight harder, wilder, not caring how I cut down the next shotani, only that each one falls. Fire tears through me and awakens the voices.

They whisper of thunder and lightning.

They whisper of firestorms.

They whisper of murder.

I clench my teeth to hold back my rage. My pores are on fire and it feels like the entirety of me—my very being—wants to burst into flames. I can stop a few shotani with my staff, but with my magic I can stop them all. In the end, I'm tired and give in to the urge to unleash my fury. The hairs stand up on my forearms as the first bolt of lightning strikes a shotani and sets him on fire. Another bolt slices across the sky and strikes again. I don't stop calling the firestorm until the rest of the shotani are dead.

RE'MEC, ORISHA OF SUN, TWIN KING

Are you ready to hear the true story of Oshin Omari and the cravens?

You're looking quite well, by the way. The wound is healing as expected.

When Oshin walked into the Dark Forest, the cravens were waiting for him. The elder was kind. She made his death quick and painless. Then she commanded her only son to shift into Oshin's form so that he could return to Tamar to influence the king. Her son took the body of a craven who had died of old age to prove Oshin's victory. He did indeed use the bones to make trinkets that protected against magic, though he himself didn't need it. For the cravens are anti-magic and immune to its influences.

I see you're taking this quite hard.

Let me make this clear to you. You are part craven, Rudjek.

I bestowed many gifts upon the cravens. You will discover them if you live long enough.

Why? Now we're getting to the heart of the matter.

A war is coming, Rudjek. It will take all our efforts to stop it from destroying this world. We cannot do it alone. You must convince the humans and cravens to ally.

We are much weakened after our war with Daho. You know him as the Demon King.

He is a clever bastard, I must admit.

While trapped in our chains for thousands of years, he's found a way to strike. He used your Ka-Priestess to do it. She's quite clever too. Had I intervened when the former Ka-Priest violated her mind, we wouldn't be in this predicament. Alas, I cannot change the past.

He wasn't always so awful. Daho, I mean.

My sister found him abandoned by his people and dying beside a frozen lake.

They were both children then, and we paid no mind when she healed him.

When he became a man, she started to understand death, not a concept that is easy for an immortal to grasp. Fram, the orisha of life and death, understands it the best of our kind. It's their nature.

Our sister didn't want to lose Daho, so she taught him how to consume kas to extend his life. The first ka he consumed was the man who had killed his father and taken his throne. Quite an unfortunate mistake.

They didn't know that consuming someone's ka would change a person's nature. Daho had consumed the ka of a very ambitious demon who would stop at nothing to gain power. Thus began his insatiable thirst for souls.

We spent too much time debating what to do about Daho. Another mistake. He became immortal and raised an army of immortals comparable to the orishas. They destroyed whole peoples in their lust for souls.

We decided to strike at his heart, our sister.

It was not an easy decision, but we knew losing her would weaken him.

Fram killed her. At least we thought she was dead.

Fram has a soft heart. We should have known better than to trust them.

I won't bore you any longer with our family problems.

But know this, Rudjek, your stake in this is as personal as ours.

THIRTY-SEVEN

The shotani lie dead at our feet. I killed them. I struck them down with lightning that set their bodies on fire. I'm shaking and Rudjek grabs my shoulders to steady me, but he's shaking too. Blood stains his tunic where the shotani's double blade dug into his flesh. There's so much blood, and his face is ashen and tired.

Magic has a price.

Even if the cost is no longer my years, it's a part of my soul. I killed those people, just as I killed Merka. Like I did to the men by the sacred Gaer tree. Yes, they tried to kill me first, but that doesn't absolve my conscience of the deed. How many more will I kill before I meet my end?

"We're okay." Rudjek rubs his hands up and down my arms and not even his warmth can stop me from trembling. "Thanks to you."

Thanks to me—the charlatan-turned-witchdoctor, willing magic that's not my own.

I want to sink into his arms and bury my face against his chest, but I want to shove him away too. I'd do anything so I don't have to remember him tangled in the furs with my sister. Rudjek reads my mood and his hands drop to his side. He's suffering too.

I turn my back to him to see the newcomers keeping their distance but watching us like hawks. No, they're watching *me*. None of them have spoken a word since arriving. More shocking is that none of them have so much as a drop of blood on their white robes.

"They're from the Dark Forest." Rudjek gestures to them. "They're here to help."

All the stories said that cravens had tree-bark skin, claws, and a horned nose. These are . . . *people*. They stare at us with as much curiosity as we do at them. They're not what I saw in my vision of Rudjek's death. But now that my nerves have started to calm, I can sense their anti-magic. Like in my vision, it's an invisible shield between them and me, and my magic feels as though it's fallen asleep. "Cravens?" I quirk an eyebrow.

Rudjek smiles sheepishly. "They've shifted their appearance so they don't scare you."

"Who's scared?" Majka glances to Sukar. "Are you?"

Sukar wipes blood from a shrinking wound on his cheek. "I'm bored again."

Rudjek grins at the cravens and they beam back at him. "Am I glad to see you."

They look about our age, no more than seventeen or eighteen. Three boys and two girls.

Seeing that we're still speechless, Rudjek coughs. "They're my . . . um . . . guardians."

"This keeps getting better." Majka puts his hands on his

hips. "You're future Vizier of the Kingdom, now you have craven guardians. Next you're going to tell us that you're an orisha too."

"Why do you need guardians?" I ask.

"I'll explain later," Rudjek says, too eager to change the subject.

He introduces the cravens, and it's easier to focus on them so I don't have to think about tonight. They've mastered their approximations of the human form, with subtle differences. Fadyi, their leader, is the best shifted of the five. He has wide-set eyes, a broad nose, and fine lines that give texture to his chiseled jaw. His hair is short on the sides, leaving a shock of black curls down the middle. Jahla's form is nearly as detailed as Fadyi's. She's added a splash of freckles across her nose. Räeke is the shortest of them with hazel eyes a little too large for her face. Ezaric and Tzaric are twins with long locs and impossibly smooth skin.

"We would've come sooner had Efiya's army not breached the forest," Fadyi speaks in accented Tamaran.

Rudjek tenses. "Is everyone okay?"

"We pushed them back"—the craven's eyes rage with pain—"but we had many casualties."

I cringe. My sister will see the cravens' anti-magic as a threat. The orishas, the tribes, and now the cravens. She's eliminating anyone who could stand against her.

"We tracked her scent here." Jahla steps closer to Rudjek, a lock of silver hair falling from underneath her hood. She sniffs the air and a streak of heat burns up my neck. She grimaces as she eyes me. "Well, this is an unfortunate turn of events."

Rudjek blanches and glances to the ground. She must smell Efiya on him.

"Someone better explain," Majka says, his voice high-pitched. "Rudjek damn near got his arm cut off, and he's fine! Sukar, your face healed too . . . What exactly is going on here?"

"My tattoos are for protection," Sukar reminds him, "and they heal minor injuries."

As Kira sees to a wound on her *ama*'s thigh, Essnai murmurs, "I should've been born Zu."

"That doesn't explain you, Rudjek." I cross my arm, waiting for an explanation.

Everyone stares at him. "I guess this is a good time to finish my story."

The blood of the dead shotani curdles on the air like sour milk. Their oppressive magic has dissipated like the ground drank it upon their death. A swarm of flies light on their bodies while vultures circle, waiting for us to clear the path to their meal. "Tell it on the way." I wrap my arms around my shoulders. "We should keep moving."

Majka jabs his finger at me. "You have a lot of explaining to do too."

We trek through the rest of the night and the next day. I keep my distance from Rudjek as he tells us the truth about his ancestor, Oshin Omari, who as it turns out had been a craven posing as a human. This explains so much: why Arti had never been able to strike at the Vizier, why Rudjek always got sick in my father's shop. The magic overwhelmed his senses and his body tried to block it. Yet Efiya had still been powerful enough to fool him. To touch him. A chill snakes down my arms as the memories rush in and I steer my mind back to obsessing about the cravens.

In the Dark Forest, the guardians helped Rudjek learn some of their skills. Although aside from healing, he failed at most of his lessons. Fadyi is exceptional at shifting, which I'd guessed from the fine details of his human features. Jahla is the tracker in the group—a huntress who can find anything. Räeke can bend space and manipulate her environment, much like a witchdoctor. Ezaric is a skilled healer, and Tzaric is the best fighter among them. All cravens have these skills, but some are better at them than others. I'm curious about what else Rudjek can do, but I don't ask. That would involve actually talking to him.

It's a shame, because I have so many questions. Why doesn't he have any of their physical features? Did he experience any signs outside of his allergy to magic before his death in the Dark Forest? There's more to his story, but I hold my questions. They can wait for now—or forever, since I will die the moment I kill my sister. Butterflies settle in my belly at the thought. It isn't fair; my life feels like someone's idea of a joke. Let's see what awful thing we can throw at her next, see if we can crack her in two. But I refuse to break. I will see this through to the end.

When I'm over the shock, I have the urge to tease Rudjek—like he's done so many times to distract me when I failed at magic. I can't deny the giddy feeling of excitement tickling my chest—even with so much that's happened. But I bite my tongue. My friend is a *craven*. I watch him as he walks ahead with his guardians flanking him. The story about his ancestor always seemed fantastical to me, but I never questioned it. The truth is so much more interesting than the legend.

Leave it to Rudjek to find a way to be even more magical, or . . . anti-magical, if there is such a thing.

Once we've both told our stories, the conversation stills. Rudjek sneaks glances at me now, but he gives me space. And with Essnai and Sukar here, it's easy for me to avoid him. We walk all day, but the pace is slow. It's near nightfall again when we reach the pass that leads up the Barat Mountains, and we're too exhausted to start the climb.

We set up camp and split into two watches, as a precaution in case the shotani come again, or worse, Efiya's demon army. The cravens take the first watch. Rudjek isn't at all pleased that I set up my pallet between Essnai and Sukar, far away from him.

Essnai and Sukar ask me how I'm doing more times than I can count, and they go out of their way to see that I get enough to eat. They're being overprotective because of *my* magic and because I'm going to die. I'm the last witchdoctor. Almost. Efiya is something else, but there's still Arti and Oshhe—my father who I left in the hands of monsters. My belly aches thinking about how I abandoned him. I can only hope that Efiya is still busy with her army and searching for the Demon King's *ka*. That should keep Oshhe safe, as long as Arti leaves him be.

The morning comes fast. I drift on the edge of sleep, tossing and turning, unable to find comfort. In my dreams Rudjek holds Efiya in his arms. He caresses her cheek and stares at her mouth like it's some delectable fruit that he must taste. They kiss, long and sensual, full of passion that makes me ache. He promises that he'll go to the end of the world to protect her. He belongs to her now—not me. He will never be mine.

I don't want this memory, and I'd do anything to forget it, but I never will. I hate Efiya for tricking Rudjek, and I can't forgive him. I can recognize the rhythm of his steps on cobblestones with my eyes closed, the musical cadence of his voice in the crowded East Market. We grew up together. Spent countless hours sneaking off to the riverbank. He should've known she wasn't me.

"Who should've known she wasn't you?" Sukar asks.

I clutch the covers to my chest as I sit up. Sleep fog clouds my mind, and every muscle in my body still hurts from the battle with the shotani. It's been a long time since I last trained with a staff with my father, and in those days I never felt this exhausted. "What?"

He peers down at me, wearing a frown that wrinkles the tattoos on his forehead. "You said he should've known she wasn't you."

My friends don't know what happened between Efiya and Rudjek, and I have no intention of telling them. Sukar looks to Rudjek, who's with the cravens on the edge of camp.

"What's going on between you two?" he asks, his voice low.

Rudjek stares at me with those eyes as dark as the hour of *ösana*, his expression pained. He isn't paying attention to whatever Fadyi and the others are saying.

I start to roll up my pallet—careful not to disturb Essnai and Kira, still fast asleep in each other's arms. "Nothing of importance."

"That's an obvious lie," Sukar scoffs, "but it's not my business."

"Exactly," I say. "It's none of your business, so don't ask."

"Someone has some bite this morning." He laughs, his face twisting in such shock and indignation that I can't help but laugh too. I need laughter. I need to forget. I don't have time to lament over what could've been between Rudjek and me. I'm going to die anyway. I'll be at peace then. I keep telling myself that to push through another day.

As we trek across the mountains, I avoid Rudjek at all costs. Maybe I'm not being fair to him, but it's better this way. Whenever we're near each other, I find something to do, or strike up a conversation with one of my friends. With Essnai or Sukar, we share our favorite moments from the Blood Moon Festival. Majka tries to cheer me up—that is, when he's not trying to woo the craven with the freckles and silver hair. When Kira isn't checking on Essnai, she lets me practice with one of her daggers. Every time I thrust the blade into thin air, I imagine my sister's face and feel sick to my stomach.

On the seventh day, we leave the mountains behind and descend into a valley on the outskirts of the tribal lands. There's been no sign of Efiya or her demons or the shotani. My *so-called* friends each feign a task and leave Rudjek and me at camp alone. I'm annoyed with them for their little trick. I wander from camp too, but he follows me to the river. I'm not ready for this conversation. Not yet. The wounds are still too fresh.

I stop without facing him. "I'd like to be alone, please."

"Are you going to avoid me forever?" Rudjek asks, irritated.

"That's the plan," I say, "so go away."

"I know you can never forgive me about Efiya . . ."

I turn and the sun catches the angles of his jaw. "You're a fool."

"I deserve that," he says, gaze flitting to his feet. "I deserve worse."

"Am I supposed to be flattered that you thought I'd give myself to you?"

"I wanted to give myself to you too." He shudders. "I should've realized . . ."

I'm so mad that my whole body shakes. "Yes, you should have!"

We stand with little space between us now. His intoxicating scent tickles my nose. How he manages to smell so amazing after days on the road is bewildering to me. He reaches for me, but pauses, his eyes asking for permission. I should say no and walk away to put us both out of our misery, but I don't. I nod because I still want him too.

Rudjek cups my cheek in his hand and I turn my face into the warmth of his palm and let him pull me against his chest. The drumming of his heartbeat echoes in my ears. The strength of it lulls me into a sense of peace. I could stay like this forever, listening to the rhythm of his heartbeat.

He buries his nose in my hair and inhales like he's taking a breath of life. "Arrah." My name is sweet music on his tongue; the call of birdsong; the hum of the ocean. His next words send a shiver down my spine. "I need to tell you something."

The chieftains' whispers startle me and drown out his voice. His hand is so hot against my face, too hot. A sharp pain cuts through my cheek and I pull away from him, half stumbling. It feels like someone just slapped my face. The magic inside me shifts, preparing to strike out at Rudjek. I draw back even farther and he does the same, an invisible barrier pushing us apart.

Rudjek glares at his hands like they're dangerous serpents.

"That's what I want to talk to you about. The anti-magic. That's why I should've known it wasn't you, Arrah." He winces. "Re'Mec said that we could never be together. Even if we can control our respective gifts—your magic and my anti-magic, there are other consequences. We would weaken each other, and eventually one of us would destroy the other. Back in the clearing, that's why—I thought that maybe he was wrong. I thought we had a chance."

"But that's never happened between us . . ." My mind races through the almost kisses, the lingering touches, and the flush of heat in their wake. Before, I didn't have magic, but now, with the chieftains' *kas*, things are different. "Efiya . . ." It doesn't make sense. My sister *is* magic, yet . . .

"I don't know." Rudjek takes another step back from me. "She's different somehow."

Dread fills my belly as the answer becomes clear. If my sister is strong enough to kill orishas, then his anti-magic would be nothing against her. The irony of our situation doesn't escape me, and I force down a bitter laugh. My entire life, I've longed for magic to mend the rift between my mother and me, but that's a foolish wish for a foolish girl. I have it now, and it isn't enough to stop Efiya, only enough to ruin any chance I have with Rudjek in my final hours.

We stare at each other, emotions raging in our eyes, a lifetime of missed chances.

I want to sink back into his arms, but this is all I can have of him, and he of me.

It's not enough.

THIRTY-EIGHT

Rudjek is afraid to touch me. He thinks I'm a flower that'll wither up and die if disturbed. He doesn't know that I've died a thousand times already. I died when my mother cursed me. I died when she stole my father's light. I died when I saw the children she'd taken for her ritual. I died when Koré told me about the *edam*. I die again every time I close my eyes and think about all the awful things my family's done.

I'm not afraid of death, but I don't want to die without ever feeling his lips pressed against mine. Even for the briefest moment. I'm haunted by the memories of kisses from the *kas* inside me. Soft, sweet ones; passionate ones. Sensual and slow ones that steal my breath. Rushed and messy ones that make my heart race.

I've avoided Rudjek since that night with Efiya. Now that we're alone, sitting beside the river, listening to the lull of the water, I don't want to stay away any longer. I want whatever my sister had of him—I want more.

"We should get back before they come looking for us," Rudjek says, his voice somber. "Essnai and Sukar will think I've stolen you away."

"They'd hunt you down." I toss a stone into the water. "Essnai might break your legs."

Rudjek gives me a lopsided smile. "I fear she'd do worse."

Fadyi, the craven leader who almost looks human, steps into the clearing. He keeps his eyes downcast like he's caught us in some lewd act. "I'm sorry to interrupt," he apologizes. "We spotted Efiya's army coming from the south, a half a day behind us."

"Can we stay ahead of them and reach the Temple?" Rudjek asks, slipping into his commanding voice. A voice that is cold and precise and ready to issue orders like he's been doing it his entire life. We climb to our feet, our backs rigid, and I suspect we both share the weariness in our bones. We've expected this for days, but that doesn't make it any easier to hear.

"If we keep moving without rest," Fadyi answers. "The demons are still limited by their hosts, but once they've consumed enough souls, we won't know what they'll be capable of."

The chieftains erupt into a deafening chorus inside my head. Their words are urgent and feverish, and my muscles tense with the need to get to the Temple. *We must go now*. There's no time. I start walking, not back to camp to gather our things first, but where they lead. Rudjek calls after me, his plea lost in the chorus too. When he and Fadyi catch up with me, their words sound like a half-forgotten dream that teeters on the edge of my memory.

The witchdoctors call me back to the Temple where they took their final breaths. Where their blood stained the grass. Where I must face my sister one last time.

I don't stop until the moon chases the sun from the sky. We walk without rest for hours and arrive at the Temple in the dead of night. I expect to find a graveyard and the smell of death on the air, but there are no bodies here. Efiya burned them so the chieftains couldn't return to their vessels. She left the grass beneath them pristine and untouched. I can't help but wonder if it's some sentimental gesture from our days in the garden in Kefu.

There's not much left of Heka's Temple besides toppled bricks and fallen columns. Through the chieftains' memories, I see Efiya destroying it in frustration after they escaped her grasp. I climb up the uneven steps with Rudjek at my side carrying a torch—the others stay behind. We step over chalices and broken statues and cracked stone. The whispers only stop when I reach a raised dais that sits upon a smooth platform. It's covered in dust and debris, but otherwise untouched by the destruction. I nudge the platform with my feet. "It's here."

Rudjek kneels and tries to shoulder the thick slab of granite aside to no avail. He pauses, sweat slick against his forehead. "It's possible I need a little help."

I kneel beside the granite. "Try now." When we both push, the stone groans as it slides away, and dust and debris drop into a bottomless pit below.

Rudjek whistles and the sound echoes in the chamber. "Now we get to crawl into the belly of the beast."

"Not quite the belly of the beast." I reach for the ladder dug out in the wall. "But close."

Rudjek lights several discarded torches and sets them about the Temple to give us more light. When he drops one into the pit, it falls so far that the flame goes out before it hits the bottom. We look at each other—his grim face echoing my own. "I'll go first. We don't know what's down there."

"Nothing living," I say. Nothing we want to see.

Rudjek secures an unlit torch across his back, then descends into the darkness. I don't tarry as I start down too. I don't want to be far from him, for fear that Efiya might step out of the void and steal one of us away. The dank air chokes me and burns my throat.

Rudjek yelps and I freeze, clinging to the rungs. Cold air snakes around my neck as his voice settles into silence. Has Efiya snatched him from the ladder like a thief in the night? Has some other demon come to claim him as their prize? Or has some new, unknowable force come to spirit him away to spite me?

"What's wrong?" I ask to break the stillness.

"I thought you said nothing was living down here." Rudjek pouts. "Something crawled across my hand."

I ease out a sigh at the incredulity in his tone, and we continue descending into the cold, dark chamber. "I amend my original statement. Nothing living *of consequence*."

"Giant insects are quite consequential."

I force down a laugh that settles in my belly. This is the side of Rudjek that I missed the most—the side of him that doesn't take himself too seriously. *I've missed you. I want you.* I don't say the words out loud, like speaking them might be tempting fate. Hasn't the universe, whether by design or not, already conspired against us? Instead, I hold my words close, and they stoke the fire already burning inside me.

Rudjek lands in the chamber with a thud and a loud crunch. "Twenty-gods."

When I reach the bottom, he strikes a flint and relights the torch. His eyes stretch wide as he takes in the room. "It's a grave."

Bones cover the floor of the chamber: jawbones, skulls, shins, shoulders, and ribs. Tiny bones and large bones of men and women who must've been giants. Suddenly time shifts around me, dragging my mind down a black hole so fast that the world turns upside down. The stack of bones shrinks until there's nothing left but a white marble floor. Sunlight pours into the open windows overlooking a lush mountain range. I blink several times to clear away the fog in my mind. I haven't moved—this is the same place. In the past it once sat upon the highest mountaintop, and in the present, it's buried in a deep pit.

The *kas* in my mind are silent.

One by one other details come into focus. The gold trim along the base of the walls. Crystal vases so fine that the red roses and water inside them appear suspended in thin air. People frozen by magic like statues, their desperate, pleading eyes finding me. They're twice as tall as me with white feathered wings that cast prisms of shadows across the room. Eyes that all glow a stunning shade of green. Their teeth are sharp points, their skin as diaphanous as the Northern people. There's some reflection of the orishas' ethereal nature in their postures.

They wear shimmering gold and silver tunics, and rings of rubies and diamonds and black opal. My breath hitches in my throat as I move closer to them. Close enough to see the rise and fall of their chests. Their panic is palpable even if it doesn't touch the unnatural smiles upon their faces. This place is familiar, from the crisp mountain air to the sweet roses, and especially the macabre art. I glance over my shoulder to ask Rudjek if he's seeing this too, but he isn't here. This is a vision of the chamber from another time. He's standing in the room as it is now, a tomb.

As I cross the chamber in the vision, the living statues make slight adjustments to keep me in their sights. A nighthawk lands on the windowsill, cocks its head, and stares at me with curious black eyes. I leave the antechamber through an archway large enough to accommodate people as large as the statues. It leads into another room of white marble—this one grand and expansive.

Steps arch over the room, where a throne floats like a cloud. It takes on a yellow hue from the sunlight pouring through the windows. I step closer, my footfalls ringing like bells in the chamber.

"You've finally come home, my love," hums a voice as smooth as the finest silks, laced with the sweetest honey. His breath is a warm breeze against my neck. It raises a deep longing in me like the first strike of a firestorm. A shadow of his power wraps around my chest.

Just like it did before, when Arti cursed me with his magic. "I've missed you," he says.

I spin around, but there's no one here. My gaze lands on the steps again and against all logic I climb them to the throne high above the room. I don't know how or when, but I've been here before, and without a second thought I sit on the throne. In an instant, I'm wearing a red dress that flows like lava at my feet. Gold bands embellish my arms, and my hands rest upon the crowns of two polished human skulls. Thigh bones shaved and strung together with gold twine form the seat. Animal skulls line the arch across the back. Ribs give the throne its distinctive curve. I have been in this chair many times. This place is a memory, and it feels as real as stepping into the chamber with Rudjek a moment ago.

"Your mother marked you with my magic to keep you safe from Efiya." Another whisper on the wind. His name tingles on my tongue; it rings in my ears. His words are full of angst and longing. "I won't lose you again, not when we're so close."

"Who are you?" I say, my voice trembling, but I know the answer. The Demon King has found a way to invade my mind when Efiya and Merka failed. Now he's whispering lies to get me to trust him, lies that only a fool would believe.

The scene changes and I sit beside a frozen lake with my legs crossed beneath me. There's a boy at my side—the most beautiful boy I've ever seen. His long hair is a shock of white that matches the wings folded against his back. One wing sits a little higher than the other, as if it hasn't healed right after an old injury. A memory flitting at the edge of my consciousness threatens to crack when I look at him, so I stare at the lake instead. Still I catch glimpses of his face in profile and my heart flutters.

"You remember nothing?" His voice is a purr, a lullaby, a hum of sweet music.

I can't trust myself to answer, and he draws his knees to his chest. "I am Daho."

He says his name like he expects a response from me, but I don't care what he calls himself. I want him out of my mind. Yet I can't stop staring across the frosted lake and the fog rising from it.

"I . . . I know this place," I stutter, feeling like I've spent eons sitting still at this very lake.

"This is our place," Daho tells me. "You found me here after my people abandoned me."

"No," I whisper, shaking my head. "This is a trick."

"Fram stole your memories," he sighs, "but they'll come back in time."

"I won't let you play games with me like you've done with my mother." I grit my teeth. "I don't know how you broke into my mind, but I'm not like Arti or Efiya. I won't do your bidding."

"I'm not in your mind, *Dimma*," he says. "You're in mine."

As I hear the name, a sharp pain slices through my head as suns and moons flash before my eyes. It's worse than the vision of Rudjek in the Dark Forest. Moon and sun chase each other across the sky so fast that they're a blur of never-ending fire and ice. My head feels like it will split in two. I squeeze my forehead between my palms, but the pain cuts deeper. I'm on the verge of recalling a memory when a calming, cleansing magic washes away the pain. I'm staring at the frozen lake again, and the name slips away.

"I'm sorry." Daho winces. "I'd forgotten that Fram took your name too. Their magic hides your mind to keep you from remembering your true self. When you were marked with my magic, I tried desperately to remind you . . ." He pauses, drawing his knees even closer to his chest. "But you kept pushing me away. I'm stronger now, and you're stronger too. Soon we'll be together again."

Fram took your name.

Fram, the orisha of life and death.

His words reel in my head and I can't make sense of them. I'm left speechless as a calming magic suppresses memories on the edge of my mind—memories that feel very old. My thoughts fall on the Unnamed orisha with the serpents coiled around her arms. The orisha with no face. The one that Re'Mec, posing as Tam, refused to speak of. The orisha that betrayed her brethren for the Demon King—she's his *ama*, his love. Did Fram take *her* name? And somehow he thinks that I'm *her*? But even as I reject this grim revelation, there's a part of me that warms to the idea. I remember how familiar his magic felt uncoiling inside my body, how it protected me, how it tried to soothe me.

No, it can't be true.

She is not *me*—I am not *her*.

I want to look at him, but now a force keeps my eyes on the frozen lake. "You expect me to believe that I'm the Unnamed orisha," I spit. "Do you take me for a fool?"

"It will take time to remember," he replies. "I'll help you."

"Stop lying," I demand, my voice a piercing echo. "I know who *I* am."

"I don't need to convince you," he says, too calm. "Time will reveal all."

"Why are we having this conversation, then, if not to convince me?"

"Selfish reasons," he admits. "I needed to see you."

I hate how his voice sends a flush of longing through me. His magic wraps around me, settling in like an old friend—no, settling in like an old lover come home. It's as familiar as my own self and comforting. I want to lose myself in it. *Twenty-gods, no.* I can't let that happen.

I can't let myself be fooled by his lies. I remember how the demons in Kefu tried to stop me from returning to my body when I was on the edge of death. How *dream*-Rudjek appealed to my heart to try to keep me there. I stare out over the lake, and the fog shifts into Tribe Litho, thousands of white-painted faces staring at me. Not tribal people, but demons taking their form again. They're a projection from my memory.

Daho gestures at the demons. "They were farm folks, scholars, homemakers, people from all walks of life. They chose not to fight in the war, but the orishas killed them and trapped their souls in Kefu anyway." There's so much pain in his words that my heart aches too.

"They tried to take my *ka*," I say, unsure now.

"They never feasted upon a single soul, but the orishas didn't care." He takes a deep breath. "They saw that you were special. They tried to save you from Efiya and keep you from ascending into death."

My stomach twists in knots. I was so sure those demons wanted my soul, but they did little more than keep me on the edge of death. Had they wanted my soul in that state, they could've taken it without even trying. He's right. They were different from the demons who taunted me in the desert after I broke my mother's curse. Different from the ones that Efiya woke. I can't believe most of what he says, but the orishas are a far cry from perfect and they're vindictive. Koré said she would've killed me to strike at my mother if given the chance. For Re'Mec, the Rite of Passage is his way of punishing the Kingdom.

Doubt and uncertainty start to creep into my mind again. It frustrates me that I can't trust the orishas either. Whatever else they may have lied about—the demons are dangerous. I saw that for myself in the alley when the demon ate that man's soul. Still I can't shake the feeling that there's truth in what the Demon King says about the orishas too.

"It's freezing in here." Rudjek snaps my connection with Daho, and my mind slips back into the present, to the chamber of bones.

I inhale, but the dank air cuts my breath short. My whole body shakes. Rudjek hovers next to me as he sweeps the torch around. The walls are black with tarnish, and somewhere water drips against stone. I cannot get Daho's voice out of my head—it's a gentle breeze against my lips, a warm embrace. If he's to be believed, there are secrets buried inside me, ones that even I cannot fathom, ones that will unravel me.

I brace my arm against the wall and close my eyes. Bile burns a trail up my throat and I force it back down. Rudjek is at my side in a heartbeat, his hand on my shoulder. Warmth spreads down my arm. A more subdued feeling than when he touched my bare skin or when he pulled me against his chest. It comforts me when I need it the most, but he draws his hand back, not lingering for fear of his anti-magic's effects.

"I'm okay," I wheeze, half out of breath.

The Demon King is just trying to distract me from finding the dagger. I won't let him.

"Say the word and we'll go." Rudjek's deep voice reminds me of why we're here.

Our eyes find each other in the half light; his stand out like black moons against his brown skin. Pieces of the past float in my mind like ashes from a fire, and another grim truth bubbles to the surface. I draw upon one of the witchdoctors' memories. It's the Zu chieftain. The greatest scrivener of his people, a historian.

"When the Demon King fell, Koré and Re'Mec collapsed an entire mountain to bury his legacy," I say. "This place is all that remains. Years after the valley formed, the first tribes who settled the land could feel the remnants of his magic. That's what drew Heka from the stars."

"What is this place to *you*?"

He says *you* like he's seen the memories too, or he hears how my heart beats two rhythms now. I fear the answer will destroy him; it will destroy me, so I leave it obscured behind the grim walls of my mind.

"A place of lies," I answer.

My chest brims with a burning ache as we enter the throne room in the present, not some memory of a forgotten time. There are so many words left unspoken, so much to say. Lifetimes of secrets stand between us, but I tuck them away for now. They will haunt me to the end of my days—but that will be very soon if I succeed in killing my sister.

The throne room is a darkened mirror image of the place from my memories. Dust clings to the stale air and coats the white marble in gray. Our shadows stretch across the floor, twice as tall, like we've transformed into the demons who lived and loved and died here.

Rudjek's torchlight catches glimpses of the steps that arch over the room and end in shadows. "What is that?"

"A throne," I say, my voice muted in the darkness.

With one hand on his shotel, Rudjek peers around the room. "This place feels wrong."

When his gaze lands on me again, I kiss him. It catches him off guard and he stumbles back, his eyes hungry for more, his mouth frozen in surprise. Warmth flushes his cheeks as he takes a step closer, then stops. A war rages in his eyes as he forces himself to stay still. "We can't, Arrah." His face twists in pain and longing. "You saw what almost happened when we touched by the river."

My lips tingle and the ghost of our embrace lingers like the aftermath of a storm. Hot and cold alternate in my body, and the combination is shocking and delightful. I take a step closer. I want to taste his lips, to explore his mouth, to feel his warmth tangled with mine. I want him to make me forget Daho.

"I may not survive tonight, Rudjek." I swallow the lump in my throat. "I don't want to die without knowing what it's like to kiss you."

Rudjek props the torch against a wall and pulls me into his arms. I sink against his warm neck, and again, longing threads through me. "You're not going to die." His declaration is low and heavy. "I won't let you."

I lift my head and blink back tears. "Do you promise?"

Rudjek cups my face in his hands and my body trembles. "I do."

I close my eyes as he kisses me properly for the first time. His soft lips are as delicate as rose petals, his tongue the hot lash of the sun. He tastes of winter and sunshine and warm springs. My hands fumble, searching for purchase as he pulls me against him. I traverse the planes of his neck, his shoulders, his back. He explores too. His fingers trace the shape of my collarbone, his touch a trail of fire that leaves me yearning for more. When we pull away, my mouth burns. His anti-magic leaves my ears ringing and my skin itching. My head spins as exhaustion settles in my limbs, but it was worth every single moment. "That was . . ."

"Amazing." A braid's fallen in my face, and Rudjek tucks it behind my ear, his fingers grazing my cheek. "Are you okay?"

"Yes," I breathe. "Are you?"

"I feel a little weak."

We stare at each other in a silence that stretches on too long— knowing there can be no more kissing, not without consequences. A stone out of place on the steps behind him catches my attention. I shimmy it from the cracked molding and remove the dagger wrapped in cloth from the alcove. It alone remains untouched by the decay in the palace. The handle is inlaid with gold and silver, symbols engraved on both sides of the blade.

Rudjek stands transfixed by the dagger, his eyes filled with pain. "Don't do it, Arrah."

"I must," I say, my voice a wisp of air. "I've made peace with it."

"Well, I haven't." Rudjek glances everywhere but my face. "I can't lose you."

"Look at these bones." I gesture with my arm. "This will happen again if my sister releases the Demon King's *ka*. I can't let it."

"There must be thousands dead here," he whispers. "He was a monster."

"He *is* a monster."

To use *was* is to pretend that the threat is gone, when Daho is very much alive.

THIRTY-NINE

"Someone's coming!" Majka hollers. I tuck the dagger in my waistband and we hurry up the ladder. Rudjek looks dusty and tattered and tired beneath the moonlight—and the kiss has left me weak too. It wasn't a good idea, but I don't care and I don't regret it. My feelings for Rudjek and this new, unimaginable memory of Daho still burn within me. The kiss only made it that much worse. If I survive this night and stay far away from the Demon King's palace, maybe this new connection will fade. I want to believe a lot of things that aren't true.

Rudjek removes his shotels in one swift draw. "We'll use the Temple as a base."

"What Temple?" Majka shrieks—his voice reaching a new octave. "You mean that pile of rocks you're in?"

Sukar lowers his spyglass. "This will be interesting."

A boy with kinky hair the color of the sun steps out of the shadows. It's Tam. Or I suppose I should say Re'Mec. Anger rises in my chest and I bite the inside of my lip. So much of what we've gone through could've been avoidable had he acted with compassion.

He's wearing a white elara trimmed in red, gold, and green thread and beaded sandals. Not exactly practical for a fight. It's near impossible to believe that *he* once defeated the Demon King. The scribes called Koré and Re'Mec the Twin Kings, but it's obvious that she was the true hero and he'd just tagged along.

"Re'Mec," Rudjek says, a bite in his tone.

The orisha grins, but the sentiment doesn't reach his eyes. When his pale blue gaze meets mine, something pricks in the back of my mind—a memory that sputters like torchlight at the first drops of rain, trying desperately to shake itself loose from some unseen chains. The same cool, calming magic washes the memory away before it comes into focus. This magic isn't from the witchdoctors. It's ancient, older than time itself, and tastes of tears.

"Do I know you?" I ask, but it's the wrong question. "Do . . . do you know *me*?"

Re'Mec blinks at me and scoffs. "Has your girlfriend lost her wits?"

Rudjek flings one of his shotels at Re'Mec's head. The sword whips through the air and the orisha steps aside at the last moment. It slams into a splintered stone column and sticks. Too bad it missed Re'Mec. He's no better than Daho. In some ways he's worse. He stood by and let the *Ka*-Priest torture my mother. He alone demanded the Rite of Passage that has broken so many families. The orishas are so removed from the rest of us that they don't bother to think of the consequences of their actions. Still, there was honest confusion in his eyes at my question, which gives me hope that Daho was lying.

"Is that any way to treat an old friend?" He makes a show of stroking his hairless chin.

"You sniveling little weasel." Rudjek grits his teeth. "Watch your tongue."

"My apologies." Re'Mec flourishes an Aatiri bow at me. "My sister is quite fond of you, or should I say *was*, since no one has seen her since she went to Kefu."

A tinge of shame warms my cheeks—still in shock that a god died to save me.

Sukar spits in the grass. "Are you here to talk or fight at our side, *orisha*?"

"I have to watch my tongue." Re'Mec presses his palm to his chest in indignation. "But insulting me is okay?"

"Stop acting like an overgrown child," I snap. "Are you here to help us or not?"

Re'Mec and Rudjek both cock an eyebrow at me.

Birds of prey squawk as they circle overhead. Like the Familiars, they await their feast. For there will be blood soon and bodies to fill their bellies. The sting of demon magic carries on the breeze. It crawls across my skin like centipedes, but the witchdoctors' magic rises to meet it. It curls around my body in a swirl of dancing light. Colors that pulse like a heartbeat.

Two falcons land at the base of the Temple. It isn't only the awareness in the birds' black eyes that gives the cravens away—it's the way their plumage gleams beneath the moonlight. Their presence mutes my magic. The dancing light dims. The falcons fold their wings, and their bodies shift into shapeless gray masses.

"Twenty-gods, Rudjek," Majka says. "Can you do that too?"

Rudjek tilts his head to the side like the answer should be obvious. I'm wondering too, but he doesn't confirm or deny it.

"They're close," Fadyi says when he's done shifting back into his human form. Räeke stands beside him, one of her too-large eyes sitting much higher than the other. We all stare at her, and she blinks, then shifts to correct the mishap. "We need to prepare."

Re'Mec beams at the cravens with sparks of sunlight in his eyes, like he'd go to the ends of the world for them. The same way they look at Rudjek. He's every bit his sister—if not even more insufferable, but they both tried to help in their own convoluted way.

Re'Mec speaks to the cravens in a language that's clipped and tonal.

"He's telling them to keep a distance from you to not dampen your magic," Rudjek says, a smile teetering on his lips. Lips that, I know now, taste like sweet milk candy. Lips I want to taste again.

He must read my expression because as heat creeps up my neck, he blushes too.

Jahla tilts her head to sniff the air. "Two thousand. Half demons, half shotani."

Kira retrieves two daggers. "I rather like those odds."

Koré and Kira would have gotten along. They both lusted for blood and loved their knives. Now Re'Mec has gifted Kira with blades almost identical to his sister's. She will honor the fallen Twin King tonight. *And I will honor you, Grandmother. I promise. I will honor all who have fallen in my mother's and sister's paths.*

"We're on holy ground." Sukar scoops up a bit of soil and lets it fall between his fingers. "Heka willing, we will come out victorious."

If only Sukar knew how unholy these grounds are, had seen the vault of bones beneath his feet.

Fadyi and Jahla move to flank Rudjek. Re'Mec stands ahead of them, all pretense gone as he faces the onslaught of night. The twins, Ezaric and Tzaric, shift into identical great leopards. One winks at me and I wink back before they move to flank our rear along with Räeke. They're so much more interesting than the stories told in Tamar to scare children.

Kira and Essnai exchange a longing gaze, an unspoken understanding between them. My heart aches for my friends—I want them to be together back home, safe like before my mother ruined everything. I can't stand the thought of them putting their future at stake to help me. It isn't fair. It isn't right. *You will lose many friends before the end*, the memory of Arti's voice whispers to me. I clench my fists against my sides. I won't let that happen.

I stand at Rudjek's back, Sukar and Majka flanking me. Essnai is behind me next to Kira with three of Rudjek's guardians at their backs. The cravens have given me a wide berth, so that when Efiya comes, nothing will block my magic. The press of Daho's dagger is cold against my waist, and though I know it means my death, it's soothing. With it, I have a chance to end my sister's reign of terror.

Majka strokes his chin, pretending to be in deep thought. "By my math, we're outnumbered by a million to one."

"Your math is bad," says Essnai, narrowing her eyes at him.

"If you can't handle your share, Majka," I tease, "I'll lighten your burden."

Shadows too coordinated to be Familiars flit in and out of the torchlight set about the Temple. They close in around us, and my pulse thumps against my eardrums. Even though the odds are against us, anticipation courses through me. The magic tingles across my skin like the light of a thousand suns beaming from within me.

"Look what I can do." Rudjek stares at his shotel wedged in the stone, and the space between him and his sword wrinkles like currents on a river. The shotel shakes loose and flies back into his outstretched hand. "Räeke taught me that." He casts a grin over his shoulder at me.

"You've been holding out on us, you bastard," Majka says.

I cross my arms. "I can call a firestorm."

"Show-offs," Sukar and Essnai muse at the same time.

The clanking of metal fills my ears as everyone readies their weapons. Sukar casts me a hopeful smile as he raises one of his sickles to me and nods. My staff is inside the Temple. I don't need it. I need magic tonight, and I have no intention of failing. Not again.

The shotani descend upon the valley first, moving as silent as the dead. The demons sweep in behind them—their eyes glowing in the night like hungry hyenas. With the shotani in black tunics and the demons dressed in red gendar uniforms, it's hard to gauge where the army ends. They have us surrounded.

"Why didn't anybody think to invite more cravens to this fight?" Majka asks.

Rudjek crosses his shotels in front of him. "You're lucky any came at all."

Re'Mec raises his hands to the sky, and the moon brightens so we can see better.

When Efiya steps from the void into the valley in front of Rudjek, time stops. He stands completely still, his hands gripping his shotels. I'm frozen too—but not my mind. Everyone else stands as still as statues. Efiya leans close to Rudjek's ear and whispers. His lips move, but the wind swallows his words. Fire burns deep in my belly. What are they saying to each other? The magic inside me pushes against hers. It rebounds and slams into my chest so hard that I cough up blood, but her grasp on me untethers.

Then my mother strides out of the shadows with Oshhe on her heels, and tears spring to my eyes. My heart both soars and falls. My father is nothing more than loose skin and bones, his face hollow. Arti doesn't look any better. She rushes toward me with urgent steps, her eyes wild.

She glances at Efiya, who is still whispering in Rudjek's ear, then back at me. "Give me the dagger," Arti hisses, desperate. "Give it to me before it's too late to stop her."

I desperately look between my father, my mother, and my sister. Arti's voice throbs in my head, poking holes in everything I know about her. I want badly for it to be true—for my mother to finally come to her senses. But no, she doesn't want to stop Efiya . . . she *wants* the dagger so I don't ruin her plans. Efiya still hasn't released the Demon King's *ka*. She needs her. I don't believe Arti has suddenly changed her mind after all the awful things she's put into motion. This is another trick.

I take a step back from her, but she moves closer. Her eyes brim with tears. "Only one touched by his magic can wield the blade," she says. "Give it to me and I'll end this now."

How can I trust my mother, who sacrificed children to call upon a demon? Why would she be regretful now? It was her hatred that started the bloodshed. But I can't deny the anguish in Arti's bloodshot eyes, the pain etched in her frown. She's hurting too. Is it because of the tribes? Did she know that Efiya would attack them too? Even if my mother isn't as heartless as I thought, it doesn't matter now. It's too late. "Get away from me," I spit.

"Arrah, please," she begs. "There isn't much time."

I shake my head. I won't be a pawn in whatever game she's playing now.

She steps closer; my magic lashes out, but hers rises up to counter. Sparks encircle us as we come to a standstill. "The chieftains were right to bind their *kas* to you," she says, relieved. I can't reconcile this broken person before me, the regret in her eyes and the pain in her voice.

I love my mother. I never stopped loving her after all that she's done, and to see her like this cuts me to the bone. I want to believe her. I want to lay my head on her shoulder and let this moment between us wash away the bad blood. Let it reverse time and erase our history, so that we can start over from that day she painted the Mulani dancers on the wall when I was a little girl. Instead of disappointment, she won't care that I don't have magic and she'll be proud of me. But all the wishing and hoping and dreaming in the world won't change the past.

"She killed them," I say, barely able to hold back my sobs. "The witchdoctors are all gone."

Arti stares at the place where the dagger rests beneath my tunic, her eyes hungry. "I didn't mean for that to happen." Her gaze meets mine again. "That was never part of my plan." She reaches her arm out to me. "You have to believe me." When I don't reach back, her hand drops to her side. "I only wanted to make Jerek and Suran and their orisha masters suffer. It isn't the Demon King we need to worry about, Arrah." Arti looks over her shoulder at Efiya with Rudjek, then says, "It's your sister."

"Why now?" I glare at her to keep myself from falling to pieces. She's still defending the Demon King after so much that's happened. My mother is hopeless. "Why the change of heart?"

Arti tilts her chin up, some shadow of the self-assured *Ka*-Priestess still left in her features. "If I have to choose between releasing my master and fixing my mistakes, then I choose the latter." She sighs. "It may not mean much now, but I want you to have a life beyond this night. Please, daughter, let me do this one thing to atone for a fraction of the pain I've caused you." The frown and anguish smooth away from her face, like she's made peace with her decision. "Give me the knife, Arrah," she says after a deep breath, her voice calm.

Tears run down my cheeks. My mother is offering to sacrifice herself to save me. The charlatan daughter who's always disappointed her. I may regret this moment for the rest of my life, but I believe that she means it. A little of the tension eases in my chest as I glance down at where the dagger is hidden beneath my tunic. I hesitate, still not quite sure if I can trust that she won't change her mind. When I look up again, the tip of a sword pierces straight through my mother's chest.

Blood splashes in my eyes. I can't breathe. I can't move. There's nothing but red—red everywhere. It coats my tongue; it burns my throat. Efiya wrenches the blade from our mother's back.

Arti's face twists in pain as she mouths, "I'm sorry."

Before her body even sinks to the ground, her *ka* rises and joins with Efiya.

Efiya smiles. "You will be with me always, Mother."

Oshhe exhales and a white cloud escapes his lips. He frowns like he's seeing for the first time. Efiya rips the shotel from Arti's chest. When Oshhe's eyes land on me, he smiles. A smile that's tired, but hopeful. Time stops and for the briefest moment, there is only my father and me. His face transforms and he's once again the proud son of Tribe Aatiri. My heart threatens to burst with joy. It's really my father. It's really him.

"Little Priestess." His voice is a vapor. "I need you to be strong a little longer."

Tears and blood cloud my vision as I stumble toward him. My eyes aren't deceiving me. My father has come back. Warmth spreads in his sallow cheeks, and his dark gaze shines with light once more. I will take him away from this pain and horror. We'll go back to his shop and dry herbs and clean bones. We'll work in the garden, eating so much milk candy that our bellies ache. I'll listen to him tell stories for hours, for days, for weeks, for the rest of my life.

Efiya appears in front of him in the blink of an eye and plunges her blade into his heart.

"No, no, no!" I scream, pain exploding in my chest.

The ground shakes beneath my feet, and I descend upon my sister like a raging firestorm.

FORTY

Efiya and I are a tangle of arms and legs lost in a plume of magic dust. We claw and punch and kick each other. I slam her head against the ground and she knees me in the belly, knocking the wind from my lungs. I struggle to catch my breath.

She's too strong.

Her magic burns against my defenses and burrows deep inside me. A blistering cold stops my heart and shreds my muscles. My skin cracks like shards of glass before a blazing heat counters her magic and mends the damage. I call lightning that sets her on fire. Our screams drown each other out, and the pain, twenty-gods, there's so much pain that it blurs my vision.

Efiya takes a step back from me like this is a game and it's time for a respite. She's got cuts and scratches and burns everywhere, and she's bleeding. She's not invincible. I allow myself a smile.

"It's like when we used to play in the gardens." Efiya laughs, delighted. "I've missed that."

As I lunge for her, my sister wraps herself into the void and disappears. In her absence, the others wake with a start. There's no time to lament as her army descends upon us like vultures. My magic stands on edge as the feeling of prying eyes peering into my soul overwhelms me. I catch sight of a demon standing in the middle of the charging army. He's wearing a new face, one that is suntanned and angular and a body that's muscular and compact, but his magic is unmistakable. It curdles my blood. Efiya has given her demon father, Shezmu, a permanent vessel. The echo of metal against metal assaults my senses, but my mind might as well be in a sunken ship deep in the Great Sea.

Bodies twist and turn around me, but I can't stop staring at my father. My pulse throbs so hard in my ears that I'm light-headed as I stumble to where he lies crumpled on the ground. I drop to my knees, my chest heaving, struggling to breathe, and then I take him into my arms. My magic wraps him in a cocoon of bright colors. It settles on him like stardust and heals his wound. His body is whole, but Efiya took his soul. The magic can't repair that.

Little Priestess, the memory of his voice whispers. *I need you to be strong a little longer.*

The rage festering inside me explodes. As I come to my feet, lightning cuts across the sky in a flash of bright amber, striking demon and shotani alike. They collapse in heaps of fire—the flames from their charred flesh sucking up the air. Hot tears streak down my cheeks. I won't stop until they all suffer. I welcome their deaths.

Rudjek does an intricate dance around me, far enough to mind his swords, but close enough to keep me in his sight. His shotels move in smooth arcs, dispatching enemy after enemy. His body is fluid as he twists and turns, slicing and drawing his swords into chests and bellies and throats. Majka does the same—although with less grace.

While Rudjek is protecting me, Fadyi and Jahla protect him. They cut down shotani with the hook-shaped knives they call *reapers* that slide through flesh and bones with ease. Re'Mec's shotels shimmer as he cuts down demon after demon. He's flamboyant and arrogant as he wields his swords.

Kira flings her knives, her aim true as she takes down several demons in a matter of moments. Behind us, Ezaric and Tzaric have changed back into their human forms. Sukar and Räeke fight side by side, but there's no sign of Essnai as a horde of demons overtakes them. My belly twists in knots, and I turn my firestorm toward the demons behind me, to help my friends. Kira runs headlong into the thicket of demons, fighting her way to Essnai. I lose sight of her too.

Thunder cracks in the sky at the same time an arrow grazes my cheek. My face burns, and blood rolls down my chin. Rudjek tries to fend off three demons at once, but he's bleeding too, his movements less fluid and less sharp.

"Are you okay?" he shouts over his shoulder, winded.

Before I can answer, the sky opens. A great beast drops into the valley and the ground shakes. I almost lose my balance, but Majka grabs my arm to keep me from falling. In its descent, the beast crushes dozens of demons and shotani.

"What in the name of the gods," Majka yells over the battle cries.

The beast is mammoth, its black hide covered in short spikes of bones, its mouth full of sharp, crooked teeth. It rolls its head back, its snout thrust to the moon, and growls—a sound that reverberates through me. It stomps toward us, shaking the ground with each step.

"My sister," Re'Mec laughs, "always one for theatrics!"

The beast disperses into a red mist and the demons closest to it drop to their knees, clawing at their throats. Rudjek catches my eye as a single figure emerges from the mist. Koré rises from one bent knee, two shotels in her hands, her long braids a writhing bed of serpents.

Not sure if my eyes are deceiving me, I whisper, "I saw you die."

Koré grins, her head held high. "I'm not so easy to kill."

Where has she been all this time? I'm both relieved to see her alive and angry that she survived when the witchdoctors did not. I look to where my father fell, but now bodies litter the valley and I can't see him. "The Demon King's *ka*?" The words are stiff on my tongue and my chest tightens. I can't have come this far only to fail. My father didn't die in vain.

"Still safe for now," she finally answers, and I ease out the breath burning in my lungs.

"I had the situation under control," Re'Mec says to his sister. Although his tone is relaxed, his posture is anything but.

Before Koré can answer, Efiya steps out of the void again and plunges a shotel into Tzaric's back. Ezaric doesn't fare any better when her sword slices through his neck. Rudjek screams—his rage palpable as he cuts down two more demons and runs to help the cravens.

My heart slams against my ribs as the sounds of the battle echo in my ears. So many good people have died already because of my mother and Efiya's quest to raise the Demon King. My father, my grandmother, the witchdoctors, even my mother herself. Still more die now. I can't let their deaths be for nothing. If I don't stop my sister here, she and the Demon King will destroy everything.

Efiya appears with her bloody swords slashing down at Sukar's head. Things happen so fast that one action blurs into the next and then the next. The air ripples with the sting of anti-magic, and a sword pierces through Efiya's chest. Sukar takes the opportunity to slide his sickle across her throat. The sword turns to ashes, and both wounds heal without spilling a drop of blood. She bears down on Sukar again with rage and murder in her eyes.

"No!" My magic flings Sukar out of Efiya's grasp, but I push too hard—he crashes into a column and falls to the ground in a heap. My hand flies over my mouth to stifle the scream burning in my lungs.

"I'm no longer amused." Efiya closes the space between us in two steps. "Time to end this game."

Rudjek charges at Efiya, but Jahla and Fadyi hold him back. Koré and Re'Mec and Kira launch weapons at her, but time stops again. By my hand. I have to get Efiya away from my friends, or she won't stop until she kills them all. The chieftains tell me what to do. I take one step backward and I'm inside the collapsed Temple. When Efiya steps into the void and reappears in front of me, a blinding light flashes, sealing us inside. There is no sound now—everyone outside remains still.

We stand in the Temple as it was before she destroyed it. Pristine pillars and columns glimmer in the torchlight. Murals engraved with stars and flowing ribbons of Heka's pure light decorate the walls. This place is another gift from the chieftains—a place where Efiya and I exist outside time itself.

"You bring nothing but destruction to everything you touch," I say. "It must end."

"Dear Arrah, I'm only beginning." Efiya smiles. "I'm life and death."

I shudder, my knees weak. "How could you kill our parents?"

"They are here!" She thumps her fist against her chest. "Can't you understand that?" She blinks back tears, her face twisted in an emotion that looks foreign on her. "They're safe with all the others inside me."

"You're mad," I spit, and the words are bile on my tongue.

Efiya frowns like my accusation wounds her. "Are you still sour about Rudjek?"

I will not give her the satisfaction of seeing how much pain she's caused me.

"I gave him a gift that you never can," Efiya answers without malice. "You should thank me."

"Thank you?" I laugh.

Efiya points a bloody shotel at my chest. "It's your face he'll remember, not mine."

Is she jealous? I dismiss the idea. If it's any emotion at all—it's contempt. But every soul she's consumed has become a part of her. It's changed her. Oshhe's a part of her now too. He loved me. Arti loved me too. "I don't hear the chieftains' voices anymore. Have the *kas* of all the people you murdered been silenced too?" When she doesn't respond, I add, "This place is special."

"I've seen visions of us entering the Temple, but I could never see inside it."

"It's not meant for you or me to see inside," I say. "Our magic will not protect us here."

Efiya considers this for a moment as she stares down at her sho-tel. Then she glances back up at me, her face set, her eyes savage. "That's very unfortunate for you."

Her blade digs into my belly before the Demon King's dagger even crosses my mind. Efiya smiles down at me through tears, her sword still piercing me. I cough, the taste of blood on my tongue. There's so much pain in my sister's gaze as she yanks back the sword and it clangs against the floor.

"It has to be this way." She pulls me close.

I let myself sag against her. In another life, we could've loved each other; we could've been best friends. We would've braided each other's hair, and fought over the last milk candy while our father told stories. In another life, our mother would have smothered us with kisses and let us cry on her shoulder.

This life flees my body and peace comes over me. I'll be able to rest soon. With a last surge of strength I slip the dagger from beneath my tunic. The hilt warms and curves against my palm as the knife reshapes to fit me. The price of using this weapon is death, but I'm ready.

In a moment that's both too quick and too slow, I plunge the knife between Efiya's ribs. It pierces her flesh with ease, splitting her open and shredding my heart into pieces. My mind settles on a memory, the most sacred I have of my sister. The first time she climbed into bed with me and curled against my side. She tried to take away my pain—her smile big, her eyes wide with wonder. She longed to be near me, but I pushed her away. I jerk the blade free and let it slip from my hand covered in blood. It clangs to the floor and rings a final note, sealing our fates.

Efiya stumbles back, and soon after, we both fall. I reach for my sister and she crawls to me, her hands and knees slipping in our blood pooling on the stone floor. Neither of us tries to speak. It's too late for words and sometimes words can't truly express the mortal heart. Tears streak down my cheeks when she collapses out of arm's reach. Firelight dances in her eyes until they go still, and her *ka* of shimmering gold slips from her parted lips. She's gone. My sister is dead, and I killed her.

Daho's bloody dagger lies between us—glowing as the first spark of his magic ignites, drawing her soul into its grasp. Darkness bleeds into my eyes until my sight fades to black, until my heart no longer beats, until I die one last time.

PART V

For *she is light and she is dark,*
For *in death her life truly starts.*
Some *deeds can never be condoned,*
For *this she will always be alone.*
—Song *of the Unnamed*

FORTY-ONE

I ascend forever into the night sky. There's no time, no beginning, no end. At death the tether between my old vessel and true self snaps. Now that I'm free, I am light and shadows, floating up, up, up. The battle rages beneath me, but it's a distant dream now. I unravel and become one with the sky, the moon, and the stars. A thousand lifetimes of memories scatter like sprinkles of stardust.

New knowledge pulses in my shapeless existence. There's no calming magic to silence my memories as it had in the palace with Rudjek—now they cleave my heart in two.

In my first life, I loved the Demon King. I loved Daho.

After the Supreme Cataclysm birthed me, I settled by a frozen lake on top of a mountain, watching the world grow old. I spent much time in the stillness of a moment until a mortal with a broken wing collapsed in front of my lake. The mortal was on the verge of death, a concept that I didn't understand until much later. I knew of mortal kind only in the vaguest terms, but when I peered into his soul, I saw his entire life.

Daho's people built towering dwellings that reached into the clouds. They mastered travel into the skies long before altering themselves to have wings. They developed cures to every illness they knew of, and learned to extend their natural lives. But no matter how advanced their medicine, they could not achieve immortality.

Under the boy's family, his people—demons—enjoyed a millennium of peace. He was their kingdom's sole heir but a sickly child. His father's enemies knew of this and used it to build support against his family. When his father died, they raided their palace and killed his mother. The boy escaped and fled to the mountains to hide. The new king did not pursue him. No one thought he could survive the cold and wild beasts.

I made a vessel to hold my soul and went to the boy, who begged me to help him. I touched his soul, felt his life pulse in rhythm with mine, saw the cosmic strings that connected us. In that moment, I glimpsed his future, sitting upon a throne with me at his side. After I healed him, Daho asked my name, but I had none. Names were another aspect of existing that I didn't understand yet.

We shared many years on the mountain together. I was very upset when he told me that one day he was going to die. I could not make him like me, so I let my consciousness stretch across the universe, seeking a solution. I discovered a people who lived very long lives by passing their souls on to another at death.

It was fitting that Daho take the life of the man who had killed his mother and stolen his throne—the false Demon King. But when Daho tasted the man's soul, something changed inside him. He became stronger and possessed magic when his people had none.

He had to keep consuming souls to live as long as me, and I grew to understand the horrible thing that I set into motion. I tried desperately to find another way, but I failed. Yet, I couldn't let Daho die. I loved him too much.

We ruled over the demon kingdom until my siblings decided to punish me for my mistake. It was only after Fram killed me that Daho gorged himself on souls until he became as powerful as my siblings. He built an army to destroy them.

I relive the endless war between the demons and my siblings. The senseless bloodshed and death. The chaos that consumed the world. Daho sits upon his throne, alone and broken, his belly full of the *kas* he consumed for an eon. He's done this because of me— because I died.

I see his real form, a shimmering silver body with wings that span the length of seas, a frame that's lean and bold. His eyes shine a brilliant shade of emerald and his chin is proud. My soul throbs from memories of running my fingers across his jaw. From memories of his sharp teeth that teased and tantalized as his *ka* sang my name. My true name. The one that only comes to me in death.

Dimma.

I am nowhere and everywhere at once. I am no one and everyone. I am her, the Unnamed orisha. I am Arrah and a thousand others who lived and died in an endless cycle as punishment for loving Daho.

I ascend beyond the stars, beyond the universe. There's only the infinite darkness of the Supreme Cataclysm—the creator and the destroyer—and the raging storm inside it. Its call is all that matters now as I draw closer. It will devour me so I can be unmade. I am at its mouth, willing and ready, when I'm whisked away to another plane.

"Hello, sister."

The voices are familiar, soft-spoken and in sync, neither male nor female. Twins shimmer into existence in front of me. They stand so close together that their bodies melt into each other. One is light and one is dark. One is death and one is life. There's duality and symmetry in the smoothness of their features. The fluidity in their gender. They are two sides of the same coin and ever changing. Their statue in the Almighty Temple doesn't do them justice. Nothing could capture their beauty.

"Hello, Fram." We aren't using words. The exchange is through the cosmic strings that connect everything in the universe. "Here we are again."

"For the last time," Fram says.

"Have you grown tired of this game too?" I ask. "It's time for it to end."

"I should've left you dead the first time." Pain flashes in their eyes. "I should've let the Supreme Cataclysm unmake you, but I loved you too much."

"We have this conversation every time I die," I say. "I don't want to have it again."

"I need you to understand." Fram's voices brim with memories that manifest as rain around their bodies. "You were very young. An infant. The Supreme Cataclysm birthed the rest of us within an eon of each other . . . Koré and Re'Mec, then the others . . . but you came much later. No one knew what to do with you, so we left you to your own devices. Such a horrible way to raise a child, but we were still learning too, even if we thought we knew everything."

"That is the failing of our kind," I say. "We think we always know best."

"I see rebirth has taught you something after all."

"It's taught me that I can never atone for what I've done."

"That's true." Fram nods, both heads in concert. "The damage can't be undone."

Silence stretches between us in this place void of time. Even here, the Supreme Cataclysm calls to me and I ache to rejoin it. It would be so easy to be unmade, to have no past or future, no memories at all. To start anew, or not. No one knows what becomes of the things the Supreme Cataclysm unmakes.

"Do you still love him?" Fram asks.

We don't need to say who they speak of; there's only always been him since that day by the frozen lake. I ache for the centuries we spent watching the world change. For the new life we created. I can feel that he's stronger than when I've died before; he's on the verge of escaping his prison. His call tugs at me, and I want nothing more than to go to him.

Supreme Cataclysm, yes, I still love him.

An echo splutters in my *ka*. A raging river, a firestorm. It refuses to be brushed aside as memories in someone else's story. I am Arrah and I am Dimma too. We are the same, but apart. She has her thoughts and I have my own. We exist as one and as two. Had I not been facing Fram, I would not understand the duality in myself—the two sides. Both broken without the other.

"And what of the craven?" Fram asks, their voices a wisp of wind.

"Rudjek." I whisper his name and memories of him flood back into my *ka*. The deep timbre of his voice, his shy smiles and arrogant grins. The feel of his soul intertwined with mine like warm water splashed against my skin. He makes my *ka* sing, and I would go to the ends of the universe to see him laugh. I love him too, in this life and in death. Daho is my past, and he is my future.

"Careful, sister," Fram warns. "An orisha's love is dangerous. You know that best of all."

"Are you going to send me back?" I ask.

They're indecisive by nature and lose themselves in thought. "No," they answer with finality. "'If you are reborn, it will give Daho hope. Once he loses hope, we can finally destroy him."

"You still don't understand." My *ka* pulses with frustration. "Sending me to my end will not quell his thirst for revenge. Have you not learned from the first time you killed me? I must be the one to stop him. I must put right the wrong that I've done. With Arti and Efiya gone, he'll have no way to escape his prison, and Koré and I can find a way to destroy his soul once and for all."

Fram shakes their heads. "You, *Arrah*, mean well, but you, *Dimma*, would go to the Demon King at the first chance. The best solution is for you to rejoin the womb. It's time for you to return to the Supreme Cataclysm."

The witchdoctors' souls are still intertwined with mine and their magic pulses in my *ka*. Dimma's magic—*my magic*—is there too, chained and bound. All this time, I thought that I didn't have any magic of my own, but Fram had locked it away, as they'd done with my mind. Countless lifetimes of frustration and longing because of them. My anger vibrates in the cosmic strings that connect me to the universe.

"Return me to my broken vessel *now*." Dimma and I are in agreement, our thoughts singular for once. We may not agree on who we love, but we both want to go back to the mortal world, the world of the living.

"No." Fram's calming magic reaches for my soul. "Your time is over."

I resist their pull with a burst of the borrowed witchdoctors' magic. A million sparks of color light around my soul, pushing back Fram's influence. The chain that binds my own magic bends, but does not break.

Fram steps closer. "Don't do this. You will cause nothing but endless death."

"I won't go," I say as my *ka* breaks their chain.

This place where time doesn't exist trembles with my fury. It tears at the seams. I slip away through a crack and descend into the world again like a falling star. Fram is with me in their shapeless form. Their magic lashes against me like a hot whip and stops my fall. They drag me back and my memories unravel as fog curls around my consciousness. My true name fades away.

"No, I won't go," I repeat, my mind less clear, less certain.

"You must," breathes two voices I don't recognize, when I knew them a moment ago.

"Let go," someone else whispers. It isn't one of the chieftains, yet it is inside me too and I understand what it wants me to do. My *ka* is akin to mist, not solid by mortal standards, but enough to hold me in this trap. When I left my body twice before, I was afraid I would travel too far and become lost in the spirit world. This is something else, something much riskier. I'm going to let my *ka* unravel, let it become one with everything. The Kes chieftain spent most of his life exploring the spirit world, and he knows how.

I push my consciousness out in all directions, stretching beyond the confines of my *ka*. At first the unraveling is subtle and slow—a new awareness that creeps into my very being. My recent memories—everything that's happened since I killed Efiya—slip away. I hold on to the idea of seeing my friends again—seeing my father one last time.

I'm falling, falling, falling through stars.

FORTY-TWO

I don't know how I've come to be here. I was in the Temple with Efiya, then awoke in the sky. I killed my sister. What I've done tears at me. I want to scream, but I have no voice and the pain threatens to burn me alive.

Rudjek's *ka* calls to me, sings my name, and I'm drawn to it.

As my *ka* pulls itself into one piece, I focus on Rudjek's song and let it guide me. His sorrow pulls me back to the battlefield, and I sweep inside the Temple and settle into my broken body. When I crack open my eyes, my gaze lands on my sister and my heart aches. She's gone. I'm dying too, but my thoughts and memories feel tangled and confused.

There's a flash of light, then the sound of hurried footfalls.

"No, no, no," Rudjek cries. "Arrah, no."

He lifts me into his arms and I stare up at his broken face. "You're going to be okay."

"She's alive!" someone shouts. It's Majka.

"That shouldn't be possible," Koré says, farther away. "Are you sure?"

"Help her," Rudjek demands.

My skin burns, and I groan in pain.

"You mustn't touch her if she's to have a chance to heal," comes another voice, the craven called Jahla.

She means that his anti-magic is dangerous. I already feel a flutter of it. A tear falls from Rudjek's eye, and when it lands on my face, I twitch from the burn. "Majka . . ." is all he says, broken, and his friend takes me into his arms. Rudjek backs away. It hurts to see his pain.

"What should we do with Efiya?" asks Fadyi.

"Burn her body before she sees fit to come back." Koré's tone is full of menace. "Do it where the demons can see, and watch them run like the cowards they are."

I slip into the lull of sleep and when I wake again, I'm lying in a tent. Koré is at my side with her hands pressed against my wounds. It hurts, but the pain is dull. Re'Mec is on my opposite side. Both stare at me like I'm some mystery they're trying to solve. Behind Re'Mec, I catch glimpses of Sukar lying on a makeshift cot. He's asleep, and the cravens are close to him. Fadyi, Jahla, and Räeke. I remember that the twins, Ezzric and Tzaric, are dead. My sister killed them. She killed Arti and Oshhe too. Tears slip down my cheeks. I'll never hear another story from my father, or collect herbs in the garden with him. We won't ride with the caravan to the Blood Moon Festival—there will be no more festivals now.

"Did Fram send you back?" Koré hisses in my ear. "I can taste their magic on you."

It takes all my effort to keep my eyes half-open, and I don't have the strength to answer. Why would the orisha Fram have anything to do with me? It makes no sense that she's asking me about them. Essnai, Kira, and Majka stand at my feet, looking anxious. Rudjek stands farther back, his arms crossed. I have so many questions, about the demons, about the orishas, about my sister.

"Can't you do something more?" Rudjek demands. "You helped Sukar."

"I've stopped the bleeding and healed her wound," Koré says. "It's the magic from the dagger that's poisoning her body now—like we expected. In truth, I may have only prolonged her suffering. And I can't do anything else without diverting my attention from more important matters."

"*More important matters?*" Rudjek turns on her, enraged. "Where were the Twin Kings when Efiya killed the tribal people? Where were you when the *Ka*-Priestess created that monstrosity?"

Re'Mec's shoulders tense. "That's not a tree you want to bark up, boy."

"Do you know where I was *not*?" Koré rises to her feet, her braids writhing in agitation. "I was not bedding Arrah's sister."

Heat creeps up Rudjek's neck and burns his cheeks. Essnai curses, and Kira glares at him. Majka looks everywhere but at his friend. Rudjek glances to the ground, his face twisted in anguish like he wants to bury himself under a slab of granite.

Re'Mec lets out a long whistle that echoes in the valley. "No need to bring up the boy's indiscretions, Koré. We were all young *once*, or have you forgotten?"

He emphasizes *once* in a way that makes it clear that there's a story behind his words, but Koré refuses to back down. Her eyes take a hard edge. "Did the others not see when Efiya leaned in to whisper to you on the battlefield?"

Rudjek doesn't answer, but Jahla speaks up. "You know as well as I that she tricked him."

"As much as I love a good spat," Re'Mec rises to his feet, "my sister and I have a horde of demons to hunt down and kill. One of them stole the Demon King's dagger and I want it back."

A shock of pain cuts across my chest. How had one of the demons taken the dagger? Had it happened right after I . . . I killed my sister? There's a blank hole in my mind and it frustrates me that I can't remember. We have to get the dagger back . . . we can't let the demons keep it. It's too powerful, too dangerous. I try to warn my friends, but the blood pooling in my throat drowns out my voice.

Koré pats my shoulder and sleep claims me again. I'm in and out for days. In my dreams, I sit with my knees drawn to my chest, staring at a frozen lake with mist rising from its surface. Sometimes I'm alone, save from the brisk breeze whipping across my bare arms, but I don't feel the cold. Sometimes Rudjek is with me and we snuggle together under a great brown fur, neither of us speaking. Sometimes it's another boy. I can only see a wisp of his silvery hair and wings.

"Do you remember me?" asks the winged boy in my dreams. "Do you remember *us*?"

My head is on his lap and it's so comforting that I could stay here for eternity.

"Who are you?" I roll over to look up at him, but the sun washes out his face.

"I'm Daho," he says, sad.

"Do I know you?"

After a long pause, he answers, choking back tears, "Not yet, but you will."

"You have a new body." I catch glimpses of his dark features, a memory teetering around the edges of my mind. A memory of him.

"Yes." He smiles down at me. "I will come for you, I promise."

In another dream a winged beast with sharpened teeth and a jackal head sweeps down from the sky and steals me away. I startle awake. "Rudjek," I say. My voice is low and broken. Shadows shift in the tent from flickering firelight.

"I'm here, Arrah." He takes my hand into his own; he's wearing thick gloves.

Rudjek runs his gloved fingers across the back of my hand, trying to smooth away my anxiety. He doesn't have the heart to tell me the truth. That the universe has conspired against us. That our touch is venomous. That there can never be more between us because of my magic, and what he's become.

"You won't let him take me, will you?" I clutch his hand—it's my tether to life. My dreams open in my mind like fresh wounds, the signs unmistakable. Sweat trickles down my back. Sometimes dreams are dreams, and sometimes they are glimpses into the future. I have Grandmother's gift of vision now, and my dreams mean more. They foreshadow a terrible truth.

Rudjek frowns, worried. "Who, Arrah?"

"The Demon King," I groan, my throat raw.

"He's still in his prison." Rudjek strokes my cheek. "You saved us."

I stare up into his bewitched eyes, knowing the truth will break him. It will break me too.

THE DEMON KING

This new body is quite small and lacks wings. I miss the wind sweeping beneath me. It will take some getting used to. Yes, I know, in due time. You don't have to remind me of that. I don't like being in this weakened state. My people need me—what's left of them.

We will lay siege to the orishas' beloved humans and cravens.

I've learned patience all these years locked in chains, and I've learned many of the orishas' secrets. I know how to destroy them, but this isn't only about bringing about their deaths. They must suffer as I have.

I will enjoy every moment of it.

What about her?

Do not ever address my wife as "girl" again, or I'll cut out your heart and feed it to you.

She's still your queen and even if she has forgotten that, it's not her fault.

Yes, she's a risk, but hear me: tread carefully when it comes to Arrah. I won't have her harmed. She will come around soon enough.

Of that I'm sure. You should be too. You know Dimma loved our people as much as I do. When she has her full memory back, she will return home. I need to find Fram. They will tell me how to break the spell on Dimma so my love can remember me.

Do you think a boy she's known for a moment in time will come between us?

I'll take care of Rudjek when the time comes too. I will make an example of him.

I warned Efiya that Koré was a trickster, but she did not listen. Look what it got her.

I don't mean to be insensitive, Shezmu. I know she was your daughter and you loved her.

You deserve revenge too. It may be Arrah who wielded the blade, but the orishas guided her hand. She didn't know what she was doing. Koré and Re'Mec tricked her. Don't you ever forget that.

Arrah loved her sister and Efiya loved her too.

Now you know how it feels to lose the one person who gave your life meaning.

It's not easy to lose a child. I should know. The orishas never allowed my child to be born and now my wife doesn't even remember our son. I must be gentle with her. She's like before, when we were young and didn't understand much about life and death. She was patient with me then, so I must be the same with her.

We will not let this break us. Not after all this time.

I'm tired of this war too. I want it to end once and for all.

I will bring peace again like we enjoyed under my father.

But for there to be peace, there must be death.

ACKNOWLEDGMENTS

The proverb "it takes a village" really comes to mind when I think of all the people who have been my support system from the moment I penned my first word to the publication of *Kingdom of Souls*. It started with my mother, who encouraged my early love of reading and storytelling, who always found a way to get me to the library, and bought books for me to devour. You read my very first manuscript with so much joy and enthusiasm that to this day, it brings a smile to my face and warms my heart. To my brothers, I am so very proud of you.

I suspect it may not be easy to live with a writer. Nevertheless, Cyril, you handle it like a pro. You've been there through the ups and downs, and the joys and disappointments. You're a champion for listening to my excessive talking about books, characters, and imaginary worlds. Thank you for always being supportive even when I'm mumbling plot points in my sleep. You keep me grounded and balanced. Your patience is boundless, and your dedication to your passion inspires me to keep pushing for my dreams.

To my literary agent, Suzie Townsend: you've been a diligent advocate from day one and a dream business partner. Thank you for all that you do, your support, and your kindness. Thanks to Joanna Volpe, the mastermind behind New Leaf Literary Agency. Pouya Shahbazian, the best film agent in the known world. Mia Roman and Veronica Grijalva for working their magic. Meredith Barnes, publicity expert, so fortunate for your expertise. To Dani, who shares my aversion to ketchup, I'm lucky to have you on my team. To Hilary, Joe, Madhuri, Cassandra, and Kelsey, you are all part of my village.

I count myself lucky to have landed two fabulous, hardworking editors for *Kingdom of Souls*, Stephanie Stein at HarperTeen and Vicky Leech at HarperVoyager UK. Stephanie, you are a world-building and plot genius. Vicky, you are amazing at honing the threads that weave a story together and ensuring every detail adds to something greater. Discussing plot and story development with the two of you is always a joy. Thank you for pushing me to find and stay true to my voice and storytelling style.

To the great team behind Stephanie at HarperTeen: Louisa Currigan, Jon Howard, and Jen Strada, I couldn't do it without your keen eyes and expertise. Marketer extraordinaire, Ebony LaDelle, and the Epic Reads team. Kimberly Stella and Vanessa Nuttry on the production side, and Haley George, who headed up publicity. Jenna Stempel-Lobell and Alison Donalty for orchestrating such a magical US cover.

Much respect to cover artist Adeyemi Adegbesan. Your work is groundbreaking and exquisite. Keisha, you channeled all of Arrah's fierceness.

Natasha Bardon, thank you for being a champion of this book

at HarperVoyager UK. Where would I be without the fabulous marketing team—Rachel Quin, Fleur Clarke, and Hannah O'Brien, thank you for your dedication. Jaime Frost, thank you for spreading the word about the book. To the wonderful design team, you created a stunning cover full of so much magic for the UK market. Barbara Roby, your proofreading notes were invaluable.

This book would still be on my computer if not for my best friend, Mickey Mouse connoisseur Ronni Davis. I wouldn't have entered Pitch Wars if not for your encouragement. It's a joy to brainstorm ideas and stories with you. So happy we started talking about books in the middle of a random meeting at work that kicked off our friendship. Thank you for your energy, kindness, and friendship.

Speaking of Pitch Wars, thank you to Brenda Drake and the crew who worked endlessly to provide an avenue to help connect writers with mentors. Thank you to Jamie Pacton and M. K. England for taking me on as a mentee, which opened up wonderful doors for me. To Tomi Adeyemi for your generosity. I will always be grateful for your support and for helping pave the way for more fantastical novels that celebrate African and black culture.

To my ride-or-die friend and critique partner, Alexis Henderson. I don't know if I would have gotten through Pitch Wars without our midnight pep talks, our virtual tears, and our sheer stubbornness. I'm such a stan for every single character you write—and I'm here for your books. Thank you for your unrivaled support, countless brainstorming sessions, and your friendship through the woes of writing.

Thanks to these fantastic authors who read early drafts of the book and said the kindest words: Samira Ahmed, Mindee Arnett, Elly Blake, Rebecca Ross, and Rebecca Schaeffer.

My #ChiYA fam, you ladies have been my stone and my inspiration. Samira, thank you for being a fierce advocate for justice. Gloria, your presence is a calming force. Lizzie, you are a joy. Anna, you are amazing, and I will never forget our epic writing retreat. Honorary member Kat Cho, I am so thankful for your generosity and friendship.

Reese, Mia, Jeff, Lane, and Rosaria, my Chicago writing tribe. I always look forward to our meetups. To the Speculators who adopted me into their family. David R. Slayton, your stories are epic, and your heart is big. Antra, I wish we lived closer so we could talk our days away. Nikki, Axie, David M, Nikki, Liz, Erin, Alex, Helen, Amanda, you are fabulous. Shout out to #SuperBlackGirlMagic and the Write Pack. To my very first critique partners, Dave and Denis. I look back on our work together fondly.

Thanks for the encouragement, Eric Francque, Kim Cavaliero-Keller, Troi Rutherford, and Kathleen Misovic. Kedest, our long-standing friendship means the world to me. Thank you for always giving me advice without filters. Alice Singleton, I've learned so much from you.

Jen (The Book Avid), you are fierce and never forget that. Rachel Strolle, super youth librarian and diversity supporter. The groups that have provided a wealth of information: Kidlit Alliance and Kidlit Author of Color. We Need Diverse Books for paving the way for more books by diverse authors.

To the writers who inspire me: N. K. Jemisin, Laini Taylor,

Leigh Bardugo, Holly Black, Octavia E. Butler, Margaret Atwood, among many others, you are masters of your art.

The biggest thanks to the booksellers and librarians who are getting this book into the hands of readers. And to the readers who've taken a chance on my words, thank you for your support. Finally, to Mrs. Okeke, my high school AP English teacher. You left us too soon—and I will always remember your passion for Shakespeare and storytelling.